Shadow

To John Lincoln Williams,

All the very best
Kind Regards,

Neil Root

Neil Root

DIME CRIME BOOKS

London

For Matthew Root
February 1969-February 2023
My amazing big brother
And to Andrea, Ellie, Ollie & Abbie
With Love and Affection Always
xxxxx

And for Tracy Medlicott
My first and best reader
With all my love always

Xxxxx

PART I

Convex

1

The long tree-lined drive into what visitors call Sunnyside, with boughs overarching and shadowing you along the way, takes just over seven minutes in a 1932 Standard Little Nine four-door saloon motorcar- I've timed it many times in my head when being taken into town.

That was when Mr Bannister was at the wheel and of course I didn't have a wristwatch like him then, but my arithmetic is strong, so counting the seconds was no problem. When Old Bannister was found at the bottom of the stairs, the face of his Zenith wristwatch was shattered, almost as much as his own.

The main house slowly comes into view as you approach, a mansion house, which Mr Baxter the history master told us was built by a tea tycoon, Sir Arthur Drummond, in the middle of the last century- the rumour is that about £150,000 was spent on building the house and furnishings.

But I wouldn't choose to live here for all the tea in China. My mother used to say, "You can't always have what you want, Edwin," but I'm still trying.

The entrance to the main house is often shrouded in mist in the autumn, winter, and early spring. The two pillars at the gate awaken your eyes first, as the house yawns into view behind the courtyard.

Then the whole huge mansion bleeds into vision, the two turrets looming above, with the gravel-walls leading up to the criss-cross black and white timber triangular frontage, which

Mr Baxter said is what's called mock-Tudor style. That just about says it all for me- the whole place is pretending to be something it's not. But I can understand that somehow.

Two stone arches lead to the main door, which is heavy and wooden, with bolts and a huge brass pull handle and a keyhole that accepts the large key on Mr Tucker the janitor's key chain.

Through that double door, the floor of the main reception dazzles up at you, black and white squares like a giant chessboard polished and reflective, the paintings on the walls of previous people who lived here before it became Sunnyside- the tycoon, his wife, daughter and son among them, all solemn and dressed in black old-time clothes, and staring out at you, almost accusingly, as if you are intruding.

Then up to the right behind another stone arch, the steep yet wide marble staircase, the central stairs of the building, the white and thinly veined stone steps climbing upwards, with more paintings all the way to the next floor. There are sixty-four steps in total, I counted them every day in my first week here.

Old Bannister was found at the bottom of these stairs with his head bashed in, and I had to laugh. Not because his fate was predestined by his name, but because he was a very nasty man and he's missed by nobody.

Sneering and controlling, he'd been a fixture here for some years before I arrived in the spring of 1931- that was over five years ago now and I've just turned sixteen.

"What *are* you looking at, young man?" That's the last thing Old Bannister said to me.

Old Bannister went down the stairs in late October, and since then Mr Leadbetter has been master of our wing, which is much more agreeable. He's approachable in a way rare here.

Somehow, I knew immediately that things were going to change for the better and that's the way it's turning out.

I feel myself for the first time since I came here, and I can finally see some light amid all the darkness.

You see, they might call this place Sunnyside, but we call it Shadowside.

*

Up on the first floor is where we all sleep. There are four main wings- North, South, East, West- each with a dormitory containing twenty beds. I live in North, along with eighteen other boys- one left about a month ago, just days before Old Bannister took his tumble. Latimer had been here since 1929. We're waiting for a new victim to arrive.

North houses the older boys, East the younger ones, South the older girls, and- you guessed it- West the younger girls. Us older boys aren't allowed to go South, nor the younger ones West. But the more creative ones among us find ways to meet girls when we want.

Between North and East are the male staff quarters, between South and West the female. None of us, boy or girl, have ever been inside either, as far as I know.

The corridors upstairs, as in some downstairs, have floors patterned with squares, circles, and hexagons, with designs within- it's a geometry lesson just walking down them.

Sporadically, the walls are lined with huge wooden cases with glass fronts containing birds- all types of stuffed birds- from the common robin and sparrow up to birds of prey and vultures.

They just sit there staring out- their eyes watching you as you pass if you pay them any attention. Terminally perched on branches and rocks, placed there when the house was built, some find them spooky, but I like them, especially the vultures. They look so majestic and knowing, ready for action, poised for prey and primed for the kill. They have a savage honesty.

At the very end of the main corridor, past South as it curves round in an L-shape like a waiting snake, is the Cavendish Wing. None of us has ever been in there either. The huge wooden double doors are always kept bolted from the inside.

Separate staff 'look after' Cavendish- I've seen them come and go, mainly female. I say 'look after' with some trouble, as the girls have told us that they've heard murmurs from in there, late at night- the cries of young children and babies. But nobody has ever seen any of them.

Back in North, I have my 'section' - an iron bed and a hard mattress, one pillow issued to each of us. A wooden locker for clothes stands next to the bed, and a small trunk for our personal possessions is kept under our beds. *They* search our trunks daily for contraband, and turn our mattresses over once a week, on Saturday mornings.

I have the best section- I'm the oldest boy in North, and I've earnt it, having been here the longest now since Latimer left. Nobody bothers me. The others, all eighteen of them, aged between twelve and sixteen, just fall in line.

Baker (never stops crying), Beaumont, Carstairs (murmurs in his sleep) , Harris, Ingram, Johnson-Pitt (twitches on and off), Kirby(still wets his bed aged fifteen), Lassiter, Murphy (his head's too big for his body), Overton, Passmore (has a nasty habit of repeating what somebody says to him), Reed, Ross, Sherwood-Ames, Taylor, Wallace (the dirtiest boy in North), Williams, and Wilson (a real cry-baby too).

And me, Edwin Castleton. I'm very pleased to meet you.

*

They say that when you pass, your whole life flashes before you- at least that's what I read in a sodden detective magazine I once found in a bush in the grounds and dried out under my bed- we just can't read such things in the library here, it's just not good for us, *they* say.

When my whole life goes before my eyes in those last moments- just as Old Bannister's must've gone before his- the day I first saw Dorothy will be one of the images dug into my memory.

That day was about eight months ago. It was only a few weeks after the King died.

I'd been taken into Milston, the local town, to have my yearly dental check, Old Bannister scowling at the wheel, Mr Leadbetter in the front next to him. I looked as glum as Old Bannister was stern, but secretly a trip to town is always to be savoured, even if it involves having your mouth clamped open. But it didn't pay to ever show any sign of contentment in front of Old Bannister as he'd shoot you right down just as the Red Baron in his Fokker doomed other pilots in the war.

I read about the Red Baron's exploits last year in a tuppenny blood called *The Wizard,* but these days I try to get my hands on *The Hotspur* when I have two pennies. That day I'd managed to slip away to buy the latest issue at a newsstand when Old Bannister left us for about twenty minutes, and Mr Leadbetter was distracted helping a lady who'd dropped her hat in the street. That's the price of chivalry, I noted.

Of course, I couldn't keep my bloods in my section, they'd have been confiscated immediately. I kept my issues in an old potato sack I stole from the bins outside the kitchen and hid the sack in the middle of the big island mound just east of the main entrance.

Covered with foliage, it has a moat around it, which sometimes collects rain in the autumn, winter, and spring, but never enough to fill it. Mr Tucker told me that it was once a prominent feature of the house's garden. Now it just sits there, overgrown and forgotten and so do I, reading my bloods there among the bushes when I have the chance to get away, usually at twilight when it's dark enough to get on to the mound unnoticed, and light enough to read the serials. It's my favourite place.

After I managed to put that new edition in the sack, I had nine editions hidden there, along with the black mask, which came free with the first number, and which, like everything I keep, proved useful later.

In that same edition, I'd wanted to send off for the offer of the electric shock machine- 'Just watch your pal's face when you give him his first electric shock!' That would've caused havoc in North. But I just didn't have enough money- I only get three pennies a week.

It was when we got back to Shadowside that same day after seeing the dental surgeon that I saw Dorothy. It was her hair which took my eyes first, black as a raven, and then when I got closer, her matching eyes took my heart. I hadn't had this feeling since I first saw Miss Jenkins years ago, but that's a story that needs no telling here.

I wanted to speak to her, but Old Bannister moved me on, giving me a push down the main reception corridor. Dorothy smiled, lighting up the musty air. We were both standing on different squares of the chessboard floor, she on white and me on black- if I'd had time, I would have planned my move, if I'd had more time, I'd have planned several moves ahead.

It was no matter. The way she looked at me gave me my new focus, the one I instantly knew was the future. I'd read H G

Wells' story *'The Shape of Things to Come'*- I wanted to see the film at the flicks a few months ago too, but we don't get to go to the pictures. No matter. I already knew that my future was Dorothy-shaped.

*

The next time I saw Dorothy was in the Great Hall, where wooden panels give way to marble which slivers up to a timber-beamed lattice roof. The fireplace, large enough to fit ten to twelve boys inside- I've seen it done- dominates the room, although it has housed no fire for generations. The wooden floor is polished every Thursday by Mr Tucker. It was a Friday in early March when I saw her there and the floor was freshly shined.

It's a hollow room and full of echoes, but I wasn't listening, just looking. Dorothy glanced at me and as I felt an irresistible pull, my inner voice ordering me into action, I went over to her.

"Edwin," I said, holding out my hand.

"D-Dorothy," she said.

"Do you have a stammer, or are you just nervous?"

She didn't answer, just blushed, but I was soon to learn that she did have a stammer.

At fifteen, she struggled to make eye contact, like many people here.

"Well, I'm very happy to meet you, Dorothy," I said.

She smiled and looked so beautiful that I wanted to hold her- I wanted her to be mine.

Everybody has a story, and Dorothy's explained why she struggled to get her words out. She told me, after just a few days, that her father had interfered with her and that's why her mother had sent her to Shadowside. Talk about replacing one circle of hell with a deeper one, but then neither her mother nor Dorothy knew what this place is like.

We began to arrange to meet in corridors at times we knew we could get away without being missed for a few minutes, usually after breakfast, keeping a lookout for Old Bannister especially, or any of *them* really- boys weren't supposed to 'fraternise' with girls, as the rule list stuck on the inside lid of all of our desks says.

Soon we were meeting in *our place,* an alcove in the corridor outside the library. It's my third-favourite place.

It was one morning there that Dorothy would confide in me that her father had just carried on as normal and her mother had forgiven him.

"T-that's why I c-can never g-g-go back home," she said, starting to cry.

I put my arms around her and promised that I would look after her from now on. I felt powerful and swore to myself that when I get out of this place, I'll pay her father a little visit, put him in line, just as I had my own mother.

Within a couple of weeks after that, Dorothy had stopped stammering when she spoke to me, but she'd still stammer when talking to others. 'It's because I feel safe with you,' she said.

Her mother came to see her every month, I saw them out in the main courtyard standing next to a chauffeured sky-blue Bentley sports saloon from the tall turret window on the second-top-floor, where I'd been sent to clean the tiles in the billiards room. I wanted to rush down and give her mother a good talking-to, but I knew that it would only make it worse for Dorothy.

I just went back to cleaning the tiles, savouring being in the billiards room, my second-favourite place. Something happened there a long time ago, and it has a unique energy.

2

My bloods are important to me, particularly my editions of *Hotspur*. I can identify with the boys in them- they're leaders, fighting the good fight, standing up to oppression, standing firm against *them*.

All the boys at Red Circle School- Jim Stacey-especially Jim Stacey, Tubby Ryan, Cyrus Judd, Rawlinson- all striking back against Mr Smugg, the best-hated teacher.

And that September, things had come to the boil in two editions. The boys were going to put the kibosh on *them*.

In one edition, a group of boys are in a graveyard with two masters, one of them pointing with his cane to a gravestone on which is written, 'To the memory of red-coat schoolboys murdered by a brutal education system.'

On another cover story, Mr Smugg is seen prowling about the school, reading small placards everywhere reading 'Strike Boys! Strike' and a larger placard reading 'Refuse to obey orders- go on strike. Refuse to do lessons until your parents take you away.... Your future is at stake. Force your parents to act now. Strike Boys! Strike!'

Every spare moment at Shadowside when I can get away, I go to the mound and read my bloods or meet Dorothy. Both let me escape from the reality of this place, and both the Red Circle boys and Dorothy help me remember who I really am.

But deep down, I know that Jim Stacey and the boys can never truly beat *them*- there has be another edition, and if they did ever truly defeat those in authority at Red Circle School, there would be no more *Hotspur*. That's the problem with fiction.

*

Now let me tell you some more about Old Bannister, and the day he met his maker.

It was a Tuesday- 27 October, the day that Mrs Wallis Simpson, the friend of the new King, was granted her divorce, as the wireless in the library told us that evening.

That morning, we'd made Kirby 'drill for oil' as he'd wet his bed yet again, and Old Bannister was called. As usual, we all suffered.

"England has the oldest democracy in the world," said Old Bannister. "We stand and fall together. Kirby has failed, and so have all of you. You are all confined to sections between dinner and lights out for a week."

As always, that meant we couldn't leave North between six and ten in the evening. That in turn meant no meeting Dorothy in the library corridor alcove or visits to the mound to read my bloods by twilight or candlelight.

Nobody betrayed their dismay in front of Old Bannister, including me. But Kirby gave a performance worthy of Sir Henry Irving in not showing his despair. He knew well what was coming to him.

As soon as Old Bannister left, I told Kirby to get into position. He went to the centre of the dormitory and bent over, placing his outstretched thumb firmly to the ground.

I chose Ross and Overton, the youngest at twelve years old, to administer the punishment to fifteen-year-old water-baby Kirby.

"Ross and Overton will keep Kirby drilling," I said, and they both immediately walked over and stood either side of Kirby.

"Spin Mr Kirby, spin, get your derrick working," I said.

Kirby complied and began to spin, and every time he became dizzy and lost balance, Ross and Overton kicked him in the backside.

"Faster, Mr Kirby, there's plenty of liquid gold to be drawn out," I said, using a story about the oil rush in Texas in one of my bloods to inform my orders.

"Put some effort in Mr Ross! Help Mr Kirby in his quest!" I said.

Ross certainly did and kicked Kirby hard so that he flew across the wooden floor, beginning to cry.

"Assume your position, Mr Kirby," I said, and sobbing, he did just that.

This time Overton got some good purchase in when Kirby floundered, causing him to fall over again. Nobody cheered or laughed, they never did, everybody watched in silence.

After ten minutes of drilling, when I knew that Kirby's backside would be red raw, I called Ross and Overton off and went up to Kirby.

"If you soil your bed again, you'll be drinking your own liquid gold," I said. "Do you understand, Mr Kirby?"

He nodded, red-faced with his head down, and then we all went to breakfast. Kirby knew just as we all did that democracies always have a hierarchy, it's just human nature.

But that was the same day that Old Bannister died, and an unyielding tier of Shadowside's hierarchy everybody thought immovable vanished.

*

I was on my way to the library when I saw Old Bannister on the stairs. I would see him three times in all that day, the first before breakfast when he punished us, and twice more, and one of those times he was alive.

He was wearing a blue woollen suit and a diamond-checked tie over a charcoal shirt, and of course his Zenith wristwatch, which would have shown it was just before two o'clock. As always, he looked different from all the rest of *them*- he was far too stylish for Shadowside.

His face was chiselled, but not handsome, and without the small moustache, which could almost have been drawn on with a pencil, he would have looked like a wood carving, but pale and unvarnished. You see, there was a hardness to his face that no amount of expensive clothes could diminish or soften.

And Old Bannister's eyes were too small for his large face, as if they were two blue pins in a new cushion in a sewing factory. Beady is not quite the word-they were like slits, little stab wounds that appeared hollow, but burrowed into you.

He thought he was something special, a fashion plate, but his lean serpent body suited his cold-bloodedness, a tightly coiled cobra ever ready to strike. Shadowside was his lair, and he was firmly embedded, as if he'd always been in the mansion, like those people in the paintings in the main reception.

He walked fast, his long worker-ant legs always having a purpose, having somewhere to go, to be. That would be one of the reasons given for his fall, he'd taken the main stairs too fast and slipped, rolling down cold marble, fourteen steps, and landing on his head.

I'd seen Old Bannister just minutes before he was found. He was at the top of the stairs as I was walking up them from the bottom. I saw him just three steps in, but it was too late to turn back. I kept my head down as I came abreast of him- I was almost half the way up, on the thirty-first step from the bottom, as I always count steps.

That's when for no reason other than to unsettle me, he said, "What *are* you looking at, young man?"

"Nothing sir," I said, looking up.

With that he continued past me at his usual fast pace. I was angry- he always made me angry- I quickened my own pace in case he should call after me again and launch a second assault upon me.

I was just outside the library doors when the scream screeched up the stairs, a female cry, high-pitched and terrible. Then for a moment, nothing. I didn't react, just stood motionless there in the library corridor, not far from my and Dorothy's alcove.

But then people starting to rush out of doors all over the first floor- a woman even ran from Cavendish Wing, a very rare occurrence- I'd seen her go *in* there before. There were more cries and groans from downstairs, and finally I joined the downward migration, all of us like metal moths to a magnetic flame.

Quite a crowd had gathered when I finally got to the bottom of the stairs. I had to push my way through. And there he was, laid out on the chessboard floor, but both the black and white squares around Old Bannister were smeared with his blood, with spatters of it on the bottom few steps too over quite an area, the veins of the marble almost looking as if they were leaking.

Old Bannister's blue stab-like eyes were open, and he had a very confused expression on his face, what was left of it. The top of his head was rather caved in, his hair matted with more blood, his forehead dented and purple. He was prone, helpless, disempowered, and quite a spectacle.

Soon Mr Leadbetter, Mr Tucker, and Miss Ambrose, who all looked saturated in shock, were telling us to move away and go back to our wings.

"Will Mr Bannister be all right, Mr Leadbetter?" I said, having moved towards him.

He looked at me with a sorrowful expression, placing his hand gently on my shoulder. "I'm afraid Mr Bannister's dead," he said.

"Oh," I said.

"But it's best if you return to your section now, Castleton. And the rest of you too," said Mr Leadbetter.

Reluctantly, I left the throng, with others following me. I managed to hold off my laughter until I was alone in the library corridor again, but not my smirk- that was already imprinted on my face.

The ambulance soon arrived, with two attendants walking a stretcher into the main entrance- we saw them from the North windows. Not long after, the police arrived. One in a long grey coat and a trilby, the other two in uniform. They climbed out of a Wolseley police motorcar- it was gleaming, and made you wonder how they had time to keep it so clean. The G-men in my bloods have no time for things like that.

The stretcher bearers finally exited with Old Bannister wrapped up in a white sheet about an hour later, but the police didn't reappear outside.

Then Mr Leadbetter came and told us to go down and assemble in the Great Hall as there was to be an emergency assembly. This had never happened before in my years at Shadowside, even after the big fire at Christmas 1932, which was started by the recently departed Latimer and somebody I know very well.

*

We were led in wing by wing, the youngest girls first, so North was the last to take pews. I could see Dorothy, seated with the other girls from South, towards the front, with her back to me, head bowed. I wanted to get her attention, but there was no way I could. I wanted to set up a meeting in our alcove.

The entire staff of Shadowside, apart from those who worked on Cavendish Wing, were seated at the very front of the

12

Great Hall in two rows. Then Mr Dodwell, in his black suit and spectacles, approached the lectern, and we all stood up.

"You will know that Mr Bannister has suffered a terrible accident," said Mr Dodwell. "This has been a great shock to all of us, but we will continue to go about our days as usual, in the manner that Mr Bannister would expect us to."

There was a pause, and a female member of staff, nobody knew who it was, as she was in the back row, was heard sobbing. It sounded unforced and real, but I just couldn't understand why anybody would be crying over Old Bannister.

"The police are still with us, and they would like any person who saw Mr Bannister between one o'clock and two o'clock this afternoon to go and see them in the library immediately after this assembly. They say this is normal practice in the circumstances," he said. "So, if you saw Mr Bannister between those times, wherever it was, please go to the library, which will be out of bounds for study for the remainder of today. Everything else will continue as normal, and Mr Leadbetter will be assuming Mr Bannister's duties for now."

It was a typical address by Mr Dodwell- straight to the point. He marched out of the room, as usual with his head held high, and one could see that he was still very much the soldier who had apparently fought at Ypres, as he'd told us in another assembly.

This had raised him in my eyes, as I knew from my bloods that the fighting there had been ferocious. But he was still one of *them*, and the lead one no less. He had been at Sunnyside since the year before I arrived, and I'd never spoken to him. But I could tell that he looked directly at me during assemblies, and only me, I just knew.

*

When I got to the library, I was shown in by a policeman, and the man who had been in the grey coat and trilby was sitting at one of the desks, close to the old Victorian globe that we all loved to spin round, but which was very out-of-date as to territories.

"Thank you for coming," he said, standing up and holding out his hand, "I'm Inspector Alexander."

I shook his hand firmly, and I could see that he was surprised by the strength of my grip.

"I'm Edwin Castleton," I said. "I'm in North Wing. I'm the oldest boy here, sir."

He sat back down, and immediately began writing in his notebook, one of those moleskin ones, lightly pressing on the expensive fountain pen. He had a long thin nose and light blue, almost grey eyes- I wondered if his wife had matched the suit to them.

"How long have you been at Sunnyside?" said Inspector Alexander.

"Over five years now," I said.

"Do you like it here?" he said.

"As much as I can, sir," I said.

"May I ask why you were sent here?" he said.

"I was told that anybody who had seen Mr Bannister between one and two o'clock today should come and see you."

"I meant, why were you sent to Sunnyside?" he said.

"Pardon me, sir. I had some trouble at home," I said.

He looked at me with no expression whatsoever. No doubt like any good detective or G-man he would be looking into my past.

"At what time and where did you see Mr Bannister?" he finally said.

"It was just before two o'clock, on the stairs."

"The stairs where he fell?" he said.

"Yes. I was walking up them and Mr Bannister was coming down."

"Did you speak to or acknowledge each other?"

"No," I said. "Mr Bannister was not one to talk to boys unless he had a reason, sir."

"Where were you going?"

"In fact, I was coming here. I had to look up some dates for my history essay."

"What's the essay about?"

"General Gordon and the fall of Khartoum, sir."

"An interesting topic," said Inspector Alexander.

"In fact, the son of the man who built this place fought in the war in Sudan and was sent to relieve Gordon, but of course never got there in time. He killed himself later." I said.

"Poor man. Did you find the dates you needed?"

"No. I didn't quite make it into the library. There was a scream from downstairs, and like everybody I rushed down to where Mr Bannister lay."

"Did you see anything strange at all?"

"No sir. Of course, we were all in shock," I said.

"Naturally. Did you like Mr Bannister?"

"As much as the other masters, sir. Mr Bannister was firm, but fair."

"That's what I've heard."

"Nobody deserves to die like that," I said.

"I certainly agree with that. Well, thank you for coming to see me, you may go now."

I stood up and walked towards the door...

"I think you'll find that the dates you wanted are 1884-85," said Inspector Alexander.

"Thank you, sir," I said, closing the heavy library door behind me as I left. A girl from West was waiting outside with a female mistress, who didn't talk to me. I'm an E6 after all.

3

She was well-heeled, stepping from the blue Bentley out on to the pavement of Fetter Lane, her chauffeur liveried and solemn. She wasn't the kind of visitor that usually attended the *Travesties* office, a pebble's toss from Fleet Street.

It was a couple of days after the new King abdicated, and every paper was leading, blanketing with the story- 'I can no longer discharge my heavy task with efficiency' King Edward had said in a message to Parliament.

Harry Rose- by-line Harold Rose- had just returned from some refreshments at the Stab, which Monk, the usually embittered-when-sober subeditor, called when drunk 'a right good hostelry'. And he was sozzled most of the time, which explained why everyone called him Monkfish.

And Rose, like most in Fleet Street, wore his drinking face and hat well. Most of the time- he'd learnt to do both on the *Daily Herald*. It was just before midday.

Mr Flanagan, the sometimes-belligerent editor of the fledgling magazine, was more fawning than fierce that day. A little later he ushered Rose into the only meeting room, flamboyantly waving his arm and almost bowing to the lady, airs he'd absorbed at some minor public school, leading to graces he turned on like an electric lamp.

"This is Mr Harold Rose, one of the top journalists in Fleet Street." Rose winced, not at his introduction, but because around the Fleet Street community he was known as 'the Hack from Hell' due to his uncovering of an occult story in his dying days on the *Herald*.

"Mrs Hopkins needs our help. Her daughter is missing," said Flanagan gravely, although in his usual high-pitched voice.

She looked Rose up and down for a second, outwardly passing no final judgement. Her cigarette was held in a gilt-silver holder, that in turn by a delicate pale hand. She wore a bottle-green day dress with a high collar and a bow at the front, her fur dangling over the chair next to her.

She was pretty, but also drawn, her makeup not quite concealing the dark rings under her eyes. Her face screamed worry, hair jet black and bobbed, striking, and didn't look as if it came from a bottle. Rose thought she was in her mid-thirties, about his own age. But he knew she looked ten years younger.

"I hope you can help me, Mr Rose,' she finally said. "I read your publication- and as it says on the cover every month *'Telling the truth, however terrible,'* I knew I had to come to you."

"Have the police not made any progress?" said Rose.

"Nothing," interrupted Flanagan. "She's vanished without a trace."

"But they did find her charm in the woods at Sunnyside- it was attached to a bracelet I gave her for her thirteenth birthday," said Mrs Hopkins.

"What kind of charm was it?" said Rose.

"You can find that out from the police," said Flanagan.

"It's all right, Mr Flanagan. It's a horse pendant, in silver. They didn't find the bracelet, just the charm."

"Thank you. What's your daughter's name?" said Rose, pointedly looking at Mrs Hopkins.

"Dorothy. She's fifteen. She's young and fragile, nervous in her behaviour. That's why we sent her to Sunnyside."

"Sunnyside is what they used to call a private children's asylum. They now call it a juvenile mental institution," said Flanagan. "It's on the south coast."

"May I ask what caused you to send her there? It can't have been an easy decision to send your daughter to such a place," said Rose.

"That's a very personal question, Rose," said Flanagan.

"That's all right- he has to know. It might help him find her…She'd been at Sunnyside for about eight months. We sent her there because she was displaying violent behaviour."

"Towards you and her father- I take it that her father is still alive?" said Rose.

"Oh yes. But Dorothy never showed any violence towards us. It was always aimed at young women. Although she only went for a particular type- out in public- she would go for any

17

young woman pushing a pram or showing any affection to a baby."

Rose and Flanagan gave each other a look so blank it looked like a cheque with no denomination, payee, or signature.

"We took her to a psychiatrist. He said that Dorothy had developed an abnormally powerful maternal instinct, and this caused her to act out like she did. He advised us to send her to Sunnyside for treatment. We felt we had no choice."

"Could you give me the name of the psychiatrist? I'll also need a letter from you authorising him to answer my questions."

"His name's Dr Sanderson and he practises in Wimpole Street. I'll have the letter sent round to you first thing tomorrow."

"Thank you. When was the last time anybody saw Dorothy?" said Rose.

"It was the evening of 21 November. She was seen by the matron Mrs Cleverly at lights out. I'd last seen her the previous Sunday."

"How was she?" said Rose. Almost three weeks had passed, he thought.

"We parted on bad terms I'm afraid. She was very emotional- she was usually withdrawn- but she was frightened, begging me to take her away. But Dr Sanderson had warned me about this and said I must always stay firm until the treatment was finished, for Dorothy's own good."

"Do you have a photograph of Dorothy?"

"Yes- here." She reached into her clutch bag and took out a small photograph album and passed it to Rose. Inside were just three photographs, all of Dorothy.

"They were all taken on the same day, at Christmas 1935, just a few months before she went to Sunnyside."

"Thank you. Are you happy for me to run a detailed story about Dorothy once I have some information? We wouldn't have to use your real names," said Rose.

"As long as you find her, I'm happy for you to do that. But discretion would be much appreciated."

Flanagan helped Mrs Hopkins on with her fur, and Rose was left staring down at the photographs.

"Thank you, Mr Rose." Her gloved hand shook Rose's hand.

"I'll do what I can," said Rose, gently. "Of course, I may have to pass information to the police if it's important, after I've informed you."

Mrs Hopkins looked directly into Rose's green eyes. "I only want to find my daughter," she said firmly. "Whether it's you or the police is no matter to me."

And with that, Flanagan escorted her out to the waiting Bentley, the colour of a summer sky, the effect of which was dulled and dimmed by grim London rain and fog.

*

Rose was in the office early waiting for the letter from Mrs Hopkins to arrive. Flanagan wasn't there, he was out trying to raise investment for *Travesties*, so he was likely to be out most of the day as funds were desperately needed. Just three issues in, and Rose knew that the periodical was operating on an almost broken shoestring.

There had never been any trouble with funds on the *Herald*, with it being backed by the unions, and later going into joint ownership with a large commercial publisher. By the time that Rose left the paper, it was selling a couple of million copies a day. Latest circulation figures on *Travesties* were 26,000 three editions in, according to Flanagan, but it was steadily building, and it was a monthly. On the paper, Rose had been on fast-turnaround news stories, often filing three a day, while now he worked on one major story a month, or two or three smaller ones if necessary.

Monkfish wrote the news-in-brief columns, grammatically perfect if workmanlike, but still impressive when you knew that he was three-quarters cut most of the time at the typewriter. Monkfish had started out years ago, working as a roving reporter, at a time when there were no portable typewriters, and hacks had to rent one by the hour or day wherever they were.

Now Monkfish was static in the office and the Stab, and no longer milking the streets for stories. But it was a different world now- Rose understood that a certain type of reader wanted more, to get under a story. That's where he came in, and why Flanagan had hired him, but Rose knew that he'd probably still be on the *Herald* if he'd had the choice.

Monkfish was hammering away at the keys in his tiny office, bigger than Rose's own. Not that Rose spent much time there-he was out and about most of the time, and when in the area he liked to pull his hat down in the Stab, where of course he had as much space as Monkfish, and every other hack usually packed in there.

The letter arrived at just before ten o'clock, the chauffeur passing it to Rose, merely saying "Mrs Hopkins wishes you all the luck," which Rose acknowledged with a non-committal smile. Within ten minutes, he was out of the office, as usual not saying goodbye to Monkfish, knowing that they would acknowledge each other in the Stab later.

A bird or somebody looking down from a Zeppelin on Fleet Street would have seen the tops of minute boaters, flat caps, and trilbies at various speeds of motion. Rose, in his blue serge suit and trilby was one of those dots making his way down the bustling thoroughfare. He dodged between two boys looking at stamps in a window and a man deftly carrying a large crate on his shoulder. He picked up speed as he saw the bus plastered with 'Capstan Full Strength' and 'Wrigley's- for your teeth' posters, moving towards the Black and White milk bar, passing a woman with a walking library on her back as he came closer to the corner of Whitefriars Street, jumping on and offering his ticket to the waiting clippy.

About half-an-hour later, Rose left the bus at Cavendish Square, walking past classical and baroque buildings, away from the green tranquillity at the centre of the square and into Wimpole Street. He finally got to the white-pillared townhouse, of the address supplied on the envelope containing his letter of introduction to Dr Sanderson from Mrs Hopkins.

Inside he was asked to sit on a couch in the reception room by a woman whose hair was tied back so tightly it looked as if it had taken two people to pull it to its extent. "Dr Sanderson will be with you shortly," she said. It was obvious that Mrs Hopkins had set up the meeting, Rose thought, meaning that the letter of introduction would be redundant, so he put it back into his breast pocket.

The man who came into the room a few minutes later looked nothing like Rose had expected. He'd envisioned an elderly

20

man with tufty white hair and a beard and pince-nez, but instead the man before him was at least thirty years younger, suntanned and athletic looking, dressed in a tailor-made suit and beaming brogues, only the doctorly red bow tie spoiling the image of a well-heeled businessman.

"You must be Mr Rose- pleased to meet you. I'm Dr Sanderson," he said, holding out a hand.

The palm was soft, and before Rose could answer, its owner said, "I believe you have a letter of introduction for me?"

Rose reached into his pocket and passed the envelope over. It took Dr Sanderson about a minute to read the contents, and then he said, "Please follow me."

Rose was conscious that he had not yet spoken, but he knew he was there to listen.

In the consulting room, which was exactly as Rose imagined it would look, all wood and lamps, flowers and bookshelves, with an almost-black desk like a giant lozenge in front of the bay windows, which looked out over a well-kept garden with a swing and benches.

"There are limits to what I can tell you, due to patient confidentiality of course, but due to the circumstances and Mrs Hopkins' authorisation, I'll help you as much as I can. So, what would you like to know about Dorothy?" said Dr Sanderson.

"Could you tell me a little about her personality, and her particular vulnerabilities- in layman's terms if you don't mind," said Rose.

"Of course," said Dr Sanderson, a little too smugly for Rose's liking. "Well, Dorothy is a charming girl, but she has a rare problem- an extreme mother complex. That means that Dorothy is fixated on childbirth, which is her only goal in life. That's not so unusual, but what is more seldom seen, and potentially dangerous, is her need to assert herself over other young women who have a child or are caring for a child. On four occasions, Dorothy physically attacked young women- complete strangers- when out and about. The worst attack occurred in Hyde Park, and Dorothy pulled a young nanny who was pushing a perambulator to the ground, slapping her around the face many times. Luckily, the young woman, a foreigner, did not wish to take it further."

"And this was when Dorothy was referred to you?" said Rose.

"Precisely."

"What's the cause of this?" said Rose.

"This behaviour is intricately linked to the daughter's relationship with her mother. It can happen with sons too- the result can often be homosexuality. In Dorothy's case, she is unconscious of her own personality, and that is why she is shy, withdrawn, gives poor eye recognition and has a stutter. Looking at her, you would think what a pretty girl, who must be well-adjusted, she looks composed and well-maintained. But if you speak with her for just a few minutes, the total lack of confidence in herself is plain to see."

"What is her relationship with her mother like?" said Rose.

"I cannot go into details, but I will say that it is strained. And there's good reason for that. You see, Dorothy tries hard to suppress her dominant maternal instinct, and having developed no conceivable personality of her own, she objectifies her mother as a sort of ideal. But there is another side to that worship, which is hatred of her mother, and the desire to control her mother, which is really just Dorothy trying to gain control over herself."

"What could be the consequences if Dorothy were not treated in the long-term?"

"That all depends on how her life goes. Living with her mother is unsustainable long-term, she must step out of her mother's shadow. The worst scenario would be her causing serious physical and emotional harm to another woman to gain control of her infant offspring, and perhaps stealing a baby."

"Could we be talking about extreme violence, murder, for instance?"

"That is unlikely, but not out of the realms of possibility. If Dorothy's condition went unchecked over a long period, she could be extremely dangerous to other mothers and female carers, and that's why I recommended that she sought treatment at Sunnyside," said Dr Sanderson.

"Does Dorothy have any other vulnerabilities?" said Rose.

"Yes- of course Dorothy has yet to have a sexual relationship, but her future prognosis largely depends on the man she meets in the future. If she meets a man whose only objective in taking a wife is having children, then she will suit him fine, and could have a contented marriage. The only danger to that would be if Dorothy's maternal instinct should be directed at her husband, and she emasculates him, treating him like a baby. But I think that unlikely for Dorothy, having treated her for several months. However, …the biggest danger to Dorothy from a man is if she meets one who doesn't allow her to indulge her maternal instinct sufficiently and tries to rein it in as it were, making her match his own projections, not hers. That could lead to a serious psychic breakdown."

"What kind of treatment did she receive at Sunnyside?" said Rose.

"A regimented existence, one-to-one therapy sessions, minimal use of medicines. This is very much a disease of the mind, not of the body. Over time, Dorothy would have been exposed more and more to babies and their mothers, getting her used to being out in the world without the need to assert herself. It's very curable, and manageable at worst. And Sunnyside is an excellent establishment. I've sent several patients there over the years, all with good results. Will you be visiting Sunnyside?"

"I intend to shortly. I just have to find a way to spend some time there discreetly," said Rose.

"Well, I know the head doctor there, Dr Sharland, who is a very good friend. I'll see what I can do. Is there a way to contact you?" said Dr Sanderson.

"That's very kind of you," said Rose, taking a card from his wallet. "If you call the *Travesties* office, they will pass any message on to me- I'll be calling in regularly."

"I do hope you can find Dorothy," said Dr Sanderson. "I worry for her welfare after all this time. You know, she would find it very difficult to get by on her own."

"I can imagine," said Rose, "I'll do everything I can to locate her."

Back out on the street, Rose felt that he had a much better understanding of Dorothy, and a possible way into Sunnyside, but above all a real sense of foreboding, which he took note of, as he survived on his instincts.

4

In the days after Old Bannister left Shadowside, *they* all looked
dazed. Nobody had ever thought that he would depart
horizontally. You see, Old Bannister had ambition oozing out of
every pore, and I'm sure that *they* all knew he would either take
over from Mr Dodwell one day or move on to somewhere
prepared to give him the control he craved.

Mr Leadbetter soothed us all, coming around each section in
turn, saying that awful accidents sometimes happen, and it was
unlikely that Old Bannister suffered for long. I held a different
opinion, thinking that he must have known what happened to
him for at least a few minutes before he passed. But I nodded
silently. Nobody cried, but some of the boys were quieter than
usual. From North, apart from me only Harris had seen Old
Bannister in his prone position, and Harris never shows any
emotion. Ever.

In fact, the bloody scene at the bottom of the main stairs
would have made a good painting, entitled 'Old Bannister
Reclining.' It could be hung in the main reception next to the
Drummond family portraits. The bearded Sir Arthur, holding a
notebook- I'd always thought he should have been drinking tea,
as that commodity had built the house. Then Elisabeth, his wife,
stout in a wire-framed dress, smiling about as much as the
Mona Lisa, although she was probably long dead by the time
that painting was stolen and found. Charlotte, the daughter, fair,
pale, and red-lipped, almost inviting you to kiss her.

But it's Lawrence Drummond, who peers out at you, that has
always transfixed me. He slit his throat with a razor in the
billiards room in 1888 because he didn't want to go back to the
war. But his father Sir Arthur, disgraced, hushed it up, and word
was spread locally that he'd died of consumption.

There's a rumour that Lawrence Drummond haunts the
building- so Latimer told me long before he left- and now that

Old Bannister had died a painful death, I wondered if his spirit could also linger here.

Drummond's ghost is said to take the final walk from the main entrance to the billiards room up on the second floor, holding his army summons telegram and an open razor he'd bought just an hour earlier from Stenson's in Milston.

I've never seen Lawrence Drummond, but I've often thought of him walking past the stuffed birds. Did he stop and look at the ravens and vultures as he made that final walk with the cutthroat in his hand? Did he admire them one last time, speak to them, asking for their help? And did they tell him to go ahead and finish it? We'll never know.

If ghosts really do exist, Drummond will pass Old Bannister on the stairs, just as I did on the day he died.

*

I'd known Dorothy for over two months when she told me the real reason she was at Sunnyside, and believe me, we all have a reason. We'd grown closer with every meeting in our alcove, and when she told me the truth, it just made me feel closer to her, and more protective.

It was a drizzly evening in May, and the rain meandered down the window in the alcove as she told me.

"I can't bear to see other girls with babies," she said. "And I react when I see them."

"You mean you pick a fight with them?"

She nodded.

"So, your father never touched you?"

She shook her head sadly. "I'm s-sorry," she said, her stammer returning.

I put my arms around her and tightened them. It felt so good that she was mine.

I asked no questions. But Dorothy did, her dark eyes looking directly into mine.

"Why are you here?" she said.

"Well...I hit my mother. Twice. Then she sent me here."

"Why did you do that?"

"She kept telling me what to do, jawing on, until I'd had enough."

"Do either of your parents visit you?" she said.

25

"No," I said. "My father's dead…He killed himself."

"I'm so sorry, Edwin. Why?"

"He had the black dog," I said.

"What's that?"

"Melancholia."

"That's terrible, Edwin. Does your mother visit you?"

"No. She sends me a little money, but that's all."

"Will you go and live with her again when you leave here?" she said.

"If I ever leave here…"

"What do you mean?"

"I'm joking," I said, smiling. "I want to go and live with my uncle in Scotland, far away from my mother."

"Can I come with you?"

"Of course," I said, holding her to me again.

It was the following week that I took her to my favourite place for the first time. We arranged to meet after dinner outside, hidden from view near the kitchens, and from there under the dimming sky I took her hand and led her on to the mound.

I had to push her up, before climbing on myself. We sat in the middle of the mound, well-covered from view, not speaking. It was enough to be together, and I made no move to show her my bloods.

That was the first time we were intimate, and it wasn't like I expected. I mean, I had secretly gratified myself once, even though onanism is forbidden at Shadowside. I'd felt weak and guilty afterwards, as if I'd let myself down.

But with Dorothy it was different.

We held each other for a long time, until we heard the bell ring inside for us all to be in sections. We kissed, dressed, and carefully left the mound in the now darkness, Dorothy slipping back inside first, with me following a few minutes later.

We were intimate several more times in the next weeks, and each time it felt the same. But Dorothy seemed to enjoy it more than me. It was almost as if I was watching myself, detached from the act. I was there, but somehow not present. But I did what was expected of me.

*

26

It was a Tuesday in early September when Dorothy told me she was up the pole. It was the day after George McMahon was sent to prison for pointing his revolver at the new King, as we spoke about it in our history lesson that afternoon. But it was in the alcove that Dorothy told me.

She was nervous, but overjoyed, and I could understand that, as it was everything she'd ever wanted, the only thing. And I was pleased as it was meant to be. But I also knew that this immediately placed the baby in danger.

"*They'll* take it off of you," I said, the following evening on the mound, as leaves brushed our faces.

Dorothy didn't need to reply, she understood. Boys and girls were not even supposed to speak to each other at Shadowside, and I'd never heard of anyone being put in the family way there.

There was no telling what *they* might do- kill the baby, have it brought up by somebody else, strangers. *They* would probably take Dorothy away somewhere too. I couldn't let this happen. Dorothy was now part of me, and so the baby was too. Letting *them* take her or the baby away would be like attacking myself, cutting off my own arm or leg.

"What are we going to do, Edwin?" said Dorothy.

"You'll have to get away, before they find out- before it shows."

"But where? I don't have anywhere to go."

"I'll think of something," I said.

"I-I c-could tell my mother and have her take care of me and the b-baby."

The return of her stammer when alone with me betrayed her fear.

"No, never. This baby is ours- your mother has never taken care of you, sending you here, getting you away from her. I won't allow that to happen."

"But-but…"

"You could go and stay with my Uncle Robert in Scotland. And when I get out of here, I'll come and join you," I said.

"Will he let me stay?"

"Of course- he has a very big farm, and a house with lots of rooms. He's not married and has lots of servants."

27

"But won't your mother forbid it?" said Dorothy.

"My mother and my father's brother haven't spoken in years. She would never know."

"I love you Edwin," she said.

"I love you too. I think you'll like the farm. Uncle Robert has over 50,000 hectares. There are hills, fields with daisies as far as your beautiful eyes can see, and a river that glints in the sun like liquid diamonds. It will be our place, away from here, where we can live with our child and be free."

"Oh, Edwin, I can't wait."

"We will have to move quickly, in the next few weeks, before others notice."

"Won't they come looking for me?"

"*They'll* have to find you first."

She nodded, and we held each other until the bell rang, bringing us back down to our present reality.

If only I had an Uncle Robert with a big farm in Scotland.

*

My father took his life in the spring of 1929. The Big Crash then was still months away, but my father's crash finally came upon him one dewy April morning, when like Lawrence Drummond, he exercised the ultimate control.

My father didn't use a cut-throat razor but threw himself from the sixth floor of the Hotel Columbus in London. When he hit the awning, the whole of Marble Arch came to a standstill.

I'm proud of my father- I miss him- he was strong enough to see his own truth, and that gives me strength too. We're only failures if we lose control.

*

It was in the library corridor alcove that I told Dorothy the news about her escape.

"Why don't you come with me?" she said.

"It would make it too easy for *them* to find you if I was with you."

"But nobody knows about us."

"That's true, we've been very careful…but *they* will tear the place apart until they know where you've gone. You never know what somebody may have seen or heard. A look between us, a sideways glance. At least Old Bannister's not around anymore- I think he had his suspicions about us."

She nodded. "Will you write to me?"

"Of course- and I'll join you as soon as I can- we'll all be together.

The next few days went slowly, and I spent a lot of time on the mound, on two evenings without Dorothy, reading my bloods. I passed more minutes with the boys at Red Circle School than with Dorothy.

But I admit there was another reason Dorothy never went on the mound again with me. It was my place, where I would think about her when she was gone, and her presence there would have been too much for me. Everybody needs a place to escape. My haven would always be the mound, where I felt most complete and in control of all around me.

But I had a tremendous shock, one evening, there in my favourite place. The sack containing my bloods had been moved, just slightly. I realised it instantly. I was furious, shaking and cursing in a whisper in the middle of my island. Something was missing.

It couldn't have been *them* though. The sack would have disappeared, and there would have been a major search all over Shadowside for the culprit who'd left such contraband there.

I knew it was Dorothy. She had been on the mound without me. At first, I felt violated, much more than if it had been *them*.

5

The White Hart on New Fetter Lane is known as 'the Stab' because it's where hacks imbibe and stab each other in the back. Half of Fleet Street's worst come through its' doors in any given week, Rose and Monkfish among them. Flanagan prefers to indulge at Ye Olde Cheshire Cheese, a longer walk from the *Travesties* office. Rose always thought that was his editor's class burden, but he was ever thankful he could water himself without Flanagan's thorny presence.

Hats on the sticky-bitter bar or on heads, it's a place to chew the gristle and above all mislead rivals. Life on the nationals was always sharp-edged, but with the building circulation wars, it was now more hard-fought than ever just to keep your place. It wasn't unknown to stuff the exhaust pipes of competitors' motorcars with potatoes to prevent them getting away, once the tip or 'gen' came in, giving you a head-start on the lead. But out of historical respect, Irish hacks usually had their paper's vehicles bunged with different vegetables. But aside from that, all sympathy stymies to a stop.

It appears to be a gang in the Stab, everybody knows one another, and Gerald behind the bar keeps a loose kind of order, but no tabs anymore, as they got out of control. Drinking there is not for the faint-hearted, even though many patrons probably already have disease of that organ by their forties. Rose was less a target now he was on a monthly- when he was on the *Herald* he was open prey, the dailies the most ruthless circle, where on one visit, you could leave the dive bar with a back like a colander, after being knifed metaphorically by peers, supposed comrades in the trade.

And that's one of the reasons- the first being that he needed a sneaky snifter after visiting Dr Sanderson- that Rose went over to the Stab after picking up his twenty pounds in expenses from Flanagan at the office. He'd asked for double that, as the Dorothy Hopkins story looked like a lengthy investigation unless she turned up quickly of course.

Flanagan had given his usual protestations about costs and funding, tapping the in-out ledger on his desk, telling Rose that more money could be wired to him if needed later, and that he was already booked into the Gables boarding house in Milston, the closest town to the Sunnyside Juvenile Mental Institute, down there on the south coast.

And the other reason he went for a fast one- and as always now, just the one- was to lay his trail for the benefit of his rivals. Just a drop of blood in the fetid ocean of Fleet Street would draw the sharks in and send them on their oh-so-merry way. Just as Rose knew he would be, Jim Buchanan of the *Express* was there at the bar, hand on cheek, elbow propping up his increasingly wizened and bald yet hatted head.

You see, Buchanan is in so much debt, with unpaid tabs in pubs all over central-and probably outer-London-that he'd sell his miserable soul for a couple of fingers of his favourite brown liquid, his own grandmother said to have already gone for a song. That's the only reason he can still drink at the Stab, selling tips for tipples. If you want every hack worth knowing to think they know what you're chasing, Buchanan is your man.

Rose peeled off a pound note from his newly acquired funds, knowing that he'd have to account for this in his notebook later as 'contact entertainment expenses'. But it was worth investing, as Rose didn't want to spend days, perhaps weeks, in an isolated seaside town to be gazumped on the story.

And the dailies would all love this, the daughter of a wealthy family goes missing from a mental home, and the Sundays too for that matter, and that's why Rose had to buy Buchanan a couple of drinks to ensure he truly did pass his exclusive on to others- Buchanan was a far-better-days-gone-by master of chomping on the very hand holding a drink that sustained him.

"You're a gentleman and a...," said Buchanan as Gerald gave him a perfectly measured double. Buchanan never had to finish his usual line when accepting a beverage, everybody knowing that what he really wanted to end with was 'and a scoundrel'.

"What you on, Harry?" said Buchanan.

"Not much."

"You have some funds- I detect a new line of inquiry."

31

"Just scouting around."

"Off anywhere nice?"

"And why would I tell you that?"

"To help an old pal?"

Rose grimaced, knowing that Buchanan had betrayed many real so-called friends over the years.

"I wish I had something to slip you, Jim, but I really have no story, just scrapping around for leftovers, like the rest of 'em who aren't on the new King."

Rose knew that Buchanan sensed he was on a new story, his hack's antennae would just know, as if Marconi had sent the signal. And that's why when he left, Rose dropped the London-Glasgow railway timetable on the floor just far enough away from Buchanan as not to be obvious, but close enough for the already half-pickled newsman to spot it. And Rose had made sure to circle a sleeper train time to ensure the point got home.

Buchanan would immediately know why Rose was going to Glasgow. Just ten days before, Simmonds of the *Dispatch* had found out that Rose was looking into a story with connections there. A man had been found dead in a house in southwest London, having been beaten badly. The rumour soon spread that the dead man, a Glaswegian from a tough area, had been over in Chicago working for the Capone gang.

Like the other hacks, Rose and Simmonds knew that this was possible, as many young Scottish men had migrated to Chicago in the late twenties to get 'a piece of the pie,' as one of them had memorably phrased it in *Reynolds News*. And many had been deported back home now. Was the beating victim really a former triggerman for Big Al as he told many, or just a braggart? It had to be checked out, as any connection to the now-imprisoned Capone was always big news.

Simmonds had seen Rose at the house where the man died, in what Rose discovered quickly from a police source was a domestic dispute which got out of hand. Rose then double-checked with a police contact up in Glasgow as to the man's true past. The answer soon came back by telegram that he'd been in and out of the city's Barlinnie Prison so frequently over the past decade that any trip to Chicago long enough to get into Capone's mob would have been impossible.

But Simmonds didn't know that, and by the time Buchanan passed the tip to every hack in need of a scoop who had the misfortune to sit next to him in front of Gerald's bar, Rose would be down on the south coast, as his peers fuelled their staff motorcars or made it to Kings Cross station for that long journey to Glasgow, and then a razor gang infested area of that city, chasing a headless herring in search of a golden goose.

*

When Rose pulled in to Milston railway station and walked past the single unmanned ticket office with a lone timetable hoarding next to it and out onto the street, the grating screech of seagulls overhead and the purity of the icy sea breeze hit him like a Jack Dempsey uppercut. He wondered if all the fresh air would kill him.

Four hours from London, Rose saw that the few winter-clad people milling around on the seafront road strolled almost as if an animator had forgotten to mobilise them, while his long strides to the taxi area and his instruction "The Gables, please," was enough to inform the driver of all that was needed, and just as well, as Flanagan had provided no street name.

Just a short ride along that same promenade, the town looked deserted, just two weeks before Christmas. There was some half-hearted bunting hanging from lampposts, but Rose couldn't tell if it was a forgotten remnant of the summer, or a reminder of the coming festivities. And with no Punch and Judy booth nor babe-in-a-manger on display, the town looked defiantly out of any season, and out on to the choppy grey sea as far as a healthy bird could fly.

"How far is the Sunnyside Juvenile Institute from here?" said Rose.

No answer.

The narrow-fronted boarding houses supported each other like standing white dominoes, only the name signs and the odd floral display in front distinguishing them, with 'Vacancies' everywhere.

"The Gables, sir."

It looked exactly as Rose had anticipated, scrubbed and soulless, except for the colour, a lime green, unique on the street. He gave a couple of pennies to the driver despite himself,

33

the coins already two kings out-of-date, their recipient grunting his reluctant appreciation, as if he were either above the largesse of strangers yet needed it or had expected a larger testament to his three-minute unresponsive service.

Rose was left on the street, in front of his new home, his suitcase in one hand and hat and typewriter case in the other. Up the three steps under the wooden porch, he tried to peer into the diamond-patterned multicoloured window in the door, stained as if requisitioned from a church. He pulled the bell rope, and it pealed twice. He only had time to look to his left to see a workman painting a fence three doors down before the door opened, revealing a tallish woman wearing a ruffle-collar, with brown hair in a bun and a serious expression.

"You must be Mr Rose. We've been expecting you."

"It's good to be here."

She waved him in, and he was soon standing in the reception area, a wooden desk above waist-height in front of him, a carpet overgrown with green and blue flowers below him. She went behind the desk, where there was a sign reading Mrs A. Smith.

"Mrs Ann Smith?" said Rose.

"Antonia, actually. Why did you think my name was Ann?"

"Ann of Green Gables?"

She smiled faintly. "You're the first guest in eight years who's made that connection. Ann is my mother's name- she named it."

"There's just one other guest at the moment, Mr Rose," she said as they walked up the stairs. "Mrs Manningham, an elderly lady, who also goes under her professional name, Madame Sosostris."

The name meant something to Rose. Not Mrs Manningham, but Madame Sosostris. "An actress?" he said after a brief pause.

"A psychic. Do you believe in the Tarot, Mr Rose?"

"I can't say that I do."

"Well, I don't think that will stop Mrs Manningham trying to give you a reading- beware, you'd have to cross her palm with a couple of bob though."

"I'll bear that in mind," said Rose.

She pushed open a door, the last on the right on the landing. "You're in number six."

34

It looked out on to the seafront with a small balcony which would have been pleasant in the summer, but the rain now pounding the closed windows rendered it less enticing.

"Dinner is at six, breakfast at eight. There are fresh towels in the cupboard and rooms are cleaned between ten and eleven every morning. The bathroom is at the end of the corridor on the left."

"Thank you."

"I'll give you the keys- this one is for your room, and this one the main door. Please feel free to come and go as you want, but please try to remember that some need their sleep should you come in after 10pm."

Rose nodded.

"Well, I look forward to seeing you for dinner at six. Welcome to the Gables."

Rose smiled and sat down on the bed as soon as she'd shut the door, and then laid back on it. It was comfortable enough once he'd removed two of the three pillows.

He was still trying to think how and where he'd heard of Madame Sosostris, but knew that it had been by professional means, as he'd never visited a psychic in his life.

Standing up again, he looked out of the window, the glass blurry with wetness, distorting the view. He looked at his wristwatch. It was just after five o'clock, so just time to have a wash and unpack his few things before his first meal, which proved to be stew and dumplings, followed by treacle pudding and custard, good stodgy traditional fare.

A young girl served while Mrs Smith- Antonia -remained in the background after saying good evening, as Rose, and then Mrs Manningham/Madame Sosostris, entered the dining room. She doesn't look like a psychic, thought Rose, having envisioned her wearing garish colours.

She looked like any elderly woman, starched, and flannelled, in a charcoal-coloured skirt and jacket, only the brooch with the blue stone and the sprig of heather in her buttonhole giving her appearance a more earthy aspect.

She made no effort to look up at Rose, despite having passed right by his table on the way in and past the five other undressed tables to take her seat in the far corner with her back to him, obviously her usual table.

Rose decided to approach her once they had both finished their meals, out of courtesy and the need to get a feel for his surroundings- from experience he knew that old ladies missed very little. But he did wonder whether he would get the Mrs Manningham of the real world or the Madame Sosostris of the spiritual world, or both if they were truly one and the same.

And then it came to him, the reason why her name had registered. The *Graphic* had run a big story several years before about fake psychics, and a Madame Sosostris, a gypsy, had been one of those exposed. There had been no prosecution, he remembered, as the police couldn't prove if she and the others were genuine or not- the publicity would have destroyed her livelihood though. But could it be the same woman, so many miles from London? She didn't look like a gypsy, but then what's a gypsy supposed to look like, thought Rose.

And then he remembered he was undercover, a furniture salesman from the city who'd moved to the seaside town for health reasons, in search of work. Nobody in Milston or at Sunnyside could know he was a hack, and as his by-line was far from being a household name, his anonymity served him well.

Just as well, he thought. If it was the same Madame Sosostris, she'd undoubtedly be less than welcoming to him if she had any sense that he was from Fleet Street.

6

Those first few days after Dorothy disappeared were chaotic ones at Shadowside for *them*. I felt calm in the centre of that whirlwind, while *they* scrambled about hopelessly within it trying to find her.

I watched like a queen ant while the worker ants scurried around with no direction, as if their hill had been disturbed. Dorothy Hopkins was all anybody whispered about in North, South, East and West, and undoubtedly *their* quarters, and probably even in the Cavendish Wing.

But I listened and learned. I feigned concern, but not too much- for why would I have such an interest in a girl from South? Dorothy and I had always been so careful, and with Old Bannister gone, our secret was safe, I was certain. Besides, I'm an E6, so I'd hardly be the most obvious person to have spent time with her.

I didn't miss Dorothy, if anything she felt much closer to me. There were no more meetings in the library corridor alcove, but I still relished my visits to the mound, my bloods, and the peace I found there.

No, I didn't miss Dorothy, but I loved her as much as ever. The way that she gives me all her attention, all of herself, mentally and physically, is the only time in my life I've ever felt so fulfilled.

Our bond is unbreakable, and that's what I meant when I said that the first time I met her, I knew my future would be Dorothy-shaped in one way or another.

That's not shaped by Dorothy, you must understand. A man- and I almost am one- needs to define himself, of course, and be sure of who he is. You see, I have a very strong sense of who I am and what I want, I always have. Dorothy understands that too, and that's why she mirrors me so well.

My mother never understood me. Sending me to Shadowside was a welcome comfort for her, I'm sure. She saw me as just a boy she couldn't control. She never had any idea of how truly developed I was, and not seeing her anymore is now a great relief to me.

But my father understood me. He would never have sent me here if he'd lived. He was a man who knew he was right- it was just those around him that made him feel so sad. He was a leader, strong and assertive, everything a man should be.

And I think my father saw his younger self in me, and knew I'd do great things one day, surpass him and all those around. He had faith in me, just like Dorothy, and that's something my mother never had.

*

It was on the following Monday morning after Dorothy vanished that I saw Inspector Alexander again, the policeman who had spoken to me about Old Bannister. He was walking through the main reception with Mr Dodwell, the latter with his hands firmly clasped behind his back, but still standing as straight as a sharp needle.

Inspector Alexander was in the same grey overcoat and trilby, and I wondered if he was looking into Dorothy's disappearance or following up on Old Bannister. Neither saw me, as I was hidden around the corner by the main noticeboard, and I moved off quickly as they approached.

That's why I made a special detour to the supplies shed after lunch, before I was expected to be back in North's form room with Mr Leadbetter. Those twenty minutes would usually have been passed on the mound or in the billiards room, and that's just how important it was to see Mr Tucker. It was an invasively cold day, I recall.

I went to see Mr Tucker, the janitor, with his sinewy, tightly coiled body and forgettable face as blank as a miser's cheque. But his simple serenity hides a mind which sees more than anyone, and not just because he spends his days all over Shadowside's main building, outbuildings, and grounds. In fact, Mr Tucker has always been the greatest threat I've felt towards the uncovering of my secret hiding place on the mound.

But as I read once in one of my bloods, 'Keep your friends close, and your enemies closer.' And Mr Tucker could be a potential enemy. Not only does he see, but his ordered mind makes calculations, and he may have not spent years poring over books like many of *them*, but he can judge most people and situations better than any other person at Shadowside, bar me.

Mr Tucker has never got to know any of the children at Shadowside, including me. You see, I know him, but he doesn't know me- yet he thinks he does. He used to feel a mixture of sympathy and trepidation toward me- the first because I'm trapped here, and the second as spending time with the children is more than his miserable wage is worth. Now he sees me as a friend.

I identified his worth as an informant early on, by the way he looked up slightly and sideways at something happening before him, his workman's clothes and jangling keychain making him seem just part of the landscape to everyone else, his rustic accent making him seem unthreatening.

Behind that, I sensed a keen mind at work, a love of detail and the gathering of information. He is obviously a man who's had to live on his wits his entire life. There are no flies, alive, dying, or dead, on Mr Tucker.

But sympathy wasn't enough. It would take more than that for him to feel comfortable enough to overcome his trepidation and speak to me, rather than just receive the nod of the head he gave boys, or a "Mornin", "Afternoon" or "Evenin", which he afforded the girls, taking off his flat cap to them as he spoke, wherever he was, with pitchfork, broom or shovel in hand.

I had to wait a few weeks before I got my 'in' with Tucker. His dog Pepper, a little yappy thing, went missing, and of course, the unmarried and otherwise alone Mr Tucker was distraught. Seven long years she'd been with him when she vanished in the summer of 1934. He'd shared his tied cottage- owned by *them* and no doubt used to control him —only with Pepper, all that time.

After Pepper disappeared, Mr Tucker's outdoorsy and unlined face seemed to grow weary, a nervous frown replacing his usual closed-lipped smile. You see, nobody had ever seen Mr Tucker's teeth as far as I know, so I can't attest to their quality or quantity. I doubt that he visits the dental surgeon in Milston as we do, but that's not the reason he never displays his ivories.

You see, an open smile is much too emotional for him. But then so was the frown he wore in those days when hand-written posters offering a £10 reward for Pepper's finder, a sizeable sum to Mr Tucker, were stuck to trees all over the Shadowside grounds and along the main Milston road. I wrote those posters for him, and I was given special permission from none other than Old Bannister himself to help Mr Tucker distribute them.

I went up to him when I saw him looking so sad in the main courtyard on a sweltering day, his braces dangling as he swept the drive, asking what was wrong.

"Nothing for you to worry about, young'un," he said, the first time he'd ever spoken to me.

I left it there, but the next day, I approached him again at his supplies shed, the place he could usually be found when not out and about.

"I want to help you Mr Tucker," I said. "But I can't if you don't tell me what's wrong."

He looked at me for a full minute.

"Pepper's gone," he finally said. He could so easily have been referring to his daughter if he'd had one, but everybody knew that his little dog was called Pepper, as he could sometimes be heard calling after it.

"Well, we'll have to find her," I said.

He looked at me again, this time for about thirty seconds.

"You really want to help?" he said.

"I sincerely do."

He told me that he would have to ask Mr Bannister for his authority to enlist my help, and I said I understood, not expecting the late Old Bannister to allow it, but he did.

For the next fortnight or so I spent every spare moment with Mr Tucker, even sometimes being allowed to return to section later than required, as I wrote and put up those posters everywhere, almost three hundred in all, including the ones I helped him distribute in Milston, a trip on which Mr Leadbetter accompanied us.

I got much closer to Mr Tucker in those two weeks, and ever since, we have had a shorthand understanding between us. I could tell that he truly appreciated the time and effort I'd made.

40

We never found Pepper. Mr Tucker recovered in time, but he's never had a dog since. He never said, but the thought of another running away would be too much for him. And I know that he couldn't comprehend that Pepper would've run away from him, so close had they been. He was sure that she'd been stolen.

So, when I walked towards the supplies shed that early afternoon, to find out what I needed to know from Mr Tucker, I knew I would be welcome. I could hear him moving things about inside. I knocked and he came to the door.

"Hello, young Edwin."

"Afternoon, Mr Tucker."

"What pleasure do I owe this visit?"

"I wondered if you could tell me why there's a policeman here today. It's just one of the boys is worried his homemade cider may have been discovered."

Tucker smiled to his personal limit, just as I thought. He's partial to a tankard or two himself at the local inn, the Golden Bell, he once told me.

"Well, as it's such an understandable crime, I can tell you it's got nothing to do with sweet applejack," he said.

"Do you know why he's here?"

"I hear he's here to look into that girl who's gone missing. Dorothy…er..."

I made no attempt to complete Dorothy's name.

"Oh, I see," I said. "And perhaps about Mr Bannister too?"

"No, I don't think so. I heard that was an accident- an unlucky fall. Those stairs can be dangerous, you know, I've almost slipped up on them myself."

I nodded. "Well, thank you Mr Tucker."

"Keep well, Edwin," he said, returning to his task.

I went back to my section, thinking that *they* had no clue as to Dorothy's whereabouts. And now her disappearance was official, something that *they* would have wanted to avoid. And with Dorothy now in a safe place, and no connection between me and her, I had nothing to fear.

*

But I must admit that I momentarily lost control of myself less than an hour later when Mr Leadbetter came into North,

41

and after admonishing Lassiter for something or other, came straight to my section displaying an uncharacteristically serious expression. He told me that Inspector Alexander wanted to see me in the library immediately.

There was no point asking Mr Leadbetter why, as I was sure he wouldn't know the reason for my summons, and with the electric-shock-like surge within me, words were hardly a good tactical move.

On the way to the library, walking three measured paces behind Mr Leadbetter, I scolded myself as I'd felt my face flush, and wondered if he'd noticed. But then I reassured myself that any boy would have such a reaction if asked to speak to a policeman.

I would deny knowing Dorothy more than any other girl at Shadowside, just a face I'd seen in passing in corridors and in assemblies. But how had Inspector Alexander linked me to her? My mind was travelling faster than a Railton sports motorcar as Mr Leadbetter left me at the library door with continuing solemnity.

"Come in."

He was sitting in the very same chair as the last time I'd spoken to him, only his suit and tie were different.

"Master Castleton, thank you for coming," said Inspector Alexander. "How did you do with your essay on Gordon of Khartoum?"

"I received a B-plus, sir."

"Well, that's good to hear. I suppose you're wondering why I've called for you?"

"I was rather sir, as I've told you all I know about Mr Bannister."

He looked at me with his illegible countenance, the opposite of Mr Leadbetter's chapter-and-verse face.

"It seems that you were the last person to be in close proximity to Mr Bannister when he was alive," he said. "Are you sure that it was just before two o'clock when you passed him on the stairs?"

"I certainly am, sir. I'm very careful about time."

"But I see that you don't wear a wristwatch?"

42

"No need, sir. All over the main building here you can hear the big clock chiming on the hour and quarter hour in every room, save the billiards room."

"But the clock was being cleaned on the day that Mr Bannister died, I'm informed."

It was my turn to look at him. "I don't recall that, sir."

"That's fine. I'm sure your approximation of the time is accurate. You seem like a very precise young man."

"I try to be aware of what's around me," I said.

"Thank you for coming to see me again. I wish you luck in all your endeavours."

"Thank you, sir."

I was just turning to leave when he put his final question to me.

"Did you know Dorothy Hopkins from the South wing?"

"No sir. Us boys can't be friends with the girls."

"Have you heard about her going missing?" he said.

"Of course, sir. Everybody has."

"And what do you think has happened to her?"

"Perhaps she ran away sir. Sunnyside can be a difficult place for some."

"And why's that?"

"It can be lonely sir."

"Are you lonely here?"

"No sir. I'm very much at home."

"That's pleasing to hear. Thank you for your time."

I quickly processed all that had been said as I walked away, and made my way up to the billiards room, the best place to think, along with the mound. At that time of the day, it's always empty, as its only used in the early evening.

I sat in the soft-to-the-touch green velvet chair, an original piece of house furniture- I was warned to be careful when cleaning it once because of its age. Since then, I'd been acutely aware that Lawrence Drummond probably sat in that same chair and may have been seated on it just before he went over to the window and then back towards the billiards table and pulled the razor across his neck, all those years ago.

Had Inspector Alexander really wanted to speak to me about Old Bannister- didn't he think it was an accident? Was he

43

looking for some assailant? Or was that to throw me off guard so that he could ask me about Dorothy? It was difficult to know.

I felt as if I'd dealt well with the daggers I was thrown. But had he singled me out about Dorothy, or was he asking every boy at Shadowside if they'd known her? What troubled me most was that I was one of the few most unlikely to have got to know her.

And my mind was far from miraged into thinking that Inspector Alexander wouldn't have checked up on me after our first conversation. He would have learnt easily enough that I'm an E6.

7

Rose walked towards the telephone box on the seafront. Freshly minted bright red beneath the white sky, he immediately saw that it hadn't been there long.

But he knew, from a news-in-brief item that had run recently in his old paper the *Herald*, that the design of this box was about to be superseded by a new model to celebrate the Silver Jubilee of the late King George V the year before.

And it would be a positive change, he thought, as this one had a post-box within it on the outside, which was fair enough, but the stamp machine next to it could be very irritating if somebody used it while you were on the blower, as it made a grinding noise.

He walked inside, pulling open the heavy cast-iron door, which always swung back on you if you didn't enter quickly enough. But Rose was glad to be out of the sea wind.

Rose lifted the receiver and put two sixpences into the coin slot, then pressed Button A. He asked the operator to be connected to the *Travesties* office number, and after a "Thank you caller, you're about to be connected," he heard the call-back signal. Within seconds, Flanagan was on the line. Monkfish was no doubt at the Stab.

"How's it going down there, Rose?"

"Fair to middling."

"I've got some good news. Dr Sanderson called..."

Just then, a grinding noise invaded the box.

"One moment," said Rose.

With the sound of the whirling wind battering the small glass panes surrounding him and the grinding of the stamp machine, he could hear little.

Rose usually prided himself on his acute hearing, a real attribute in Fleet Street, but not mandatory- one old reporter on the *Express* who'd gone almost deaf in the trenches in the war had become an expert lip-reader to not miss any 'gen'.

Rose could see the old lady patiently waiting for her stamps, undoubtedly for the Christmas postage, and she smiled at him through the glass. He managed to smile back as Flanagan got impatient on the other end of the line.

"Are you there, Rose? Rose…?"

Rose fed another sixpence into the slot and filed a memo to himself to make a note of all this on his expenses form- 'waste less of thine own money, spend more on thyself,' he always thought.

"Rose?"

"I'm here. Some old biddy buying her stamps. Did you say Dr Sanderson called?"

"Yes. You're to go to Sunnyside tomorrow morning. A Dr Sharland will be waiting for you in front of the main entrance of the building at ten o'clock sharp."

"That's very good news. Please thank Dr Sanderson for me," said Rose.

"Good luck, Rose. This could be a big one for us- make sure you bring it in."

With that, Flanagan was gone. The editor always exited conversations before the matter of expenses could be raised. Rose habitually made sure that he asked for more expenses immediately after first greeting, but he couldn't ask for more just yet.

Rose pressed Button B and a sixpence fell out of the bottom of the apparatus, which he pocketed in his heavy coat.

He opened the door, pushing hard against the now riled wind, and walked against it towards the sanctuary of the parade of shops on the other side of the road, away from the sea.

He was scanning the street for a place to shield from the wind, and then he saw her. She was fighting the wind like him but meeting less opposition on the other pavement. It was Madame Sosostris, her long blue-bottle coloured scarf flying up behind her, almost suspended mid-air for a second or two.

She walked into the Grecian Tea Rooms, its hanging sign flapping violently from side to side. Rose knew he just had to follow her inside, after waiting a required couple of minutes. But then of course, her wicked deck of cards may have already told her that he would enter after her, he thought, smiling to himself.

*

As if the force of the wind as he pulled the door closed behind him, making it bang twice, wasn't enough to announce his arrival at the Grecian Tea Rooms, the ring of the bell above the door offered final confirmation.

The two women behind the long white formica counter and the assortment of elderly and out-of-work patrons on that Tuesday morning all looked up and around depending on where they were seated or standing.

But Madame Sosostris, already seated with her back to the door at the rear of the long and narrow room, didn't pay him any attention.

Rose took a seat at a table for two towards the front. Covered by a plastic lacquered tablecloth, easily wipeable at the end of a visit- his was red-and-white checked, while other tables had the same pattern in blue-and-white and Rose spotted a ghastly yellow-and-white one draped over a table near to the cutlery racks.

A man (blue-and-white checked) looked at Rose and raised his flat cap slightly, Rose responding with a nod, and then a second more pronounced one when the man, who had seen many other days, lifted the cap from his head and put it back on.

"What can I get you?" said the youngish woman in a green apron who had come from behind the counter, pad in hand, as if his order was going to be so long that she needed to record it in detail.

"Cup of tea please and a couple of rounds of toast."

"Butter, jam, marmalade or honey?"

"Butter please."

"Is that all?"

"Yes," said Rose, almost apologetically. He wasn't usually one for eating much during the day- he often sustained himself liquidly at the Stab or another hostelry, but he hoped to find a good one in Milston in the coming days.

"Coming right up."

"Windy isn't it," he said.

"It's a little gusty today, yes."

47

In fact, Rose wasn't hungry at all, having had breakfast at the Gables. Although the tea would hopefully warm him after surviving the extreme weather he'd just endured. Everybody else in the room, including his waitress, seemed to act as if it was just a slight breeze.

But then, coming from London, he knew he was used to buildings blocking out the wind, with smog being the main hazard there. In Milston you had all the fresh air you could ever want, if you could stay upright to enjoy it, he mused.

He wondered how Madame Sosostris found the weather in her new home, having come from London herself. How long had she been there- did she move to Milston immediately after the *Herald* exposed her and several others' psychic services as probably fraudulent, or did she settle there after trying other towns or cities? And why Milston?

She sat, still in her coat and scarf, only her tilt hat removed, and seemed to be eating something, and he knew she'd missed breakfast that morning. Rose decided to go over and introduce himself.

He stood up and walked towards her table and around, so that he was facing her.

"Hello, I believe that you stay at the Gables too. I'm Harold."

She looked up, and he held out his hand. Madame Sosostris looked distinctly unimpressed.

"Yes, I saw you in the breakfast room the other day."

"Have you been staying there long?"

"A couple of years now."

"Do you like it there?"

"I wouldn't have stayed there if I didn't."

She spoke good English, heavily accented, with Rose guessing she was Greek. She made no effort to invite him to sit down at her blue-and-white checked table.

"Well, I hope to see you again soon, perhaps at breakfast."

"You probably will."

"Goodbye now."

When he got back to his table, the tea and toast had arrived, and he had to pat the bottom of the sugar shaker quite aggressively to get it flowing, his loud stirring raising a few weary eyebrows around him.

He took a sip, and it was a good strong brew. He needed it, as Madame Sosostris's reception had been colder than the wind outside. He paid at the counter, leaving a few pennies on the silver tip tray, and then went back out into the whirlwind.

Walking down the road, he saw a chemist shop, which looked as if it had been there for many years. It had a black and gold enamelled frontage, with its name 'Stenson's' written royally in italics.

Rose went inside as he needed a new shaving brush. He might just be able to put it down on expenses- personal grooming on professional business? The next day, he was going to Sunnyside, and he wanted to look as presentable as he could.

After making his purchase, he followed the sign to Milston library, the wind now abating a little. He wanted to find out a little about Sunnyside. To understand the present, he needed to delve a little into the past.

*

Back at the Gables, Rose went straight to his room, putting his new shaving brush on the glass plate above the small washbasin. He slipped its receipt into his notebook and sat down on the bed, looking out of the window and the unused balcony. The wind was still strong, attacking the window frames. Rattle, rattle.

He laid back on the bed, crossing his arms behind his head, closing his eyes, thinking about his coming meeting with Dr Sharland at Sunnyside. And then came a knock on the door, quiet yet pronounced. It must be Mrs Smith, the owner, he thought.

Standing up, he straightened his suit jacket before opening the door. But there in front of him stood Madame Sosostris.

"Please forgive me for bothering you. And my apologies for not being more friendly towards you earlier, but one cannot be too careful when meeting strangers for the first time. Mrs Smith tells me that you are a gentleman looking to improve his health, and that's why you came to Milston."

"That's true," said Rose. "And there's no need to apologise. I was perhaps a little forward in the café."

49

"Not at all. But I want to provide you with a service. I hope you do not mind me saying, but I sense a restlessness around you, a negative energy, and I'd like to read you."

Rose winced internally but smiled enthusiastically. He had nothing to lose, and little to do that afternoon, and had decided not even to go for his one fast one, so to be fresh for the morning, an impulse alien to every other hack he knew, and if Monkfish and the rest of the boys at the Stab could see him now, they'd think that the sea air had gone to his head. But he felt a real responsibility to Mrs Hopkins and to Dorothy, as well as getting the story.

"I'd be honoured. Would you like to do it here?"

"I'd rather you came to my room. It's the second from last on the left. Perhaps in five minutes?"

"I look forward to it," he said.

She turned away immediately, and Rose closed the door. Negative energy around him, restlessness? I bet she says that to all the boys, he thought. He drank a glass of water and after the allotted time knocked on her door.

"Come in."

He opened the door, and inside was half-dark with curtains tightly drawn and no electric light, but six candles evenly placed around the room gave off enough glow to make out things in close to them.

"Please have a seat," said Madame Sosostris, waving him towards a sofa, which he saw was covered in a bright purple velvet blanket, soft to the touch, with a gold silken tassled trim.

She sat in a wooden upright chair behind a large coffee table, which looked like it was made of walnut wood in the half-light but could have been a cheap imitation- it was the Gables, he remembered.

On the table was the expected deck of face-down cards, larger than the normal kind of cards that Rose had previously used to play rummy and poker.

"These cards will help tell you who you are and give you a guide in the current maze in which you find yourself. Are you a little lost?"

"I suppose I am." He thought that this was because he was in a strange town, a goldfish out of its bowl.

"These cards may also reflect those who can influence your life. Those forces of course have an impact upon you."

He nodded.

She picked up the cards with a face showing no discernible emotion, and with the displacing of a whiff of perfume, she passed the deck to him.

"I'd like you to shuffle these four times. And at the same time, please think about a problem on which you are dwelling."

For the first time in that room, Rose felt comfortable. He was a great shuffler, having perfected the skill over countless card night lock-ins at the Stab and other selected hostelries where the beer runs, the spirits are sunk, and money is occasionally won and often lost.

And the problem came easily too: where is Dorothy Hopkins? He had countless problems, but that was the most urgent at that moment.

"Very nicely done," she said. "Now please cut the deck."

He did as she asked, and then she took the bottom deck from him. He placed the top deck back on the table near to him.

She took three cards off that deck, and dealt three down on to the table, placing one centrally and two others either side, but closer to her.

Despite himself, Rose took an intake of breath as she turned the two outer cards face-up from the sides, revealing strange archaic illustrations.

Madame Sosostris looked at him intently, her large blue eyes glinting in the candlelight.

"You have the Hanged Man," she said. "But it's reversed."

"What does that mean?

"It means self or needless sacrifice, and points to a persecution complex, and feelings of being a victim."

Rose gave no reaction but knew that this wasn't how he felt at all, and somehow this was a relief to him.

"And then you have The Devil. This signifies a move in the direction of darkness and obsession."

Cheerful stuff, he thought.

Finally, she turned over the central card.

"You have received The Lovers. But again, it is reversed. You see here is the angel looking down on the woman and the man."

She looked at him again. "Are you in emotional turmoil?" she said.

"Not that I am aware of at the moment."

"This card represents emotional chaos, and a choice which has been made with regrets."

She continued looking at him, with a grave expression.

"Beware. You are entering a dangerous phase. Take the utmost care."

He looked back at her, and began to be drawn in a little, no doubt influenced by the suggestive lighting, her solemn demeanour, and cautionary words. But when she next spoke, that spell was broken.

"That will be ten shillings please."

The commercial aspect- which he knew would come- still made him bridle a little. But he reached into his jacket pocket and pulled a ten-shilling note from his wallet.

This was going on his expenses, as research. He almost asked for a receipt, but stopped himself, as Madame Sosostris would never supply one after her trouble with the police in London.

"Thank you," she said. "I will never do a reading for you again, and we shall never speak of this reading again either."

"Understood. And thank you."

She opened the door for him, and he was soon back in the natural light of his own room. Ten shillings! Quite a lucrative business, he thought. He thought about her words of warning for some time that afternoon and evening but concluded that he couldn't identify the observations within himself.

He had no lover- chance would be a fine thing with his lifestyle, the closest he'd ever come to a hangman was when he interviewed the country's number one executioner Thomas Pierrepoint a few years earlier when on the *Herald*, and he was sure he felt as near to the devil as the next man.

But he was restless, as she had said before the reading. He was beginning to become emotionally involved in the Dorothy Hopkins story, a rare occurrence for him on an assignment.

He could only hope that Madame Sosostris's reading of emotional chaos and making a choice with regrets was dishonest, and that the papers and the police had been right in thinking her a charlatan.

*

Rose sat beside the same voluntarily mute driver in the Austin motorcar which had taken him to the Gables on his first day in the town. He'd walked to the only rank in Milston to find a taxi and was met with the same response- nothing- when he asked to be taken to Sunnyside.

As they meandered along the Milston Road, Rose questioned internally if it was the only taxi in town, but provided he got there on time, it didn't truly matter.

Past the Golden Bell inn, which he filed under refreshment/research in his mind, and then the small red posting box on the side of the road, at which point the wordless wonder turned the Austin round sharply in the middle of the road, two large pillars supporting the open wrought-iron gates before them.

The sign, written in weather-beaten black letters signalled it was Sunnyside, and that was all- there was no mention of it being a children's asylum, or a Juvenile Mental Institution as Flanagan had labelled it. It looked merely like the entrance to a very big house, the kind to be found dotted randomly around the English countryside.

But then it had been a private house it seemed, and was now a private institution, he reminded himself. A state-run place would surely have trumpeted its purpose, but here he saw only wilful discretion.

There was a low mist which blew over the motorcar's bonnet as they cruised up the gravel drive, the trees arching around them, blocking the light, but the winter-scrubbed faded green of the grounds was evident.

Rose imagined how beautiful it would look in the summer. But a Leica-clear image invaded his mind, in colour, rather than in sepia or black-and-white. The fields around them were deep green, trees a rich chestnut brown, and the sky above them clear blue, in that snapshot of the approach to Sunnyside on a summer's day, over six months or two seasons ahead.

But it was now just eight days to Christmas, and as the trees gave way to the open white sky, Rose knew he had little time to get to the truth, if there was a chance that Dorothy could still be found and brought home to her mother.

And then the house appeared ahead, a vast mansion, built with obvious love and the pockets of a rich man. At Milston library he'd read about the house, and the Drummond family, but there were no photographs. Although what he saw now illustrated all he'd read in that local history book.

It was five minutes to ten when they pulled up in the main courtyard, the turrets looming above, which somehow seemed both foreign and at home in the surroundings.

Then he saw Dr Sharland approach- Rose gathered it was him because of the white coat he was wearing. A small man, but well-proportioned, hair the light beige colour and substance of a beach at high tide, receding sharply.

"Will you wait for me here?" said Rose to the driver. He had no idea how long he would be, but as it was going on expenses, it was worth the retainer, although Flanagan would have winced manically at the cost. But what Flanagan didn't see, he'd never know.

The driver nodded as Rose got out of the gleaming black door of the Austin, and it closed heavily behind him. Dr Sharland was by now next to him, and they shook hands.

"Welcome to Sunnyside, Mr Rose. Please come with me."

"Dr Sharland."

They walked through the main door, and onto the black-and-white checked and highly polished floor. The paintings on the wall must be members of the Drummond family, Rose thought, but he had no time to have a good look at them as Dr Sharland whisked him past the cold and sharp looking marbled stairs on the right, and through another door, where they turned left at the well-pinned and papered noticeboard.

Two women, one in a nurse's uniform, the other in a grey flannel jacket and skirt walked past them, smiling at Dr Sharland and, by default or courtesy, Rose.

There was a hollow feeling in the corridor, as no children seemed to be around, and Rose concentrated on the ornate patterns on the floor, which seemed to contain every kind of shape and design and must have taken a long time to produce all those years ago.

"The children are all in classes or treatment at the moment, and that's why I chose this time for you to come, to give us some peace," said Dr Sharland, as if he knew what Rose was thinking.

"They must be quite a handful sometimes," said Rose.

"We have our moments like any provider of care services, but generally the children are happy to be here as they know it's the best place for them to get better."

"That's reassuring," said Rose.

They came to a large wooden door with 'Dr Sharland-Senior Consultant' written on a nameplate, which looked less than permanent as it could be slid out and easily replaced.

"Have you worked here long?"

"A little over three years. I used to work in a London teaching hospital- that's where I met Dr Sanderson."

Dr Sharland opened the door and let Rose walk in first. It was oak-panelled, high-ceilinged, and spacious, with the requisite large desk, a couple of filing cabinets against a wall, two leather chairs and a dark blue sofa.

"Of course, I live at Sunnyside now, so this place is very much my life."

"Do you miss London?" said Rose.

"Occasionally- but I do make trips back there to do research and see old friends. I'm originally from this part of the country, so it was like coming home here in a way. And my work is very satisfying- we see real progress every day."

"Watching children getting better must be very rewarding."

"It is, and that's why I decided to specialise in juvenile psychiatry years ago. It's the area in which you can have the most profound impact. With new theories, treatments, and medications, we are developing the tools to stabilise and heal children mentally. But of course, some cases are harder than others."

"I can imagine," said Rose.

They were seated now, and Dr Sharland arched his hands under his chin as he spoke, almost as if he were praying.

"Dr Sanderson told me all about your quest to find out what happened to Dorothy Hopkins. I welcome that, and the police have made little headway, it seems."

"Did you treat Dorothy?"

"Yes. I oversaw her care here, as I do with all the residents. We don't call them patients here, by the way. We try to keep this place as much like a boarding school as possible. These children aspire to normalcy and their surroundings can have a real impact."

Rose nodded. "That makes sense."

"You will have to spend some time here, I know. So, I've been able to arrange a temporary job for you. It's as a kind of orderly."

"That's very kind of you. But I have no medical training, you understand."

"None required," said Dr Sharland. "It really is a dogsbody job, but it will let you spend some extended time here. The wages are low, but the opportunity is good in the circumstances, I believe."

"It certainly is. And I won't be requiring any pay." Rose could sense Flanagan wincing uncontrollably now.

"We will have to pay you every week as you'll have a job, but what you do with the money is up to you."

"Do you have a charitable foundation? I'd be happy to donate it there. I have my expenses and salary you see."

"That's very generous of you. Yes, we have the trust for developing new medications- that's part of our remit here, and we work in tandem with several hospitals in London and Exeter."

"That sounds perfect."

"By the way, there is also a grace and favour cottage with the post if you should need it. Wages may be low here, but because of the extensive grounds and numerous outbuildings, accommodation is always offered to staff. Most of the medical and teaching staff are housed here in the main building, but as a casual worker you would live in the grounds."

"That would be ideal," said Rose, "It will really give me the best chance of locating Dorothy."

"I take it that you accept the job and the accommodation then?"

"Yes, I certainly do- thank you for doing this."

"It's for a good cause, and Dr Sanderson vouches for you, that's enough for me. When would you like to start?"

"I'm ready to move in tomorrow?"

"That's fine. I'll meet you at the same time in the same place, in the main courtyard."

"Thank you, Dr Sharland."

"It's a pleasure."

As Dr Sharland led him back towards the main door, Rose was amazed at how helpful he had been, and how much easier it had made his job working undercover.

Just before they got to the main door, Dr Sharland turned and said, "This is strictly between us of course. Only you, Dr Sanderson and I know about this arrangement."

"Fully noted," said Rose, as they shook hands, and he made his way back out to the waiting taxi and its silent driver.

PART II

Concave

8

It was in the first week of December that I noticed her look at me.

It was in an assembly in the Great Hall, the first time that Dorothy's disappearance was mentioned by Mr Dodwell in front of the whole of Shadowside.

"One of the girls from South, Dorothy Hopkins, seems to have left us recently. If anybody should know anything about Dorothy's whereabouts, please speak to your head of section as soon as possible."

It wasn't the theme of the assembly that day. The theme was the need to understand yourself before you can understand others, a waste of time if you ask me. You either understand people and what they need and how they can help you, or you don't. It's got nothing to do with you at all.

But it gave Mr Dodwell the opportunity to say Shadowside's Latin motto once again: et verum est intellectus preparatnem cordisio, which we all knew meant 'the real motivation is understanding.'

I had no doubt that *they* had already spoken to the girls in South as soon as Dorothy departed, and the policeman who'd now asked to see me twice had more than likely interviewed the older girls too.

The decision of Mr Dodwell to inform us all officially that she was missing wouldn't have been taken lightly, for fears of others absconding.

It was disguised as almost an afterthought at the end of the assembly, while really being the main reason for it. But it certainly meant one of two things.

Either *they* were becoming increasingly desperate and were checking if a worm would turn in the wind, or *they* thought that a boy had been involved. Knowing *them* as I did, it was probably a mixture of both motivations.

I felt no fear. I still knew that there was nothing to connect me to Dorothy. But then she looked at me, and I realised I had a problem.

I'd seen her before with the other girls from South, and I knew her name was Isabel. She was fifteen like Dorothy, but pale and fair-haired. I'd never seen them together particularly, and Dorothy had never mentioned her to me.

When she turned around on the pew where she sat and looked over at me behind her, it wasn't a random glance, or in any way accidental.

Mr Dodwell had just said his piece about Dorothy, and that's when the look came- it was scornful and spiteful, but when I looked back, she swiftly looked away and ahead of her again.

As always, the girls filed out of the Great Hall first, and I didn't look at Isabel again. There was no need. I'd identified a problem, and now I had to deal with it.

You see, I understood her, but my motto is quod motus realis salvos: the real motivation is survival.

*

Dr Sharland stood by as Mr Tucker the janitor opened the heavy wooden door of the workman's cottage with a large key from his chain. Rose watched, taking in his new home from the outside.

Mrs Smith at the Gables had said she was sorry to see him go but understood if he had a more permanent place to stay. He didn't tell her where he was going, and she hadn't asked. She was probably used to guests coming and going with no backstory. And Rose was especially glad that he'd avoided Madame Sosostris on his last night there.

It was a small, cobbled cottage, with a long chimney and a thatched roof, with a small sitting room downstairs at the front, a kitchen behind that, and rickety stairs, which Mr Tucker warned them about as they ascended.

"Watch your step here, mind," said Mr Tucker, "this wood is about eighty years old." At least he'd have advanced warning if anyone broke in and went upstairs when he was asleep, thought Rose.

"I hope it's comfortable enough for you," said Dr Sharland, as Rose looked around the small bedroom with the large bed, which looked as if it might have once been a four-poster but had been decapitated.

"It's fine," said Rose, knowing that his new abode would please Flanagan as it was free, although Rose already had designs on spending some of the money he saved at the Gables at the Golden Bell down the road.

The window looked towards the main house, the turrets and roof visible, but the view of the lower part of the building was partially blocked by a kind of overgrown island, with what looked like an old moat around it, about a hundred yards from where they stood.

"Right, I'll let you get settled in," said Dr Sharland. "Shall we say we meet at my office at two o'clock this afternoon? I can give you a proper tour."

"That would be very useful," said Rose.

Mr Tucker nodded slightly, but not hesitantly, and Rose thought he seemed like a man who probably did little spontaneously.

After he heard the front door shut downstairs, Rose unpacked his suitcase and put his toiletries, including his new shaving brush from Stenson's, in the bathroom, which had a white sunken bath with taps that must have once shined.

"These are the main stairs which take you up to all the wings on the first floor. Be careful- they can be slippery- we had a very nasty accident happen here just a few months ago."

Rose was following Dr Sharland after leaving the office.

"Did somebody fall here? Were they badly hurt?" said Rose.

"I'm afraid so. Mr Bannister, a popular member of staff, unfortunately died after tripping down them. The marble is of course hard and unforgiving."

"How did he manage to fall down these steps and not stop himself- and fall hard enough to injure himself so badly?"

"It seems he bounded down them too quickly, tripped and bounced down. It was a terrible sight, I'm told, but I was away in Exeter that day."

"Was he an elderly man?"

"Not at all. And he was in vigorous health. But that may have been his undoing, moving so fast. I can attest to his long pacy strides."

Rose felt reassured that he was currently walking up them. He was no physicist but falling upwards had to be more difficult. And bouncing down them would take some doing- the steps were wide, if deep.

"The poor man," said Rose.

"Quite."

They turned left and Rose was taken aback when he saw the huge cabinets with the eyes staring out. Dr Sharland saw his reaction and smiled.

"Yes, this is the bird collection, although when this place was a house it was called the aves collection. Two hundred and eighty-nine species are on display, although few people know that a further sixty-four are stored in the basement."

"They're very arresting," said Rose.

"Yes, and especially at night."

As they waked past the glass-fronted cabinets, Rose read some of the name tags: the common raven, common blackbird, peregrine falcon, snowy owl, bald eagle, the Monk vulture, which momentarily brought a smile to Rose's lips, but this soon subsided as its stare was terrifying, and made him stop reading and look away.

"Sir Arthur Drummond, who later built this house, started his taxidermy collection after visiting the Great Exhibition in London in 1851 where he saw an amazing mounted display, I'm told," said Dr Sharland, noticing Rose's interest in the birds.

After showing him the library, which looked as Rose would have imagined it to have looked when it was still a private house, they walked on and Dr Sharland pointed out the four children's wings- North, South, East, West, and the staff quarters.

"It's very quiet," said Rose.

"The residents are all in classes or treatment again, but when the bell goes, you'll see them. Of course, you are not encouraged to communicate with them more than necessary. Your role is to assist me and it's not resident-focused."

"Understood," said Rose.

Then they made their way up a wooden spiral staircase to the second floor, and Rose was shown the billiards room, a game he was a little partial to playing when he had the chance.

"All the other rooms up here are treatment rooms and classrooms," said Dr Sharland. "As with the resident and staff quarters, you're not authorised to enter without my permission."

"Understandable." But Rose knew that rules had to be broken to get answers.

Just then, the shrill ringing of the bell sliced through the air. Immediately, doors began to open, and children of different ages and sizes, both boys and girls, began to appear. All wore blue blazers, black pullovers over white shirts and blouses, and black trousers or skirts.

But they didn't seem like normal children, as they all moved in silence, a black and blue with a hint of white throng which descended the stairs towards wings at a measured speed, neither rushing nor dawdling.

"They're very well-behaved," said Rose.

"We run a tight home for them here. Mr Dodwell insists on it, and clinically, stability and calm are always sought. Some of these children have tics and disorders, but you will never see the worst afflicted."

Rose looked at their faces. They neither smiled nor frowned, and nobody acknowledged either him or Dr Sharland.

It wasn't what Rose expected at all. He wondered where the high jinks happened, as they had to occur somehow, somewhere, sometime.

*

In the book *The Great Gatsby*, which I read last year after finding a copy in the library, the man telling the story begins by saying 'In my younger and more vulnerable years my father gave me some advice that I've been turning over in my mind ever since'.

The advice given is righteous- not to criticise anyone and to remember that not everybody had been given the advantages he had. And from that very first page, the narrator is carved and set in stone- a weak man, to whom nothing directly happens- he's an observer, not a doer.

If I were to write that book myself, my late father's advice would be very different, and I'd be a far stronger narrator. You see, my father would have told me- in my younger years, I was never vulnerable- 'to get *them* before *they* get you.'

My father knew that he never caused problems for himself, and that they were created by *them*. But he never stood by and just watched and waited to be tossed around by *their* vindictive will and the random winds of fate. He did unto *them* what *they* would do to him before *they* could.

Like my father, I recognise that there is no right and wrong, only right. One makes one's choice and one follows that path to the end, no matter where it goes. He would tell me that 'limits are for lesser men than you or me.'

My father always lived his life the way he wanted, and only when he did not wish to live that life anymore, did he end it. His example is branded within me at my very centre. Everybody is a predator, but some are stronger than others.

The Red Baron had eighty 'kills' in the air, and on his last flight when he was downed over the Somme, he came to the aid of his cousin, caring nothing for danger. My father valued loyalty too, and I always gave it to him.

Now my only loyalty must be to myself, the struggle against *them* at Shadowside, and then my future outside it.

*

After he'd left Dr Sharland in Sunnyside's main cobbled quad, Rose heard a voice behind him, a strange voice, very slow and resonant, but one still undecided on how low or high in pitch it would eventually be.

"Are you lost- can I help you sir?"

The owner of the still-breaking voice was almost the same height as Rose, and well-built. But his dark blonde hair and baby face, along with his uniform, identified him immediately as a boy 'resident'.

"I think I might be," said Rose.

"Where would you like to get to sir?" said the boy.

"I'm not sure to be honest. I'm just having a look around."

"I like to… have a wander sir."

The boy pronounced every syllable strongly, yet still spoke with some hesitation, as if he were trying to justify his words to himself.

"There's nothing wrong with a wander," said Rose.

The boy smiled without showing his teeth, but it was his eyes that transfixed Rose. One was of the clearest lagoon blue, the other also blue, but darker and opaque.

"I'm Mr Rose. I work with Dr Sharland."

"I guessed that sir. Because I saw you with him earlier."

"Well-observed," said Rose.

"I don't miss much sir. I see things nobody knows I've seen."

Rose couldn't help but stare at the boy's eyes, as they were startling.

Suddenly, as if the boy had sensed it, he reached up to his right eye, the darker misty one, and took it out, leaving the empty dark cavity of the eye socket where it had been. Rose visibly shuddered with the shock.

"Please don't be alarmed- I only need the one eye sir."

That's just as well, thought Rose, but he merely nodded.

"I'm Carstairs sir, it's a pleasure to make your acquaintance."

And with that the one-eyed boy with the body of a man ambled off across the quad, head down, as if deep in contemplation.

Rose watched Carstairs go under the arch beneath the clocktower, still a little shaken by what he'd just seen.

But he knew that his priority was to find out about Dorothy's horse charm, and just where it had been found. That would be his starting point.

9

She had no idea of what normal was, but after almost three years at Sunnyside it had become her normal. Before that everything had been so different, and Isabel was conscious of having shed her previous unwanted skin and left that life far behind her.

She was twelve years old when she carried out her experiment to see how long her sister could hold her breath underwater. Imogen was five then, and Isabel hadn't seen her since.

But Imogen's confused and then desperate face under the cold bath water, her fair hair splayed out and framed by the white porcelain around her was an image which still often returned to Isabel's mind, as if it were a macabre picture within a locket. Just Imogen's head in portrait, but with her eyes closed, cheeks swollen with air and bubbles furiously coming from her closed lips.

Imogen's body had been held down too tightly to move or even squirm. And then Mummy came in, pulling Isabel off her sister, saving Imogen, who had only been under for a minute-and-a-half. At the time, Isabel felt that she could have safely kept Imogen under for a further minute, but she now understood how close her little sister had come to dying that afternoon.

Before that it had been Imogen's dolls- their smiling faces and heavy eyelashes over fluttering eyes just too much for Isabel to bear. How sweet Imogen looked with them visitors to their house would say. "Angelic" little Imogen- "What a poppet", "The most beautiful little girl in the world" and "Such a gentle temperament too".

Isabel ripped off the dolls' arms, legs and heads and hid them around the garden before inviting Imogen to do a treasure hunt to retrieve the plastic limbs. And Imogen wailed for hours when she found her dollies' decapitated heads in her toybox, to Isabel's astonishment and relish.

Indeed, Imogen had never seemed to cry or sulk before that, as Isabel had herself at that age. That was why she'd put her sister to the ultimate test, to see just how perfect she truly was, in the bathroom that day in their home, surrounded by the white tiles with a diamond-patterned trim.

Within a fortnight, Isabel had been sent to Sunnyside, having spoken for hours to a doctor, the same one whom her friend Dorothy Hopkins would later see.

Isabel missed Dottie being there more than she could ever say. They understood each other without even needing to speak much. It was as if Dottie had been a foothold allowing her to keep some sort of a grip on the everyday at Sunnyside. But now she was gone.

It had all happened so quickly- one day Dottie was the happiest she'd ever seen her, and the next the most despondent and frightened she'd ever been at Sunnyside. And one night not long after, she simply disappeared.

*

Smoothing down his hair with his customary daily dip of Brylcreem, Rose wiped his fingers on the mouth of the bottle before replacing the cap. Looking in the mirror in the cottage's bathroom, he knew he looked as good as he could.

He walked across to the main building, where Dr Sharland had told him that breakfast was available every day at eight o'clock. There were a few people in the queue in the small staff dining room, two men and a woman, and the woman turned and smiled at Rose as he waited behind her.

"I'm Mrs Benson," she said.

"Harold Rose, nice to meet you."

"Have you just joined the staff- teaching or clinical?"

"Yes, I've come to assist Dr Sharland."

She nodded nonchalantly, as if new staff arriving was a daily event. Rose could see that she liked asking two questions at once, with the second one seemingly half-answering her own first question.

"It is all a bit new. I've just moved down from London."

"Oh, you'll get used to it and it'll be plus ca change soon enough."

67

Rose nodded knowingly but had no idea what she meant as he couldn't speak French.

"Are you on the teaching staff?" he said.

"Yes. I teach French and German. Are you a doctor- a consultant perhaps?"

"Nothing so grand. I'm afraid I'm just an orderly come to help with the mundane tasks."

She smiled, but the way she turned around again and faced the back of the man in front of her told Rose that he'd lost her interest.

After taking his coffee-white, two sugars, well-stirred- and picking up two pieces of toast, he made for one of the wooden tables. There were only two, but he was the first to sit down, as the others seemed to be going for the cooked breakfast option.

He smiled as he spied some newspapers at the end of the table, and reached across to pick up the *Herald*, but instead chose the *Daily Graphic* when he saw the front-page headline.

'Was man killed in London Al Capone's gunman?' It was by-lined 'Our Staff Reporter' but Rose knew that would be Dick Blythe. He grinned to himself and wondered how much or how many drinks Buchanan had got out of Dickie.

Then he retrieved the *Herald*, and sure enough on page four, there was 'Was Scot found dead Big Al's hired gun?' This time Rose's old drinking partner Bobby Martin had his name on the piece.

He looked up and noticed Mrs Benson had decided to sit on the other table, and another of her colleagues soon joined her. Finishing his coffee, he gave her a slight wave as he left the room, not expecting it returned, which it wasn't.

Just as he'd thought, Sunnyside had a strict hierarchy, and he was very much at the bottom. But at least he now knew that his associates in Fleet Street didn't know where he'd gone, and with any luck it would remain that way.

*

Rose's first task after being given his obligatory white coat- a little tight under the arms- by Dr Sharland, was to move some boxes from a storeroom on the ground floor up to another almost identical storeroom on the first floor.

"Take your time- there's not much more for you today," said Dr Sharland with a smirk, Rose reading it as telling him to focus on why he was really at Sunnyside.

He sat on one of the boxes and composed his thoughts. Dorothy had disappeared on 21 November, almost a month earlier. She's been living in the South wing with the other older girls or 'residents' as Dr Sharland had told him.

Rose knew that he had to find out who had been closest to Dorothy, amongst the other girls and the staff. But as he wasn't supposed to be interacting with the residents, and none of the other staff apart from Dr Sharland and Mr Dodwell, this had to be done on tiptoes, like most undercover work.

She was a fifteen-year-old girl-it was inconceivable to him that she wouldn't have confided in somebody. Had there been any romance, with a boy resident, or a father-figure among the staff? This would take time to find out.

But firstly, as well as visiting the woods where the horse charm had been found, Rose would need to look at the deeper background to Dorothy's disappearance. What had been happening at Sunnyside in the weeks and months before she vanished? Was there a trigger there to explain what had happened to her?

The death of the member of staff on the stairs was his starting point. This incident was out-of-the-ordinary, and Rose had learnt from experience that every action has a reaction, and every extraordinary action has an extraordinary reaction.

But he couldn't speak to the police about the man's death. They would try to get him out of there- they wouldn't want a national journalist hampering their local investigation. The local newspaper? Hacks thrive on rumours, but any benefit he'd get from talking to them would be outweighed by them trying to beat him to the story.

Then he remembered that in Milston library he'd seen shelves of archive copies of the *Milston Argus*, the local newssheet. That would enable him to build gen without alerting anybody.

Once he had finished with the boxes, he returned to Dr Sharland's office, but he wasn't there. Rose waited for a few minutes, and then decided to use the telephone.

69

Taking the card from his battered wallet, Rose dialled the number of the taxi-office, asking for a car to pick him up in half-an-hour on the slip road on the other side of his cottage-after all, it was best not to announce his comings and goings.

It was a different driver this time who took Rose into Milston. He spoke in between sucks of mint imperials, emitting a menthol smell all around him. Rose learnt all about how much Milston was changing for the worst, and began to miss the other driver's non-verbosity, but he asked the driver to come and take him back to Sunnyside in two hours.

The librarian, whose hair matched her grey clothes give or take a shade, took his order for copies of the weekly *Argus* going back four months. After taking a seat opposite her desk, they were soon delivered by an elderly man who looked as if life had got the better of him as he unloaded them from the wooden trolley.

"Seventeen copies of the *Argus*. Please leave them in the condition you found them."

"Thank you," said Rose.

"No marking, tearing or smudging."

Rose nodded, wondering if he was looking at the local rag or one of the remaining original copies of the Magna Carta. As the trolley faded into the distance, he decided to start with the oldest copy, from August that year and work towards the latest edition.

When he left the library just over an hour later, Rose had learnt more details about the man who'd died at Sunnyside just over three months earlier. Bernard Bannister was forty-one years-old, and had been at Sunnyside for seven years, arriving there from another institution in the north of England in 1929.

He taught classics and worked his way up from being a lowly assistant to be one of the senior members of staff at Sunnyside. Rose copied down a quote from Mrs Benson, who had snubbed him at breakfast that morning. "He was a good man, we are all so sad, he was liked by one and all." He wondered if that was how she really felt.

Unmarried, Mr Bannister's relatives remained in the north. The paper covered the story as an accident from the beginning, with headlines such as 'Tragic Fall at Sunnyside' but Rose could see that as the police had investigated his death for over five weeks, the case last appearing in an edition in late October, there had been enough possibility of doubt to warrant keeping their minds officially open.

But there was one mystery. Mr Bannister's wristwatch, which he always wore, according to other staff members and both his mother and brother, was not on his wrist when he was found at the bottom of the stairs. Nobody could remember its make, and a search of his living quarters and inquiries made at the town's two clocksmiths had failed to turn it up.

But that was all. It seemed that Mr Bannister had been extremely unlucky. For Rose, though, it wasn't enough. It may well have been an accident, but it was still an unnatural death.

If he were to have any chance of finding Dorothy, he needed to find out what everybody at Sunnyside really thought about Mr Bannister's demise.

He had almost an hour until the driver came to collect him, so Rose decided to pay a visit to the clocksmiths mentioned in the paper. The first was G. Wheeler's on Argyll Street, but that was closed. Ten minutes later, he arrived at Timely Timepieces on Charteris Mews.

The window was covered in gold and silver clocks, and as he opened the door, the metronomic ticking of scores of clocks filled the air.

The young man behind the till on the wooden chair, with watch parts in his hand and holding an eyeglass to his eye, looked up as Rose approached.

"I wondered if you could tell me if you have ever repaired a wristwatch for a certain person?"

"Why would you be asking?"

"I'm trying to find a friend's watch- he's lost it."

"I'm afraid that's confidential. I'd need the owner's permission to give you that information," said the clocksmith, putting down the innards of the mechanism on the counter.

"That's just it. My friend has passed away, and I'm trying to locate his favourite wristwatch- I just need to know who made the watch so I can buy another for his mother."

"You just want the make?"

Rose looked at the man more closely.

71

"How confidential is it?"

The man paused and stared at Rose and then said, "Fairly confidential."

"Five shillings confidential?"

"Oh, a little more secret than that."

"I'll give you ten shillings if you can find my friend's name in your records and tell me the make."

Without a word, the man went under the counter, pulling up a large entry book, and then opened it.

"My friend's name is Bernard Bannister," said Rose.

The man looked up at Rose with a look of recognition, probably as he'd already had a visit from the police, but then casually flicked to the 'B' section of the book, and then ran his finger along a handwritten line.

"Bernard Bannister, c/o Sunnyside, Milston Road?"

"That's him," said Rose.

"Ten shillings?"

Rose went into his wallet and pulled out a ten shilling note, knowing that this was going on his expenses claim to Flanagan.

"Your friend had his watch repaired here last year and collected it on 27 February 1935."

"And the make?"

"It was a Zenith in yellow and white gold, with seventeen jewels, gilt silver hands and Arabic numerals. A very stylish piece."

Rose wrote down the details in his notebook.

"Is it a common wristwatch?"

"Not around here. It's pricey."

"Thanks," said Rose, handing over the money.

"It's a pleasure," said the man.

As he left the shop, Rose knew that the whereabouts of the watch was a small puzzle which needed solving on the way to unravelling a much bigger mystery.

*

Up in the billiards room, built for relaxation and chosen by Lawrence Drummond to end his life, I watched again out of the bay window from where I used to observe Dorothy meeting her mother. It was a Wednesday.

But this time, I was looking out for Isabel. I hadn't seen her since that day at assembly in the Great Hall, and I hoped to spy her. If I knew who she walked with and where, I would be able to find and approach her, and most girls walked through the main courtyard in the late afternoon on Wednesdays and Fridays on their way back to sections before dinner after playing field hockey- the boys played rugby on Tuesdays and Thursdays.

But if Lawrence Drummond's ghost really did linger in that room, neither he nor I saw Isabel that day. Although sometimes, when you are focusing on something, you notice something else, or in this case, somebody else.

I'd never seen him before. Tallish and lean, with slicked-back dark hair, he wore a white coat and no hat or cap. He was talking to Dr Sharland, that evil man, and they were oblivious to me up in that domed window high above them between the turrets.

I like to know who everyone around me is, and this man, who didn't look like he belonged at Shadowside, was a real curiosity. Was he just a visitor, or if he were a new member of staff, why hadn't he been introduced at an assembly?

He looked different, somehow more worldly than the rest of *them*. I couldn't see his face close-up, but the way he stood and moved was relaxed, almost languid, unlike the wind-up soldier-like *them*. He was natural, unforced, unhurried, somehow at ease with himself.

You see, Mr Tucker the janitor is a physical man who moves fluidly with no effort. But this man wasn't physical, yet his gestures and motions- there were no gesticulations- just flowed. I could tell he was a man who knew himself very well, as I do.

He wasn't a policeman, that was obvious. He was far too unobtrusive, a blender into the background, a man who could disappear into a crowd, or a room of two people. It wasn't that he was forgettable, he was just there.

Should I see him again, I would have to identify him.

After the man and Dr Sharland left the courtyard, I looked up at the darkening sky, fading from grey to black now, having already bled from white.

73

Lawrence Drummond opted out of his personal struggle in the winter, and I knew as I stood there that this was what he looked at before he took the blade out of the handle and pulled that straight razor across his throat.

Did it gush and feel warm and sticky, like it does in my bloods? Or was it cold and painful, as breathing became more difficult and he gasped before dropping to the floor around where I stood many years later?

Then I heard the long double peal of the second bell, which meant dinner for the boys, and I left the billiards room and made my way downstairs.

10

As he made his way down the corridor from Dr Sharland's office, through the double doors towards the main entrance, Rose was intending to locate the woods where Dorothy's horse charm had been found by the police.

But then he stopped and glanced up, taking a closer look at the stairs on the left, with their off-white-almost-yellow-in-places-mottled-with-green steps, which slowly and surely wound themselves upwards in a reversed L shape from the ground, like the number seven, unlucky for some.

Ascending from the ground floor, around two thirds of the steps went straight up, at a reasonably steep gradient, but not one of dizziness or folly. Then after the turn to the left, there was a marble balustrade which overhung the ground as a bridge, perhaps forty feet up, which supported the steps until they reached the first floor.

On top of the banister was a carved handrail, also in marble, which ran from the very bottom to the top of the stairs. When taken with care, even the most infirm climber would find it difficult to fall upwards, with gravity and the well-defined handrail offering support.

But on the way down, Rose could see that a fall was possible. The steps were well spaced out, and deep and wide enough to easily hold any human foot, and even if one were to trip, it would likely be just one or two steps, resulting in grazing, minor bruising or perhaps damage to the knees.

Any person tripping downwards would be able to balance again and rectify their position quickly, he was sure. Mr Bannister was certainly able-bodied, and by all accounts in good condition, so how he could have failed to stop himself from toppling over so severely that he wasn't able to save himself took some imagination.

But Rose remembered what Dr Sharland had told him about the late Mr Bannister- he'd walked very quickly with long strides. Could he have danced down those hard and cold steps with so little care as to cause him to plummet with enough momentum to cause his fatal injuries?

In the years he was at Sunnyside, Mr Bannister must have taken those stairs hundreds, no thousands of times- could he have felt so comfortable coming down them to allow him to be so careless as to almost leap down them- for that is what it would take for a person to fall so violently, Rose surmised.

It was both possible and improbable, but so much depended on Bannister's state of mind that day in late October-was he rushing for a reason? The newspaper reports made no mention of him being late for anything.

Or had he seen something up on the first floor that startled him and caused him to run away down the stairs? These were things that Rose knew he had to find out.

And then there was the missing wristwatch- a Zenith- an expensive make and model, it seemed. Why wasn't Mr Bannister wearing it that day as he always did, and if he was, who had taken it from him while he was dying, or from his dead body?

Or could it have come off in the fall and been thrown somewhere, to be found later by somebody who kept it? Unlikely, thought Rose.

And if somebody had taken it from Mr Bannister in his final moments, or from his lifeless corpse, it was probable they'd also pushed him down those stairs. Had there been an altercation or fight of some sort on the marble?

Or had it been wilful- a mere push, enough to send the unaware member of staff off-balance and toppling, or a forceful two-handed push? If another was involved, Rose was sure that it wasn't an accident, as the wristwatch would never have been taken if so.

But who would want to kill Mr Bannister? Another member of staff out of jealousy as he was a rising man at the institution, or a 'resident' out of consuming and hidden hatred for him, with the possibility of mental instability playing a hand?

Or was it just one of those unlucky turns of fate for Bernard Bannister, a tragic accident that nobody, including Madame Sosostris, could have foreseen.

Rose wished he could see the police file on the case, but he knew to ask would lead to a rebuttal, as he had no contacts down there. He could ask his police contacts in London to make discreet inquiries, but that risked exposing him and could lead to him having to leave Sunnyside.

But Rose couldn't forget Mr Bannister's missing wristwatch. It was unexplained, and such things needed answers.

Although Rose also knew that he had to remember why he was there. He was there to find Dorothy or what had happened to her, to make a chain of connections. And Bannister's death could be a link in that chain or nothing at all.

*

Rose had little contact with the residents in his first days-aside from the boy Carstairs who removed his eye- just as Dr Sharland had stipulated. It wasn't difficult- when the other boys and girls walked past him in the corridors, he wasn't given any acknowledgement or any facial recognition at all. It was as if he wasn't there.

This concerned him though. He would have to somehow penetrate the stony silence of Sunnyside if he were to find out any more about Dorothy. It would surely have to be another girl who could help him, he decided, one who lived alongside her in the South wing.

On his third day there, he casually asked Dr Sharland in his office whether he knew of any girl whom Dorothy had been especially friendly with, or to whom she was even close.

"Nobody in particular, I'm afraid. Dorothy always seemed alone to me, and with her thoughts. Remember that she'd attacked young women before coming here. Granted they were older and taking care of babies. But Dorothy still had a marked aversion to other females and was still very much working through her issues."

"Did you encourage her to make friends with other girls?" said Rose.

"No-she wasn't ready for that. Dorothy was in the early days of her treatment, and it's a slow process. Perhaps in a few months, when I'd seen her making progress, I would have urged her to form female attachments. But not yet."

"How would she be coping in the wider world, away from Sunnyside, in your opinion, doctor?"

"That's a worrying question, to which I'm afraid I have no answer. It all depends on circumstances, her exposure to triggers and her state of mind. But of course, she was far safer cocooned here."

"Was she being given any medication before she disappeared?" said Rose.

"No. I can divulge that to you. She was on a therapy programme, which involved daily sessions and a gentle talking through of the issues. Her problem wasn't acute enough for medication as it stood, unlike some of the other residents."

"Are any of the residents potentially violent?"

"There are some, perhaps twenty percent of the residents have had violent episodes in their pasts and could regress to those behaviours again."

"Could Dorothy have become friendly with a boy here, or even a male member of staff?"

"From a psychological point of view, that would be more likely than her attaching herself to another female, but practically, it would have been very difficult at Sunnyside, where such fraternisation between male and female residents is strictly prohibited."

"But is it possible?"

"It's not impossible, but highly improbable. Such an attachment would have been noticed very quickly by the staff, including me. We keep a close eye on the residents of course. But, on the other hand, Dorothy wasn't an E6."

"May I ask what an E6 is?"

"Forgive me. It's a clinical classification. It basically means that a resident is classified as opposite-gender sensitive, so an E6 is forbidden to fraternise, get to know or spend time with residents or staff of the opposite sex."

"And I can see why this wouldn't apply to Dorothy- as you said, her vulnerabilities lie within her attitude to her own sex."

"Quite right," said Dr Sharland. "Her sensitivities stem from maternal envy of her own gender."

"Please excuse my persistence, but in a hypothetical situation, would a friendship, either platonic or romantic, be more likely between a fifteen-year-old female resident and a boy, or with a male member of staff?"

Dr Sharland looked at Rose intently, as if he were slightly stunned by the question. "I really cannot see any member of our staff building an illicit relationship with a resident. It would be highly unethical. But if I had to make a choice, I would have to say that Dorothy would be more likely to form a friendship or relationship with a boy than a man. She was fearful of authority, you see."

"Thank you, doctor. That's clarified matters nicely."

"Not at all. We both want Dorothy found safe and well, the sooner the better."

As Rose left the office, he felt quite drained, and the words 'safe and well' replayed in his mind, in Dr Sharland's voice, not his own inner voice.

He decided to make his first trip to the Golden Bell that evening, for the purposes of refreshment, but in his expenses, it would be marked down as research. Flanagan couldn't question that he needed gen- that was why he was living at a mental institute, after all.

*

Rose felt like a flailing fish on a riverbank as he ambled into the Golden Bell for the first time. The atmosphere was so different from the Stab and his usual London haunts, and above all, he knew nobody.

A man of routines, he didn't expect a brass band to play as he entered or the publican to hold out both brawny barrel-rolling arms in welcome, but after standing at the beermat infested bar for over ten minutes, when there were no other customers waiting, and the man manning the fort continued to engage in an undoubtedly meaningless conversation with an old farmer who nursed what looked like a triple whiskey, Rose wished he was back at the Stab ignoring the sozzled Monkfish.

And then there were the three other customers, or 'patrons' as a sign above the bar called them, warning them that asking for a tab was unwise as the reply could offend them. The three men scattered around that saloon bar in high-backed chairs, swathed in smoke and the smell of earlier deployed polish on the tables, just sat there and stared. At Rose.

Not a sound from them- they were all seated at different tables in one-man cliques, only the whispered mumbling of the barman and farmer could be faintly heard, only decipherable by a dog, Rose thought.

"What can I get you?" finally said the centre-parting-haired barman, who was more than likely the owner or at least the manager of the establishment, as he moved with the unhurried nonchalance of authority.

"A pint of your best stout please," said Rose, his mouth now dry, causing him to clear his throat.

"Old Belter OK for you?"

"I'll give it a go," said Rose.

The warm light brown liquid was soon delivered, and Rose paid up and moved away from the bar, his head grazing against one of the battered tankards hanging down from above.

He took a seat as five eyes watched him, one of the men sitting down having one eye which looked in another direction, Rose couldn't fail to notice, and knew that the man wasn't showing off his ability to look two ways at once.

The barman-manager-owner was straight back into his conversation with Old Macdonald at the bar. And then another customer entered.

"Evening Jim," said none other than Sunnyside's janitor Mr Tucker as he approached the bar.

"Usual Lionel?" Rose couldn't help but be slightly annoyed at how quickly a regular was served.

Tucker nodded. "It's getting fierce cold out there now Jim."

"Looks like a bitter one, it really does."

Tucker moved away from the bar, and although he was taller than Rose, managed to avoid all contact with the tankards.

He saw Rose, and nodded slightly, which Rose reciprocated, expecting Tucker to go and sit with one of the other solo imbibers. But he didn't- he went and sat all by himself at a new table. There were now five men seated at tables, all on their own, all looking at Rose.

"Bill," said Tucker to the man whose left eye was now trained on him instead of Rose, his right eye still looking at the main door. That was it, and Bill raised his half-pint glass a fraction on the way to his mouth.

Rose looked around at each of the men in turn, and his focus only shifted when Old Macdonald went to relieve himself and his glass was refilled automatically.

For the first time he could remember, Rose was truly thinking about leaving after just the one, so stifled was the atmosphere. And then, Tucker got up and came over to his table.

"Mind if I join you," he said. It was a statement, not a question.

"Please do."

Tucker's powerful manual hands were wrapped around his glass on the other side of the table.

"Just finished work?" said Rose.

"Yep. Done for the day, I hope."

"Are you looking forward to Christmas?"

"It's all the same to me," said Tucker. "I'm working."

"Even on Christmas Day?"

"Yep. Most of the children will still be there, and the staff."

"Apart from one child," said Rose. "I hear that a girl disappeared not long ago." He'd taken his chance in bringing up Dorothy, and now waited for Tucker's response.

"Yep. It's been a while now."

"What do you think happened to her?"

"Who knows? All I know is one or two other children have run away in my time there, but they were brought back within hours."

"Boys or girls?" said Rose.

"Boys."

"Did you know the girl?" said Rose.

"Why are you so interested in her?"

"Just curious. Seems strange that nobody has heard anything from or about her."

Tucker sat up slightly, his lean and muscled body tensing a little.

"I don't really know the names of any of the children, bar one or two who chat to me sometimes."

"What's the local feeling on what happened to her?" said Rose, knowing that if he couldn't get Tucker's own view, he

81

might get an idea of what people who lived around there thought.

"I suppose many think a local boy might have put her in the family way."

"A local boy? From Milston?"

"And thereabouts."

"Could she have regularly met up with a local boy?"

"Children have ways and means- I know I did," said Tucker.

Rose nodded. Looking round, he noticed that the other customers were no longer looking at him. It seemed as if the fact he was talking to Tucker had made him less of an alien.

"Hopefully, she'll turn up," said Rose. "But the same can't be said for Mr Bannister."

Tucker looked again at Rose, but with no expression whatsoever.

"You've heard about that too?"

"Yes. A tragic accident."

"Yep, most think so."

"Most think so?"

It was Tucker's turn to nod.

"Some think it wasn't an accident?"

"So I hear."

"What do you think?"

"I have no opinion." Tucker gulped his beer, looking down into the glass until he'd drained it.

"I really should be going," said Tucker, and with that he stood up and held out his hand to Rose, who offered his own and they shook, with Rose's handshake no match for Tucker's powerful grip.

"It's been nice having a chat. Could you show me where the woods are at Sunnyside sometime- I've heard they are nice to take a walk in," said Rose, making no mention that he was going there to see where the horse charm had been found, as this likely hadn't been publicly released by the police.

"I certainly can," said Tucker, "Tomorrow morning at eight o'clock- I can meet you in the main courtyard?"

"That would be perfect, thank you."

Then Mr Tucker walked towards the door, nodding at Bill, and calling out "Jim," to which Jim replied "Lionel."

It was Rose's turn to look down into his glass as he drank the remains of his Old Belter, not a bad brew as it happens, he thought.

As he left, he said "thank you," and Jim nodded at him. Old Macdonald, Bill and the other two customers said nothing, as Rose made his way out into the cold.

11

It was just at the top of the main stairs, paces away from the stern gaze of the Indian vulture in his cabinet at whom I'd been gazing, that I finally came face-to-face with Isabel.

She was alone, just like me, making her way back to South, while I was on route to the billiards room. I saw her before she noticed me, and I knew what I had to do.

As I slowly walked towards her and she gazed to her right out of the big narrow window onto the main courtyard outside, I timed the moment we passed alongside one another to perfection.

So much comes down to timing. Not happenstance, I don't believe in that. But you can bend reality to your own will if you know how to do it.

I had to calculate the exact moment that Isabel would turn again to peer ahead of her, so that I would dominate her vision and there was no time for her to look down or away.

If she knew something about me and Dorothy, I needed to force her silence to others who could cause damage.

I was a mere two yards in front of her when she turned, her face expressionless and unknowing, and then I gave her my cutting look.

You know when the look has worked. Isabel's body flinched, her pale face seemed to grow paler, her lips seemed to quiver momentarily, and her eyes widened and blinked in a form of terror.

I had just two or three seconds to gauge her reaction- a cutting look cannot be sustained, it must have a short, but very sharp thrust.

She looked down as soon as she could and hurried pass me towards the main stairs where Mr Bannister took his last steps down and Lawrence Drummond his final walk upstairs.

No words were spoken, there was no need yet.

You see, there's more than one way to cut a person. A look will slash the will of some, carefully chosen words can stab at the heart of many, and a knife will pierce the flesh of anybody.

*

Rose found himself in the main courtyard with an empty stomach and his coat collar turned up, missing breakfast, and facing the whirling face-cuts of the wind in pursuit of Dorothy.

It was a little before eight o'clock, earlier than necessary, but punctuality had been ingrained in Rose since he was a small boy.

The Jesuits said that if you gave them a boy when he was seven, they would give you the man. But Rose knew that his father, who certainly wasn't a Jesuit and scorned any other religious sect, had done an even better job, having moulded his son from the age of three, or from as early as Rose could remember anyway.

Mr Tucker appeared just a few minutes after the hour, and Rose said nothing. He never reprimanded others for tardiness, only himself, an anomaly which he felt strange.

"Thanks for coming out so early, Mr Tucker."

"Oh, I've been up three hours already- it's midmorning to me. Shall we make our way to the woods now?"

Rose nodded, and a crunching sound punctuated their every step as they walked down the path scattered with dried-out leaves, towards the west of the main building.

"This'll really need the daily sweep later," said Tucker.

Rose didn't answer, but felt sorry for the janitor, knowing that in the gusty weather at Sunnyside, it was a fruitless task, and leaves would once again paper half the path's cracks within an hour or two.

"I met a boy yesterday who removed his eye," said Rose suddenly.

"That's Carstairs- he's always around the place."

"Is he allowed to wander around so much?"

"He's allowed to please himself for much of the time- he doesn't do as many lessons as the others- he's a little slow you see."

"I see," said Rose. "How did he lose his eye?"

"No idea I'm afraid. When he first came here, he wore an eye patch. It made him look like a boy pirate, but he's had the glass eye for a while now."

"He's a big strong lad."

"That he is," said Tucker. "I'll show you the shortcut."

They didn't speak again for some minutes, as they made their way across a field, the mist allowing Rose no view of what came ahead of him. But the grass was wet and smooth beneath his feet, and he was almost gliding along.

"Not far now," said Tucker finally.

A minute or two later, Rose looked up to see the twirling shapes of tree branches just in front and above him. It was as if the woods had come to him. He wondered if Dorothy had felt the same sensation when she went there weeks earlier- it was probably misty then too, as it always seemed to be at Sunnyside.

"Here you are- Sunnyside's woods," said Tucker.

Rose glanced at his wristwatch and realised that it had taken about eight minutes to walk there from the main entrance.

"Would you like me to take you to where I found the girl's little trinket?" said Tucker.

"You found the horse charm?!" said Rose in a shocked reflex, blowing his cover story of wanting a walk in the woods.

"I certainly did."

"But I thought the police found it?"

"Is that what they told you?" said Tucker.

"Not exactly- somebody else said that they had."

"Suits me. I just came across it one morning when I was up here gathering some kindling for the fire. Caught my eye, it did. I gave it to Mr Dodwell of course."

"He must have passed it to the police," said Rose. "Can you show me roughly where you found it?"

"I can show you precisely."

Rose followed as Tucker took him a little deeper into the thick woods. Soon they came to where a tree had fallen. Tucker duly sat down on it, as if it were a makeshift bench.

"I found it just there," said Tucker, pointing at a space heavily bedded with leaves just in front of him.

"And you found nothing else?"

86

"Not a dickie bird."

"Do many other people come up here?"

"Not really- maybe some poachers from time to time, some of the residents on organized trips, and perhaps one or two *secretly*," said Tucker.

"Like Dorothy Hopkins?"

"Perhaps."

"Could you cut through these woods to leave Sunnyside's grounds, to go to Milston for instance?"

"You certainly could- by walking for about fifteen minutes that way you come out on to the Milston Road," said Tucker, pointing north.

They then sat in silence for a while on the tree-bench until Rose felt he had to speak.

"You're probably wondering what I'm doing here?"

"I rarely wonder. I take life as it comes and go with it. What I don't know can't bother me, you see."

"That's a good philosophy," said Rose.

"As good as any I suppose. I must be getting back now- I have my rounds to do. Are you coming or can you find your own way back?"

"I think I've seen enough of the woods for now. And thank you, Mr Tucker."

The two men walked back through the mist towards the main building, the size of which still caught Rose off-guard as it emerged almost ghost-like from the haze, disturbing his thoughts, which were all about Dorothy.

Did she go to those woods alone or if not, with whom? Was she making her way out of Sunnyside? Did she lose her charm in her rush, or was there some kind of altercation with somebody? Did she also lose the bracelet on which the charm hanged, or was she still wearing it, wherever she was now?

There were just too many questions for Rose's liking.

*

Mr Tucker was wheeling his wooden barrow across the quad courtyard below the library's window. It was the day after I'd given Isabel my look.

In his heavy, buttoned-up coat and battered trilby, which he alternated with his flat cap, he was going about his daily chores without a care in this world or the next.

I wondered what the janitor of the house would have been like in the days that Lawrence Drummond stalked the corridors, both before and after going to the war, up to the day he opted out in 1888.

I imagined Mr Tucker's predecessor, the keeper of the house and grounds then, similar in temperament and demeanour, but dressed in old-style clothes.

It was while I was looking through the books on the military history shelf, with Carstairs, Reed and Ingram caught up in their arithmetic on the large table nearby, that I saw it.

It was a large folder, made of leather, which was laid down on the top shelf above, high enough to be missed, which I had done for years.

Embossed in gold letters in fine calligraphy on the cover were the words '*A History of the House*', and the smaller letters beneath read '*Compiled by Elisabeth Drummond*' who I knew had been the wife of the owner and builder of the house, Sir Arthur Drummond, and the mother of Lawrence.

I leaned the folder on the wooden ledge beneath the shelves, and proceeded to open it, a small puff of dust springing from it and evaporating into the air. It looked like everybody else had missed it too, which made me feel better.

The inner frontispiece had a flowery pattern, which showed a feminine touch, but as I turned it over, that womanly feeling dissipated, and the eye of the folder's creator took on a sense of no specific gender.

Each turquoise page made of stiff card had four photographs on it, with tiny captions beneath written in fountain pen by a fine hand. So, while the cover was formally produced, the contents of the folder showed a homemade and loving touch.

The photographs had obviously been produced with an old-fashioned daguerreotype camera, not the latest Beau Brownie and Brownie No 2 cameras which I'd recently seen in Shadowside's darkroom.

I could visualise whoever took the pictures, standing behind the heavy box on a tripod, waiting for each shot which would require laborious patience to materialise.

The first three pages I turned over showed the house under construction, piles of debris and wooden planks everywhere, and one picture, taken from the vantage of looking out from the main construction site itself, revealed that there was no mound- it must have been built a little later, when the grounds were landscaped. It seemed desolate and incomplete with my favourite place missing. The pages were captioned '*The Grand Project 1857-1868*'.

On the fourth page was written '*The Grand Project Completed, 1868*' and the pictures showed the main house from the front, just as you see it now as you approach it. Not much seemed to have changed- the two turrets and mock-Tudor frontage and gravel walls were all in place if you looked carefully.

But it was the page following that one that really interested me. As I lifted the protective tissue paper covering them, the four photographs revealed the Drummond family, and this was confirmed at the bottom of the page with the caption '*The Drummond Family, 1876*'.

It must have been taken when the house had stood completed for eight years, the family all moved in, a working family home, with the huge range of furniture and interiors of the rooms undoubtedly still being added to regularly as the Drummonds increasingly moulded the place in their image, or at least the one they wished to display.

I had the uncanny feeling that I'd seen the four pictures before, but I knew I hadn't, as I was looking at the folder for the very first time. Then I realised why I recognised them.

The four members of the Drummond family, the inhabitants of the house fifty years before, were shown in the very same poses which were to be found in their portraits in the main reception. The painter of those portraits must have used the photographs as a template, I thought.

But there was a marked difference between the photographs and the portraits too. The pictures in the folder, which nobody ever saw, while old and sepia-tinged and taken on antiquated plates, had far more facial detail than the portraits, which every visitor and resident was aware of every time they walked past them.

The portraits were typically Victorian, staid and formalized, with the subjects firmly in control of themselves, showing no emotion, a style adopted by the painter, and no doubt expected by the family when the paintings were commissioned. But the photographs in the folder, the basis of those portraits, contained a hundred times more humanity within them.

Sir Arthur Drummond, while still stern looking, had a smugness in his expression, a pride in his face not seen in his portrait. And he wasn't holding a notebook, a prop added by the artist, it seemed. Elisabeth, the creator of the folder, had a knowing smile, showing satisfaction in the photograph, as compared to the glum look rendered in her painting. Their daughter Charlotte, enticing and forthright when seen hanging in the main reception, looked far more vulnerable and delicate as captured by the daguerreotype camera.

But it was the picture of Lawrence Drummond which kept my attention. In 1876, I calculated that he must have been in his middle twenties. He looked worldly, perhaps having already been on a European tour, as was the custom for young men of good family then.

He looked serious, strong, almost fierce- ready to take on the world, the kind of man with whom I could identify. Taken around five years before he went to fight in the Mahdist War in Sudan, which had affected him deeply, causing him to take his own life in 1888 rather than return to those bitter battlefields so distant from home.

In the portrait, he looked weak and sensitive, Byronic in demeanour. Was this license used by the artist, or an evocation or a premonition of what Lawrence would become once the war had extracted much of the will from him?

But it wasn't the difference in Lawrence Drummond's countenance which really held me for the long minutes I stared at his photograph. It was something I had read about in my bloods which caused me to quiver nervously. It was all starting to become clear to me now.

*

Rose was back in Milston to make a call to Flanagan, but this time he chose a different telephone box. The one on the seafront was too exposed to the elements, and the one in which he now stood, in the square behind the library, was sheltered on all sides by buildings, both Victorian and Georgian in design. There was Parsons & Parsons the solicitors, the Unity Assurance insurance company offices, a rock and bucket and spade shop, the Milston bookshop, the Antiques Emporium, and the back of the library all around him as he placed a sixpence in the slot and waited to be connected.

"*Travesties.*" It was Monkfish, sounding peculiarly sober, although it was just after nine in the morning, and Rose knew that would soon be remedied.

"Flanagan in?"

"Not yet,"" said Monkfish.

"How's the Stab?"

"Magnificent. One or two of the boys have been asking after you."

"Anyone in particular?"

"Dickie Blythe. And Bobby Martin."

"What do they want?" said Rose, knowing full well that they had realised they'd been led astray on the Capone gunman story.

"Dunno. But Bobby says he has a skeleton to pick with you. And Buchanan has been picking my considerable brains as to your whereabouts."

"What did you tell him?"

"That I was a subeditor, not your flaming mother."

"If Buchanan asks again, tell him I'm looking into a prostitution ring in Manchester, will you?"

"You'll owe me a tipple for that."

"I'm sure Buchanan will wet your whistle if you play your cards right."

With that, Monkfish was gone, no doubt to get ready for the Stab once Flanagan had arrived- somebody always had to be in the office to answer the telephone -that was something Flanagan got uptight about, although he refused to invest in a secretary.

Rose left the telephone box and made his way towards the Grecian Tea Rooms on the promenade. He'd missed breakfast

91

at Sunnyside, which he often did, due to the less than welcoming atmosphere there.

He'd been living there for more than a week now, but the most he got from other members of staff was a nod, and from Mrs Benson, who had introduced herself and then blanked him on his first morning, he barely got that.

But Rose knew that he had to find a way in and become accepted if he were to learn what the people who worked at Sunnyside really thought about Dorothy's disappearance and the death of Mr Bannister.

He needed a way to ingratiate himself, without obviously trying to do so, which would be out of character for him anyway. If he could show them that he was worth knowing and talking to, he could begin to make inroads.

He knew Mr Tucker a little now, but it was obvious that he didn't mix with the other members of staff, and Dr Sharland, who held the highest position on the clinical side, was aloof from the fray.

Rose had learned over the years that the best insights don't come from the frosty top of the tree, but from those who toil in the middle of it, among the tangled branches.

And now that it was just three days until Christmas Day, Rose knew that if he were to find out anything significant before the new year arrived, he would have to find a way in quickly.

Dr Sharland had mentioned that there was to be a staff Christmas party on Christmas Eve, and while he wasn't attending himself as he was going to be in London over Christmas, Rose should go and get to know everybody.

It seemed like the perfect opportunity. He presumed that the alcohol would be flowing at the event, and that could loosen workplace inhibitions as well as tongues.

Rose would just have to ensure that he stayed sober enough himself to pick up on anything he heard, something he would have struggled with just a few years earlier.

He was still sure that the death of Mr Bannister had some relevance in Dorothy's disappearance- two such extraordinary and rare events at Sunnyside close together had to have some connection, somehow. And he remembered what Mr Tucker had said at the Golden Bell- that some didn't believe that Mr Bannister's death was an accident at all.

12

Carstairs was peering closely at the noticeboard in the corridor outside Dr Sharland's office when Rose appeared from that door and was about to walk the other way.

But Rose had been turning over and over in his mind something that the boy had said last time- 'I see things nobody knows I've seen'- and that made him walk towards the noticeboard instead.

"Good morning Mr Rose." This startled Rose, as Carstairs hadn't turned around but knew it was him, as if he had a kind of extraordinary peripheral sense.

"Hello Carstairs, how did you know it was me?"

"I usually know what's going on around me sir."

That explained nothing, but Rose mused about whether it could be true that those deprived of sight or hearing developed greater sharpness in other senses. Either that, or Carstairs had seen him enter the office and waited there until he heard the door open again and somebody walk near him.

"What are you reading?" said Rose.

"It's the rugby sevens team for the New Year's match against the Denton Institute," said Carstairs.

"Are you playing?" Rose thought that the strapping boy would make a good forward player.

"I can't sir- I'm not allowed to since my accident."

"What happened to you?" said Rose.

"I don't like to talk about that sir."

"I'm sorry I asked."

"That's quite all right, you weren't to know. Goodbye now sir."

"Goodbye Carstairs."

And then Carstairs walked off and went through the double doors, into the main reception corridor by the stairs at the foot of which Mr Bannister died.

Rose looked at the team list- Castleton (Captain); Beaumont; Ross; Harris; Kirby; Lassiter; Passmore; Sherwood Ames & Baker (Reserves). It was signed by Mr Lewis.

The names meant nothing to him. But Rose still wondered if Carstairs had some information about Dorothy, or at least about Mr Bannister's death.

*

I sat on the mound, reading an edition of one of my bloods that I hadn't read for over a year. All was deadly quiet as I took in the words again after all that time, which now had gained a much deeper meaning.

It is 9 November 1888. The streets of Spitalfields in London are subdued. Ever since September, far fewer people have been out at night up this way east. The menace is a man, a fiend, and nobody knows who he is. The sound of faint footsteps can be heard, and the echoes of puddles splashing ripple through the wind from Commercial Street, as a trader makes his way to market pushing a handcart. If he stopped and walked down Dorset Street and under the archway into Miller's Court, he would see nothing. But he would never stop, as he has to set up before sunrise.

Almost four in the morning and the shadows of wet chimneys almost glisten and the silhouettes of makeshift washing-lines dance in the light rain, every drop which hits the cobblestones making reflections clearer. The stench, such a stench, so putrid it turns the stomachs of even locals daily, the sewers fetid and pungently aggressive.

Then there is a cry from Miller's Court, under the archway just off Dorset Street. It came from No.13, a ground-floor room in a lodging house. Then another horrible cry rings out. The first was full-bloodied, the second cry is muffled. No lights go on in the room or anywhere else. Nobody else seems to have heard, and if they did, they are too afraid to do anything. These are hysterical times.

A scraping sound becomes louder and louder. The window of No. 13 is firmly closed, but somehow the sound travels. And then it stops just as suddenly, as has the rain, but the glistening will continue for some time.

More footsteps- a flower-seller is pushing her wagon up nearby Brushfield Street, moving towards Bishopsgate to get ready to fill the early morning buttonholes. The sky is now turning milky blue and becoming paler by the minute. Night will soon give birth to the new day.

A stooped man in Artillery Lane is also up and about, methodically sweeping the street for cigar stubs, ready to be remade as cigarillos later. At his current speed, he will reach this end of Dorset Street in about half an hour.

The door to No.13 Miller's Court slowly opens. A man in a bowler hat steps out, and pulls the door shut behind him, before locking it and pocketing the large single key.

His face cannot be seen, as he is looking down. He is carrying a case and his bloodied clothes are inside it. He is wearing the clean ones he arrived with in the case. He walks briskly yet calmly through the Court, which is lit by a gas lamp.

He walks around a large puddle, and his reflection can be seen momentarily, but too quickly to gain a lasting impression. He walks through the archway, after glancing back at the room from which he came. This will be the last prostitute he kills. He kills for pleasure, but this is the last wretched woman he will slaughter.

The sky is white now, succumbing to grey in places. The surrounding streets will soon be bustling with activity on this cold November morning as people make their way to make a hard living.

In just over six hours, at around a quarter to eleven, a man named Thomas Bowyer, a former soldier in the Indian Army who lives in Dorset Street, will arrive at No. 13 Miller's Court. Sent by his employer John McCarthy, who is the landlord of No.13 and other rooms in the building, and also has a chandler's shop close by, Bowyer has to collect rent arrears from Miss Kelly, who lives in the room at the front on the ground floor.

Bowyer will walk past the dustbin, outside toilet and water tap and knock on the door but get no answer. Knowing that Miss Kelly could well be inside but not answering, Bowyer looks through the window.

There he sees the human remains within- a murder room of unimaginable horror- what is left of Mary Jane Kelly is unrecognisable, ferociously murdered, mutilated and eviscerated in a hyper-frenzied attack.

The shaken and repulsed Bowyer will run and tell his boss McCarthy, and McCarthy sends Bowyer to fetch the police, who will arrive soon, after Bowyer rushes breathless into Commercial Street police station.

A little later, Inspector Beck, Inspector Abberline and Detective Constable Dew, the latter of whom more than twenty years later will catch another infamous murderer, Dr Crippen, are on the scene.

And the man who left No 13 Miller's Court is soon far away, in an affluent part of London, walking down a well-heeled street. Wait. He is quite tall, pale and angular.

And when he looks up, others can see his face beneath his bowler hat. His face is mournful, and almost morose. He is well-dressed, with a touch of dishevelled grandeur. As he walks away, his footsteps fade into the past.

Nobody here knows his name or who he is. Nor do they have any idea that he is the terrible Whitechapel fiend known as Jack the Ripper.

I looked up from the now-battered pages of my blood, smiling to myself. I had seen the face of the man in that street before.

It was the wilful face I'd seen the day before in a photograph, not the controlled and muted one I'd seen for years in the portrait in the main reception.

I could see that the man who finally showed his face all those years ago in London was Lawrence Drummond.

*

Isabel ran her long pale fingers through her fair hair. A small bald patch had again appeared on her scalp, which she managed to hide by brushing her hair across and over it.

The hair plucking had started again just recently, in the last few days. She'd twist a few hairs around her finger and just pull them out, whenever she felt the urge. This had happened twice before- when she was sent to the infirmary for two months the time she got scarlet fever at seven, and on first arrival at Sunnyside, and in those early weeks there, she'd half removed one eyebrow too.

Sometimes she'd also chew her plucked hair, having already bitten her fingernails down to their quicks. But she tried to make sure that neither Mrs Benson nor Dr Sharland noticed her nervous habits. Because that's what they were- she just knew it.

Ever since Dottie had told her about Edwin months before, she knew that there would be trouble. She'd never spoken to him, but she was well aware of who he was *before* he began courting Dottie and put her in the family way.

She'd tried to warn Dottie…there was something just not right about Edwin, she could sense it. But Dottie hadn't listened- she'd been over the moon for some weeks, and then suddenly, she'd become frightened and anxious, just as Isabel felt now. And then Dottie disappeared, and Isabel was sure that Edwin knew her whereabouts.

As she lay on her bed in the South wing twiddling and pulling at her hair, the lights out so that nobody could see her, tears trickled from her eyes.

And as more hairs fell onto her blanket, Isabel was consumed by dread.

*

Rose had never really enjoyed Christmas. He was often working during the holiday, while others ate and drank and forgot why there was a holiday. Not that this offended him, although when he was a boy it would have been a mortal sin.

He always remembered the few times in his life when he'd said a silent prayer when in trouble since leaving his childhood home. He often wondered if a muttered "Please God" was from a deep hidden belief or just blasted into him as a boy, what his parents and the Brethren expected.

Either way, at such times of perceived peril, from being caught looking out over the garden fence when he was seven to being chased by a sect of occultists he'd exposed just a couple

97

of years before, which earned him the dubious nickname 'the Hack from Hell' in Fleet Street, he knew that his mind and mouth were not joined-up somehow at such times.

If he wasn't working at that time of year, he'd make the trip to visit his mother, who was always lonely, his father having died many years before. It would just be him and his mother, and they'd sit beneath the crucifix in the dining room and eat well and talk little. But it meant a great deal to his mother.

This year he'd sent her a card from Milston's post office, with a picture of the Christ suffering on it, once he knew that he would be spending Christmas at Sunnyside. But he was getting restless, he needed to dive into this story, and find out all he could about Dorothy and where she had gone, not just for the exclusive if there was one, but for her mother, who would be spending Christmas filled with worry.

It was now Christmas Eve, and the staff party was set for that evening. Dr Sharland, who was going to London, had said goodbye to him that morning, wishing him the greetings of the season, as he got into his Ford in the main courtyard.

It was then that Rose had got the feeling that they were being watched. Just a sense that eyes were trained on them. As Dr Sharland pulled away and the gravel crunched beneath the motorcar's wheels, Rose looked up above at the windows behind him.

Somebody in a large bay window swiftly moved away, which caught Rose's eye. He didn't see who it was- it happened too fast.

He made some calculations, counting the windows across. It was the window just below the right turret, and he knew by now that this was the North wing, where the older boys lived. Could it be Carstairs, who seemed to hover around so often?

As he walked back into the main building, walking past the portraits in the reception, Rose thought just how alone the children must feel at Sunnyside at Christmas, and undoubtedly bored, so that such a mundane action as saying goodbye to somebody could be so exciting.

*

A sprinkling of tattered tinsel doesn't evoke any true Christmas spirit, thought Rose, as he stood alone in the meeting room on the first floor, with hastily hung yuletide baubles liberally festooned around. But it was the first overt sign of festivities he'd seen at Sunnyside.

The large oak conference table in the room's centre was covered in a burgundy tablecloth, and two punch bowls with cups were laid out next to plates containing on-the-turn sandwiches, sausage rolls and biscuits.

There was no music- Rose wished that somebody had thought to bring a gramophone -of all parties he'd ever been to, this one was in dire need of accompanying sound.

There were around twelve members of staff there, almost half of whom he'd never seen before, and even less of whom he'd met. There were four islands of people- Mrs Benson was at the heart of one, talking excitedly to the sheepishly beaten Mr Leadbetter, as four other teaching/pastoral staff looked on.

One of the men in that group was strikingly handsome, blonde haired and dark-eyed, a fine physique making his torso look like an inverted triangle under his white linen shirt. Then Mr Leadbetter introduced Rose to him- "This is Oscar Lewis, the physical exercise instructor for the male residents."

Mr Lewis smiled, showcasing perfectly even white teeth, although saying nothing as they shook hands. Rose guessed that he was in his late twenties and could have been a matinee idol in a different life.

Looking around, Rose suspected that Mrs Benson had been responsible for the miserable decorations, but he had nothing to corroborate that. He smiled at her, and she nodded back. Another group of three nearby, a man and two women, were wearing white coats, and were obviously clinical staff.

The best-suited Mr Tucker stood alone, eyeing the punch bowls, as did Rose, two men with a thirst, both for refreshment, but Rose for information too.

Mr Tucker cracked first, going for the nearest punch bowl, while Rose walked over to Mrs Benson's group, holding out his hand to Mr Leadbetter, as Mrs Benson looked at Mr Tucker with a scolding look for not waiting for her cue to start imbibing.

Mrs Benson was something of a busybody and an organizer it seemed, and Rose noted to himself that she was probably one of the best sources for Sunnyside gen if he could break down her formidable barriers.

"It's good to see you here," said Mr Leadbetter. "How are you finding Sunnyside?"

"Oh, I'm settling in," Rose said, "but it took a few days to adjust."

"It does. I remember my first week, it all seemed very strange."

"Won't you have some punch?" said Mrs Benson to Rose.

"I really don't mind if I do," said Rose, smiling as he did so.

As he moved towards the punch bowls where Mr Tucker was still hovering alone, Rose noticed that Mrs Benson was looking at him as she spoke conspiratorially to Mr Leadbetter.

"What's the poison like?" said Rose.

"I won't answer that," said Mr Tucker, his eyes expressing the opposite of the licking of lips. "But beggars…"

Rose grinned as he ladled some of the almost translucent red liquid into a cup, a slice of cucumber floating on top. He took a sip, and he could see why Mr Tucker was less than impressed. It had an acrid taste, and calling it poison no longer seemed just a manly joke. Still, a few cups of that should get them talking.

Rose was especially hoping that Mrs Benson would have a cup or two when there was a new arrival, which made the lacklustre party atmosphere even more subdued. It was Mr Dodwell, and the effect he had on the room was as if the Almighty had entered.

His jet-black suit was spotless, old school or club tie perfectly knotted, and the button-down white shirt ferociously starched, his black brogue shoes having almost achieved a wet look through dedicated polishing.

Along with his perfectly erect posture, most impressive for a man of his age and considerable height, he had a distinct military aura, and the firm clasping of his hands behind his back as he walked towards Mrs Benson's and Mr Leadbetter's little group showed he had certainly been of the officer class.

Rose and Mr Tucker shared a glance as they both abandoned the punch table- Mr Tucker seemed to melt into the background as far away in the room from Mr Dodwell as possible, while

Rose purposefully went and stood close to the man who ran Sunnyside.

"So much more amenable than last year," said Mr Dodwell. "I must congratulate you on your organisational skills, Mrs Benson."

She blushed, and Mr Leadbetter was about to speak to his boss when Mr Dodwell turned around sharply to face Rose, cutting Mr Leadbetter as if in a deliberate show of power.

"You must be Mr Rose. Dr Sharland has told me all about you."

Rose was still processing how terrible last year's staff Christmas party must have been if that year's one was more 'amenable', and the social castration of Mr Leadbetter, so he was a little taken aback at the speed of Mr Dodwell's introduction, causing him almost to spill his punch, which he was sure would burn a hole in the carpet.

"It's a pleasure to meet you, Mr Dodwell. It's a shame Dr Sharland's not here too," said Rose.

"Indeed. Although he's never much of a one for such occasions, a little like me, I'm afraid. Are you comfortable in the cottage?"

"Very much, thank you. And I'm getting to know your staff now."

"They're a good bunch and they really care about this place."

Rose could see that Mr Dodwell had a warmth in his eyes, a counterpoint to his rather supercilious demeanour and the chilly tactic he'd just used on harmless-looking Mr Leadbetter. Rose also noticed that Mrs Benson was listening in very carefully to his conversation.

"You will be attending present-giving tomorrow morning, won't you? It's in the Great Hall at nine. We give all the residents their Christmas boxes."

"I'd be delighted to attend," said Rose.

"And perhaps you would come up and see me in my office for a chat afterwards, perhaps at ten?"

"Certainly."

"My office is on the first floor, just past the Cavendish Wing on the right. Do enjoy your evening."

101

"I will, thank you." With that, Mr Dodwell moved away just as abruptly as he had turned around just minutes before. After sharing a few pleasantries with the members of staff he couldn't identify, Sunnyside's custodian left the gathering.

Mrs Benson was now suddenly interested in Rose again, perhaps since he'd been invited to Mr Dodwell's office for a private chat.

"If you need anything, any help at all, please don't hesitate to ask, will you?" she said. "It's good to have you here with us."

Rose could tell that she really wanted to know why he- a lowly and unqualified clinical dogsbody – should be granted a private audience with the man she was obviously desperate to impress, either professionally or romantically, or perhaps both.

But it was Rose's turn to take control.

"I must be going now," he said, as Mrs Benson was about to interrogate him further. "Thank you for the invitation."

And with that, and a nod to the still-wounded Mr Leadbetter and the ever-handsome Mr Lewis, Rose left the room, noticing as he placed his punch cup down on the table that Mr Tucker was now having another cup himself, seated alone over in the far corner. Probably the best place to be at this party, thought Rose.

13

"It's that time of year again when we all come together at Sunnyside, to give thanks to what we have and to celebrate the life of Jesus Christ, our saviour. Amen."

"Amen." The word was spoken by almost everybody in attendance, as they bowed their heads, but my lips didn't move at all.

The Reverend Barnes stood at the lectern at the front of the Great Hall, the lectern higher than his pulpit in Shadowside's chapel. With his wispy grey handlebar sideburns and bald pate gleaming as he leaned over to read, dog collar tightly arranged, I looked at him with nothing less than contempt.

Everybody knew that Rev Barnes liked to give private divinity lessons to certain boys at his cottage, who went there to collect the few pennies he offered at the end of each visit for attendance. He'd never asked me- he just wouldn't dare.

"But it's also the day- the 25th of December- when Christ was born, that we remember the tragedy which befell us here on this day just four years ago, when the chapel caught fire and claimed the lives of three innocent boys. The work of the devil, no doubt. He was amongst us then, and he's never too far from us. We have to be watchful and keep him at bay."

I wondered how innocent those three boys had truly been. Nobody explained why they were in the chapel that evening with the good Reverend, and why it took him so long to raise the alarm, before the smoke engulfed them and they began to burn to death.

"So, before we accept the fruits of the season, and say our grace, let us not forget those three boys- Samuel Jamieson, Peter Thirby and Anthony Simpson-Jones. May peace be with them. Amen."

"Amen."

Behind Rev Barnes sat most of *them,* and to their right a Christmas tree, a real, but ailing one, although the threadbare branches were decorated with baubles and tinsel, and a lonesome silver angel sat atop the skeletal summit. Underneath was piled scores of small cardboard boxes, one for each boy and girl.

I scanned the ranks of *them*- Mr Dodwell took his central seat as usual, with the teaching staff around him, and the doctors and nurses, aside from those in the Cavendish Wing who I knew would be continuing their terrible work.

And then I saw *him* again- there was no Dr Sharland, or Mr Tucker, who never came to assemblies, but the recently arrived man who looked out of place was sat there. He didn't bow his head like the others, but looked out at us, taking in the room in front of him, all the boys and girls gathered.

I looked at him, but I'm sure I was just another anonymous face among many from his vantage. I had to know who he was, this man sitting there in a white coat like the other doctors, this man who had become a fixture at Shadowside so suddenly and with no announcement.

Then my focus was derailed by Rev Barnes being replaced as speaker by Mr Dodwell, towering over the lectern, as Mr Leadbetter forced a nervous cough out behind him.

"Now we will receive our gifts and show our usual appreciation for the fortune we possess. Let us say Grace."

"For what we are about to receive may the Lord make us truly thankful, Amen." Again, almost all the room joined in, while I looked again at the man I couldn't identify, whose lips didn't seem to be moving.

"We will now come up one by one, by wing, as always West first, followed by South, then East, and finally, North," said Mr Dodwell, as Mrs Benson and Mr Leadbetter began to pick up the small boxes from under the tree in piles and then took their positions either side of him.

The youngest girls went up first and received a box each from Mr Dodwell, who reached down and smiled at them. Then the older girls of South, minus Dorothy of course, who was in a quite different place now, but Isabel walked back with her box, head down, meaning I couldn't give her another look.

I kept my eyes on the man at the front as much as I could- he was intently watching the proceedings -he was either naturally very curious or was looking for something, I just knew it.

The younger boys from East were soon returning with their boxes, and I was in line. Like the others, I returned Mr Dodwell's aggressive smile with the saintly half-smile I used for *them*, and I was soon back on the bench with all the others.

"Please open your boxes and Happy Christmas to you all," said Mr Dodwell.

The sound of the boxes opening in unison echoed around the Great Hall, and sighs came from some of the younger boys and girls. I opened mine, and as usual it contained an apple and an orange and a book, this time *Black Beauty*!

I wanted to protest- surely this book should have been given to a girl from South. But when I saw that Kirby had been given a copy of *The Black Peril* by W E Johns, I knew that I would be reading about Biggles by the end of the day. Just for amusement. I'd like to see him take on the Red Baron- he'd blast that pretender Bigglesworth out of the blooming sky.

Then my gaze returned to the man at the front of the room, who was now standing, and talking to Mr Dodwell, which immediately accelerated my curiosity to concern.

My mind was still on Lawrence Drummond and his murderous deeds, and this was an unwelcome distraction. But something was going on, and I had to find out what it was and the true reason for the man's sudden appearance at Shadowside.

*

Rose could sense that he was being watched as he began to climb the main stairs. It was just a feeling, but a strong one.

As he walked up the shining marble steps, which had presumably been recently polished, he wanted to look behind him, but decided it was better to keep going for now- whoever it was would show their face eventually.

As he reached the first floor, he stopped in the corridor and looked at the stately yet static birds in the cabinets, hanging back to see if anybody appeared before he made his way to Mr Dodwell's office.

Two girls materialised at the top of the stairs and took an immediate right turn towards the residential wings, failing to give him even a momentary glance.

But he could still feel somebody close, and began to wonder if he were imagining it, as there was nobody there. And the

105

staring eyes of the birds in front of him only increased his trepidation.

It was unsettling to be the focus of unknown attention, and he decided to make his way down the corridor, past the many doors, following the geometric patterns beneath his feet, punctuated by looking up and around.

Rose could hear movement behind him, from where he had just come, but had no idea if it were one or more people. He looked around, and nobody was there.

Then he came to South wing and passed its large door- he knew that this was where Dorothy had lived and would have liked to have gone inside to get a sense of her quarters but knew he couldn't go in there.

The corridor curved around to the left and immediately opposite him were two huge and heavy-duty double doors, which dwarfed South's single door. Unlike the other wings and rooms, there was no nameplate outside on the wall.

Suddenly, there was the sound of a key turning, and one of the doors opened from the inside, vigorously creaking. And a woman in a white coat appeared, stepping out and closing the door immediately behind her before Rose could peer inside.

"May I help you?" she said sternly, as she saw him standing there.

"I'm just on my way to Mr Dodwell's office actually."

"It's the last on the right," she said, pointing in its direction.

Rose realised that she'd been one of the staff members at the party whom he hadn't been able to place, and she hadn't been at the assembly that morning.

"Thank you," said Rose. "And Happy Christmas."

She didn't return the greeting and failed to move away. It was as if she was suspicious of him, wanting him to leave that vicinity before she went about her own business.

As he walked down towards the end of the corridor, Rose realised that the room with the huge double doors which the woman had come out of must be the Cavendish Wing, as Mr Dodwell had said that his office was just past it on the right.

Rose could still sense that someone was looking at him, and assuming it was the woman, he turned around abruptly expecting to see her still there, but she wasn't. And neither was anybody else.

He finally got to the single door, which had 'Mr Dodwell, MA Cantab' printed on the nameplate. Rose knew that there was no need to state his position there. Mr Dodwell sat at the highest point of Sunnyside's tree, and everybody knew who he was and what he did.

Rose knocked twice cleanly, glanced to his right and saw nobody again, even though he was sure that somebody was in that corridor somewhere, and could see him.

When he heard a female voice saying, 'Come in please,' Rose entered at once, pleased to be out of that corridor and the uncomfortable sense of being the focus of somebody unknown.

*

When I saw him enter Mr Dodwell's office, I knew that he was truly one of *them* and as such he was my enemy.

I'd tracked him all the way from the Great Hall, up the stairs where Jack the Ripper walked on his final day on this earth and down which Old Bannister met his maker and witnessed his altercation with one of the monsters from the Cavendish Wing as I leaned into an alcove.

Like a good G-man I stayed just out of sight, although the furtive glances he made behind him told me that he felt a presence around him. But he had no idea who it was following him. Like a wriggling worm on a fisherman's hook he squirmed, helpless.

Whoever he was I needed to find out. His sudden and unheralded appearance at Shadowside was unexplained. I was sure that he wasn't a policeman, but could he be a private detective hired to find Dorothy?

This man who seemed so alien to his surroundings was there for a specific reason. There had to be a connection to Dorothy, and I needed to go on the offensive without revealing myself to him.

*

"Although I can't say so openly in front of the staff for obvious reasons, I want you to know that I'm glad you're here and looking into Dorothy's disappearance."

Rose was seated opposite Mr Dodwell in a blue Victorian upright armchair which looked very well-used and was surprisingly comfortable.

"Has there been any progress with police inquiries?" said Rose.

"Not as far as I know. Inspector Alexander, the officer in charge of the case, updates me weekly by telephone, although he's had very little to report so far."

"No sightings of Dorothy since the night of the 21st of November then?"

"The last time she was seen was at lights out at 9pm, when she was in her section in the South wing, as she should have been," said Mr Dodwell firmly.

"May I ask which member of staff saw Dorothy at lights out?"

"It was Mrs Benson, who always puts the girls to bed in both South and West."

Rose made a mental note of that. "Were there any further sightings?"

"Apparently not- nobody saw her leave South or Sunnyside after that, and no witnesses in Milston and the surrounding area have come forward to seeing her either. She didn't buy a ticket at the train station, nor call for a taxi to take her away from here."

"So, she could have left here on foot, which is unlikely as she would have surely been seen by somebody, or she might have left by private means."

Mr Dodwell gave a pronounced and solemn nod. "All I can say is we know that Dorothy Hopkins left here at some time after 9pm on that night, and before seven the next morning, the 22nd of November. The grounds have been extensively searched, all members of staff and girls in South questioned by the police, and I'm told we are none the wiser."

"Do you have any feeling about where she might be and why she left?"

"As I told Inspector Alexander, I believe that Dorothy ran away, and had the help of someone from outside, somebody with access to a motorcar I presume. She'd only been with us since the spring, and sometimes new residents take a while to

108

settle in, but I'm sure that Dr Sharland has told you about Dorothy's treatment."

"Indeed, he has," said Rose. "So, you are happy for me to dig around and find out what I can?"

"Of course. But please tread carefully. We have been very discreet about Dorothy's disappearance- we wouldn't want more runaways – and in my experience, one thing can lead to another."

"I'll be careful I assure you. I think that vital information about Dorothy may well come from the residents themselves. Could I perhaps speak to one or two of the girls who knew Dorothy best?"

Mr Dodwell paused for a moment and looked out of the long window at the bare boughs of a tall tree outside, blowing in the wind. When Rose looked out too, he could see the island of foliage in front of the school, which blocked his cottage from view.

"While it's contrary to normal procedure, for a male member of staff to speak to female residents, I think that in the circumstances we will have to bend those rules- not break them- just loosen them to accommodate the needs of this exceptional situation. I'll ask Mrs Benson to draw you up a list of the girls to whom Dorothy was closest."

"Thank you."

"And then you can speak to them in a private place. We don't want to alarm the other girls- it could affect their treatment. We always have to put the residents first- we're a care provider, and parents have entrusted us with their children."

"That's well understood," said Rose, although he was thinking that Mrs Hopkins had been sorely let down by Mr Dodwell's institution.

"Apart from that, please take your directions from Dr Sharland. As the clinical lead, he knows the most effective way to deal with residents. I will of course brief Dr Sharland on his return in a few days about you having limited access to any friends of Dorothy."

"Will Mrs Benson be told the true reason I am here?"

"I think it's best to keep that between you, Dr Sharland and myself, and of course Dr Sanderson in London, who I believe was Dorothy's original psychiatrist?"

"Yes, I've met him," said Rose.

"Mrs Benson can be told that you are doing some research into the impact of Dorothy's disappearance on those closest to her in care, purely for clinical purposes."

"That sounds a good cover," said Rose.

"I don't enjoy misleading my staff, believe me. But if we are going to locate Dorothy and bring her back here for treatment, one must take such measures."

Rose nodded.

"Just remember to please tread carefully and report any progress directly to me, and I can decide whether the police should be informed. I can usually be found here in my office, but if I'm not and around and about the place, my secretary Mrs Furnival next door will take a message for you in confidence."

"Thank you."

"Good luck, and let's hope we find Dorothy quickly- God speed to you."

As Rose left the quietly calming office, past Mrs Furnival who had ushered him through about twenty minutes earlier, he wondered just how much he could share with Mr Dodwell, who naturally always put Sunnyside first. He, on the other hand, had a story to scoop and a desperate mother to help, both of which were of equal importance to him now.

Walking back down the corridor, Rose felt for the first time since he left the Great Hall earlier that morning that no eyes were upon him, enabling him to think clearly about what had just been said.

The fact that Mr Dodwell was granting him some access to the girls who knew Dorothy was a breakthrough, but Rose was clear in his own mind that his allegiance was neither to Mr Dodwell nor Sunnyside.

14

The rare glimpse of winter sun that fell across the main courtyard could have looked like a summer's day from an upper window if anyone was watching him, thought Rose, but it was actually still bitterly cold out there in the wind.

It was late afternoon, and he was about to go back to his cottage as Mr Lewis appeared on the gravel. He walked over to Rose, at the speed of a stroll, but there was nothing slow or pedestrian about the physical exercise instructor.

Lewis walked like the panthers that Rose had seen on a Pathe newsreel before the main feature presentation at the Ritzy near the *Travesties* office back in London, where he sometimes leaned back in a seat when ruminating on a story. There was something feline about how Lewis moved, almost gamine, although his body was decidedly masculine.

"Afternoon, Mr Rose." Lewis held out his hand and smiled simultaneously, his perfectly even dazzling teeth like the man that Rose had seen on the Macleans toothpaste poster under the caption 'Did you Maclean your teeth today?'

"Hello Mr Lewis," said Rose, shaking firmly as he was sure that Lewis would have a strong grip, which he did.

"Please- call me Oscar."

"I'm Harold." Rose had never called himself Harry. As a boy, he was always Harold at home, and that had stayed with him. Only on Fleet Street did people call him Harry.

"Beautiful day for it isn't it?" said Lewis.

"It certainly is, but it depends on what you're doing I suppose," said Rose.

"I'm off to do some practice in the nets myself."

"Cricketing man, are you?"

"Yes, that's my sport really. I used to play at county level."

"That's impressive," said Rose.

"It was until I injured my shoulder. And my arm was my main weapon."

"I'm sorry to hear that," said Rose. "Were you a bowler?"

"Right arm over, fast-medium. But more like slow- medium now!" said Lewis.

As they spoke, three of the older girls walked past, and Rose couldn't help but notice how they looked at Lewis. There was a mixture of awe and adoration on their faces as they smiled shyly at him.

"Good afternoon girls," said Lewis, his model smile brought into service once again. The girls responded by smiling back and giggling nervously, walking away, yet looking back at him as they did so.

"I think they like you," said Rose.

Lewis laughed. "Well, they haven't got much choice here, present company excluded of course!"

It was Rose's turn to smile, if not laugh.

"Well, I'd better be going if I'm going to get an hour in at the nets before dark," said Lewis. "Bye now."

Rose raised his hand and smiled, still marvelling at the girls' smitten reaction to Lewis as he moved across the courtyard, his strides ones of controlled laziness, smooth and almost balletic.

But as well as admiration, Rose could identify a touch of envy within himself, while knowing that he would never possess Lewis's magnetism, no matter how hard he tried.

Although he was also struck that the girls' reaction to Lewis was by far the most natural behaviour he'd seen any of the children at Sunnyside display.

*

When that hypocrite Rev Barnes brayed on about the chapel fire at assembly, I must confess that I felt a stirring down below. But unlike some of the other boys in North, who thrash around at night under blankets in their sections imagining Carole Lombard or, in the case of Sherwood-Ames, Mrs Benson naked, I didn't want to waste my seed, so controlled myself.

My rise at Shadowside began one day in the Great Hall when I was twelve years old, and that Christmas night will forever be emblazoned in my mind. But I'd wanted to make that charlatan priest suffer months before that, when he read a Proverb from the King James Bible in assembly. I knew I had to do something.

That was over four years ago now, and the words still burn into me.

"Do not withhold correction from a child, for if you beat him with a rod he will not die," he said.

It was everything that I stand against- *they* are the oppressors- keeping me in line when for as long as I can remember I've known that my destiny is to set that line.

Latimer agreed with me, and we made sure that Rev Barnes and *they* suffered, with those three imbecile sycophants who got charred getting what they deserved too.

But I couldn't have done it without Latimer.

You see, Latimer, who was my only pal here until his release, is a master of the fire arts. Indeed, that was why he was sent here in the first place, for setting things alight.

But I had to convince my pal to utilise his skills once again, and this was helped by the fact that Rev Barnes had once propositioned him, you know, invited him into the vestry, which Latimer wisely declined to do.

We'd been talking about how it was all a lie for a few months, how Rev Barnes was a fraud, more interested in his own desires than anyone else, and I'd decided to get at him somehow. But Latimer didn't share my depth of hatred, to my frustration.

Although when Rev Barnes winked at Latimer at Midnight Mass that Christmas Eve of 1932, it finally lit Latimer's short fuse, and all was set to put the kibosh on the reverend the next day.

We knew that Rev Barnes and his trusty little choirboy lackeys would be in the chapel that Christmas Day afternoon and evening, as there had been a call for helpers at the last assembly to ready the chapel for the New Year's services.

After Latimer told me the ingredients I'd need, I started preparing for a fire attack, so that I'd be ready when my pal felt his old craving again.

It hadn't been difficult to sequester some paraffin from Mr Tucker's supplies shed- he really can be very careless, leaving the door open for me. Then it was just some matches, which I managed to pilfer from Mr Baxter's desk when he left an almost full book of them, along with his stinking pipe, as he left the

113

History classroom one day. Then there were the ten milk bottles taken over time from outside the kitchens, as well as a crate in which they were stored. Finally, I'd gathered assorted socks from the laundry basket over several weeks, until I had five.

We made our little fire-bombs in the morning, knowing that we could use them later that day. We assembled them on the mound- Latimer introduced me to my now favourite place, as it had been his too for some time. We often sat there, idly conspiring about how we could attack *them*, and latterly sharing the stories about the boys at Red Circle School and their own fight against oppression in my bloods.

But we were very industrious that day, operating a system that would have made Henry Ford proud. Latimer cut up the socks into wide strips using the penknife he kept hidden on the mound, while I half-filled the milk bottles with paraffin. Next, we stuffed the cloth strips into the open bottles, so that one end was submerged in paraffin and the other end came out of the bottle top. We put them into the crate and left them there on the mound and went about our daily Shadowside business until it was dark.

Returning to the mound a little after five o'clock, while the younger boys and girls in East and West were probably reading their sad little books given out by Mr Dodwell as presents, we put on our gloves and went to war.

We soaked the top of the cloth strips in paraffin, and then placed all our fire-bombs back into the crate. After checking that I had the matches and all was clear, we ventured off the mound, carrying the crate between us in silence. We passed nobody as we made our way over to the chapel, the out-of-condition Latimer breathing heavily with the exertion while I sailed along.

In the graveyard outside the chapel, we could see that the lights were on downstairs, and hear a constant scraping sound.

Me and Latimer knew that four boys would be inside along with the Rev Barnes, as three had especially volunteered to help the dog-collared devil with his chores- Simpson-Jones, Jamieson, and Thirby- while water-baby Kirby, who had been Barnes' special little helper ever since he arrived at Shadowside the previous year, would naturally be there too as always.

We quietly carried the crate down the steps towards the chapel door, which was half open. I looked inside and could see some boys at the far end leaning over pews and sandpapering. I didn't have time to see exactly who was there or where Rev Barnes was, as we had to go into battle.

I gave Latimer the matches to light the cloth strips- it had been decided that I would do the throwing as I have a good overarm spin bowling action and can throw a good distance, but I wouldn't be in need of my googly.

The zealous choirboys kept sandpapering as the first bottle smashed near them, followed by a whoosh and a flame which spread out as it hit the floor. The sandpapering stopped as the boys must have looked around in fear, but I was focusing on the next missile. Each one had the same effect, and we were delivering them at thirty-second intervals, just as we had planned- smash, whoosh... fire, fire, the chapel's burning!

By the time I'd thrown the final three bombs, the whole far end of the chapel was ablaze, as were the boys, and the fire was working its way towards us at the door. And the sound of the boys' high-pitched whimpering and murmuring like mice in an oven was thrilling.

One called out for his mummy as the flames took hold and that will forever stay with me as a highlight of my life. But none of the boys cried out to God or Rev Barnes, supposedly in whose service they were in the chapel.

Latimer and I shut the door on them and rushed back into the graveyard with the crate, which we abandoned there, having kept our gloves on throughout. The G-men in my bloods always make great use of fingerprints, you see.

For a few minutes me and Latimer stood there amongst the gravestones, more energised than we'd ever been, smiling at each other in triumph, watching the glow of the flames through the stained-glass windows at ground level, which soon began to smash outwards.

When the wailing stopped, we knew that the boys inside would be burnt to cinders, the wood panelling and furniture having turned the chapel into their tomb.

We dared stay there no more, and began to run back towards the main building, removing our gloves and putting them into our coat pockets as we did so.

We'd covered about a hundred and fifty yards when sneaky Old Bannister appeared and called us over. Neither he nor Mr Dodwell could ever prove that we were involved, although we were gated to sections for two weeks for being out in the grounds without permission.

Our only lasting regret was that the Rev Barnes and Kirby had missed their cremation, and we never found out where they were while those silly boys burned.

*

As Rose expertly dissected the first five pages of each newspaper over breakfast, he wasn't surprised to see that they were all still leading on the new King George's sudden elevation to the throne.

Edward had stepped down a fortnight earlier and was now in Austria staying at the home of a baron, while Wallis Simpson was in the south of France. Rose was wishing he could be in either place rather than at Sunnyside, but he also knew he had real work to do there.

He'd hoped that Mrs Benson would make an appearance in the staff dining room, but she didn't, so after exchanging some words about the weather with Mr Leadbetter, Rose suddenly changed the subject.

"You worked closely with Mr Bannister, didn't you? Terrible what happened to him, wasn't it?"

"It certainly was, and quite a shock for all of us," said Mr Leadbetter.

"Those stairs obviously give you little chance if you slip."

Mr Leadbetter's usually relaxed features took on a troubled look. "If you were to slip, yes."

The response intrigued Rose, so he continued probing. "Mr Bannister is said to have walked very quickly, so I suppose he could have missed a step quite easily."

"It could have happened like that. But although Bernard walked faster than most, he was also a man who took great care. He had fine balance- he'd been a champion university athlete when he was younger, you know."

116

"I didn't know that," said Rose. "Perhaps he was distracted in some way, which made him lose his footing?"

"Most of us think that. Of all the staff, Bernard was the one least likely to have had such an accident. You see, he was always very much in control of himself, and he was in good physical condition."

"Did you tell the police that?"

"Oh yes. Many of us did. But nobody saw what happened. How did you know about Bernard's death anyway?"

"Dr Sharland told me as he was showing me around. What was Bernard Bannister like?"

"He was very professional, firm but fair. We all respected him, and he was a kind man when you got to know him. But he didn't suffer fools."

"That has to be a good quality," said Rose. "How did the residents react to his death?"

"They were all in shock too. Some of the younger boys cried in assembly. As I said, he was respected. He kept a tight rein on them- he was a stickler for the rules- but they knew that he treated them all equally."

"Some of the children cried?"

"That's not surprising," said Mr Leadbetter. "Whilst we maintain a healthy barrier from the residents emotionally, they have to feel free to come to us with their problems. They have what they call psychiatric problems, but I prefer to think of them as emotional ones. And being away from home, some of the younger residents especially come to see us as surrogate parents. We're all they have here at Sunnyside."

Rose decided to go all the way, even if he sounded like a policeman. "Did Bernard Bannister have any enemies that you know of?"

"No- as I told the police, he wasn't a man who created enemies. He was very good at what he did, you see, and he was always willing to help other members of staff. Why are you so interested in Bernard anyway?"

"I just find it sad that a man in his prime could die in such a strange way while just going about his daily business."

"They say that accidents happen, but I agree that it was an unusual way for Bernard to be taken from us. But then death is something that not even Bernard could control."

"That's very true," said Rose. "None of us knows when that will come."

As Rose said goodbye to Mr Leadbetter, he realised that they were both solemn faced now, having gone from an innocuous chat about the weather to the subject of mortality. A Happy Christmas to all, he wryly thought.

But a clearer picture of Bernard Bannister was forming in Rose's mind now- a man in full charge of himself and what was around him, perhaps even the people around him. Just like Mr Dodwell.

And Rose wondered if Mr Leadbetter would share their conversation with Mrs Benson, and whether she would tell Mr Leadbetter about his need to speak to Dorothy's closest friends. If so, he was bound to become the subject of their gossip. But he couldn't let that concern him. He had to keep digging.

*

1st December 1888

He walks in a strange sideways motion, as if picking up thoughts from the left of him. He has an erect, angular presence otherwise, and his pale gaunt face is framed by immaculate, slicked- back hair, parted in the centre, his moustache punctuating his symmetrical face.

His dress is clean and smart, the young and professional aspirant in the flesh. But when you look into his eyes, you will see a sadness and sense of loss deeper than you have ever seen before.

Those eyes are dark, shining and reflecting all around him. Walking down High Holborn in London, he is one of the teeming crowd, their arms flapping like penguins. He looks purposeful, going about his business, but aimless in his mind. He's a soldier, but unfit for war now, and unfit for life.

He sees himself in the window of Simpson's Cakes on the corner, without really seeing himself. A carriage speeds past him, spraying mud over his striped and pressed trousers, but this elicits no reaction from him either.

Two red and purple-ribboned schoolgirls saunter past him and giggle at his misfortune with the carriage, and the angry-looking man with the seasoned face selling copies of The Strand magazine permits himself a smirk- he knows how it feels to be lonely- he lost his wife of thirty-four years to pneumonia last winter. But he's never felt as lonely as the man with the mud on his trousers.

When he tries to speak, to scold the schoolgirls, tears fall within his voice, drowning a once resonant tone.

He suddenly starts walking back in the direction from where he came, as if retracing his own footsteps. He wants to end it all, and he momentarily believes he has the courage.

But during the next days he will be tortured by the fact that this last stab at free will could be just another delusion, as he disappears from the London streets forever.

I knew exactly what happened to Lawrence Drummond after he was last seen in the city as I again finished the last instalment of the Jack the Ripper serial in my tuppenny blood. The second reading made me understand him so much more.

His terrible work was done, and he came back to his family home, which is now Shadowside, then going on his final errand to Stenson's in Milston to purchase that cut-throat razor.

And back at Shadowside, he walked up the main stairs where Old Bannister descended almost forty-eight years later, up to the billiards room, where he felt most at peace, and where he made his final bold statement, just as my father would too.

There was little wonder why that room with such a pedigree of courage had become my second favourite place after the mound.

119

15

The following morning, Rose breathed in the bracing winter air as he walked up the path from his cottage, navigating the island overgrown with bushes and shrubs and made towards the main building.

As he approached the main building, Rose could once again feel eyes upon him, and he instinctively looked up at the large bay window below the right turret where he'd seen somebody moving quickly away just a few days earlier. He saw nothing this time, but wondered if it could be Carstairs, who always seemed to be around somewhere looking on.

The surveillance seemed to continue as he walked through the main reception, past the portraits and the Great Hall and then the deadly main stairs. Through the double doors and then a right turn- still there was nobody in sight.

Dr Sharland was in his office when Rose arrived there.

After exchanging greetings, Rose's new boss informed him that he'd seen Dr Sanderson in London.

"He sends his best to you and said he will help you in any way he can to find Dorothy."

"That's very good of him," said Rose.

"He cares about his patients, as I do. He helps me design the clinical programme and he regularly looks at the progress of a sample of residents. But of course, he's available to talk to you about Dorothy too and offer any more psychiatric analysis of her he can. As her first and primary psychiatrist, he has a profound insight into her mind and motivations."

"That could be very useful," said Rose, although he felt as if Dr Sanderson had already given him a good insight into the girl.

"And that brings me to the matter which Mr Dodwell briefed me about by telephone- your access to Dorothy's closest acquaintances. I wish you'd asked me instead of going to Mr Dodwell," said Dr Sharland, a little stiffly.

"My apologies for that. But I was called to his office for a meeting, and we were discussing the need to locate Dorothy and finding out what those closest to her know seemed important. I wasn't meaning to go over your head."

"No offence taken. But this will be unprecedented access to residents- only those involved directly in their treatment usually have such access. So, I would like to be present when you speak to anybody from the South wing."

"With respect, is that a good idea? It may make them feel less able to be forthcoming with a man in your position in the room."

"On the contrary, I think my presence will help any resident to open up, as they know me and will feel more at ease."

"May I ask if you were present when the police interviewed them?" said Rose, imagining that if so, they probably got next to nothing from the girls.

"Of course. It would have been unethical of me to have allowed strangers to badger those girls. My job is to protect them and make them better and any outside hindrance to that must be minimised."

"But these are exceptional circumstances, as Mr Dodwell said to me..."

"They certainly are. But that doesn't mean that we stop following the correct protocols. I do have a lot of experience in this field, and I think you would find that Dr Sanderson agrees with me."

Rose knew that he couldn't press it any further. "I understand. You know your business best."

"I'm glad that's settled. Mrs Benson is on her way here now and she will be filling you in about the girls you'll be meeting."

Rose nodded, and a long silence followed, probably only lasting a couple of minutes, but which felt interminable. Suddenly there was a slightly strained atmosphere in the room, and Dr Sharland seemed less of an ally somehow.

The knock on the door was most welcome when it came to shatter the still and steely air, but when Mrs Benson appeared, Rose was hardly overwhelmed with relief. She wore her usual smug and cloying expression.

"Dr Sharland, Mr Rose."

"Thank you for coming Agatha," said Dr Sharland.

Rose was startled to hear her name, especially as she didn't look like an Agatha at all. But then he knew that he certainly didn't look like a rose either. He nodded and smiled.

"As I think Mr Dodwell has informed you Agatha, Mr Rose here is doing some research about the impact of Dorothy Hopkins's disappearance on those who knew her best. It's part of a larger project we are working on."

"Yes, Mr Dodwell gave me a thorough briefing," said Mrs Benson, with a knowing smile bursting with self-satisfaction.

"Could you tell Mr Rose which residents he will be speaking to, and a little background about them?"

"Certainly," she said, turning to Rose. "There are two girls who were closest to Dorothy- not exactly close I suppose, but they knew her best anyway. They are Caitlin Whitaker-Davies and Isabel Haarman."

Rose nodded. "I'd like to speak to both girls separately if possible."

"That's no problem at all," said Dr Sharland. "But both girls are fragile and must be treated with care. Could you tell Mr Rose about the girls' sensitivities and a little about their histories, Agatha?"

Mrs Benson smiled at Dr Sharland, as if she was part of an elite club with privileged access to information, which Rose knew in a way she was.

"Caitlin suffers dizzy spells and comes over faint," said Mrs Benson. "She came to reside here after collapsing several times. We're still trying to work out the cause of her fainting spells- she doesn't suffer from epilepsy though, we know that."

"Quite so," said Dr Sharland. "There are no convulsions or foaming at the mouth. Caitlin just passes out. She has attacks of severe anxiety, but they have decreased in frequency considerably since coming under treatment here. Still, she must be spoken to softly and calmly to avoid any spell coming on."

"Understood," said Rose.

"Isabel is a more serious case though, I'm afraid…" Mrs Benson was interrupted by Dr Sharland, and looked mildly upset as she was curtailed.

"Isabel has a capacity for violence if threatened. She has a history of lashing out- in her case at her younger sister at home.

122

It started with her breaking up her sister's dolls. And then one day her mother found her holding her sister's head under the water in the bath."

"Was she trying to kill her?" said Rose.

"We can't be sure what would have happened if her mother hadn't appeared and stopped her at that moment. It could have been a game to her, and she may well have let her sister breathe again. But her parents rightly took her to a psychiatrist- Dr Sanderson in fact -after that episode."

"It sounds a little like Dorothy in a way," said Rose, "getting angry and violent when she feels threatened."

"There are similarities," said Dr Sharland. "But Dorothy and Isabel are very different characters, aren't they Agatha?"

"They certainly are. Dorothy is easier to control than Isabel. If Isabel doesn't like what is going on around her, she can become angry very quickly- she's much more self-possessed than Dorothy."

"So, Isabel needs a particularly careful approach. If she feels that she is being blamed for anything-and it may not seem logical to you- she will either shut down or become belligerent," said Dr Sharland. "Neither girl is currently on medication, and we would like it to stay that way if possible."

Rose nodded once again, and Mrs Benson smiled at Dr Sharland.

"If you could bring the two girls here tomorrow morning at nine o'clock, Mr Rose and myself will speak to them in the office."

"Shouldn't I be present too, to make them feel at ease?" said Mrs Benson.

"That won't be necessary Agatha, I can take it from there."

That was something, thought Rose. Mrs Benson being there could only complicate the situation.

Mrs Benson left the office first, looking somewhat annoyed. Rose departed soon after, Dr Sharland telling him he wouldn't be needed again that day, but that he should prepare his questions for the girls carefully and sensitively.

And as Rose walked down the corridor, he had the sense of eyes following him again. Somebody was certainly interested in him, and he needed to find out if it was Carstairs, and if not, just who it was, so that the watcher became the watched.

*

I sat in the back of the Standard Little Nine, which was already four years old. Kirby was next to me, doing his usual thing of counting on his fingers, looking down and saying the numbers to himself.

Mr Leadbetter was driving, and we were cruising slower than Old Bannister used to go, down the drive and out the gate. It took eight minutes and two seconds, around a minute more than Old Bannister could achieve, but then Mr Leadbetter is a man who has limits and knows it.

Unlike Kirby, I timed the motorcar from the main courtyard to the main gate in my head, I didn't need any finger displays- not that Kirby was counting his fingers for a reason. It was just his way of surviving. Many at Shadowside have such ways of coping, they just don't have my strength.

It wasn't difficult to negotiate a trip to Milston, once I heard that it was Kirby's turn to visit the dentist that afternoon. I approached Mr Leadbetter, who is far more accommodating than Old Bannister, and told him that I needed to make some notes from a book at the town's library, one which Shadowside's library didn't carry.

"Which book is it?" Mr Leadbetter had said.

"It's a book about the Anglo-Zulu War of 1879," I said.

Mr Leadbetter didn't even check up on whether I was studying this with Mr Baxter, the history master. Old Bannister would have done so but wouldn't have let me go into Milston anyway. He would have taken the book out for me and brought it back.

If Mr Leadbetter had checked with Mr Baxter, he would have found that we were studying that war and had just looked at the Battle of Rorke's Drift, a victory for the Empire, but at some cost- although Mr Baxter had emphasised that victory and the heroism of our soldiers.

It made me think of Lawrence Drummond, fighting in another war with the British Army, just five years later, another hero who came back from that campaign and went on his

124

murderous rampage before taking the honourable way out. A man finally in control of his own destiny.

Mr Leadbetter wasn't a man in control of his destiny. He was obviously a man washed around by life's currents, but not panicking or drowning as he lacked either the intellect or strength of character- and probably both- to see his terrible truth.

Kirby didn't look at me all the way to town, but just continued to count. I glanced across at him several times, and the recount would begin again immediately one was finished.

I wondered whether he was counting to a high number or starting again each time, but I favoured the latter view, for a continuous count would have entered the millions, perhaps even billions by now, as he did it for many of his waking hours and wet his bed for some of his sleeping ones.

"I'll pick you up in an hour. Please don't leave the library," said Mr Leadbetter as he pulled up outside Milston Library.

"Yes sir, I will be waiting at the door here in an hour, thank you."

"Very good," he said.

Kirby didn't look up or speak as I got out of the motorcar. He would never know for sure how close I'd come to killing him in the chapel fire, but he must have heard the whispers.

Mr Leadbetter sat and watched me as I went into the library. As I waited just inside the door, I realised that I almost liked Mr Leadbetter- he was almost human- but then I remembered that he was one of *them*.

And as soon as I heard the car pull away and the sound of the engine faded into the distance, I came back out of the library and made my way into the square.

I had some urgent business to attend to.

*

As soon as Rose walked into the main reception the next morning, he knew that something was wrong.

On his way to Dr Sharland's office to speak to the two girls from the South wing, three members of staff, including Mrs Benson and Mr Leadbetter, were hanging around there, an unusual sight. And they were also talking excitedly.

"It's just terrible," said Mrs Benson.

125

"I don't know how it could have happened," said Mr Leadbetter.

"It must have been a resident," said a woman whose name Rose didn't yet know, but he knew she looked after the younger girls in West.

"But why would they do it, Susan?" said Mrs Benson.

"God only knows," she replied.

"Has something happened?" said Rose.

"Yes, something rather ghoulish I'm afraid," said Mr Leadbetter.

Before Rose could learn any more, Dr Sharland appeared through the doors from the direction of his office and hurried towards them.

"We'll have to cancel our meeting this morning," he said, looking at Mrs Benson and Rose as he spoke. "Mr Dodwell has called an emergency assembly for nine o'clock."

Mrs Benson, Mr Leadbetter, and the woman called Susan from West suddenly left without saying anything. Rose assumed that they automatically knew that they had to return to their wings and marshal the residents from their sections where they always returned after breakfast.

Rose looked at Dr Sharland, looking for an explanation, but none came.

"What's happened?" he finally said, the second time he'd asked the question that morning.

"It's rather strange. One of the orderlies was cleaning early this morning and they came across a rather macabre object- a razor, covered in blood."

Rose hadn't expected that. Perhaps a fight between some boys, or even a bad accident, but not that.

"And the razor is very old, a Victorian cut-throat razor," said Dr Sharland.

"Nobody uses those anymore."

"Quite."

"Where was it found?" said Rose

"Up in the billiards room."

"Why would anybody leave a razor in a billiards room?"

Dr Sharland seemed genuinely perplexed as he looked at Rose. "Those of us who've been here for a while know that the billiards room has a tragic history- one of the original occupants of this house killed himself in that room."

"With a razor?"

"Yes."

"Who was he?"

"Lawrence Drummond, the son of the owner of the house."

"Why did he kill himself?" said Rose.

"It's said that Lawrence, a soldier in the Sudan campaign, didn't want to return to the war."

Rose was imagining the battle-scarred young man, when just then, the residents began to make their way down the main stairs, and walked past Rose and Dr Sharland, deadly quiet.

West, then East, then South, and finally North. As if on a silent march, they filed into the Great Hall, Mrs Benson, Mr Leadbetter, Susan, and the man who looked after East behind them.

It was all so organised, thought Rose, especially for an emergency assembly called at the last moment.

And as he and Dr Sharland made their own way into the Great Hall, Rose wondered just who would want to plant a bloodied razor for somebody to find. Just a rather sick prank played by one of the boys, he thought, to unsettle everybody who knew what had taken place in that room.

And looking around him, Rose could see that it had created the desired effect.

*

I hate biology classes- it's all about the body, which is weak, and nothing about the mind, which is all that matters, as it conditions the body too.

Mr Townsend the Biology master is everything I despise, flabby in mind and action, thrashing around in his make-believe world of anatomy and botany, all so useless in my real life.

But last year I learned something from Mr Charles Darwin, well, in fact, I was reminded of something I already knew deep inside me. He wrote that 'Man selects only for his own good- Nature only for that of the being which she tends.'

You see, I agree. I tend to nobody but myself- Dorothy is part of me now. Mr Darwin was thinking of those rare beings such as I when he had that thought. And he had no need to go all the way to the Galapagos Islands to discover his theory- I'm sure that if he'd met my great grandfather, he'd have had all the proof he needed of the survival of the strongest.

Lineage matters, and while I never met my great grandfather, he would undoubtedly have shared the unique strength of me and my father.

I am *et perfectum hominem*- the perfect human, but also God of all around me, both king and kingmaker, any son I have when I'm ready a future king.

There will come a time when the weak will no longer be there. As Mr George Bernard Shaw has written, 'If we desire a certain type of civilization and culture, we must exterminate the sort of people who do not fit into it.'

Until then, I'll see the plebeians all around me, weaklings, slaves of their own minds, floundering and sinking in their cesspool of failed existence.

Others will dare to step up to me, and try to beat me, steal my crown, but I'm no King Duncan, easy prey for a deluded Macbeth. I slay those who stand against me before they can strike.

Take Old Bannister- when he stopped me on the main stairs, warning me that I had to stay away from Dorothy- "You're an E6 after all," he said- he had to go. That alpha fraud took little more than a heavy shove to topple down.

His face was a picture after his mouthful of marble, I can tell you, his eyes like two blue and tiny lacerations in his face, opened as wide as they could! How dare he take me on- he should have known his place like Mr Leadbetter.

If I'd had time, I would've ripped out his intestines and fed them to him through his gaping open mouth in his dying moments. He just stared up at me as I took his wristwatch from him- I'd always wanted his Zenith, and it didn't matter if it was smashed or not. Possession is nine points of the law as Thomas Draxe wrote years ago, you know. Ownership is control, and control is all.

That's why I was understandably enraged when the Zenith disappeared from my sack on the mound- until I realised that only one person could have taken it- Dorothy. But as she was already mine anyway, nothing was lost.

Out here on the mound I can tell the time by the sky, and inside the main building the ringing of the bell punctuates my day- I've realised that I don't need a gaudy timepiece like his at all.

I'm the real thing, whereas Old Bannister was as fake as a plastic mannequin in a haberdasher's window- he had no substance, no spunk at all when it really mattered, and it was the end of him.

Part III

Plane

16

"Earlier this morning, there was an object discovered in the billiards room, one which has caused a great deal of distress to the member of staff who found it there."

The whole of Sunnyside seemed to be there, apart from Mr Tucker, as far as Rose could see. Perhaps he was out and about in the grounds doing his chores and had no idea what had occurred, or maybe he just wasn't invited to such gatherings, pondered Rose, as Mr Dodwell spoke to the large room.

His voice echoed a little, as he was projecting it more loudly than he had at the Christmas Day present-giving assembly. There was no anger in his voice- Mr Dodwell was too self-controlled for that- but there was a steely firmness.

"I won't talk about the object found this morning, and there really is no need to. For the person who put it there knows exactly what it is of course, and exactly why he or she put it there. And I have no doubt that the person responsible is present in this room right now."

There was a long pause as if for effect, to let the culprit feel the fear of possible discovery. If that person were there in the Great Hall, thought Rose.

"And let me give a warning to that person. If he or she fails to come forward to the master or mistress of their wing by lights out tonight, the police will be informed, and they will find out who did this horrible and irresponsible misdeed."

With that, Mr Dodwell left the lectern and almost pranced out of the room, his hands clasped firmly behind his back as usual.

Rose looked around him at the other members of staff and at the rows of children- he still couldn't bring himself to think of them as 'residents'. And he was sure that nobody would come forward to own up to the placing of the razor.

And whilst he felt a strange fascination about the person who had killed themselves in the billiards room, what really

131

troubled him was a more practical puzzle- just where had the blood on the razor come from?

*

I sat there and watched as everybody listened rapt to Mr Dodwell, *their* leader. Like sickly spiders caught in the sticky web of a black widow, or should I say false widow, as he's as fake as they come.

The cut I'd made was still sore under the left arm of my shirt and pullover. I'd had to cover it at first with a Willard's adhesive bandage I requisitioned from the sanitorium some time ago, as it just wouldn't stop bleeding. It was quite deep, but I'd needed enough blood to smother the razor. Lawrence Drummond hadn't spilled just a few small drops after all.

With its bone handle and ruthlessly sharp clean blade, I'd chosen a razor I could afford, but I also felt that Stenson's the chemist in Milston, where Drummond bought the implement of his death, would have stocked a cheaper range of cutthroats.

Manufactured in Sheffield in 1885, three years before Drummond pulled one like it across his throat, the stainless steel still shone, although there was just a little rust around the rivet which connected the blade and handle.

It had to be authentic, it had to make an impact. And now that it had, it was time to follow-up. I knew how, but just needed the opportunity.

*

The chance to talk to the two girls from South now postponed, Rose was at a loose end, and a little frustrated. Just when he thought he was getting somewhere, everything at Sunnyside had been temporarily thrown into chaos.

But he had to admit to himself that he was now thinking about the bloody razor too. If it was a prank, how had somebody got hold of such an old cutthroat? And the biggest question remained- whose blood was on it?

To escape the tense atmosphere about the place and with Dr Sharland preoccupied, he decided to take a trip into Milston to make a call to Flanagan back in London.

He wouldn't tell Flanagan about the little box left outside his cottage- it might still lead nowhere, and there was no point drowning his editor with detail, as Flanagan would forget much of what he was told by the next time he spoke to him.

Flanagan always returned to the *Travesties* office as soon as he could after Christmas- that's what an unhappy marriage does to you. Rose imagined him telling his wife that he had a magazine to run, but in truth there was little point in being at the office in those few days between Christmas and the New Year. Even Monkfish never showed his seasoned yet distinctly unseasonal face there then, although he might well be at the Stab.

It was wet and cold, and the same driver who'd ferried him around so many times still had nothing to say. Rose asked to be dropped at the square behind the library, as he wanted to use the telephone box, telling the driver to collect him there in two hours.

"Flanagan." Rose's editor sounded less harassed than he normally did when answering the phone.

"It's Rose. Just reporting in."

"About time too. What's going on down there? I've had Mrs Hopkins on the phone twice in the past week asking what we've learned about her daughter."

"It's coming slowly. It's a very insular place, but I'm making progress. I'm interviewing the two girls closest to her in the next day or two."

"That doesn't sound like there's a sense of urgency."

"Well, something happened today that has thrown the whole place into uproar, but I don't think it has any connection to Dorothy. And it will settle down."

"Anything else?" said Flanagan.

"One of the members of staff died in a suspicious way a few months ago- he fell down the stairs- either a very nasty accident or he had a little help."

"What's your reading?"

"Could be either way, but I think he might have been pushed or at least distracted or frightened in some way."

"Did he have any contact with Dorothy?"

"Not directly, but he may well have spoken to her at some point."

"Any idea how she might have left the institution?"

133

"I think it was most probably in a private motorcar. The police have found no witnesses after she left her room on 21 November and she didn't take a train or a taxi," said Rose.

"So, somebody else picked her up?"

"It seems likely. Unless she's hiding somewhere in the grounds, but every inch has been searched by the police I'm told."

"Have you spoken to the police then?"

"No. I'm still very much undercover- just the doctor who has given me the job and the principal know why I'm really there. I've been to the place where the little charm from Dorothy's bracelet was found, but no more on that yet.

"Well keep at it and let me know if anything turns up. I can't keep you on this story forever. We may run your gunrunning piece in the new issue, but after that I'll need copy within a fortnight, as you know."

Rose knew only too well, and when the pips went, he put another sixpence into the slot.

"Understood," said Rose. "And could you wire me some more expenses? I'm in the local town now and I could go and collect it."

"Already? How much do you need?"

"Another £20 perhaps?"

"Christ Rose, are you Puttin' on the Ritz? I'll wire you £15 and that's generous. It'll be with you within the hour."

"Thank you, Mr Flanagan." It pained Rose to have to say those words, but he knew that Flanagan had yet to see his expense account claims written down, so it was best all round to remain civil.

Flanagan hung up the receiver and Rose walked out into the square and past the Antiques Emporium, deciding to have a rummage around in the nearby Milston Bookshop before he went to the post office to collect his money.

*

After finding nothing of interest to him in the bookshop, and with the dusty air in there stifling, not helped by the assistant's constant puffing on a Player's Navy Cut, Rose made his way to the post office.

Flanagan was as good as his word and the money was ready at the Western Union desk. The lady cashier counted out two five-pound notes and five one-pound notes, which Rose signed for and placed in his wallet.

"Just a moment, please. You have a telegram too, sir."

She passed him the message, and it read 'There you go-look after the pennies. F.' It was typical Flanagan, it gave him the final word, but was totally unnecessary.

Rose thought about making a quick visit to the Grecian Tea Rooms for a cup of coffee but decided to walk back to the square, as the driver would return there in about twenty minutes.

It was really blowing up outside and he walked against the wind almost as if he was pushing a piano down the street. Once there, he planned to shelter in the library until the taxi came, but as he went past the Antiques Emporium, something in the window display captured his attention.

On red velvet cloth, which due to the faded colour, had likely acted as a bed for trinkets and small ornaments for many years, lay an array of cigarette lighters and cigarette cases, some antique spoons, and a few clocks. But in the middle of the display, Rose had spotted several razors. As he got closer, he could see that two of them were of the old-fashioned cutthroat variety. And next to them, there was still an indentation in the velvet where another had probably been.

They were the very same type of razor that had apparently been found splattered with blood in the billiards room. He walked into the shop, and the bell above the door rang more loudly than would be necessary, even for the hard of hearing. Rose felt like a prize cow as two browsers looked at him curiously.

It was cavernous inside, the old lamps for sale providing much of the light- some had shades made of stained-glass, others gaudily carved cherubs hanging from them. He wandered through the shop carefully, and then, looking ahead, Rose almost shook his head when he saw the same man who had served him in the bookshop earlier seated behind the desk.

"Didn't you serve me in the bookshop about half-an-hour ago?" said Rose.

"No, that wasn't me. I've been here since this morning," said the man. Rose could see that he was wearing a different jacket, and there was no smoke clouded around him.

"That's very strange. He looked just like you."

"Oh, he does. He's my twin brother. But we're different in two ways…"

Rose waited for the rest of the sentence, but it never came. "How are you different then?"

"I don't smoke and I'm much better looking," he said, before laughing a little too much at his own obviously well-used joke. "Are you after anything in particular?"

"Well, in fact, I need to know if somebody has bought a Victorian cutthroat razor from here recently."

"And why would you like to know that? Are you with the police? I don't stock stolen goods, you know."

"No. nothing like that," said Rose. "It's just that somebody played a prank with it, and we need to find out where it came from,"

"May I ask who 'we' is?" said the man.

"I'm a teacher at a local school and one of our pupils left it lying around to frighten the other children."

"But if I had sold a dangerous cutthroat to a child, wouldn't I be in trouble?"

"No. We just need to know who bought it."

"Well, we don't sell many of those, I must say, perhaps only a couple a year. Not much need for them now of course. How far back are we talking?"

"In the last month or so?"

"There was a boy, who came in here a few days ago. He chose a razor from the window. Told me it was for a school project about Victorian times when I asked him why he wanted it. Honest, I checked."

"That's fine," said Rose. "Do you have any details for him?"

"Let me just have a look. I make a note of all sales in this ledger, and customers write their name and address. Just in case of any problems later, if you understand me."

"I certainly do." The man turned the page back and ran his finger across a line.

"There we are. Two days ago, in the morning. He gave his name as W.E. Johns, and the address is Drummond Lane, Milston."

"Do you know where that is?" said Rose.

"Never heard of it, to be honest."

"Hardly a fail-safe system you have here, is it?"

"I take people as I find them."

"How much did it cost him? Said Rose.

"Three pennies- I wanted a shilling, but he told me he only had thruppence. It had been in the window for some months, so I let him have it."

"Can you remember what the razor looked like?"

"It had a bone handle- bit of wear and tear, but the blade was still in good nick. Late Victorian, around 1880-1890 I'd say."

"Do you remember what the boy looked like?"

"I don't want to get him into any trouble, really I don't."

"No need to worry about that- he's done that himself. He'll just have a few detentions, that's all."

"Oh, I remember those. And no harm done, although you'd better ask my wife. He was tallish for his age, slim, pale skin, dark eyes, light brown hair, spoke well, if you know what I mean- a little posh."

"I know exactly what you mean. Any idea how old he was?"

"Difficult to say- fifteen, sixteen, seventeen. But he was very confident. Boys that age are usually all over the place, but he was very much in charge of himself."

"Thanks for your time, you've been very helpful."

The man nodded, and Rose left the shop wondering how many of the older boys at Sunnyside looked like the description. But he knew one thing- the boy had a sense of humour. W E Johns was the writer of the Biggles books about the adventures of a pilot.

The twin brother who worked in the bookshop would have known that, thought Rose.

17

The billiards room was out of bounds, and although that was a high price, it was worth paying to enjoy all the commotion around Shadowside. And I still had the mound.

Mr Leadbetter was even less sure of himself than usual, and *they* were all walking around with a confused look, *their* usual complacency falling from *them* like scales from a fishmonger's knife.

Even Mr Dodwell, Shadowside's emperor, usually the bee's knees, had looked troubled at assembly in front of his unwilling subjects. The head snake was shaken, although to kill a serpent, you must cut off its head.

But I read in my bloods that you need to be careful- a snake can still bite for a long time after being beheaded, it's cold-blooded you see, and harder to kill. You either make sure you destroy it or take flight quickly.

I know I'd destroy it- running isn't in my nature. But my whole purpose now is survival- I'm sixteen now, and I'll be able to leave here by the end of the new year, perhaps even by next summer. But that all depends on nobody making a connection between me and Dorothy.

If *they* found out about our relationship, I would be under serious incoming fire.

And if the relationship between me and Dorothy were discovered, I would never tell *them* where she is. *They* couldn't keep me here for much longer, as sixteen is the age limit at Shadowside, but there are other places for young men, and although I dread to think it, some may be as bad as it is here.

*

Rose was standing at the window in the small kitchen of his cottage looking idly out at the bare winter trees, dark boughs silhouetted against the darkening sky, thinking how quiet it was there compared to his life in London.

Looking down at his wristwatch, he realised that he would probably be at the Stab on his way home at that moment if he were in the city. He didn't exactly miss it as it was too much like work, but he somehow felt at home there.

And he already knew that he would never feel comfortable at Sunnyside. It wasn't the fact that strange things happened there- the death of Bernard Bannister, Dorothy's disappearance, the razor in the billiards room, and the terrible fire in the chapel that killed some children on Christmas Day a few years before he'd heard the priest talking about in assembly. Then there was the constant background presence of all those uncannily quiet children.

No, it wasn't those events- almost all the stories he covered for *Travesties* and had on the *Herald* were crime-related, and some of them were truly diabolical. There was the Dr Buck Ruxton case of just a few months before, the Indian doctor who killed his wife and maid, dismembered their bodies, parcelled the parts up, and threw them from a train window when travelling through Scotland.

Rose had been on that case for over a month, and the expenses had nearly given Flanagan a heart attack. But he'd got an exclusive interview with the boyish doctor, who was still on remand in prison awaiting trial. The November issue of *Travesties*, the third one, had sold the best so far.

No, he was used to the terrible things that people did to one another by now. But it was the atmosphere at Sunnyside which meant he could never relax there. It was something he couldn't define- he'd never admit it to anyone, but it sometimes sent a slight shiver through him.

There was the feeling of often being watched. A pair or pairs of eyes trained on him at times- who was it? He knew that the answer could lead to Dorothy, or that it could just be a busybody such as Mrs Benson nosing around to see what he was up to. Although he couldn't truly imagine her being able to stay out of sight like that. It was somebody nimble, quick-thinking, and persistent.

That was it, he thought. Sunnyside was full of unpredictability. You never knew what would happen next, so there was never really a time to let up and feel at ease.

He hadn't forgotten that he was undercover, and that was never easy. But since the day before, when the news of the razor's discovery whirled around the place, Rose had seen the same tenseness and anxiety on the faces of other members of staff. Dr Sharland, Mrs Benson, Mr Leadbetter, even Mr Dodwell.

It was as if they'd felt that way many times before at Sunnyside, and to sense that uneasiness again filled them with disquiet. What could be considered a rather grisly prank was being taken very seriously, and it wasn't just because rules had been broken. There was something more, an inertia of helplessness, the sickening worry of the true unknown.

He looked down at his wristwatch again. It was just past six o'clock, and he was going to make himself some onion soup for dinner. But when he looked up, he saw something through the window, something that moved very fast.

It had been on that island covered with overgrown bushes and foliage, which stood between his cottage and the main building. He couldn't say what or who it was, but something or somebody had moved over there.

He watched for a few more minutes, but nothing. Then he put it out of his mind and went over to the table to peel an onion.

*

When I saw Inspector Alexander from North's window that morning having the door of the Wolseley police motorcar opened for him by a feckless-looking flatfoot, I knew exactly why he was there of course, and that Mr Dodwell had been as good as his treacherous word.

I also understood why the police had been called. It wasn't the placing of the razor, or the history of the billiards room, but the blood on the cutthroat.

As the hours laboured on that morning, I was three-quarters-expecting to be called by Mr Leadbetter to report to the library for my third meeting with the unsuccessful detective.

That's what Inspector Alexander was- he'd gained no grip on Dorothy's case, I'd outwitted him along with every bobby under him and so every charlatan in white tie and tails that outranked him.

He had no reason to connect me with the inspired re-enactment of Lawrence Drummond's suicide scene, I'd made sure of that, but I wanted to tell him that I'd solved the mystery of Jack the Ripper, a case which had defeated London's finest almost half a century ago, so certainly couldn't have been solved by Milston's rural plods.

But no summons was given, and I was left feeling somewhat removed from the action. So, before my mathematics class with Mr Strickland, I decided to find out what was being said around the place.

Mr Tucker was where he could often be found at that time of day, removing the gravel from the path near the main courtyard, which eventually leads down to the terrace at the back of the main building. Every time a motorcar pulls in and out, little pieces of grit are flung across the narrow walkway, adding to the fallen, trodden-in leaves covering it, requiring the daily sweep.

With each motion of the broom, the keys on his chain jangle like unmelodious wind chimes. I walked up to him, knowing exactly what to say.

"Hello Mr Tucker. I remember when Pepper used to jump around you as you swept the path."

He turned and looked at me, at first a little startled- not because of my sudden appearance, but at the mention of his beloved dog that had run away.

"He certainly did," Mr Tucker said finally. "Pepper loved to play."

"I'm sure he's still playing somewhere," I said. "Have you heard about the razor they found?"

"How could I not- it's the talk of the place, and Miss Lane is off work with the worry."

"Did she discover it up in the billiards room?" I said.

"Yes, poor woman. She had quite a turn. She knows what happened in there."

"We all know," I said. "The story gets passed down every year."

"I don't know who would do such a nasty thing."

"Well, perhaps it could have been Mr Lawrence Drummond who returned and left it there himself?" I said.

It was the first time I ever heard Mr Tucker laugh, or should I say chuckle. "Do you believe in ghosts then?"

141

"There are more things in heaven and Earth, Horatio, than are dreamt of in your philosophy," I said. "Shakespeare."

"He said a lot of other things too I'm told, but it doesn't mean they're true."

"Shakespeare didn't say it, he wrote it. Hamlet said it."

"That doesn't make it any truer. I've never seen a ghost in my thirty-eight years," said Mr Tucker, a little forcefully.

Before I could continue making my case, I heard a deeper and measured voice behind me, one I'd never heard before.

"Coming up chilly now, isn't it?" I spun around, and standing there was Shadowside's new arrival, the strange man in the white coat whom I'd seen go into Mr Dodwell's office.

"It is just, Mr Rose," said Mr Tucker.

I felt my heart beating a little faster- I finally had a voice and a name to go with the man I'd been watching.

"I don't believe we've met," said Rose, holding out his hand to me. He was looking at me closely.

"I'm Edwin, it's a pleasure to meet you."

"Edwin's in North wing," said Mr Tucker. "He helped me out a while ago when my dog Pepper ran off."

"Did you find him?" said Rose, still looking at me.

"Her," said Mr Tucker. "No, she never returned."

"We tried everything we could. We searched everywhere, put up posters, but nothing," I said.

"Edwin made the posters himself," said Mr Tucker.

"I'm sure Pepper's playing peacefully somewhere," I said.

Mr Tucker nodded wistfully.

"We were just talking about the razor they found in the billiards room," I said.

"Yes, awful thing. Apparently, a man killed himself in that room many years ago," said Rose.

Mr Tucker nodded silently, but I spoke. "He cut his throat from ear to ear there in 1888."

"Why did he do that?" said Rose.

"He didn't want to go back to the war- he was a soldier," said Mr Tucker.

"That's what everyone says, but I think it was a much bigger reason than that. He had the black dog, but he was also out of his mind," I said.

142

"How do you know that?" said Mr Tucker.

"I just do. His father, Sir Arthur Drummond, put it about that Lawrence had died of consumption. So, don't believe what anybody says."

"Edwin thinks that Lawrence Drummond's ghost may have returned and placed the razor there," said Mr Tucker, not scornfully, more playfully.

"I heard it was a Victorian cutthroat razor, an antique," said Rose, ignoring the paranormal direction of the conversation. "With a bone handle."

I said nothing, knowing that details of what the razor looked like hadn't been released to the rest of Shadowside, and knowledge of such details could cast suspicion on me.

"It was definitely an old one, and covered in blood," said Mr Tucker.

"I must be going," I said, "I have mathematics class. It was nice to meet you Mr Rose. Mr Tucker."

"Goodbye Edwin," said Rose, while Mr Tucker just nodded.

I was glad to be away from there- I didn't want to become too friendly- and never had a double mathematics class been so appealing. But as I walked into the main reception, I realised that the meeting I thought I'd have to engineer had just occurred by happenstance. I could now approach Mr Rose whenever I wanted.

After wishing Mr Tucker the best of weather for the rest of the day, Rose made towards Dr Sharland's office. He was a little shaken, not as if he'd seen a ghost, but having encountered a living person he'd heard described in the flesh for the first time, somebody he hadn't expected to meet so easily.

Rose remembered the words of the man who worked in the Antiques Emporium in Milston. He pulled his notebook out of the breast pocket of his sports jacket which was under his white coat, and soon found the page.

The man had said that a boy had come into the shop who was 'tallish for his age, slim, with pale skin, dark eyes, light brown hair, spoke well, a little posh."

It was Edwin. The intense-looking boy he'd just met matched that description perfectly. That boy had bought the razor, he was sure of it.

143

*

Dr Sharland had nothing for Rose to do for the rest of the day, and he realised that he could no longer put off visiting the chapel, the domain of Reverend Barnes, who had spoken so movingly about the terrible fire there at the Christmas Day assembly.

The hairs on the back of Rose's neck bristled with the thought of entering a place of worship, something that he tried to avoid and had managed to except for a few occasions when his job called for it. But he knew he had to find out more about that fatal fire, which like Mr Bannister's death was a ghastly occurrence, particularly at a place called Sunnyside.

Down there in the basement of a large brown-brick outbuilding close to the main building, which looked nothing like a place of worship at ground level apart from the small and unobtrusive Church of England cross above the door, yet morphed into a truly holy shrine downstairs, Rose saw the memorial plaque for the three boys who'd died in the fire there.

It was a simple plaque, and if you weren't aware of the tragic circumstances in which those boys died, you would never know. But outside of an epidemic like the influenza of 1918, the deaths of three children in one day indicated either an accident or foul play, and Rose wondered just which one it had been.

"It's nice to see you down here, it really is." Rose wasn't physically startled, as he'd heard the footsteps behind him first, but he couldn't bring himself to say that he was pleased to be there.

"It is very sad," said Reverend Barnes, his voice gentle and rich. "I remember those three boys very well. But God had other plans for them it seems."

Rose winced internally- he'd never understood 'God's Plans.' It reminded him of the Brethren, who thought everything was held in the hands of the Lord, with no room for free will except when it came to prohibiting things.

"It is tragic," said Rose, "so very young."

"The Lord giveth and he taketh away," said Rev Barnes.

"Why were the boys in the chapel that day- Christmas Day?" It was a question that Rose just couldn't resist.

144

"They were sandpapering down some pews for me, ready for Mr Tucker to give them a glaze. Those boys often helped me out in here. Lovely little chaps."

"The fire must have caused a great deal of damage too," said Rose.

"Yes, it was dreadful- it almost completely gutted half the chapel. It took more than two years before we could worship here again. We had to have all our services in the Great Hall during that time."

"It was obviously arson-have you any idea who started the fire?"

"I came to think over time that it must be some unruly local boys," said Reverend Barnes.

"So, nobody from within Sunnyside?"

"I very much doubt it. Two boys were seen not far away in the grounds that evening, but no connection between them and the fire was ever found, and I don't believe that they would do anything so wicked."

"Which two boys?"

"I'd really rather not talk about that very sad day anymore, if you don't mind," said Rev Barnes, a firmness overlaying his usual avuncular tone.

The priest moved away from the plaque and Rose instinctively followed.

"Have you been the chaplain here for a while?"

"Oh yes. I've been Sunnyside's priest since 1911 when it came into being. And I've lived on the grounds since 1882. My father was the priest here when it was a private house, you see."

"When the Drummond family lived here?"

"Yes- Henry Drummond died in 1894, but his wife Elisabeth and daughter Charlotte lived here until they sold the house and grounds in 1908. It became Sunnyside three years later."

"Have you seen a lot of change since you first came here?" said Rose.

"Not really- Sunnyside is one of the only places I've ever been that remains timeless- that's exactly why I love it so much. The familiarity gives me the time and energy to concentrate on higher, more important things."

145

"Do you remember Lawrence Drummond? I'm sure you've heard about the rather nasty discovery in the billiards room."

"I certainly have. A very horrible occurrence- to play with the memory of a man's very painful death is sacrilege. Lawrence Drummond deserves the respect due to any of God's creatures."

"What was he like?" said Rose.

"I didn't know him very well of course- I was the son of the priest who worked for his father in the name of God. But he would say hello and pass the time of day. I was just a young boy then of course. But Lawrence, or Mr Drummond as we called him, was far more approachable than his father Sir Arthur. He was a thoughtful man, and that's why I was never really surprised that he took his own life- he always seemed troubled, you see, felt too much."

"About the war? He must have seen some terrible things on the battlefield, in the Sudan War I heard."

"I'm sure he did, but it was more than that. He was a sensitive sort, you know. I must be getting on now. I have a service to prepare for this evening. I do hope to see you here again," said Rev Barnes, with a soothing smile which Rose wasn't quite sure was genuine.

"I'll be down here again," said Rose, trying to look as positive at the prospect as possible.

"That *is* good to hear," said Rev Barnes, smiling.

Rose walked through the aisle and then out of the chapel, up the steps and then across the well-tended garden outside, under the grey, darkening sky. It was only two in the afternoon, but it felt much later.

As he made towards the main building, he thought about the fire- who were those two boys seen nearby that evening?

And then there was the boy, Edwin. If he had placed the razor in the billiards room, there was every reason to follow up on that too.

But for now, he was glad to be out of the confines of a place that stood for something which brought back many painful memories.

*

It always happened in the small pantry in the kitchen, his father's stern yet expressionless face terrifying to Rose, as he assumed position with his trousers and underpants around his ankles, afraid that the vibrations might cause the rattling pots and pans to come crashing down from the shelves above. But they never did.

"He's had enough now Arthur!"

Rose's mother Anne would sometimes say those words after the belt had come down on his behind multiple times, the leather stinging more than enough, but when the buckle slipped from around his father's wrist and the metal hit his skin, it really was agony.

And his father's words, his voice almost breathless from exertion as he administered a beating, came flooding back to Rose often- "Penance more."

"Let Harold be, Arthur, he's taken enough now."

His mother would allow an ample amount of punishment before interceding, but his father never listened anyway, and would go on striking him several more times.

Although more than the pain or his parents' words, it was his father's smell that stayed with Rose- he knew that smell better than any other, and when he smelt it, his whole miserably repressed boyhood was evoked.

It was the toxic whiff of varnish that came from his father, which clung to him after a day's cabinet making, where Rose would also work as an apprentice from the age of fourteen for two years.

He was too young for Kitchener's call-up to the war, but he still managed to escape, to the deep despair of his mother. He became a messenger boy on the local rag, which was made possible when his father's heart suddenly gave out when Rose was fifteen.

His mother wasn't able to hold him like his father- after three years he applied for a messenger position on the *Daily Herald* in London, upping and leaving one morning in late 1919 when he was accepted, after intercepting the letter before his mother could dispose of it. He was a mere tadpole in the big stream of Fleet Street, but he was finally free.

He didn't speak to or see his mother again for some years, until he was in his early twenties and starting out as a reporter. He felt secure enough in his new life by then to go and see her, and they had managed to salvage the relationship, after a fashion- she was still in the Brethren and financially supported by its members, but she'd long realised that her only child could never be part of it again. Although he only visited her once or twice a year now.

Many triggers remained to take him back to his dark boyhood again though, almost twenty years after he left home. Organised religion, the Bible, authoritarian preaching, and injustice, all brought back sharp flashes of his early emotional torments.

But it was that acrid smell of vanish that still made Rose bridle most- it brought back all the unhappiness and feelings of entrapment he'd felt so deeply, as his father represented all that had confined him, even though he now understood that Arthur Rose was misguidedly trying to protect him from the unholy fornications of the ordinary world.

Rose often wondered if his early removal from sin had led him to become a crime hack, a job in which he saw the very darkest of the human soul every day. But he tried to stop analysing his reasons for becoming what he was, as it could only lead to introspection, something he'd almost drowned in as a boy.

And there really had been no escape- Rose's childhood world was one of isolation, attending the home of another Brethren member with four other boys for schooling, chaperoned by his mother to and from that house. Apart from that, only the weekly visit to the plain and austere nearby chapel on a Sunday, then straight back home.

"Depart ye, depart ye, go ye out from thence, touch no unclean thing…be ye clean, that bear the vessels of the Lord."

Those words from Isiah were always quoted by both his parents, when he asked why he had to stay in the house or garden, with the towering ten-foot fence around it, which Arthur had erected to keep his son away from the evils outside.

Those regular beatings were for the smallest of transgressions- helplessly jumping to try to peer over the fence,

148

questioning the Bible's teachings that only Jesus coming back again could heal everything, looking at his parents in an unworthy manner, all led to that belt in the pantry.

And until his father died there had seemed no hope, at least not until the return of Christ, and the world was certainly still waiting for that.

18

Everybody needs somebody to admire, no matter how accomplished they are- I have several idols, all men, as women lack the strength and resolve to live on the high and treacherous summits of existence.

There's my father, who stood against this miserable world on his own terms, and never surrendered to it. There's the Red Baron, who night after night placed his own life in peril in pursuit of enemies, and too perished on his own terms.

There's Jim Stacey and the other Red Circle boys, who fight the impossible battle against oppressive and most-hated teachers, just as I wage my secret war against *them* at Shadowside.

And now there is Lawrence Drummond, also known as Jack the Ripper, the most famous killer of all time. Like my father, he opted out of this wretched life when he had fulfilled his destiny, neither victims, but both martyrs to their own causes.

These men were all leaders, and if I was wearing a hat, I would certainly tip it to them. Within their worlds they were omnipresent, and lords of their unique landscapes- my father in the world of banking, the Baron in the fierce skies of war, the Red Circle boys within the human zoo of their school. Lawrence Drummond, the master of mutilation, a truly depraved artist.

Old Bannister wasn't a leader- he thought he was, but he never had the stomach for the real fight. Like Mr Dodwell and that deadly doctor Sharland, he controlled his very limited realm with uncreative zeal and no intelligence. He was, and they are, faux leaders.

Mr Leadbetter meanwhile is a true follower's follower, a bleating farmyard animal sheared by those stronger than him, as is Mr Tucker, who is physically robust, yet mentally lacking. Dorothy, like almost all females, a follower too, of mine.

The new man Rose doesn't look like one of *them*, but whether he's a foe or usable friend we shall see. An idol he almost certainly isn't, nor will ever be.

*

"Mrs Benson will be bringing the female residents, Caitlin Whitaker-Davies and Isabel Haarman, here shortly," said Dr Sharland.

Rose always felt it odd that they were referred to as residents, as they were only girls. Just because he was the head of the clinical staff, it didn't mean that the doctor had to be so coldly clinical in manner.

"Fine, I've got my questions for them ready," said Rose.

"I don't think I need to remind you to be gentle with them."

"That's well understood, I assure you. Any developments on the find in the billiards room?"

"That's in the hands of the police now," said Dr Sharland, slightly abruptly, as if speaking about the bloody antique cutthroat was no longer acceptable, although it had been discovered just two days before.

"That's reassuring." There wasn't the lightest drop of sarcasm in Rose's tone, having been filtered from the considerably sardonic well within him. He'd begun to wonder just how effective Milston's police were, as they had made very little progress on Dorothy's case, it seemed, apart from finding the horse charm, which he now knew had been handed to them by Mr Dodwell via Mr Tucker.

The telephone on the desk rang, and Dr Sharland spoke briefly before turning to Rose and saying, "I'll be back with you presently," and leaving his office.

Rose reached for his notebook where he had scrawled down the questions he'd prepared, and not wanting to read them out as he asked them, he went through them to himself to keep them to mind when the girls arrived.

Over the years he'd interviewed many people, from the famous and infamous to the anonymous, from a duke and a lord, killers, criminals, and occultists to victims and witnesses of crimes big and small, as well as those famished for recognition or short of a few shillings.

The two girls, Caitlin aged 16 and Isabel, 15, very much fell into the potential witness category, but Rose hadn't ruled out that both or either could be accomplices in Dorothy's disappearance, in helping her to get away.

The sad words of Dorothy's mother, Mrs Hopkins, were still engraved on his memory from the day she said them in the *Travesties* office, about two weeks before, but which now somehow felt like half-a-lifetime ago.

When she last saw her on the Sunday before she vanished, Dorothy had been "frightened, begging me to take her away," Mrs Hopkins had said. For Rose, this pointed to a young girl desperate to leave Sunnyside and running away might have seemed her final option when her mother didn't answer her plea.

Dorothy couldn't have disappeared voluntarily and stayed that way by herself.

The other alternative, that Dorothy was dead, was a real possibility, with the appearance of her bracelet increasing the chances of that, but Rose had to focus on her being alive and in hiding in case she was and could be helped.

Dr Sharland suddenly returned, a little breathless. "There's been a change of venue, I'm afraid. We'll talk to the residents in the South wing. Isabel Haarman is feeling somewhat tense, and Mrs Benson thinks it better if we speak to her in the most familiar surroundings possible. We have just under an hour before the other residents return to the wing."

"Fine, that makes good sense," said Rose, secretly relishing the chance to get a look inside a residential wing as he followed Dr Sharland out into the corridor with the geometrical shapes patterned on its floor.

*

The Indian vulture looked back at me with its usual forceful expression. If I were carrion or a small mammal, I knew it would swoop down and take me away if it could, and if I were dead or dying as Edwin, I'm sure it would feed on me too.

But perched there in the glass case, where it had been since Lawrence Drummond stalked those corridors, next to all the other birds of prey, it was motionless in the moment forever, its eyes trained on the observer.

152

I wondered just what it had seen all those years ago and if Jack the Ripper had found solace in those eyes as I do. It might have been stuffed by the hand of an expert Victorian taxidermist like all its static neighbours, but it lived on in my eyes.

The problem with living beauty is that it fades unless captured and preserved, just as true majesty withers bodily too, alive to the moment and at the mercy of a lifespan, but unlike beauty, it has a spirit which remains.

I could feel that in the Indian vulture- it may have left this mortal coil, but like Lawrence Drummond it was now immortal at Shadowside, just as the Red Baron is in the skies from which he fell, and my father's majestic fortitude circles all around me. That was where I would be one day, omnipresent and as all-seeing as the eyes of the avian colossus before me.

I've touched him before. The glass cabinets can be slid across, they're not locked, as I suppose *they* see no need as the birds can hardly fly away. A warm musty sensation hits you as the glass recedes, the contents trapped with no air in such an enclosed space since the last time it was opened.

Old Bannister nearly caught me once, bounding up the stairs that would later claim him, and I had to walk away toward the library, leaving the cabinet open until I could return and pull it closed again.

The Indian vulture's feathers feel smooth, remarkably soft considering their age. I didn't pet him- that would never do-he's due respect and is not a tame creature. No, just a touch, a connection with greatness before I went about my daily grinding business. You see, for moments I can live on those high plains of greatness, but then I must return to the sordid reality of Shadowside and *them*, with their sparrow brains, until my time comes.

And I'm sure that spending time with the Indian vulture is meant to be. It's almost the perfect place hiding place too.

It was while I was standing there looking at my favourite bird that I saw the Cyclops walk past, a little like Boris Karloff as Frankenstein.

And then, a short while after, Dr Sharland rushed down the stairs and returned minutes later with the new man Rose in tow, an evil shepherd herding a willing sheep down the corridor, where I noted they turned into South's doorway.

*

It was a large room, about half the size of the Great Hall Rose estimated, set out as a dormitory, chestnut-coloured wardrobes and desks alongside small beds arranged in rows, each one self-contained territorially, but affording very little privacy.

"This was Dorothy's section," said Mrs Benson, as she pointed to a set of furniture with no personality, just like the rest of the South wing. Rose thought that the term 'section' was wholly appropriate to describe the missing girl's living space.

Dorothy had slept on the right side of the room, away from the three large bay windows facing out on the large sprawling terrace at the back of the main building, beyond which through the mist, upon a faded baize of sodden grass, an unwelcoming pond sat like a glacier mint which had been dropped on a dirty floor, one yet to be tended to by Mr Tucker's broom.

Mrs Benson walked into the section next to Dorothy's, and as Rose walked around the corner, he could see a girl sitting on the bed behind the wardrobe, mousy-haired and with a very healthy complexion.

"This is Caitlin," said Mrs Benson. "This is Mr Rose who wants to have a few words with you."

"Hello Caitlin," said Rose.

"Hello sir."

"That'll be all for now Agatha, thank you. We'll send Caitlin out for Isabel to come in when we are finished," said Dr Sharland quietly, but Rose heard every word. Mrs Benson paused and made a sound midway between a sigh and a huff, before walking towards the door.

"Mr Rose wants to ask you a few questions about Dorothy, to see how it has affected you and the other residents," said Dr Sharland.

"Did you know Dorothy well?" said Rose.

Caitlin nodded. "A little."

"What kind of girl was she?"

Caitlin looked at Dr Sharland for a moment, as if she was waiting for his permission.

154

"Do go ahead, Caitlin," said Dr Sharland.

"Dorothy, or Dottie as we called her, was very kind. A little shy, but we all loved her."

"She hadn't been here as long as most of the girls in South, had she?" said Dr Sharland.

"No- Dottie was one of the last to arrive, apart from Cecilia who came only last month."

"Did you notice any change in Dottie in the last days and weeks before you last saw here?" said Rose.

"She was quieter, and more serious- she very much went back to how she had been when she first arrived here in the spring."

"You mean she became more relaxed and happier as time went on, but then went back to being more tense in the weeks before she disappeared?"

"No-only days- in fact, about a week before she disappeared Dottie was happier than ever, laughing and smiling all the time, as if she'd had some good news that none of us knew about."

"Did you ask her why she was so happy?" said Rose.

"No- I was just glad to see her like that- I didn't want to question it."

"How did Dorothy spend her free time in her last days here?"

"She went to library a great deal alone, to read."

"What was she reading?" said Rose.

"*Little Women* by Louisa Alcott."

"Did you ever see Dottie spending time with anybody else apart from the girls in South and Mrs Benson?" said Rose.

"No. Dottie was very much independent of others. Even though I slept next to her for months, I never got to know her very well. But what I knew of her, I liked."

"Did she spend any time away from the wing, apart from meals, assemblies and classes?" said Rose.

"Yes, actually- she would sometimes go off for half an hour or so, usually in the morning after breakfast before class, or after dinner."

"Did she ever say where she was going?" said Dr Sharland.

"No sir. And I never asked, honestly."

"Did you ever see Dottie distressed?" said Rose.

"When she first arrived, yes, she would cry at night in the first week, but just softly into her pillow. She had a stammer you know, and could be quite nervous, although she had a beautiful smile."

"That's nice," said Rose. "Did you see her cry in the week before she disappeared?"

"No. But she was jumpy, like I told the policeman. One evening I walked behind her when she was brushing her teeth leaning over the sink and touched her on the shoulder for a joke, and she almost jumped out of her skin."

"A normal reaction?"

"No- it was more than that. She was really shaken, and she scolded me and didn't talk to me at all the next day. That wasn't like Dottie, she was usually so mild like that."

"Did you see her behave like that on any other occasions?"

"Well, she was very down after her mother visited her on Sunday."

"The Sunday before she disappeared?" said Rose, knowing that to be the case, as Mrs Hopkins had told him that.

"Yes, I think it was."

"How did she seem in herself?"

"It's hard to explain. She hardly spoke for the next few days, and her stammer got worse when she did. It was as if all her hopes had been dashed in some way, I suppose."

"Can you think of any reason why she might have been so anxious?"

"No. As I told the policeman, there was nothing particularly going on at the time."

"When was the last time you saw Dottie?" said Rose.

"It was just before lights out. I said goodnight, but she didn't answer. When Mrs Benson rang the bell at six o'clock and turned the lights on, Dottie was gone."

"Was her bed made?" said Rose.

"No, it wasn't."

"That'll be all Caitlin, thank you for your time- please go and join Mrs Benson outside," said Dr Sharland.

"Thank you, Caitlin," said Rose, "you've been very helpful." But he was a little annoyed as the girl left the room, as he had more questions.

"My apologies, but the other residents will be back for morning break soon," said Dr Sharland.

Isabel was ushered in by Mrs Benson, who walked her into the section on the other side of Dorothy's, showing Rose that the two girls were indeed Dorothy's closest neighbours.

Rose focused on Isabel- she was quite tall and walked gracefully, but with her head firmly down. She had blonde hair, real honey-yellow-auburn.

When she finally looked up when Dr Sharland greeted her, Rose saw that she had the clearest-blue eyes, along with the palest skin he'd ever seen outside of a tuberculosis ward, and a slightly upturned nose which gave her a look of both sweetness and precocity. Then he forced himself to remember that this girl had almost succeeded in drowning her younger sister.

She said nothing as Rose introduced himself with a smile to relax her, which also had no visible reaction.

"Did you know Dottie well?" said Rose.

There was no answer, and she looked down at the polished wooden floor as if checking she still had a reflection.

"Mr Rose would like to ask you a few questions," said Dr Sharland, "to help us understand the impact Dorothy leaving so suddenly has had on you all."

"I really have nothing to say." The voice wasn't surly, but gentle.

"What do you think happened to Dorothy?" said Rose, deciding to go straight to the nub.

There was no response.

"Were you good friends with Dorothy?" said Rose.

"I told Mrs Benson and the policeman I know nothing weeks ago," said Isabel.

"But you were one of Dorothy's closest friends here, I believe," said Rose.

"Who told you that? It's not true. I'd like to go now please."

"All right Isabel, thank you. Please go and join Mrs Benson outside," said Dr Sharland.

Rose stood there thinking that sometimes no words are worth more than the complete works of Shakespeare, as they infer so much meaning.

19

Rose had just helped Dr Sharland carry out the annual inventory of resident maladies at Sunnyside, a task apparently usually performed by Mr Bannister.

In fact, it simply amounted to Rose writing the number of cases in boxes on a form next to a disorder- dementia praecox, manic-depression, depression, epilepsy, anxiety disorder, obsessive disorder, organic disorders, other neuroses, etc, while Dr Sharland called out the figures.

It was already dark at just after six o'clock when Rose decided to walk up to the Golden Bell just outside the grounds to see in 1937 with a drink or two, and it really would just be that. But he had to keep telling reminding himself why.

Despite always carrying his hip flask that usually contained whisky and from which he rationed himself to a swig when needed, in pubs he never drank more than a couple of drinks now, as he'd learned that any more could lead him back down a dangerous path.

He had a real taste for liquor, one that he'd built up in his years on the *Herald* drinking in countless hostelries with older hacks who held their drink just like the law sometimes held those same old-timers in contempt of court for refusing to divulge sources.

It made Rose feel alive like nothing else- others in Fleet Street coped with the long hours, broken marriages, and the terrible sights they saw with amphetamines, but he'd never taken to them.

Although the drink was bad enough. Until he was almost twenty, he'd never tasted alcohol- his parents and the Brethren would never have allowed that, it would've meant a severe beating.

And he'd worked in London for almost a year before he took his first drink, and it had crept up on him unknowingly and slowly, like a snake on its prey, costing him his livelihood.

"Hello Mr Rose."

Carstairs was standing there in the courtyard as Rose walked out of the main doors, awakened from his thoughts by the boy's slow and monotonous voice.

"Good evening Carstairs. What are you doing out here in the cold?"

"I like the cold sir- it wakes me up."

"It certainly does that," said Rose. "Will you be singing Auld Lang Syne tonight?"

"Oh no sir, we don't do anything like that here. Will you sir?"

"That's very doubtful." As he said that, Rose could feel somebody watching him again, and he could be sure that it wasn't Carstairs, who was standing right there in front of him.

"Well Happy New Year to you Carstairs, I wouldn't stay here too long, you'll catch your death."

"That's what my mother would say sir. By the way…"

Carstairs didn't finish the sentence and looked confused. Rose waited upwards of a minute before he finally spoke again.

"Do you want to tell me something Carstairs?"

"No sir, nothing at all. Goodbye now."

And Carstairs walked back into the main building, still looking rather perplexed, while Rose, a little frustrated, wondered what the boy was going to tell him.

Then Rose began his long walk up the drive towards the Golden Bell, still feeling eyes on him. But he didn't even bother to turn around this time.

*

On the mound yesterday evening, my lips chattering but to nobody, I finished rereading the Jack the Ripper serial in my bloods which helped me to forget how cold it was, and that it was New Year's Eve.

I was making my way quietly back to my section, skirting around the main courtyard ensuring that I avoided the gravel, when I saw that man Mr Rose talking to the Cyclops.

That's what we call that oath Carstairs, but never to his face. We all know how he lost his eye- Old Bannister came and told us the day before the Cyclops arrived here, almost two years ago now.

The Cyclops' father is an Admiral of the Fleet, not a Rear one, nor a Vice one, but a full-bloodied one. And that is why the Cyclops is so dim.

When he was twelve, he was taken on a tour of his father's ship, and while exploring the upper and lower decks with little supervision- tut-tut- the Cyclops managed to bring a hatch down on his head. He damaged his brain and had to have a metal plate fitted into his bonce.

But that's not how he lost his eye! Old Bannister told us boys in North that the Cyclops began to have terrible tantrums and could lose control at any time. And that he'd been sent to Shadowside because he'd stabbed himself in the eye with a fountain pen when angry in a calligraphy class at his old school, and his eye had to be removed. That's how he became the Cyclops!

Old Bannister warned us to be nice to him, but of course, I just couldn't- I had to find out what makes a monster tick. I just threw a naval jibe at him whenever I saw him, 'Ship ahoy,' but after a few days he just snapped and pushed me away, so hard that I fell back a good ten or twelve feet.

He's a strong boy- nobody else in North could or would do that to me. But I know that I could beat him if I put my mind to it, and of course, he's no match for me mentally. Anyway, since then I've given him his leeway, as he keeps himself to himself.

So, the Cyclops doesn't trouble me, he's just a nuisance. But the man Rose does. He's now allowed into South, and I've never seen a member of staff other than Mrs Benson, Dr Sharland or on one occasion after Dorothy disappeared, Mr Dodwell, enter there, and the only other stranger I know to have been admitted was the policeman I'd been interviewed by twice in the library. And now he was chatting openly with the Cyclops, a resident!

Something isn't right, and the mound is where I've always thought most clearly at Shadowside. It's my haven, an island cut off from *them*. But just feet away, there's danger everywhere, *they* all want an answer to Dorothy's disappearance so that *they* can return to *their* cocoon of oppression.

"It's time to take the offensive," I said aloud to myself. It was time to put the kibosh on Mr Rose, *their* new weapon.

And I knew where he lived- the old cottage, just the other side of the mound from the main building. So, this morning before breakfast, and being prepared to miss that meal and any attendant punishment Mr Leadbetter would give me, I waited on the mound again, taking vantage in a bush with a clear view of the path to Mr Rose's front door.

After twelve-and-a-half minutes he appeared- I counted carefully- and I saw him lock the door and place the key in the mouth of one of the stone guard dogs which sat to attention either side of the cottage's entrance.

It didn't surprise me that he entrusted the key to the useless jaws of an ornamental canine. Mr Rose struck me as an urban character, one misplaced in the murky, waterless goldfish bowl of Shadowside, floating around, out of sorts. Everything about him roared of the city, and metropolis dwellers always seem to think it's much safer in the countryside. I'd read him so well.

Once he'd walked down the path, his coat pulled tight around him and hat down in the rain, I waited precisely two minutes before I emerged from my island and ran towards the door, grabbing the key from the dog's open mouth.

The key turned noiselessly but the handle with a slight creak. I had a quick scout around downstairs- a kitchen and bathroom, a small living room, all with no personality connected to the current occupant, which either meant Mr Rose wasn't staying long or he had no interest in homemaking, like most professional men, and I was sure he was one of those.

But he was no doctor or scientist, he was much too 'real' for that. He was among *them*, but he wasn't one of *them*. And he wasn't a policeman- he seemed too clued-up for that, even for Scotland Yard, I'd wager. A private detective was a possibility, but as most of them are ex-plods, I was reserving my considerable judgement on that.

The stairs creaked more than the front door handle, but the sound sprang from the same acoustic family. Upstairs there was just a sort of store cupboard and a bedroom in which the bed was about four times as big as the one in my section in North. The bedside drawers and wardrobe yielded nothing, including the pockets of the suit, sports jacket and trousers hanging there, and the underwear and socks randomly thrown on a shelf too.

I confess I was beginning to think my visit had been a waste of time when I decided to look under the mattress- that's where I'd hide something important if I didn't get mine turned over every Saturday. Nothing there either. But when I put my mind to it, one thing usually leads to another.

As I lowered the mattress again, I saw that the carpet, a thin and mottled affair, was slightly lifted in the corner of the room. I went over to it, and carefully pulled it up a little.

And there, on the bare floorboard, was a small notebook, which when opened revealed rows of numbers, pounds shillings and pence, with explanations next to them- 'taxi; 'research'; 'interview entertainment'; 'sundries'. It was a kind of expenses book.

But it was in the back flap of the notebook that I found what I was looking for- a business card, on which the words 'Mr Harold Rose, Special Writer, *Travesties* magazine- Telling the truth, however terrible' with '12 Fetter Lane, London EC4' and "Telephone: Holborn 3210' beneath it. And, also in the flap was a battered membership card for the National Union of Journalists in the same name.

I put the notebook back, consigning the contents of the business card to my memory, replaced the carpet, ensuring that it was slightly raised in the corner once more, and left the cottage quickly, this time not entering the mound, but walking around it the other way.

Only Mr Tucker saw me walk into the main building, just a few minutes late for breakfast. He was sweeping the path again, a little earlier than usual, and nodded when I waved at him.

I was as happy as a sand-boy who'd sold his last grains of the day from his hamper. So Rose was a scribe, a 'gentleman' of the press, a muckraker no less! And such men have a very real weakness- they have large egos and want to be famous, just like Gary Cooper. Oh, super-duper!

*

162

Rose was wandering through the main corridor, just going past the stairs, killing time. It was Saturday morning, the day after New Year's Day, and he wasn't expected to work at weekends, not that he did much for Dr Sharland anyway. He just had to remain visible enough to keep his cover as a clinical assistant, and that required extraordinarily little endeavour.

But he was very aware of the passing of time too, and the need to get some real answers about Dorothy- he'd been at Sunnyside for over a fortnight now, and both Mrs Hopkins and Flanagan were sure to be asking questions again about his progress soon.

But he had a real lead now, he felt. Isabel Haarman certainly knew something about Dorothy's disappearance, and her refusal to say anything told him more than a full set of the Encyclopaedia Britannica.

From his experience of interviewing many criminals and witnesses, Rose understood that those who won't speak at all are hiding some knowledge of a crime, those who speak too much know little of real relevance, and those who speak just enough to not appear uncooperative are generally guilty or are protecting somebody else.

Isabel certainly had a medical history of mental instability and impulsive attacks of anxiety and a propensity to violence- towards her own sister no less. But Rose's hack antennae, finely tuned after over twelve intense years on the job told him that she was holding something important back.

He was about to go upstairs, the main stairs where Bernard Bannister's head hit the cold unforgiving marble, to hang around near- but not too close to-the South wing, hoping for Isabel to enter or leave so he could approach her, as perhaps on her own without Dr Sharland present, she might open up a little. He'd had the feeling when he spoke to her that the doctor's presence made her more uneasy.

And then a boy appeared, as if from nowhere, but really from just around the corner, but it wasn't Carstairs.

"Hello, Mr Rose," I said. "Happy New Year, sir."

"Happy New Year to you too, Edwin."

"Too late for the pinch and the punch," I said.

"What exactly is that?"

163

"It's what you do on the first of the month."

Rose smiled, realising he must appear rather slow in comprehension- Flanagan would certainly groan if his star journalist was less than pin-prick sharp in the field, especially with the mounting expenses, which would be submitted at the end of the assignment against what he'd received.

"I'm about to go up to the billiards room. We're allowed to go in there again now," I said. "It's one of my favourite places here."

"So, where's your favourite place, may I ask?"

"That would be telling," I said, gently tapping my nose twice with my right index finger.

"I've never been in there actually," said Rose, less than truthfully. "I'd like to come up there with you if I could."

He knew that he wasn't supposed to be getting too close to 'residents,' but nobody seemed to be around. And perhaps sensing his slight reluctance or for his own protection, the boy offered a less troubled path to the room where he himself had left the bloodied razor just days earlier.

"Of course. I'll go up first and meet you on the second floor at the head of the winding stairs," I said. "It's probably best for me if we aren't seen together, there's rules here you see."

"That sounds like a good idea."

And with that I made my way up the stairs. I almost leaped up them like Old Bannister once did, and with shorter legs too. At the top, after I'd counted the sixty-fourth step, I looked down and saw Mr Rose still on the twelfth, proceeding to the thirteenth step.

Then I commenced my next ascent, up the winding iron stairs that lead to the second floor, where Lawrence Drummond walked his last into the billiards room. I wasn't even out-of-breath as I waited on the narrow landing for the scribbler.

*

I opened the ornately patterned wooden door, which had a panel just above my head-height with two cues and a ball carved within it with '*The English Game*' written underneath, and Mr Rose followed me inside.

Just as he'd thought when Dr Sharland gave him a cursory look at the room while giving him the brief tour of Sunnyside

164

on his arrival, the oddest thing about it was there was no billiards table within it. He assumed that when it had been a private house there had been, but Edwin was ready to explain that, as if he could read minds, just as Madame Sosostris claimed she could tell futures.

"It's said they had to move the playing table out of here because Mr Drummond bled all over it," I said.

"Lawrence Drummond, the son of the house's builder?"

"That's right, he spilled himself all over the baize."

Rose could see that Edwin recounted the story with some relish, like any boy of his age with a penchant for the macabre- if only he knew what real violent death looked like, he thought, having seen a good few murdered corpses himself at crime scenes.

"Is that why you put a razor in here last week?" said Rose, going for all or nothing, as there could only be a denial.

I was mildly taken aback, I admit, but naturally didn't show it. There was perhaps more to this man than I'd foreseen.

"And why would you think that?"

"The man who sold it to you described you well. Are you a fan of Biggles by any chance- as you gave the name of Biggles' creator for the shop's records?"

"Not exactly a fan- it just came to mind- I'd just read one of the books in a sitting."

"That's impressive."

"Not really- it's for children- I'm far beyond that now. I've read Mr Aldous Huxley, you know."

"Why did you plant that old razor here- as a prank?"

"As a reminder," I said.

"For whom?"

"Anybody and everybody I suppose."

"And the blood?"

Rose watched as Edwin pushed the sleeve of his navy pullover up his left arm and unbuttoned the cuff of the white shirt below, before folding that back up his arm too. There was a cut on the back of the forearm about two inches long, still quite red, which didn't need the boy to point it out.

"It bled like the dickory it did," I said.

"Do you usually suffer so much for a practical joke?"

165

I laughed again. "I like to give birth to mirth!"

Rose smiled weakly. "What did you use to cut yourself?"

"Why, the razor of course- I'm all for authenticity."

"Was there any particular person you wished to shock with that 'reminder' of the man's tragic passing?"

"No- as I said- anybody and everybody."

Rose's gaze was momentarily taken by the black-and-white diamond-shaped patterned tiles which covered half of one wall behind the boy, which Edwin noticed immediately.

"They're a bugger to clean, you know- please excuse my cursing, I didn't mean to, Mr Rose."

"Apology accepted under the circumstances."

"And may I ask what those are?" I said.

"You've come clean about placing the razor here, so a mild profanity seems less of a crime."

I paused for a moment. "It wasn't a crime in my eyes, but a service."

"To frighten Miss Lane half-to-death when she found it? You must've known it would get a strong reaction due to what happened in this room."

"Did she find it? So disappointing- she's only a minor figure here..."

"She's only just come back to work and refuses to clean in here anymore I'm told."

"Well, I had to draw everybody's attention to far graver crimes than a man taking his own life. You see, I know something about Mr Lawrence Drummond that nobody else does."

"Which is?"

"With respect sir, how do I know if I can trust you with this privileged information?" I said, meekly.

"How about if I promise not to tell Dr Sharland about you being the culprit?" said Rose, making an offer that really wasn't a concession from him as he had no intention of informing the doctor nor Mr Dodwell about what he'd discovered days before, at least not yet.

"That seems reasonable. Shall we become blood brothers? I said.

"What does that mean?"

166

"It's a show of loyalty- a small incision in each of our palms, and then we place them together, mixing our blood. It binds you like brothers- they do it in the old world still, in parts of the Empire."

"I think we'll have to make do with a shaking of hands."

"That'll have to do then, I'll take your word as a gentleman."

"And I yours as a scholar," said Rose.

They shook hands, and Rose was startled by just how strong Edwin's handshake was- he'd softened his usually only firm handshake to accommodate the boy.

"Do you know the gazebo close to the terrace behind us?" I said.

"I can find it."

"Please meet me there tomorrow morning at ten o'clock."

"Can't you just tell me here- we *are* in the appropriate place for me to learn Mr Drummond's secret, I'd say."

"That's true, but what I'm going to tell you requires a place of objective contemplation."

"Ten o'clock tomorrow at the gazebo it is then."

"It'll be worth it, you'll see," I said, taking a seat in the green velvet chair.

"You seem at home in here."

"It's one of my favourite places, remember."

"Is the gazebo another favourite of yours?"

"Not at all. It's simply perfect for serious secret-sharing."

Edwin suddenly sprang up from the chair. "I'll go out first if you don't mind, Mr Rose. I should be back in my section now."

With that, the boy was gone, and Rose himself sat down in the chair, which was much more comfortable than it looked in its' Victorian uprightness. He welcomed the rest- he couldn't take much more melodrama.

20

Rose saw the gazebo through the mist before he even left the terrace the next morning. Towards the west, just before the dense woods in that direction where Mr Tucker found Dorothy's horse charm.

The gazebo lay at the edge of the rectangular envelope of a grass plateau, behind which to the south there was a dangerously steep decline as the crumbling cliff gave way to the sea.

In Lawrence Drummond's time, half a century before and more, Rose imagined that the land mass would have been far greater past the terrace. But nature's erosion had eaten into it, unseen in motion over time.

It was silent-still as he walked across the terrace, wondering if anybody was watching him from any of the many windows of the main building, as his dark trench-coated and hatted figure weaved in and out of the moving shield of fog around him.

Just the occasional cawing of crows broke the hush, and he wondered if the calls were aimed at him or other birds, but certainly not the stuffed example of a crow he'd seen in the glass cabinet in the 'Domestic Species' section on the first floor of the mansion.

The gazebo appeared before him as he walked towards the trees and the cawing got a little louder. It was at least thirty feet in height, made of grey stone, but half-covered with vines and leaves wrapped around its dome, which had a turreted spike on the top of it.

It was presumably built there about a third of the way through Queen Victoria's reign, as the house opposite sprang up, thought Rose. It too must have provided echoes of past grandeur even then.

He was looking at the gazebo's large portholes and the criss-crossing stonework above them when the boy's voice said 'Mr Rose.' Not a man to flinch easily, he did just that.

"Morning, Edwin."

"You found it then," I said.

"I just followed my nose," said Rose.

I laughed a little.

"Is something amusing?" said Rose, in a tone not irritated, but curious.

"Please forgive me for having a lark, but I was just thinking 'Mr Rose follows his nose,' and it tickled me."

Rose smiled, remembering that he was talking to a boy, which was easy to forget sometimes as Edwin had a better vocabulary than most men and women he knew, with the obvious exception of Percy Johnson of the *Telegraph*, whom everyone in the Stab called 'Dr Johnson' as he was a walking dictionary.

"Shall we go inside?" I said, moving towards the gazebo without waiting for an answer. Mr Rose followed me in, and I sat down on the stone bench, the muckraker taking a seat next to me.

"It's well-designed," said Rose, "the wind might be whistling, but it's not reaching us in here."

"Sir Arthur Drummond hired only the best architects for the house and all the outbuildings they say."

"It must have cost him a pretty penny then."

"About £150,000," I said, not needing to divulge my source, which was Mr Baxter, the history master.

Mr Rose showed his astonishment at the figure by touching the brim of his hat, a mannerism I would come to see was habitual when he was mildly startled. But I was waiting to see what he did when he was truly shocked.

"I may as well not beat around the bush," I said. "The reason I've brought you here is to talk about Mr Lawrence Drummond, also known as Jack the Ripper."

Then I saw his reaction to amazement- unlike many people, Mr Rose's eyes didn't widen, but narrowed. A pause of over a minute followed before the scribbler recovered.

"And *why* do you say that?" said Rose.

"Mr Drummond was in London on the dates of all the murders, and after he went into the billiards room with his razor there were no more killings."

"Coincidence-there must be many people who were in the city on those dates and left after the last woman was killed."

"But Mr Drummond was deeply unhappy, and when he realised what he'd done, and that he couldn't stop himself, he took the honourable way out," I said.

"But those five murders were truly terrible, and we're probably talking about the most infamous killer in history. What would lead Lawrence Drummond to commit such horrible crimes?"

"If I knew that I'd have Dr Sharland's job," I said, lying- as if I'd want to be one of *them*!

"You need more evidence than that- there have been many people suspected of the Whitechapel killings."

"I have more evidence, but that's enough for today- I need to be back in my section, I'm afraid. I'll be outside the library at about four o'clock this afternoon- in the alcove there- if you'd like to hear some more."

"I'll do my best to be there," said Rose.

"I must be off now- good morning to you, Mr Rose,' I said, as I walked out of the gazebo and into the rising mist, hearing his "Goodbye, Edwin," as I left.

Mr Rose not believing me, or should I say, not pretending to believe me, told me something especially important about him- he had morals. Many muckrakers, from what I've read in my bloods, would be as happy as Larry to take my word and print it. He was more like TinTin than I'd thought. And having proper morals is certainly a weakness.

And I already knew that I was going to enjoy playing with the scribbler.

*

Rose had been inwardly startled by the Jack the Ripper revelation- it was something he could never have anticipated. But Edwin was a boy, a weaver of tales it seemed, and dark ones at that.

And he may have left the razor in the billiards room, but that had nothing to do with the search for Dorothy, his reason for being at Sunnyside.

Although there was also something intriguing about it- the way that Edwin told him was as if he genuinely believed that

Lawrence Drummond had been the awful predator of London's East End in the late 1880's.

Rose recalled speaking to an old hack years before when he was starting on the *Herald*- Gerald Taylor had worked for the *Illustrated London News* and reported on the hunt for the Whitechapel fiend when he too was a young man.

Taylor had by then been unhappily retired for years, but still hung around Ye Olde Cheshire Cheese and other public houses a cut-above the Stab around Fleet Street, yearning to still be part of 'it.' Taylor had told him that the police thought they knew who the killer was, but that he'd died soon after the last murder in an asylum, after having a complete mental breakdown.

Yet Rose knew that he had to follow it up- it was the story that every editor wanted, every journalist craved, decades after the gruesome murders that took place over the space of seven or eight weeks that autumn and early winter of 1888.

Who was the ogre, the monster, the demon? He knew only too well that Flanagan would be salivating, and although he didn't believe that Drummond had been Jack the Ripper, his interest was awakened, one eye half-open, anyway.

He wouldn't be telling Flanagan yet, but he would make a few inquiries. Then he wanted to focus on Isabel Haarman, who he was sure could help lead him to Dorothy, given time and effort.

Rose waited for Edwin outside the library in the alcove at four o'clock that afternoon as he'd been asked to, in fact he waited for over half an hour. But there was no sign of Edwin, so he made his way back to the cottage.

*

There was no need to keep my second appointment with Mr Rose. As my mother used to say, 'It's sometimes better to bite your tongue than to continue to hold forth.' Although she never took her own advice, sadly.

But in this rare instance she was right- I already have Mr Rose almost on the line- he's about to take the bait, the wriggling maggots of a killer story about a murderous legend. He won't bite his tongue, but into the hook, and hence I can keep him dangling and thrashing around, away from Dorothy.

I have no more evidence to offer of the sort he wants confirming that Mr Lawrence Drummond was Jack the Ripper. You see, I *know*. It truly doesn't matter if Mr Rose really believes me, that's neither here, there, nor anywhere.

What matters is that every day that Mr Rose doesn't think about Dorothy- the reason I'm sure he's here and conferring so closely with Mr Dodwell and Mr Sharland -is a day when he comes no closer to finding out about me and Dorothy and where she is now. And it's another day when he can't report it to *them* and write the story for his magazine, '*Telling the truth, however terrible*,' as his business card stated.

I must keep him from that truth, until he leaves Shadowside. And that's why I had to creep around North last night with a pair of heavy scissors I borrowed from the arts supply cupboard.

It was all quiet on the North front as I crouch-walked along the wooden floor like a trench-bound soldier on the Somme. That is except for the unintelligible mumblings of the Cyclops in his brain-damaged stupor, whose section was my target.

His section lies opposite Kirby's, and that was my main concern as rousing the water-baby suddenly could cause him to cry out and soil his sheets and blanket. But I'd carefully planned my approach to the Cyclops's bed, allowing me to remain kneeling while I carried out my mission.

And it all went as splendidly as predicted. The Cyclops's breathing remained shallow and his guttural moaning continued, with no sign of incoming fire from Kirby's section at all.

With the Cyclops's head on its' side, his good eye closed shut on the thin pillow and glass one staring open at his desk and glinting in the near-dark, I leaned up and took a small lock of his dark blonde hair at the nape of his neck in one hand and placed it between the scissor blades in the other. Snip! That's all it took, one cutting motion.

There was no reaction from the one-eyed monster or the water baby nearby, so I crouched back bent-doubled to my section, knowing that I could have given the Cyclops a full haircut if I'd so wished.

*

Rose was back in Milston the next morning after telephoning his usual mute driver from Dr Sharland's office, who took him there in good time and without using any syllables.

It was a Monday, just four days into the year, but Rose was very aware that time was passing quickly. He had to buy some more time at Sunnyside, and that was why his first errand was to call in to Flanagan at the office from the square behind the library, which would be his second port of call.

He waited for the elderly woman to try to open the telephone box door against the wind before performing the action for her, for which she thanked him and he told her it was his pleasure, which it really wasn't.

He slotted a couple of sixpences and gave the office number to the operator, who he knew might well have been sitting at the switchboard at Milston's post office, and could listen in to the call, so he would have to be careful what he said.

When he was connected, the voice was unmistakably that of the Monkfish, and strangely, for the first time he could remember, Rose was pleased to hear it.

"He's not here," said Monkfish, undoubtedly watching the minutes count down and chafing to get down to the Stab when it opened but having to man the office.

"Where is he?"

"Investor's breakfast at Claridge's."

"Claridge's- breakfast?"

"Some rich foreign gentleman with blue blood, he said."

"Any idea when he'll be back?"

"He said by eleven- I bloody well hope so."

"Tell them at the Stab that I'm visiting my mother now, as she's unwell."

"Will do. By the way, everyone's on the case of a missing little girl up in Nottinghamshire and Flanagan's been fretting that you should be on it too."

Rose inwardly groaned- once Flanagan got a whiff of a big story, he always followed the Fleet Street herd, irrespective of what was already being covered.

"Well, he'll have to let them feed on it for now, I'm still busy down here."

"Right-o."

But Rose had to smile to himself as he replaced the receiver. Flanagan had done this before- he'd met one of the earliest investors in the magazine at a party where editors go, a sort of hellish Valhalla in the newspaper world, with canapes, champagne, and a liberal dashing of ruthlessness.

That gentleman was Turkish and had once visited the *Travesties* office in a Rolls Royce and a fez and was apparently so shocked at the meagre size of the offices that he paid for a new Bluebird typewriter for Monkfish. To his irritation, Rose had been out of the office as usual that day and just got a compliment from the gentleman about his latest story, relayed by Flanagan in his inimitably uncomplimentary manner, instead of the latest Underwood.

Although Rose knew that while sipping his tea from the finest china in Claridge's, Flanagan would be calling him one of Fleet Street's star journalists, just as he had to Mrs Hopkins, and showing the man copies of the magazine, while inflating the circulation figures. Still, investment meant that the magazine continued, and so too Rose's job, one that gave him far greater latitude and freedom than most hacks, he begrudgingly had to admit to himself.

He left the telephone box and walked towards the library, where he had some reading to do.

21

The easiest way for Rose to check up on details about Jack the Ripper's 1888 rampage would have been to telephone contacts in London to dig up the gen for him, but due to the competitive nature of his rivals on the nationals, that just wasn't a possibility- they'd sniff the scoop and once they'd located him, half of Fleet Street would descend on Sunnyside.

There was Monkfish, whom he could trust, but Rose needed information fast, not the following week. Monkfish wrote and edited quickly, but when it came to finding facts, he was a snail whose trail led in and out of public houses.

So Rose was in Milston library to painstakingly go through the old newspapers. As well as old copies of the *Milston Argus*, there were old editions of the *Times*.

After ordering copies of the *Times* covering August, September, October and November 1888, the months he knew covered the Whitechapel murderer's reign of terror, Rose went and sat at the same table, glumly realising that as the Times was a daily, he'd have to wade through over sixty editions, although the articles would almost definitely all be on the front page at least.

He waited at the table, and it was twenty minutes before the same bent-over elderly man who'd brought his order last time appeared pushing his wooden trolley.

"The *Times*, August 1888."

"Thank you, but I ordered September, October and November 1888 too."

"All in good time, sir. These older papers are right at the back of the archive room. I shall bring them to you month by month."

"I understand. Thank you."

"Please leave them in the condition you found them."

"No marking or tearing?" said Rose with a smile, remembering the man's instruction on his last visit.

"Or smudging." The man walked away with a roll of his eyes, as if Rose had stolen his big moment by pre-empting his words.

Rose decided to look at the first three pages of each edition. He went through every yellowed and brittle copy on the table before him and found no reference to the murders at all. He was sure that the murders had started in the August of that year, so why was there no mention of them?

He remembered the old hack Gerald Taylor saying that the big nationals were on the story from the beginning, due to the ferocious nature of the slayings. Realising that he would have to wait for the next batch of newspapers to be pushed through by the now slightly irritated elderly archive man, Rose decided to see if there was anything about the killer on the library's shelves.

Deciding that he wouldn't ask the grey-clad librarian at the main desk- she seemed so stiff and proper that despite being a crime writer he felt embarrassed asking her, a rural bookworm, for a book about Jack the Ripper. That was something in Rose firmly instilled by his mother- a self-conscious sense of decorum.

When he saw a young man shelving books around the corner, he asked if they had any books on the killer.

"Oh, we certainly do- It's in British history- it's one of our most requested books actually."

This showed Rose that most other people didn't share his sense of noble gentility.

"There you go- *The Mystery of Jack the Ripper* by Leonard Matters."

"Thanks," said Rose, taking the book and returning to the table. He could see on the inside flap that the book was published in 1929, so was already almost eight years old.

He had no interest in the writer's theory as to the identity of the killer- he just wanted the dates of the murders, and in the appendix at the back, he found a timeline. He quickly scrawled down the dates of all five killings. Then he realised why there had been no piece about the murders in the August 1888 editions- the first one had been committed on Friday, 31

August, so the next edition of the *Times* when it could be reported was on Monday, 2 September.

He was about to go to the librarian to cancel the rest of his newspaper order when he saw the elderly man and his trolley approaching again. Before Rose could speak, the man said, "The *Times*, September 1888."

"Thank you, but I won't be needing them now, or October and November."

The man gave a truly champion eye roll- not worthy of the Berlin Olympics the previous year, but the kind that could win a much sought-after ribbon at a village fete.

"My apologies," said Rose, as he walked past the man, hoping that he wouldn't have to use his services again.

It was a little after eleven, as the chiming of the clock in the square reminded him, so Rose entered the empty telephone box, asking to be put through to the office for the second time that day.

"Flanagan."

"It's Rose."

"What the devil's going on? Mr Monk says you need more time down there."

"I'm getting closer. I've spoken to one of Dorothy's best friends, and she's hiding something."

"I need something solid now, Rose, time's getting on- there's a missing ten- year-old girl called Mona Tinsley and rumours of a strong suspect yet to be arrested- I'm sure you can get to him. I've heard that the *Express* may be offering a sizeable public reward."

Rose said nothing about Monkfish having mentioned that earlier.

"I need at least another week here," said Rose.

"I can give you two days, and that's all. I'll have to pull you out after that."

"But what about Mrs Hopkins and Dorothy?"

"Perhaps there's no answer. If the girl ran away and doesn't want to be found, we may never know where she went. We've got an edition to put out, and a new investor to impress."

So, the breakfast at Claridge's had brought results.

"But I won't have the story ready in two days..."

"So be it. Sorry Rose, the Mona Tinsley story's just too hot to miss."

Rose knew that tone in Flanagan's voice- it was lower than usual, and one of finality. There was only one more thing he could do to gain more time, and he'd have to take the risk that the operator could be listening in.

"There's something else I'm working on here. A suicide, about fifty years ago. Claims are being made that the man who killed himself, the son of the man who built the mansion here, was Jack the Ripper."

"What?!!!" said Flanagan.

"One of the boys living here says he has evidence, and so far, the days fit."

"What evidence? This could be the story of the century."

"That's what I'm working on, but I need another week."

"That does rather change things. You have a week- mine the Jack the Ripper story for all it's worth. Even if it's not true, it would be a great lead story for the next issue. See if you can find out anything about Dorothy too, of course."

"I certainly will," said Rose.

Flanagan was gone, and Rose suspected that he might get straight on the telephone to the swanky new investor, bragging about the big story being worked on about Jack the Ripper.

Every professional instinct Rose had wanted to go back to London that day and away from Sunnyside's stifling atmosphere, returning to his own normality- he felt cut off from his usual way of working. He hadn't even heard about the Mona Tinsley story, and normally he'd have been all over it.

But he was invested in Dorothy's story now, emotionally- he had to find the answer, or at least get further than he had.

He needed to find Dorothy, and if that meant covering the Lawrence Drummond/Jack the Ripper story too, which he was already sure was Edwin's fantasy or at least unprovable, it was the way it had to be.

But Rose felt conflicted, as every minute he spent thinking about Lawrence Drummond was one lost in the search for Dorothy.

*

I was a wolf cub once, before I came to Shadowside- I was too young to be a cub scout. I say 'once,' and I mean it. I only attended one meeting of the pack.

It was unbearable- all the little boys gathered around, being asked to believe a fantasy. I'd already read *The Jungle Book* and knew before I'd reached page five that Mr Kipling was a liar and a fraud. You see, in his jungle, there are rules, and codes of honour and loyalty, but I understood very early on that there are no rules in nature. In life's jungle, it's just me and *them*.

I couldn't kow-tow to Akela, a man who was probably a fawning shopkeeper or salesman by day, a lackey falsely endowed with the power of a leader one evening a week. I saw right through him, the organisation's founder Mr Baden-Powell and its inspirer, Mr Kipling. I wasn't about to say 'bwana' to any of *them*, like some tuppence minion of the Empire.

I refused to stand in the semi-circle, and glowered at Akela, causing him to tell my mother when she came to collect me that I wouldn't be welcome back! I wasn't the kind of boy who would be a credit to the uniform- as if he were an officer in the army, like Mr Lawrence Drummond's commanding officer, who truly must have had the power of life and death over his men in the Sudan.

My mother was most unhappy, and told me that she was ashamed of me, and that I'd gone there to build my character, as if that were ever needed! But my father understood- it was just two months before he ended his life, and he didn't reprimand me over it. He died of honour, while my mother wailed that she would die of shame because she'd been socially embarrassed by me once again.

She thought she was significant in the world with her blood-red Flame Fatale lip stain, a hog in a silk waistcoat. I always knew she was like a shell, but dead inside.

"Everybody has to die of something," I said to her, before she sent me to my bedroom. Within six months she would be free of me and I of her, but the price was coming to Shadowside.

Although there was one thing that Akela said that early evening with which I agreed- "Be prepared." Ever since I can

179

remember I've planned every move, knowing that he who does the digging sets the path taken.

That's why when I saw Isabel outside the Great Hall, I made sure to give her a little nudge. Just a gentle push as I walked past her, not far from where the Drummond family stare out at you from their gilded frames.

She looked at me, and I saw the fear exposed in her lost-in-the-ocean eyes, and I knew that she was sinking almost as fast as the Titanic had. The smile I momentarily gave her flickered into my sternest, teeth-clenched expression, a treacherous iceberg ripping through her. She looked down at the chessboard floor where Dorothy and I had once stood on different squares.

Isabel was at once dejected, tense and frightened, no match for me and my iceberg look, which remains submerged until required.

*

It was a small wooden box, rough and unfinished as if made by inexperienced hands, two inches by two inches, which lay just outside the door of Rose's cottage when he returned there that evening. He picked it up but didn't open it until he'd gone inside.

After taking off his hat and coat, he sat at the gnarled and heavily knotted kitchen table and lifted the box's lid. Inside was a delicate silver bracelet, plain yet expensive looking, with a tiny ornate clasp, from which Rose knew that the horse charm had been attached, as he realised immediately that it was Dorothy's bracelet.

And once he'd taken the bracelet out of the box, he saw a small piece of white paper folded up beneath where it had been. Swiftly unfolding it, a tuft of blonde hair fell out, landing on the table, which was only slightly lighter than the coiled strands. He instinctively placed the hair back into the box before he lost it.

Rose then read the words on the paper, which were written in blue ink.

My Darling D,
I will love you forever my angel
Ever Truly Yours,
O

Reading it again, he focused on the initials, the addressee obviously being Dorothy, and the author's name seemingly beginning with the letter O.

And it certainly wasn't Dorothy's hair, which Rose knew was jet black, like her mother's. It had to be a lock of her lover's hair, but who could that be, and why would they leave it outside his cottage? They wouldn't- somebody else had left it there as evidence of this person's involvement in Dorothy's disappearance, whose name began with the letter O, he surmised.

Perhaps somebody close to Dorothy at Sunnyside, who had her interests at heart knew why he was there, and was trying to point him in the right direction, but who could that be? Or could it be a bluff, implicating an innocent person?

The horse charm had been found by Mr Tucker in the woods, and now the bracelet was there before him, but why would Dorothy have taken it off, especially as it was a present from her mother? This could be a bad sign, Rose mused.

He sat there looking at the note, hair, and bracelet in turn again and again, taking in this unexpected yet welcome development.

And Rose now knew that somebody, for whatever reason, was secretly trying to tell him whom Dorothy had been romantically linked to before she disappeared, and that this could lead him to wherever she was now.

22

Overnight, after mulling it over in his mind, Rose had come to suspect that it was Isabel Haarman, the girl closest to Dorothy at Sunnyside, who'd left the box with the hair, note and bracelet outside his cottage.

He sensed that she wanted to help him find her friend Dorothy but was emotionally unable to do so openly.

And going through Dr Sharland or Mrs Benson to speak to Isabel wouldn't be worth it, Rose well knew, as she wouldn't tell him anything in front of either of them, as he'd seen when he spoke to her and she became upset. But he had no choice- he had to get to Isabel alone.

It was the following morning in the staff dining room when Mr Leadbetter inadvertently told Rose where Isabel could sometimes be found when she wasn't in classes or her section in South. It was the first time he'd gone there for breakfast for some time, and finding Mr Leadbetter alone at a table, Rose sat down next to him.

"Morning, Mr Leadbetter," said Rose.

Mr Leadbetter shrugged and half-smiled as he ate his porridge before speaking.

"And how are you this Tuesday morning, Mr Rose?"

"Fair to middling."

"Are you a horse-racing man?"

"Only within the form pages," said Rose.

'Beautiful creatures, horses- we've got several here at Sunnyside you know."

"I didn't know that. Does Mr Tucker take care of them?"

"No, the older girls in South do as part of their therapy. It's what Mr Dodwell calls 'Trust Time'."

"Because only the trusted girls can take part?" said Rose.

"Not really- it's because the girls are allowed to muck out the stables and groom the horses unsupervised in the afternoons after classes."

"Sounds like a good idea."

"It is very calming for the girls, but no riding of course," said Mr Leadbetter, as he added several teaspoons of salt to his porridge.

"The Scottish way," said Rose.

"And that's the way it should be," said Mr Leadbetter, but as if trying to convince himself.

After Mr Leadbetter left, Rose made a point of scanning the newspapers, to catch up on what was going on, still subconsciously amazed that he'd become so removed from his own world.

*

I was on the way to the billiards room when I saw her again, having been reading *Newnes' Pictorial Knowledge* in the library, which I often do- ipsa scientia potestas est, or knowledge itself is power, as Mr Norrington-Davies the Latin master told us. But he got it from Sir Francis Bacon of course.

There Isabel was, her usually deathly white skin becoming ashen grey as she became aware of me.

We were all alone, at the bottom of the winding stairs that take you up to where Lawrence Drummond entered the spirit world, if unlike the late Mr Houdini you believe in that sort of thing.

It was obvious what she was thinking as we stood close to one of the bird cabinets- that I knew where Dorothy was, and that I'm an E6, and you only become one of those for good reason. I gave her my iceberg look again, calculated to rip into her. Then I counted to five in my mind, before I said the words I'd prepared, to deliver maximum damage.

'There are some birds that fly high and fast like the peregrine falcon and are able to escape more cunning birds like the Indian vulture which swoops down on its prey.' Then I counted to five again. 'But you're not one of those... You're the common robin, easy pickings for a vulture like me, just waiting for you to die.'

She was visibly trembling by now, looking down at her shoes, which were almost as polished as the geometrically patterned floor.

And that's how I left her, as I walked up the stairs.

*

183

Rose was directed towards the stables that afternoon by Mr Tucker- he'd waited until after three o'clock when he knew the children's classes finished.

The newspapers were leading on the war in Spain, and just two days earlier President Azaña had ordered the evacuation of all Spanish citizens from Madrid.

But Rose's thoughts were very firmly confined within Sunnyside, and the identity of 'O' in the note. Although he knew that he likely had just a week to find Dorothy before Flanagan sent him up to Nottinghamshire on the Mona Tinsley disappearance, or some other story that meanwhile emerged.

"Just follow the path past the chapel and you'll get to the stables after about three hundred yards by my measure."

"Much appreciated. Hope to see you in the Golden Bell soon," said Rose.

Mr Tucker nodded in a non-committal fashion as if to say he would be there when he *was* there.

Rose walked faster than usual towards the chapel, not due to urgency, but because of the hostile wind attacking his face.

As he got to the chapel, he considered going inside for some respite, telling himself that he needed to ask the Reverend Barnes more about Lawrence Drummond, but decided to keep going as Barnes could be found anytime, while an opportunity to speak to Isabel unsupervised was rarer than a blue moon.

The air froze in front of Rose as he exhaled and continued up the muddy path, rain beginning to gently fall, but the cows in the field to his right remained standing.

The stables appeared on the left, red-bricked and functional, with a sloping roof. He assumed that the four gated arches each housed a horse, and that the girls would be working inside out of the cold and rain. But there was no sound or sight of anybody.

He waited just to the side, under a large English oak, its leaves dripping metronomically in front of him as he sheltered from the now pouring rain. He could feel odd raindrops hitting his trilby, and he was almost smug in his green cocoon until he leaned forward and felt a cold sensation running down his neck to his shirt collar.

He wished he were back in London, where there was always a door to enter to escape the elements, while also debating whether he should run across and enter the stables and wait there. And was Isabel one of the girls allowed 'Trust Time?' Then the rain dropped to a drizzle, and he heard footsteps coming down the path.

Gazing across, he saw that there were four girls- he didn't recognise the two in front, but when they got closer, he saw that Caitlin and Isabel were walking behind them.

Knowing that he couldn't just appear from behind a tree and call her name- a strange man jumping out of the undergrowth would undoubtedly frighten them- Rose stayed still. He watched them enter the stables, each girl unbolting the wooden door below an arch.

He waited some minutes and could make out the sound of raking from inside. There was no giggling or talking, it was as usual silent among the children, or 'residents' as Dr Sharland called them. He could understand that when a member of staff was around, but these girls were alone.

Rose walked towards the arches, knowing that Isabel was inside the third one down. Peering through, he saw her pulling the rake over the hay with little effort, as if she was just combing it rather than turning it over.

"Miss Haarman, I wondered if we could have a little chat," he said in a gentle voice.

Isabel span around by reflex, but Rose could see that her anguished expression was ingrained. She looked tired and disturbed, worn down, and not manic as she had when he'd first seen her with Dr Sharland and Mrs Benson just a few days earlier.

She said nothing, and just looked at Rose.

"I really need to talk to you about Dorothy."

There was no reply.

"Please Isabel, we need to find her."

"I-I've got nothing to say," she said.

Just then, Caitlin appeared from the next gate, apparently having heard Rose's voice. "Are you all right Izzy?"

"I'm fine," said Isabel, at which Caitlin returned to her part of the stable, giving Rose a stern look as she did so.

"Where are the horses?" said Rose.

"They're still in the field," said Isabel.

"Please...I really need your help."

"I can't help you, I really can't."

"I know you know something about what happened to Dorothy, you're the only one who can help...I know you left the box with Dorothy's bracelet and the note with the lock of hair outside my cottage."

Isabel looked both confused and ready to explode, but Rose felt he had to push a little more.

"Who is 'O,' Isabel? Does he have something to do with Dorothy's disappearance?"

"If you don't go, I'll...I'll scream," said Isabel, her eyes filling with tears.

Rose knew when he was beaten. "I will go, but you can find me at the workman's cottage close to the main building. If I'm not there, just slip a note under the door saying where you want to meet and when. Please Isabel...for Dorothy."

Isabel was still staring vaguely at him as he left the stables and walked back up the path, into the wind this time. He didn't expect her to appear at his cottage- he'd have to find another way to get her to share what she knew.

Rose was worried now- it was obvious that Isabel knew something about what happened to Dorothy, and probably who her admirer or lover 'O' was- and the strain she was showing was a definite sign of a deep-rooted fear.

He knew that If Isabel was so afraid, almost anything could have happened to Dorothy.

*

Dorothy never saw it coming.

It was just before two-thirty that morning of the 22nd of November when I slipped on my shoes and coat over my pyjamas and climbed out of the washroom window and on to the roof, before dropping on to the gravel below with a stony splash.

Dorothy's route to our rendezvous outside the kitchens was easier than mine- she just had to walk down the scullery stairs and take care not to make too much noise as she pulled the bolt across.

But I'd oiled it earlier that evening after leaving the mound, using some butter I'd wrapped in a handkerchief and messily pocketed at dinner, so that the bolt slid across with little effort. And it worked, as Dorothy arrived exactly on time.

She was wearing her favourite green dress with the white flower pattern, under her black winter coat. I'd told her not to wear her best red coat to leave Shadowside, as it was indiscreet, and she's obeyed me. But she was wearing her most-loved bright red lipstick, which she'd never been able to sport openly at Shadowside.

She was distant as I took her hand and we walked across the field towards the woods in the dark mist. It seemed to take forever, but I'd timed it in my head the day before during daylight, when it took six minutes. Having allowed for Dorothy slowing me down and it being night, the eight and a half minutes we covered the distance in was only just outside my calculations.

She'd agreed to run away with me, to Uncle Robert's farm in Scotland, where she'd have our baby and we'd live happily ever after as in a fairy tale, the only problem being that neither my uncle nor his farm existed of course.

We got to the fallen tree on which I sometimes sat, surrounded by standing oaks, and I told Dorothy that we should rest there for a few minutes before resuming our journey.

It was all quiet save for the rustling of woodland animals and birds. She looked at me, and although it was impossible to see, I knew that her dark eyes were staring at me.

We held each other. Dorothy was trembling, and began to cry, so I hugged her closer to me. The embrace lasted a few minutes before she spoke, her voice filled with trapped tears.

"I don't know if I can go with you," she said.

"Because you found Old Bannister's wristwatch on my mound?"

There was no response. As anticipated, Dorothy was shocked that I knew.

"Did you...did you push Mr Bannister?" she finally said, her voice almost a whisper.

"Of course not. I found his wristwatch on the main stairs- it must have fallen off when he fell."

"How could that have happened?" she said, her voice stronger now.

"It must've been the force of the fall I suppose."

There was silence for at least a minute,

"Do you promise me that you had nothing to do with his death Edwin?"

"I promise you on our child's life."

"I love you," said Dorothy. "I've been very worried about this, you know."

"There's no need to be. I swear we will be all happy on my uncle's farm, you, me, and the baby."

"Oh Edwin," she said, and we put our arms around each other, remaining locked together alone among the concentration of trees, which could make entire orchestras of woodwind instruments if wished.

No, Dorothy didn't see it coming.

When we eventually broke apart, I had my hands around her neck within seconds. I still couldn't see her beautiful eyes, but I could feel the fear within her.

"Oh no! Please Edwin!" she said, as she began to choke.

Her last word was "Why?" before the gurgling sound drowned out any more words. I counted to just over three minutes before she went limp and dropped to the ground, the faint sound of a final expulsion of air coming from Dorothy's lungs.

I leant over her, pressing my left ear to Dorothy's chest, listening to her fading heartbeat. After about seven more minutes there was no more heartbeat, and I knew that Dorothy was dead.

Then I lowered my ear to Dorothy's stomach and could hear the dying pulse of our child for a couple more minutes before it also failed. I felt at peace.

I sat there on the wet ground for some time, thinking and sweating with adrenaline in the chilly air, my breath visible from my mouth. I understood why she had invaded my mound without permission and took Old Bannister's wristwatch.

She loved me so much that she wanted to be as close to me as possible. But she had to go, and so did our baby. It wasn't because she knew about my putting the kibosh on Old

Bannister- that was only a minor irritation. I knew that she would never dob me in. Dorothy loved me too much to do that.

She had to go because I have so much more to do before I start a family, a world to conquer. As soon as she told me that she was up the pole she signed her death chit.

In the darkness, I searched through her pockets and found the Zenith wristwatch and slipped it into my coat.

It was about an hour before I stopped savouring the moment. I hid Dorothy's body under the hollow beneath the tree, piling leaves and scattered branches over her.

She'd remain there until I came back for her, just as I'd planned the day before.

*

Rose woke up to a heavy frost next morning, the grass outside the kitchen window of his cottage glistening in rare rays of early morning sun.

It was just after eight o'clock and he felt despondent, as he knew that he'd really learned nothing really solid in his weeks at Sunnyside except a fantastic theory about Jack the Ripper's identity.

He needed a break on the note, hair and bracelet- he had started to suspect that Isabel had left it the box containing them outside his cottage, But he felt thwarted and could find no way forward unless Isabel unburdened herself to him as to the identity of the person's name beginning with 'O', a prospect he thought as likely as Monkfish becoming teetotal.

Isabel was obviously distraught and close to a breakdown, and he was sure it wasn't because of the underlying psychiatric condition that had brought her to Sunnyside. She may have once tried to drown her own sister, but she was now paralysed with fear over something she knew, and he was certain it was about Dorothy.

But Rose knew he had to pull himself together. He'd worked almost impossible stories before and got results, and answers sometimes came from nowhere.

It was in that mindset that he put down the teacup that looked as if it had been in the cottage since Lawrence Drummond was alive and went into the hallway to put on his hat and coat.

He would have to try to speak to Isabel again, and as soon as possible, as his instincts told Rose that she could unlock the mystery of Dorothy's disappearance.

*

We never play the Yank game baseball at Shadowside, and with Mr Lewis being a failed and frustrated cricketer, it will never happen here. But I know a little about the game from my bloods, and the exploits of Satchel Paige, the negro pitcher with a dangerous curveball, which often deceives batters.

And there was the wooden box I made in carpentry class, which had been in my section for over a year. I always knew I'd find some use for it, and it proved perfect for delivering my own curveball to the scribbler.

The lock of the Cyclops's hair and the note linking him to Dorothy were the first items to fill the box. But then I decided to add her bracelet to them, the one that she never took off for some silly reason.

I'd searched high, low, and high again trying to find the little silver horse that always hanged from it- retracing her route through the scullery, the main courtyard, the way we walked towards the woods and around the tree-bench where she died, even around the place where I'd finally laid her to rest. All to no avail. So, it seemed fitting to give the muckraker Mr Rose the bracelet too.

You see a man like him needs steering, a helping hand in the direction in which you need him to go.

*

Mr Leadbetter was bending his tall frame into the Standard Little Nine when he saw Rose coming out of Sunnyside's main doors and hollered across to him.

"I'm going into town if you need a lift?"

"That would be very kind of you," said Rose, who needed to report into Flanagan again, so he began to walk towards the motorcar.

"Perhaps you could sit in the back seat if you don't mind? Oscar's coming too and he has rather long legs like me."

"Of course," said Rose, getting into the back and onto the coffee-coloured leather seat. "Oscar?"

"Oscar Lewis- you met him at the Christmas party?"

190

"Yes, that's it." Rose remembered that he'd seen the physical exercise instructor since the party in that very same courtyard, but his first name hadn't really registered. But it did now, and the feeling was reinforced when Lewis got into the front seat.

"Thanks for waiting, Charles," said Lewis, then turning round to Rose in the back, his perfectly symmetrical face breaking into his ever-infectious smile, he added, "Good afternoon, Mr Rose…"

"Hello again Mr Lewis."

"Oscar, please," said Lewis.

The fact that his name began with the letter 'O' preoccupied Rose, along with the recent memory of the day when he'd seen the older girls looking at Lewis as if he were the bees-knees. And his hair was the same colour as the lock in the box too.

In fact, Rose was so side-tracked that he forgot to offer his own first name to Lewis again, who was soon making conversation with Mr Leadbetter.

"About time they replaced this jalopy don't you think?" said Lewis.

"It still runs fine," said Mr Leadbetter," but I heard Mr Dodwell say that he had his eye on a Morris Big Six or the new Flying Nine coming out soon."

"Terrific. Although I can't drive myself, it'd be nice to be ferried up and down in something new- not that this one's infra dig, you understand."

"Is this a staff car then?" said Rose.

"Yes, we book it on the noticeboard in the staffroom," said Mr Leadbetter. "Of course, institute business comes first, but we can use it for personal reasons when we have some time off and its free."

"Do you have business in town, Harold?" said Lewis, as they travelled down the Milston Road.

"Yes, just a few bits and bobs, Oscar" said Rose, surprised that Lewis, or Oscar, had remembered his own first name.

As Lewis and Mr Leadbetter made conversation about where they were planning to take holidays that year- Leadbetter staying close to home and Lewis to the south of France, Rose

191

decided not to call Flanagan that day, but to carry out some surveillance on Oscar Lewis.

Rose liked him personally so far, but if the handsome ex-sportsman had anything to do with Dorothy's disappearance, he had to get more gen. Somebody, likely Isabel Haarman, could be trying to point him the right way, but hopefully time would tell the truth.

They got to the centre of Milston, and Mr Leadbetter dropped them off in the car park by the promenade, telling them to meet there two hours later if they wanted a lift back, which Rose said that he would, but Lewis announcing that he had plans to stay in town that evening.

"Tally-ho," said Oscar Lewis rakishly, as he walked away from them, his broad shoulders slightly swinging as he made his panther steps into the near-distance.

Rose thought about what Dr Sharland had told him soon after he arrived at Sunnyside, that Dorothy was more likely to have formed a romantic attachment with a boy than a man, as she was afraid of authority.

But Oscar Lewis wasn't an authority figure, like Dr Sharland and Mr Dodwell, nor what Mr Bannister appeared to have been, and what Mr Leadbetter plainly wanted to be. Lewis's easy manner was boyish and approachable.

Rose let Lewis get about thirty yards away and said goodbye to Mr Leadbetter, who was walking towards the promenade.

Having followed many people over the years, including suspected murderers and other assorted criminals, Rose knew that the trick was to stay in sight but maintain a healthy space between you and your subject, but always staying alert for them to turn around and suddenly change direction, and to be able to fade into the background to stop them spotting you.

Not that he'd always got it right- he remembered closely following a drug-addicted pimp into a spieler in London's Soho once while working on a white slavery story for the *Herald*, being noticed by a Sabini mob henchman and held against the wall with a stiletto flick-knife to his throat.

It was one of the biggest professional lessons he'd ever learned, and after being a little roughed up and let go, he'd never trod on the heels of a target again.

Oscar Lewis was hardly a gangland thug, but if he was involved in Dorothy's disappearance, he might very well have a hidden dark side, so Rose was taking no chances.

Lewis was walking on the opposite side of the street when Rose saw him go inside Stenson's the chemist. Having been in there before when buying his shaving brush, he knew the shop's layout and that he could hide behind the centre shelving, on the other side from where Lewis happened to be. Rose also understood that it was a low-risk static tail, as it would scarcely appear strange if he were shopping in the chemists too.

He paused for a minute after Lewis entered Stenson's and waited for a lady to exit the shop, remembering that there was a bell which sounded when the shop door opened, and that could well cause Lewis to look to see who had come in after him.

Rose's timing was perfect. The bell rang once when the lady opened the door and again as he closed it, and there was no sign of Lewis. Rose went to the far side of the shop, shielding behind a high and wide stack of Vicks cough syrup.

"How can I help you today sir?" It was the voice of the chemist at the back of the shop.

"I'd like some prophylactic sheaths, please," said Lewis confidently.

"Any particular brand sir?"

"Do you have Phantasma?"

"We certainly do sir. How many would you like?"

"Just one packet, thank you."

Rose was almost holding his breath, knowing it meant that Lewis was planning to have intercourse. Could it be with Dorothy?

Lewis said goodbye and made for the door. Rose knew that he would have to buy something, and quickly, or he would lose his quarry. He picked up a bottle of Vicks, noting to himself that this would go on expenses, and having paid for it and exchanged very rushed pleasantries, rushed out onto the street.

Luckily, he could just see Lewis turning the corner, so Rose sped up and went left at the end of that stretch of road himself, further into Milston's main shopping area. Lewis was about twenty-five yards ahead of him now, on the other side of the road, and Rose was content with that distance.

193

Then Lewis went into a tiny Victorian pub called The Harp, in which Lawrence Drummond might have once imbibed, Rose thought. He positioned himself on the opposite pavement, holding back, but also ensuring that Lewis didn't exit. After a few minutes, Rose cautiously walked into the pub himself.

It was thankfully quite dark inside, all wood and lanterns, with a small circular bar at the rear and a line of booths against the far wall. There was no sign of Lewis as Rose approached the bar, and only a handful of patrons at several tables by the front windows, the air around whom was filled with cigarette smoke.

At the bar, Rose scanned around and finally spotted Lewis in the far booth, opposite another man with dark hair. After ordering a half a pint of beer, Rose made his way to the adjoining booth, as Lewis was fortunately facing the other way.

As he sat down on the long wooden seat of his booth, Rose got a quick look at the man opposite Lewis. He was handsome in a boyish way, wearing a sports jacket and looking as if he was in his early thirties at most. The man momentarily glanced back at Rose before going out of view.

Lewis and the man were speaking in hushed tones, but Rose thought that he might be able to make out some of what they said with some effort, as the pub was also quiet.

"But you promised," said Lewis.

"I tried, Oscar, I really did."

Rose couldn't understand what Lewis said next, but the other man's voice was slightly louder.

"It's just too risky, Oscar. Pauline would suspect something."

"I don't know why you married her in the first place," said Lewis, his voice a little sullen and unlike his usual cheerful tone.

"I had to keep up appearances for God's sake, you know that."

"Indeed, I do, but I can't wait forever, Mark. I just won't be able to bear it."

And with that, Lewis stood up and walked past Rose's booth and out of the pub. Rose sighed with relief.

The other man, who was tall and athletic, got up and left a few minutes later.

Rose looked at his wristwatch and saw he had another hour before he had to meet Mr Leadbetter. He surmised that Lewis would want a lift back to Sunnyside too now, as it sounded like his plans had been dashed.

But Rose now knew that Oscar Lewis couldn't be Dorothy's beau, the 'O' who signed the note in the box. It was obvious to Rose that the ex-bowler batted for the other side.

23

It had started out in the Stab on a Friday lunchtime, and ended on a muggy Tuesday morning in July 1934, in a warehouse near the East India Docks in East London.

Rose's stock, having recently earned his dubious sobriquet of the Hack from Hell for breaking a major story about an occult ring for the *Herald*, had never been so high in Fleet Street.

But that all changed that mid-morning when he and Bobby Martin woke up, both now hatless, among palettes of packing crates, with violent avalanches falling within their heads, their suit jackets, and loosened ties crusty with dried bile. The hair of a pack of dogs that bit them couldn't have made their headaches go away.

Once they'd managed to pick themselves up and walk to Canning Town underground station, a newspaper boy at his stand outside confirmed that it was the start of the working week for most, and Rose and Martin realised that their bender had lost them four days.

And when Martin handed over a penny for a copy of the *Daily Mail* and they saw the front-page splash, it all came rushing back, along with the painful knowledge that they were in serious trouble.

Arthur Cranfield, the assistant editor of the *Daily Mail*, who they both knew a little, would be licking his ever-moistening lips at their headline, they well knew- 'Arrest in Trunk Murder Mystery No 2- Man with the Scar Found in London After All Night Search'.

While their own editor on the *Herald*, Will Stevenson, a mild Welshman but with the quietly steely backbone of somebody who had once worked the seam down the pits, would be less than pleased, as the ever-understated Bobby Martin put it to Rose as they caught a tube train into the centre of London to face the music, which Rose knew could well be Mahler's Symphony No 1, the Funeral March.

Rose and Martin had been in the Stab the previous Friday, enjoying a couple of chasers before lunch, when they got the police tipoff about Tony Mancini, a man whose girlfriend Violette Kaye's body had been found in a trunk in his lodgings in the seaside town of Brighton, not far from London.

The off-duty Sergeant had come into the pub to find them, earning himself a crisp tenner for the advance gen that Mancini was being sought. They'd then called their news-desk, who'd got the go-ahead from the news editor to get down to Brighton pronto to find Mancini and speak to him for a scoop before he was pulled in for questioning.

But Mancini was the 'man with a scar' who had just been arrested in London, and the fact that it was on their own patch was even more troubling for Rose and Martin. But what made it a double-barrelled nightmare was that they'd been primed for this scoop, having already been sent down to Brighton the previous month to look into another woman's body found in a trunk there, that one cut up and unidentified, her killer not found.

Now they had to face their editor, and they knew that they were in for the high jump. And all this with a grade one hangover, the kind that required rest, loving care, or a swift resumption of liquid intake. Not that they dared sneak in a snifter of brandy on the way to their respective homes to have a quick wash and change of clothes before going on to the *Herald's* offices, no matter how much they wanted one.

In the end, it was brief but brutal, for Rose anyway. On the tube, they'd decided to come spring-clean about the drinking spree, as they were supposed to telephone in once a day at least but tried to soften their landing by saying that they'd been drinking with a contact in Brighton to gather information on Mancini's whereabouts.

And Rose had offered to take the larger share of responsibility for their missing four days- Bobby Martin was a little older and had two children to feed, while he had none. So, Rose told Stevenson that Martin had tried to tear him away from the pubs in which they drank in Brighton, but that he'd insisted that they keep drinking with his 'man.'

In fact, there was no contact in Brighton, and they'd never left London, as far as they knew.

Rose was immediately dismissed from the *Herald* that day for having 'missed his man while inebriated', and Bobby Martin was demoted to the subbing room for almost a year before being made a reporter again, hardly a teetotal, but not a drunk anymore.

Rose immediately knew that the drink had caused him to lose his job, but he had to admit to himself that he and Martin had allowed the drinking to happen. He'd floundered jobless and antsy for over a year, staying away from pubs, until Flanagan had eventually hired him for *Travesties* on a firm promise that he'd keep his drinking in check, the tale of his firing having made the rounds of Fleet Street.

He'd never been on a bender since, but the welcoming shadow of the bottle still loomed sinister in his mind at times.

But try as he might, Rose could never recall what he and Bobby Martin had done aside from drinking, and where they had been during those four lost days, between sitting in the Stab and waking up on that cold warehouse floor miles away, while Tony Mancini went to ground in the same city.

Mancini was acquitted of his prostitute and ex-dancer girlfriend's murder while Rose was on the dole, but Rose had always thought him guilty.

*

When keeping control of my environment in North, I take a measured approach, but it's different from the one taken by *them*. In my book, the punishment shouldn't fit the crime, but the culprit.

And with my limited resources at Shadowside, I need to be imaginative in providing suitable correction.

For instance, Mr Strickland the mathematics master really has no idea how to teach his subject, but he has his uses. The minutely squared graph paper he issues serves as a fine punishment for Overton and Sherwood-Ames.

You see, both have terrible eyesight and wear milk bottle glasses, so when they have to colour in alternate squares, starting a new page again if they should cross the printed line with ever-blunter red pencils, it truly is a worthy penalty.

It would be an even more perfect punishment for the Cyclops- I'd pay a few shillings to see him cover the graph paper one-eyed, but he's best left alone face-to-face.

And when Wallace, the least athletic as well as dirtiest boy in North has to run-if you can call his waddle that- down the cliff to the beach three miles there and back to bring me some seaweed as proof of arrival there, he won't ever forget it.

Like many who are slovenly, Wallace thinks he's cleverer than he is. Yesterday when I ordered him down to collect more at four in the morning for talking after lights out, he presented me with what seemed like a fine specimen after breakfast.

But Wallace's scheme was ruined when Kirby the grasshopper informed me that two weeks ago, when I sent Wallace on his bracing quest for seaweed, he gathered a supply and then soaked it in cold water with some salt pilfered from the dining hall.

Nobody likes a grass, and Kirby will still drill hard for oil next time he soils his bed, but that water-baby did the right thing for once, and I sent Wallace back to the seashore early this morning, where he will return every morning for a week to pay his penance.

I'd just accepted the beetroot-faced Wallace's latest offering and made my way in the direction of the library, stopping on the way to admire the Indian vulture once again on his perch, when I saw Dr Sharland and Mr Rose coming up the main stairs together.

They walked silently away from me, down the corridor past South, towards Mr Dodwell's office. It had to be there, as Dr Sharland surely wouldn't be taking the scribbler to the Cavendish Wing?

There was little point following them, as I would hear nothing outside at the keyhole, as Mr Dodwell's office is behind his secretary's room at the front of the building.

But I had to wonder what was afoot as I saw them disappear around the corner.

*

Rose was still trying to work out who 'O' could be after ruling out Oscar Lewis, but his concentration was interrupted by a new and unwelcome development.

He knew that something was wrong as Dr Sharland had been acting very detached towards him in his office that morning. Not that the doctor was ever particularly one for bonhomie, but there was now a marked coldness to his manner.

"We have a meeting with Mr Dodwell presently," he said.

"May I ask what about?"

"You'll find out soon enough."

Without another word he led Rose out into the corridor and through the double doors, then up the stairs to the first floor. Past the mysterious Cavendish Wing, where Rose had had an uncomfortable encounter with a member of its staff on his last visit to the principal's office.

After knocking on the outer door, Rose saw that Mrs Furnival the secretary was at her desk.

"Mr Dodwell is expecting you both. Please go straight through," she said.

"Thank you," said Dr Sharland, who gave a courtesy knock and received the expected 'Come in.'

Mr Dodwell was seated behind his desk as last time, and Mrs Benson was in front to his left in the blue chair.

"Please take a seat," said Mr Dodwell, firmly as ever, and both men did, in markedly less comfortable wooden chairs to the right of the large desk.

"This isn't a pleasant meeting I'm afraid, Mr Rose. The last time you were here I told you to tread carefully, I remember, which you have obviously ignored. I'll come straight to the point- Mrs Benson and Dr Sharland have been telling me that they have been made aware that you have been upsetting a female resident," said Mr Dodwell.

"Isabel Haarman? Is that what she told you?" said Rose, equally bluntly.

"Perhaps Mrs Benson could tell us the details."

"Isabel had a breakdown late last night and began hitting her head against the wooden headboard of her bed. I rushed and stopped her as I was on duty in South, but she managed to badly bruise her forehead," said Mrs Benson.

"And then I was called," said Dr Sharland, "and I found Isabel in a hysterical state, with the tremens. I had to sedate her with morphine- the first time that I've administered drugs to her since her arrival. And we have little choice but to put her on a long-term drug treatment from tomorrow…"

"We don't like to medicate residents unless absolutely necessary," said Mr Dodwell, suddenly. "We prefer a non-medicated approach at Sunnyside."

"Indeed, we severely limit the use of Luminal and other barbiturates, as well as various other invasive procedures. So, this will be an extremely negative change in Isabel's treatment plan, as she had been making steady progress," said Dr Sharland.

"Could you tell Mr Rose how you learned he had been harassing the girl, Mrs Benson?" said Mr Dodwell.

"I hardly think I've harassed her," said Rose, his voice raised a little.

"Oh, but you have terribly," said Mrs Benson. "According to Caitlin Whitaker-Davies, you ambushed Isabel at the stables during her Trust Time."

"Forgive me, but I hardly think I ambushed her- I merely went to see her there and asked her a few questions."

"Which has completely disturbed her equilibrium. You've set her back months, I'm afraid," said Dr Sharland.

"Thank you, Mrs Benson, that will be all for now," said Mr Dodwell.

"Anything to protect the residents in my charge," said Mrs Benson, rather too smugly as she smiled at Mr Dodwell, making Rose feel like a predator as she left the room.

There was a pause before Mr Dodwell spoke again.

"I've a good mind to ask you to leave Sunnyside immediately, but then I know why you are here. Have you made any progress in learning what happened to Dorothy Hopkins in the last weeks? You certainly haven't reported anything to me, as I requested of you."

"I have nothing solid yet," said Rose. "But I know that Isabel, the girl closest to Dorothy, is terrified of something, and I truly believe it's about Dorothy."

"Do you have any proof of that?" said Mr Dodwell.

"No- it's just a gut feeling- my instinct just tells me."

"We don't work by instinct here, we go only on facts," said Dr Sharland.

"And *my instinct* is, as I mentioned before, to tell you to leave Sunnyside at once," said Mr Dodwell, "but I'm going to give you one more chance. Providing you leave all residents alone and have no contact with them whatsoever- I mean whatsoever- you can stay and see what you can find out about Dorothy."

"Thank you," said Rose, like a little boy, apologising for nothing except for his presence.

"And Dr Sharland, I'd like you to try to find out what is at the root of Isabel Haarman's disturbance, as well as keeping a close eye on Mr Rose here."

"I certainly will do both," said Dr Sharland, before turning to Rose rather menacingly "you can be sure of that."

"That's settled then. I hope that the next time I see you in this office you will be telling me what happened to Dorothy Hopkins, Mr Rose. Thank you for coming both of you," said Mr Dodwell.

The atmosphere was very taut as Rose followed Dr Sharland out of the room, past Mrs Furnival and out into the corridor, and it remained that way as they walked in silence until they reached the bottom of the main stairs.

"I won't be requiring you for the rest of the day. But do take care and stay away from the residents," said Dr Sharland

Rose gave him a solemn shrug, as Dr Sharland smoothed down his white coat before walking back through the double doors towards his own office.

Rose now knew that he would have to find another way to approach Isabel- it was imperative or Dorothy's whereabouts could remain a troubling enigma.

*

I do my best thinking on the mound but lying in bed in my section I can still think clearly. I don't dream, I never have. There's no need to when you control the thoughts of those sleeping around you.

I know that all the boys in North are afraid of me and I will be in their nightmares often. Kirby always wets his bed at night after I've given him a look, Johnson-Pitt has said my name aloud while asleep more than once and drilled for oil for it, and

Reed stammers only when he speaks to me, just like Dorothy stammered when talking to anyone apart from me.

You see, I've known from a very early age that the whole world has a will for power, and it's up to me to seize it and spread my influence, or *they* will use *their* power over me.

My mother couldn't handle me, and neither can anyone here. My rise at Shadowside began one day in the Great Hall when I was twelve years old.

When that charlatan Rev Barnes read that Proverb from the King James Bible in assembly, I knew I had to do something.

That was over four years ago now, and the words still burn into me.

"Do not withhold correction from a child, for if you beat him with a rod he will not die," he said.

It was everything that I stand against- *they* are the oppressors- keeping me in line when for as long as I can remember I've known that my destiny is to set that line.

Latimer agreed with me, and we made sure that Rev Barnes and *they* suffered, with those three imbecile sycophants who got charred getting what they deserved too.

As Machiavelli said, 'it is far better to be feared than loved if you cannot be both.' Once others thought that I was involved in the chapel fire, I had their attention and fear- it's not difficult to gain such power at a place like Shadowside, where whispers become the word.

And as well as power, I now I have Dorothy's love and I will have my boy's love too. But while their love is unconditional, power must be maintained.

Just like the boys at Red Circle School in my bloods, I won't stand by and watch *them* abuse me. But I'm past that make-believe stuff now- this is real life and I deal with every obstacle I face, just as the Red Baron did when he had *them* in his sights.

I make things happen, I always have- while others remain in line, I define my own line, just as my father did his whole life, before he opted out. Just as Lawrence Drummond did, after he had asserted himself over the weak and lost. The powerful will inherit the Earth, no matter what Rev Barnes may say.

Nobody will dictate my future- I won't let that happen. And if anybody gets in my way, may his or her God have mercy upon their soul.

*

Rose was contemplating approaching Isabel again at the stables that afternoon, as he walked in through the main doors of Sunnyside.

His destination was Dr Sharland's office for his morning check-in, and he was just passing the marble stairs when Carstairs appeared once again, coming through the double doors.

"Good morning, Mr Rose."

"How are you Carstairs?"

"Fine and dandy, sir." But the boy's expression and voice were as emotionless as usual.

"Do you have classes today?"

Before Carstairs could answer, the double doors opened behind them, and Mrs Benson appeared.

"Mr Rose, you know that you shouldn't be talking to the residents. Off you go now Carstairs."

"Yes, ma'am," said Carstairs, as he meekly walked away and back through the doors, head down.

"Please don't let me see you engaging with the residents again, Mr Rose, it truly is to their detriment, and Mr Dodwell would *not* be pleased."

And Rose knew from observing her that Mrs Benson wanted to please Mr Dodwell more than anything else.

She walked up the stairs, while Rose followed Carstairs through the double doors, resuming his route to Dr Sharland's office, his wrist very firmly slapped.

*

I saw her walk from South and through the door of the library after Wednesday morning break, during which we return to our sections.

I hadn't gone back to North but was waiting seated on the large wooden window ledge outside the staffroom to see Mr Lewis. He wanted to talk to me about his game plan for the big rugger sevens match against Denton coming up in a fortnight.

204

Naturally, I'm his captain, and Mr Lewis is lucky to have me. Denton's boys are older and mostly bigger than us, and we need strong leadership. And Mr Lewis hardly provides that.

But my plans changed when I sighted Isabel, my eyes following her down the corridor. I positioned myself in the alcove outside the library, the very one where me and Dorothy used to meet, which seemed fitting somehow.

After standing there looking out onto the quad for more than sixteen minutes, I knew I'd missed Mr Lewis's poor tactics briefing. Then Isabel came back out of the library.

She saw me immediately and tried to get away, turning quickly on her heels to get back to South, but I was too fast and cornered her, corralling her back into the alcove like a cowboy his cattle in my bloods.

If eyes really are the windows to your soul, then Isabel's were shuttered, all life gone from them now, as if she were in a trance. The expression on her face was pained, but just not desperate enough for my high standards.

That's when I knew that no more words would do, and action was needed. So, after looking around to make sure nobody was nearby, I pushed her into the wall, held her there with my left hand at arm's length, before moving closer and pressing my right fist into her right cheekbone.

I pushed her against the wall hard, screwing my fist into her cheekbone, grinding her head against the cold wall, pushing it in tighter and tighter. There was no way she could move, as if she were in a vice.

There was no sound from her, not even a murmur- it was as if she was unable to use her voice anymore. But tears were trickling from her eyes.

After kneading my knuckles into her pale skin for just over three minutes, the same length of time it had taken Dorothy to die, I released her, and she almost fell over with the sudden freedom of movement.

There was a red mark on her cheekbone. That would vanish within the hour, leaving no trace of physical contact, but the emotional damage would be permanent.

As she scampered away, almost slipping on the geometric-patterned floor in her frightened haste, I went into the library to improve my knowledge, my task completed.

*

When Rose saw the Wolseley pull into the main courtyard and a detective and two constables stepped out of it, he knew it was serious.

She'd been gone since Wednesday night- nobody had seen her. Dorothy had been missing for over six weeks, but Isabel was found within twelve hours.

It was Mr Tucker who discovered her body that early Thursday morning while he was doing his daily rounds around the grounds.

She was floating face-down in the large pond in front of the terrace at the back of the main building. He'd thrown off his key chain and pulled off his scuffed boots, jumping into the almost freezing, stagnant water.

"She looked so calm once I got her out," said Mr Tucker over a pint of beer at the Golden Bell the following evening. "As if she was at rest."

For a moment Rose thought of Ophelia in *Hamlet*, who after becoming insane, drowned herself in a brook- not as she'd been imagined in the painting by Millais, floating on her back with a wistful look on her face, flowers scattered around her. Aside from the fact that Isabel was floating on her front, Rose had seen that pond and only weeds would have surrounded her in there.

Rose was concerned that if foul play had been involved there may have been a perverted motive, one which he'd seen to terrible effect when reporting on the case of little Vera Page five years earlier in his *Herald* days.

"Was she fully clothed?" he finally said.

"Yes, she was wearing a blue dress and a coat, a heavy coat, it must have weighed her down, and then there were the stones in her pockets."

That didn't necessarily mean that Isabel had killed herself, Rose knew only too well. The placing of stones or rocks in pockets was common in drowning suicides, but he'd once covered a case where a man had battered his business partner to

206

death and then thrown him into the Thames near Greenwich, weighted down with bags of coin, an ironic touch as the motive had been financial.

"Did you see any injuries or bruises on her?"

"There was a dark bruise on her forehead," said Mr Tucker soberly, as he took a long swig of his beer. "And she had a patch of hair missing on her head. Apart from that, she was very pale, very cold to the touch and a little bloated, that's all."

Rose knew that the bruise had been caused by Isabel herself hitting her forehead against her bed in South, but he had no idea why she had hair missing. He could however see that the usually impassive Mr Tucker was deeply troubled by what had happened and asked him if he'd like another drink.

"I really must be going now," he said, and stood up, nodding to Rose and a few faces around him as he left the pub, the barman calling "Mind how you go, Lionel."

Everybody knew about Lionel Tucker finding Isabel's body- it had been the front-page splash in the *Milston Argus*, the article explaining that the police were busy investigating, but Rose already knew that of course.

Rose sat there alone, the fire crackling in the corner, no longer a total outsider, the other customers having lost interest in him as an invading curiosity. And when he stood up to leave, he got a nod himself from the man with an eye which looked in the other direction, although he still had no idea what he was called.

Rose felt terrible too, or terribly guilty. What if Mr Dodwell, Dr Sharland, and Mrs Benson were right and he'd put too much pressure on Isabel? He could well be morally responsible for her death. But he'd tried to be sensitive to Isabel, he really had.

*

Rose was truly shaken by Isabel's passing and how unnecessary it was for such a young girl to die, perhaps by her own hand. But he had to press on- he felt a real urgency within him now, to find Dorothy wherever she was, especially as he was sure that Isabel's death and that of Mr Bannister before it were linked in some way.

He'd been meaning to visit the library again ever since Caitlin, Dorothy, and Isabel's neighbour in South, had

207

mentioned that Dorothy had been reading the book *Little Women* there in the days before her disappearance.

As often when working on a story, Rose didn't know exactly what he was looking for, but he had to retrace Dorothy's last individual movements at Sunnyside as much as he could.

He'd never read the book himself, and Rose wondered if the story could give some clue as to what Dorothy was thinking in those days leading up to the 21st of November when she left her section after lights out.

A group of seven uniformed young boys were sitting at the biggest table quietly reading from storybooks when Rose entered, with no master in sight. He guessed that they were from the East wing, and they barely looked up at him. As he'd often thought when he saw them, the children at Sunnyside were the calmest and most disciplined he'd ever seen.

Rose walked around, unable to stop himself giving the old globe a slight twirl as he passed it, causing a creak which made a couple of the boys look up at him, at which he shrugged an apology in reply.

Looking at the labels on the shelf, he saw that the fiction books were arranged by wing, so obviously by age and gender. He assumed that a book that Dorothy was reading would be within her wing, so went straight to the three shelves labelled 'Novels: South'.

And there it was, at the far left of the first shelf, alphabetical by author, *Little Women* by Louisa M Alcott. The cover was bright yellow, with a girl in Victorian clothes wearing a bonnet and looking wistfully upwards, and the spine carried the words 'the famous book that has made a famous film' below the author's name.

There were three copies, all the same, with 'H&S Yellow Jacket' embossed on them, all quite new, published just three years earlier, and obviously bought for the library together. Rose took all three off the shelf, and single copies of two other books by Alcott, *Little Men* and *Jo's Boys* fell flat on the shelf with a thud, the East boys looking up and Rose shrugging once again.

Rose lowered himself carefully and noiselessly into a leather upright chair by the window, and began to look at the books, not knowing which one Dorothy had been reading.

Not much of a reader apart from the news, Rose forced himself to begin reading- "'Christmas won't be Christmas without any presents," grumbled Jo, lying on the rug. "It's so dreadful to be poor!" sighed Meg, looking down at her old dress.'

He managed to read the first two pages, wondering if he would be able to finish the book and how long it would take him, when he noticed something slightly sticking out of the pages of one of the other copies of the book.

He changed copies, and on opening the second one at page one-hundred-and-forty-nine, a piece of paper fell to the floor, which he quickly picked up. He knew that Dorothy could've left it there. And then a voice interrupted his thoughts.

"I didn't take you for a *Little Women* type." It was Mr Leadbetter, standing there looking pleased with himself.

"Oh, I like to read all sorts," said Rose, his face feeling a little flushed, a sensation he'd rarely felt since he was a boy and was caught doing something by his parents, which would then soon turn to fear. Now, he just felt embarrassed, as he was sure he looked very unlike the average Alcott reader.

"Well, and why not I suppose? I won't disturb your enjoyment." And with that, Mr Leadbetter moved off towards the big table, checking on the boys from East.

Rose looked down at the piece of paper, not quite daring to read it yet, but he could see that it was an article, which had been ripped out of a magazine.

He returned to reading the book, but now he was pretending, as his only interest was in the article in his lap. As soon as Mr Leadbetter left the library, he picked it up and started reading.

It was obviously an article from a magazine or journal for women, entitled 'Childbirth and Nurture,' giving advice to pregnant women! He scanned down and saw the subheadings 'Twilight Sleep Pain Relief,' 'Forceps Delivery',' Cleanliness,' 'Good Nutrition,' 'Maternity Apparel'…

Rose put down the article, realising that Dorothy's obsession with having a baby had remained as strong as ever in the days before she disappeared, so much so that she was secretly reading up on maternity advice.

But then Rose's face became flushed again, this time with shock, the hairs on his neck also raised. And both his heart and mind were racing...Dorothy *was* pregnant!!!...she'd finally got what she'd so long craved...that was why she'd disappeared, it had to be...and where could she have gone to have a bastard child, to shield herself from being shamed and shunned by others...

Rose understood the ostracism that Dorothy would face, much more than most. But then his understanding was clouded by the Brethren's influence, still within him from childhood, even though he didn't believe it anymore.

He remembered his mother and father around the dining room table, quoting the scripture from Deuteronomy, that a bastard child, one born out of wedlock was forever cursed, along with its' parents and descendants. But even outside the Brethren, many people would judge Dorothy and whoever the father was very badly.

Then a terrible feeling came over Rose, his hands becoming clammy, as another revelation having hit him. The bracelet, which Dorothy never took off, which was now in his possession...was Dorothy still alive, and if she wasn't, what had happened to her baby...had it been born, or had it perished too? He could only hope that she and her baby were safe somewhere, away from Sunnyside.

But if she were pregnant, why had Caitlin told him that Dorothy had been withdrawn in her last days, after a period of elation? Why had Dorothy begged her mother to take her away from Sunnyside on that last Sunday visit before she disappeared, as Mrs Hopkins had told him and Flanagan?

As Dorothy had been desperate to have a baby to mother for so long, why would she have been so tense before she vanished? What or whom was she so frightened of that it affected her whole bearing?

Rose pocketed the article, placed the three books back on their shelf, and after leaving the library, he walked down the corridor, trying to compose himself.

But his brain kept turning the same question over again and again- Who was the father of Dorothy's child? If he could identify the father, he could probably find Dorothy.

Part IV

Cracked

24

Shadowside hasn't been so alive with activity since Dorothy died, and everybody seems to be blowing their wig.

I saw the same police detective in his grey coat and matching trilby along with two plods in the main courtyard yesterday morning, greeted by the snivelling Mr Leadbetter and taken inside. I don't think he'll be asking to see me this time somehow.

It's fitting that Isabel ended up floating in the pond like a piece of random debris as she was always just flotsam and jetsam, useless and unwanted, a momentary snag in my current.

We were all confined to sections from after breakfast until dinner time yesterday, but today's another day. It's Saturday, and we can move around the building now, although not go outside, but here on the mound there are no rules anyway of course.

It was easy enough to get here after breakfast, lowering myself out of the washroom window and on to the roof, and then jumping to the ground, the same route I took to meet Dorothy on her final night here.

The sun keeps trying to break cover and take control of the sky today, but the clouds are too strong for it, as if I were the clouds and the sun Isabel before she met her watery maker.

*

Rose was managing to endure a very cold wet shave when the knock came.

He rushed downstairs tieless and with braces hanging, but whoever it was triple rapped firmly twice more before he opened the cottage door to see Dr Sharland standing there, his face emotionless.

"Mr Dodwell and Inspector Alexander wish to see you Mr Rose."

"The police want to see me- about Isabel?"

Dr Sharland didn't answer the question when he spoke.

"They're waiting for us in Mr Dodwell's office *now*."

213

"Let me just get my coat if you would."

Rose went through to the kitchen, adjusted his clothes, then reached up to where his hat and coat were hanging on the back of the slatted wooden door and grabbed them, putting them on in the small hallway as Dr Sharland looked on.

There was no apology from Dr Sharland about it being a Saturday, his once courteous manner now replaced by a marked detachment. Shutting and locking the door behind him, Rose placed the key as always in the mouth of the ornamental stone dog just outside.

I heard their footsteps before the scribbler's voice got closer...

"I do hope that you know that I never hounded Isabel at all-she was already in a very bad way."

I stayed statue-like and listened to the one-way conversation as they passed the mound.

"She knew something about Dorothy, and it frightened her."

There was still no answer from the dangerous quack as they walked out of earshot towards the main building.

I could see that Mr Rose was still a potential thorn in my side, and my little box implicating the Cyclops seemed to have had no discernible impact.

They were halfway up the main stairs before Dr Sharland spoke.

"Just tell them the truth, it'll be best for you in the long run."

"That's exactly what I have been doing."

They passed the doors of the Cavendish Wing, Rose preparing himself for whatever was coming, but he was sure it was about Isabel, it just had to be.

Dr Sharland gave the same triple knock on Mr Dodwell's outer door, but Mrs Furnival didn't answer. Instead, within seconds the principal himself appeared.

"Please come through," said Mr Dodwell.

This time a bogey, what Rose and everyone in Fleet Street and much of the underworld called a police detective, was sitting in the blue upright chair.

"This is Inspector Alexander," said Mr Dodwell, looking at Rose intently.

"Mr Rose," said Inspector Alexander holding out his hand, which Rose accepted and shook.

"The inspector wants to ask you a few questions," said Mr Dodwell, waiting for the policeman to sit down again before taking his own seat. Once again, Rose and Dr Sharland were in the uncomfortable wooden chairs, which suited the atmosphere.

"I understand that you spoke to Isabel Haarman on the day before her death, and she became very distressed," said Inspector Alexander.

"She was already a bundle of nerves before I spoke to her," said Rose.

"That's why she's at Sunnyside," said Dr Sharland.

"Quite," said Mr Dodwell.

Rose could see there was a pincer movement operating against him.

"Could I ask why you wanted to speak to Isabel, and what you said to her?" said Inspector Alexander.

"After a specific warning to stay away from her and all residents," said Dr Sharland.

"I believed, and still do, that Isabel knew something about the disappearance of Dorothy Hopkins," said Rose.

"And what made you think that?" said the policeman.

"The fact that she was Dorothy's closest acquaintance here, and her very jumpy demeanour when I first met her with Dr Sharland present."

"That was quite normal for Isabel, I'm afraid. When she first came here, she was suffering from what was once called acute mania but which we now call severe hypertension," said Dr Sharland.

"What did you say to her?" said Inspector Alexander.

"I asked her what she was holding back about Dorothy."

"And her response?"

"She told me nothing and became agitated."

"And her state of mind deteriorated to panic in the following hours, by the time I saw her that evening," said Dr Sharland.

"Do you think that Isabel Haarman died by her own hand, Mr Rose?" said Inspector Alexander.

"I'm keeping an open mind on that for now, as I hope you are too," said Rose.

215

The policeman looked at Rose, running his finger over his lips as he did so, before speaking.

"I've experienced problems with the press before, on a local level of course."

"I didn't go in hard on Isabel- I was gentle with her," said Rose.

"But she still committed suicide soon after you spoke to her," said Mr Dodwell.

"Perhaps she took her own life," said Rose.

"I fear you overstepped the mark here, Mr Rose, and I must warn you to stay away from police enquiries, regarding both Dorothy Hopkins and Isabel Haarman," said Inspector Alexander.

Mr Dodwell interceded before Rose could defend his ever-decreasing corner.

"And Mrs Benson informed me recently that she had seen you talking to Oliver Carstairs from the North wing too, it seems that you have a problem staying away from our residents."

"But Carstairs approached me," said Rose.

"That doesn't mean that you can have conversations with the boy, though, does it? Anyway, there won't be any more chances for Mr Rose to interfere with police inquiries, Inspector, as he will be leaving Sunnyside tomorrow morning, and will not be welcome within the grounds again."

"But…"

"There's no point in trying to change my mind, Mr Rose. Against my better judgement, I let you in here to try to find some answers about Dorothy, with her psychiatrists Dr Sanderson and Dr Sharland here vouching for you, but it just hasn't worked out, and it's resulted in a girl's death," said Mr Dodwell with finality.

"I must agree that your presence here has become detrimental to the treatment of residents," said Dr Sharland.

"I require you to leave the premises tomorrow morning," said Mr Dodwell. "Good day to you now."

Rose knew that further protest was pointless and stood up to leave.

"Mr Tucker will come to your cottage at half past eleven tomorrow morning and pick up your keys and Dr Sharland will arrange a taxi for you from the main courtyard at a quarter to twelve. Goodbye now."

Inspector Alexander sat silently, scribbling something down in his open notebook as Rose left the room and found himself out in the corridor and out on his ear.

But he had taken something useful from the meeting- it was Carstairs' first name, Oliver. And he had dark blonde hair, matching the lock in the box. Could he be Dorothy's lover, 'O'?

*

His goose now well overcooked at Sunnyside, Rose spent the rest of that day wandering around the place, trying to find Carstairs, very aware that his time there was now extremely limited. But for a boy who often seemed to appear out of nowhere when you least expected him to, there was no sight of him, to Rose's deep frustration.

And then, just after five o'clock, when he was about to give up and go back to his cottage, and he was just coming up to the bird cabinets at the top of the marble stairs, he saw Carstairs there, gazing into the glass.

"Hello Carstairs."

"Good evening, sir."

"I was wondering if you knew the girl from North who disappeared, Dorothy Hopkins?"

"I can't say I did, sir. I saw her around sometimes, but I never spoke to her."

There wasn't a hint of emotion betrayed on Carstairs's honest face and his voice was as slow and monotonous as usual. Rose, who'd met many guilty people and some innocent ones, believed him.

"Do you speak to any of the girls from South?"

"No, never, Mr Rose. They don't understand me, I'm afraid."

"Females are often a mystery to me too, Carstairs."

The boy gazed into the glass of the cabinet again.

"Do you like the birds?" said Rose.

"I like to look at them sometimes, sir. Most people here don't seem to like them, but I do. So does Edwin."

217

"Edwin?" said Rose, surprised at Carstairs saying that name, one that Rose now knew well.

"Yes, Edwin Castleton. He's in the same wing as me. He spends a lot of time staring at the Indian vulture, almost as if he's looking for something, sir."

"Really? The Indian vulture?"

"Yes, sir."

"What do you think he's looking for?"

"I don't know sir, but he only ever looks at the Indian vulture, as if its' special for some reason."

"That's strange," said Rose.

"I suppose it is, sir. I must go now, sir- dinner's at half-past in the dining hall. But I'd be happy to show you sometime."

"Enjoy your meal, Carstairs. Goodbye now."

"Goodbye, sir."

Rose knew that there was something about the Indian vulture and Edwin's fascination with it that needed proper investigation.

But there was too great a chance of being seen by somebody at that time, so he'd have to come back later when all was quiet.

25

By the time Rose got close to Sunnyside's main building, it was almost ten to eleven at night.

He remembered that Mr Tucker locked the main doors at eleven o'clock every night and opened them again at six o'clock in the morning, so unless he found another way in or got locked in all night, he'd have to wait until the next day.

Finding an open or faulty window was unlikely, he thought, as security had been tightened since Dorothy's disappearance and the place was virtually in lockdown after lights out now following Isabel's death, as both girls seemed to have left their sections in South on the nights they departed, but nobody knew how they had got out of the main building.

Breaking a window was another option, although with Mr Dodwell having put him on a final warning on threat of being banished from the premises, Rose decided against that.

Mr Tucker usually appeared from the grounds at five minutes before the hour to pull the big bolts across the doors, so he had a few minutes to get inside and hide and wasted no more time in doing so.

It was pin-drop silent as he walked briskly across the chequered floor in the main corridor, past the portraits of the Drummond family now eerily shrouded in the gloomy light, and then up the main marble stairs, where Bernard Bannister had met his death just a few months earlier.

At the top of the stairs, walking past the bird cabinets, he made for the shadow of the alcove outside the library, and within a minute of getting there, the rattling of the rusty bolts thundered through the air as Mr Tucker performed his last duty of the day downstairs, the final shudders of metal meeting metal sounding like billiard balls being pocketed, but much louder.

Rose stood there, looking out of the window onto the main quad below, and then at the facing tower opposite which he had seen twitching boys being forced to abseil down a few weeks earlier when he first arrived.

After several minutes with no sound except wind on windowpanes, he moved just a few steps to his right. It was near-dark, the corridor's lights now all out, but with some glow offered from the electric lanterns overlooking the nearby stairs which had been left on, and he assumed, always were at night.

Directly in front of him, Rose saw the beginning of what he was looking for, and slowly walked down the corridor back towards the stairs, looking to his left with every step.

It was the bird cabinets he was interested in, and the glistening of pairs of narrow-set eyes like marbles in the dark sent a chill through him, additional to the already cold and draughty air.

He reached into his coat pocket and pulled out the brass Zippo lighter which a fellow hack from his *Herald* days had brought back from America for him the previous October, causing great excitement in the Stab as nobody else at the bar had seen one before.

He knew from looking at the stuffed bird displays in daylight that the exotic birds came first, and the 'Domestic Species' were closest to the main stairs. He flipped back the top of the Zippo and flicking the wheel, making the wick ignite, the smell of petrol rising immediately.

The diluted light from the lanterns and the close illumination offered by the lighter enabled him to just about read the labels. It wasn't long before he came upon the Indian vulture.

It had a long bill and a huge wingspan, its' pale feathers darker on the wings, and angry eyes that drilled into you. Rose was mentally holding his breath as he shone the Zippo towards the forbidding-looking bird on display,

He pulled at the cabinet door, hoping that he wouldn't have to break into the ornate Victorian case, and was relieved when it slid stiffly open. And then he suddenly jolted, the lighter's flame flickering, but not going out.

It was more of a shriek than a murmur, a cry from the far end of the corridor, past the South Wing where Dorothy and Isabel had slept, in the direction of Mr Dodwell's office. Rose knew that otherwise only the Cavendish Wing could be found down there.

Then there was another longer high-pitched wail- it was difficult to tell if it was that of a child, man, or woman, but it certainly sounded as if somebody was in pain, frightened, or both.

Rose stood there, lighter still in his hand, shaking slightly. He stayed as still as he could, wondering if anybody would come running towards the desperate sound, but nobody did. But if it had come from the off-limits Cavendish Wing there would be staff in there to deal with it, he thought.

When about five minutes had passed, he decided to focus on the Indian vulture again. Moving the Zippo around the bird, its eyes looking directly into Rose's, he scanned around the perch and saw nothing. He had no idea what he was looking for but was sure that Isabel had been trying to draw his attention to that bird in particular- there just seemed no other explanation for her choice of words.

Then he held the lighter almost upside down and gazed at its mocked-up habitat just below. It seemed like a nest, not the kind you could see in gardens and parks, but in wilder domains, on faraway mountains and plains, he imagined. And this one had something shiny within it...

Moving closer, he moved the Zippo into his left hand, using his natural right hand to retrieve the object, a delicate operation with all the other bird displays just inches away.

He pulled it towards him, and having stepped back slightly from the cabinet, examined it under the lighter's very concentrated gleam. It was a wristwatch, yellow and white in colour, its face shattered, but with jewels and symbols in the Arabic style still discernible. And Rose could just make out the inscription on the dial.

Zenith

Favre-Leuba

It was Bernard Bannister's missing wristwatch, the one that had been repaired in Milston the previous year that he had been wearing when he died, but which had vanished.

The silver hands had stopped at two minutes to two o'clock, undoubtedly the time he fell down those cold marble stairs, less than fifteen yards from where Rose now stood.

221

Where could Edwin have got Bannister's watch? Had he taken it from his body before he was found? But Rose saw the obviously purloined smashed timepiece as near-proof that Bannister's fall hadn't been an accident, and he was sure that Edwin had put it there because of his obsession with the Indian vulture.

And if Edwin had killed Mr Bannister, had Isabel known? Also, if Dorothy was pregnant, had she told Isabel about it before she disappeared, and perhaps even who the father was?

Was that why Isabel had been so terrified, because of what she knew- had she felt in danger herself?

It also struck Rose that Bannister's probable murder and Dorothy's disappearance were more than likely linked in some way, but Isabel had taken whatever that link was with her now. Was the link Edwin?

Rose had no evidence that Isabel had left the box with the note, hair, and bracelet outside his cottage, but he still had the feeling that it was her. And if that were the case, Edwin couldn't have been Dorothy's lover or the father of her child, as his name didn't start with 'O.'

The various permutations of the puzzle consumed Rose until he suddenly remembered where he was, standing there at night in the dark corridor.

After he put the Zenith watch carefully in his inner jacket pocket and then placed the lighter back in his coat, Rose slid the cabinet door back into closed position and retreated back to the alcove, before trying the library door, which was surprisingly open.

He decided to wait the night out in there, until he could sneak back out when Mr Tucker unlocked the main doors again at six o'clock. In the meantime, sleep was impossible, as he came up with speculative answers to the multitude of urgent questions running through his mind.

But Rose was very aware that he only a few legitimate hours left at Sunnyside now. He felt thwarted, just as he seemed to be getting somewhere, but he would find a way back inside.

26

Rose also had something else to do before he left, and it wasn't to do with Dorothy.

He'd decided not to tell Flanagan about being banished from Sunnyside, as he'd only be recalled back to London to work on another story immediately. He only had a few days at most left anyway, but he resolved to continue trying to find the answer from outside until then.

Flanagan would want something on the Jack the Ripper story, and there was only one person he could think of to find out more about Lawrence Drummond's final days and whereabouts during the terrible killing spree- the Rev Barnes.

Rose was sure that Drummond was as likely to have been the infamous murderer as the Monkfish, who hadn't been born in 1888, and as unlikely too. But it was a story that Flanagan would want- a quest piece, like the one for Dorothy, although this time needing no resolution as the Jack the Ripper myth would be enough to sell the magazine.

He was still reeling after the attack by Mr Dodwell and Dr Sharland, partly from a sense of indignation that he was being unfairly persecuted. But he was also questioning in his mind whether he may have contributed to Isabel's death if it truly was a suicide, and because of this he did feel a sense of guilt.

Knowing that he had to hand over his keys to Mr Tucker and leave Sunnyside by taxi at a quarter to twelve, Rose arrived at the chapel just after ten in the morning hoping that the priest would be inside preparing for Sunday service the following day, knowing that as Rev Barnes wasn't a 'resident', he wasn't already pushing his luck in talking to him.

Rose walked through the now windswept but obviously well-tended graveyard and down the steps.

He heard a voice from inside the room- a boy's voice.

"Should I place the candlesticks on the altar, father?'

"Please do Master Kirby and remember to space them evenly apart."

It was a boy- he looked younger than Carstairs or Edwin and lacked the latter's confident presence. Kirby looked around when Rose walked down the aisle towards Rev Barnes, who had his back to him.

"I'm sorry to disturb you again, Father," said Rose.

Rev Barnes turned. "Not at all. What can I do for you, Mr ------?"

"Rose."

"Forgive me. Yes, I remember now, we spoke about the Drummond family."

"That's right. I just wondered if we could have another little chat about Lawrence Drummond?"

"Certainly. Master Kirby, perhaps you should be making your way back to your section now- it's past ten o'clock."

Kirby went red in the face, looking down at his feet.

"Go along now…and thank you for your help this morning."

Kirby walked slowly towards the door, obviously not wanting to leave.

"Poor boy- it seems like he's being bullied, but he'll never tell me by whom," said Rev Barnes.

"It can't be easy fitting in with the other boys at that age, all having different problems and needs too," said Rose.

"Especially in the North wing, it seems- several boys have told me about the hectoring that goes on in there."

Rose said nothing, realising that North was where Carstairs and Edwin lived too, but mentioning that he knew them so soon after being warned away from speaking to the children would be the act of a blind moth to a naked flame, as words were passed fast at Sunnyside.

"Please take a seat," said Rev Barnes as he carefully lowered himself onto a toffee-coloured pew.

"Thank you. I wondered if you could tell me something more about Lawrence Drummond's final months," said Rose, sitting down himself.

"May I ask why you are so interested in Mr Drummond?"

"Oh, just purely out of historical interest- I find the history of this place fascinating."

"It is a unique place. I'll help if I can."

"Did Lawrence Drummond spend any time in London during that final autumn before his death?"

Rev Barnes fell into thought for a moment. "No- Mr Drummond never left this area in the last five or six months of his life. He had deep melancholia and was under a doctor's treatment. He only ventured as far as Milston."

"Really- so he never left the local area?"

"Yes, I'm sure of that- and he probably only visited Milston a handful of times in the last months of his life. We saw him every day you see- he would walk around the grounds- he particularly liked the island in front of the main building and would stroll around that many times, deep within himself."

"I know the island you mean, it's near the cottage I'm staying in- I thought I saw something move within the undergrowth there a few weeks ago actually."

"Oh, I doubt any living thing would be amongst that tangled mess, unless a bird was rummaging in there perhaps. In Mr Drummond's day it was beautifully landscaped of course."

"I thought it must be my eyes playing pranks on me. You've been very helpful. Thank you," said Rose.

"I'm glad to be of help- you know Mr Baxter the History master has often asked me about the Drummond family too- they were a colourful bunch in their own way."

"They seemed to have been, by all accounts."

"I do hope that you'll be joining us for the service tomorrow, by the way. I haven't seen you worshipping here yet."

"I'm afraid that I won't be able to attend tomorrow, but I will try to make it soon," said Rose, lying on the job, but also fully aware that his ostracism from the grounds would thankfully have started by the time the chapel bell rang the next day anyway.

"I do hope so," said Rev Barnes. "We all need spiritual nourishment, you know."

Rose nodded but felt distinctively queasy- his father had given him enough 'nourishment' to last several lifetimes. He really did require rejuvenation of some sort, but it certainly wouldn't come from the church.

"Goodbye now," said Rose.

"God bless you."

225

As Rose made his way up the steps, he smiled bleakly to himself- the confirmation that Lawrence Drummond hadn't been Jack the Ripper, and was just Edwin's fantasy, would make no difference to Flanagan at all.

But if he were unable to get to the real truth about Dorothy very soon, he would be writing that lame story up for *Travesties*, and it would be all he had to show for his stay at Sunnyside too, having failed in his quest, and let down Mrs Hopkins too.

27

I'd just been up to the billiards room for the first time since I was in there with the scribbler, as I've had other things to do recently. I was peering out of North's upper window, thinking about the sleazy scribe, and having seen him walking along to Mr Dodwell's office with the deadly doctor, when who should appear beneath me in the main courtyard?

He was standing just in front of the main doors, a suitcase and what looked like a typewriter case by his side- it seemed that Mr Rose was taking a trip. Needing to know more, I left North quickly and made my way downstairs. We were still 'gated,' meaning that we couldn't leave the main building, but I knew there was no need to go outside.

Opposite the Great Hall, just to the right of the Drummond family portraits, is a small door which opens into a small cloakroom, very rarely utilised, and only as a storeroom. There's a window in there, which can't be used to exit the building as it's barred from the outside and barely opens four inches. That's probably why Mr Tucker never has to lock the door.

Once down in the main corridor I scanned around me, but as usual on Sundays it was deathly quiet before chapel. Everyone was in their sections still, polishing shoes for inspection before being led down to listen to the Rev Barnes' poisonous musings- the boys first at ten-thirty, and then the girls at eleven after we'd left, filled with the lies of the Church.

Mr Leadbetter would give us his once-over in our sections at ten-fifteen- so much less thoroughly than Old Bannister's draconian scrutiny- which gave me plenty of time to get the scribbler's attention.

Once through the cloakroom door, I pushed past the piled boxes and made for the window, unlatching the ornate metal arm from its hook, and pushing it away from me, the old wooden window-frame making its usual grating sound when opened narrow to its full extent.

"Pssst…Mr Rose…"

He had his back to me and showed no recognition of having heard me.

"Mr Rose sir, it's Edwin," I said, my voice raised as far above a whisper as possible without attracting attention from *them*.

This time it worked, and he span around, comically looking around him almost like Mr Chaplin, momentarily dumbfounded.

"Mr Rose," I said, my voice now modulated lower, "are you leaving us?"

"For a while," said Rose. "What are you doing in there?"

"I saw you from upstairs, and as I need to talk to you, I came down here- it's always unlocked and hardly anybody goes in this room."

"What do you need to talk to me about?" said Rose, acutely aware that if any member of staff saw him talking to a resident, it would probably get back to Dr Sharland, Mr Dodwell, or both. He might already be banished, but he didn't want to worsen his situation even further unnecessarily.

"I have some powerful new information," I said.

"I have all I need to know about Lawrence Drummond now…'

He turned around again mid-sentence at the sound of a motorcar and its tyres pressing against the gravel.

"That's my taxi," said Rose, facing me once again.

"It's not about Lawrence Drummond… it's far more important than that, believe me."

"I've been warned not to talk to any residents, and asked to leave Sunnyside," said Rose.

"That's even more reason for you to hear what I have to say-*they* are closing ranks on you, sir. I'll be at the gazebo at ten o'clock tomorrow morning-you can get there across the terrace in the mist through the farmer's field at the other side of the wood."

"Who are *they*?"

"I'll explain it all tomorrow at ten o'clock, Mr Rose. It's time I told you the truth."

I closed the window as he moved away and walked towards his taxi, knowing that as the doors of Shadowside were now locked to him, his mind would be clearer for me to enter.

*

It wasn't Rose's usual mute driver, but a garrulous one, and as he could have done with some silence to take in and think about what Edwin had just said, for once the conversation was less than welcome.

"Not long til spring now- still, if only Milston was in a valley like Greathampton, we'd always escape the worst of the weather, I suppose."

"But it's still early January," said Rose.

"The saplings will be out in no time, you'll see. The wife'll have me out in the garden in a jiffy, for my sins, ha-ha."

Rose grunted as amiably as he could.

"Been working at Sunnyside?"

"Just visiting."

"Big old house, isn't it? A real manor."

"It certainly is."

"Don't get too many calls out there though."

"I can imagine."

"Where to in Milston, sir?"

"The Gables, please. A boarding house on the seafront."

"Oh, I know it well. Antonia who runs it went to school with my wife."

"It's a small world."

"And getting smaller all the time with all those aviators setting records."

Rose made an affirmative noise.

"You'd never get me up in one of them airplanes, mind you. And I doubt the Yank Lindbergh will again after what happened to his baby, tragic that."

"It was very sad," said Rose, not mentioning that his former paper the *Herald* had reported just a few months earlier that Charles Lindbergh and his wife were actually now living in England, in Kent, to escape all the publicity surrounding the kidnap and murder of their infant son almost five years earlier.

"And I heard on the wireless that some woman was planning a round-the-world flight- only in America!" said the driver.

229

"Amelia Earhart?"

"Something like that. She'll never do it anyway!"

Rose was just starting to enjoy the closest he'd had to a normal chat with anybody since he arrived at Sunnyside when the taxi pulled up outside the Gables on the promenade.

"Here you are sir. Mind yourself- it's blowy out there today."

"Thank you," said Rose, giving the driver a tip on top of the fare on the meter, and asking for a receipt.

"Thank *you*, sir," said the driver as he wrote it out.

"Can I book you for nine o'clock tomorrow morning, to go back to Sunnyside?"

"Of course, sir- I'll collect you here then."

Rose thanked the driver again as he walked up the path to the door of the Gables, the 'Vacancies' sign luckily still out as he'd hoped.

He looked through the stained diamond-patterned window as he knocked, just as he had weeks earlier when he first arrived in Milston, when his world had seemed a different place.

28

The stone bench was cold through my woollen long trousers, but thankfully I didn't still have to wear shorts in winter as *they* make the younger boys do in their buster suits, as well as a peaked cap, as I did until I turned fourteen two years ago.

I'd arrived on time, as always, but the muckraker was late.

I looked at the wall of mist, but couldn't see more than ten feet away, just as I'd expected. The scribe emerged- first his outline, then his hatted head and face.

"You made it through the mist," I said, "at last."

"This is nothing compared to the peasoupers we get in London I can tell you."

"I know, Mr Rose, I used to play hide and seek with my father in those fogs- I lived in London before I came to Shadowside."

"*Shadowside?*" said Rose. "Don't you mean *Sunnyside?*"

"Not at all. That's what *we all* call this terrible place."

"I've never heard it called that- why Shadowside?" said Rose.

"Because it's full of darkness- there's no sun here, no light."

"It is winter, you know."

"It has nothing to do with the sky," I said. "But everything to do with the negative shadows and evil forces all around us."

"Evil forces?" said Rose. "Like Lawrence Drummond?"

I shook my head. "I'm talking about living forces, not ghosts."

"What on earth are you talking about?"

"*Them.*"

"Meaning who?"

"Those with the power."

"I think you might have been reading too many fantastic stories for boys, Edwin."

"There's nothing fantastic about this, it's as real as you and I sitting in this gazebo."

"Who has the power?" said Rose.

"Mr Dodwell of course, and Dr Sharland, and all those who work under *them*. The very people who I'm sure asked you to leave here."

"And why are they evil?"

"It's all a charade Mr Rose, all a smoke and mirror illusion here at Shadowside."

"And why is that? It's an institution to make boys and girls better- what can be wrong with that?"

"That's the illusion- *they* want you to think that- when in actual fact, it's all about control."

"And what's the purpose of this control?"

"To enable *them* to carry out *their* true work," I said.

"Which is?"

"I don't know exactly- but the answer lies in the Cavendish Wing- some kind of terrible experimentation goes on in there, you know."

Rose looked at me in silence for several moments.

"Supposing something was happening in the Cavendish Wing- how does that affect you?"

"Many of us are controlled- haven't you seen how quiet the boys and girls are here?"

"And how are they controlled?"

"Dr Sharland's drug, which he calls 'the remedy' when giving it to us."

"But you aren't quiet, at least not with me."

"I haven't taken the drug since I was thirteen- only those of weak character are given it and they soon learned *I* wasn't one of those- the few of us with strength of character just have to stay in line."

"But that doesn't make sense. Surely the stronger characters would need more doping to stay in line."

"You would think so, but that's not how they work here, it's all jumbled up. The weaker ones are better for testing so *they* can experiment and make better drugs- then eventually *they* will be able to control everyone. *They* see themselves as a higher level of being."

"That all seems a little unbelievable, Edwin. And I must say- Dr Sharland and Mr Dodwell seem quite normal to me."

"Wolves in sheep's clothing, as they say. *They* gave the remedy to Dorothy Hopkins and Isabel Haarman, you know."

"The missing girl and the girl that they said killed herself?"

"Oh yes. And nobody's seen Dorothy for weeks and weeks now, but I've heard that she was on the remedy before she went missing."

"Where do you think she is?" said Rose.

"Nobody has any idea for sure, but there are rumours that she might have ended up in the Cavendish Wing."

"Why?"

"That's for you to find out," I said.

"And why would I want to do that?" said Rose.

"Because I can tell that you're a good man."

The scribbler's eyes narrowed, and it was several moments before he spoke again.

"So, Isabel- why did she kill herself then?"

"It could have been a side-effect, a bad reaction to the Luminal."

"Luminal?"

"That's Dr Sharland's remedy," I said.

"What is it?"

"I don't know, but it makes you drowsy and slows you down."

"But I heard that Isabel was more manic in her final days," said Rose.

"I can't explain that, unless it was a side-effect as I said, or perhaps a higher dosage?"

Rose was immersed in thought now, looking down at his feet, hands firmly in his trench-coat's pockets.

"I have to go now," I said. "I have my Latin class- it killed the Romans, and now it's killing me!"

"Will you be here again?"

"Tomorrow at five o'clock."

"I'll be here," said Rose.

"And please try to be on time, sir," I said, as I walked out into the mist, without looking back at the muckraker, knowing that I'd got his full attention anyway.

29

Once back at the Gables, Rose returned to his room, the same one he'd stayed in on first arrival in Milston, which he thought of as *BS* or Before Sunnyside, but after what Edwin had told him that morning, he now wondered if that should be Before Shadowside.

Laying on his bed, his feet just hanging off the newly added flowered eiderdown and with two pillows once again removed, he stared out at his balcony view, which consisted only of the white sky from that position.

He marvelled at how Edwin had moved from his Lawrence Drummond/Jack the Ripper yarn to this new conspiratorial story. But what if there was some truth in it? Mr Dodwell and Dr Sharland had become hostile, and the children at Sunnyside *did* seem to be unnaturally quiet.

What if there were drug experiments going on, preying on the most vulnerable as the boy had said, with the worst of them in the Cavendish Wing? Could Dorothy really have ended up in there?

And had Isabel been doped to shut her up, perhaps as she knew too much? If so, was her 'suicide' an unforeseen reaction to the Luminal, or a planned overdosing, leading to her taking her own life, which would be murder of course.

Or was it all a schoolboy's fantasy, a boy who was also a mental patient, something that was easy to forget when talking to the very articulate Edwin.

Whatever was true, he knew he had three things to do- investigate Luminal and its effects, call in to Flanagan with developments to gain himself more time there, and meet Edwin again the following afternoon.

But he decided to speak to Edwin again before he called Flanagan, as there was bound to be more to come. And in the back of his mind, there was still Mr Bannister's wristwatch- and Rose now saw Bannister as a definite murder victim with his killer unknown.

*

It was back in Milston library that Rose was able to discover more about Luminal, in a 1935 drug directory on the Medicine shelves.

He found that it was the trade name for phenobarbital, and was used for treating seizures and insomnia, the side-effects being dizziness, sedation, and if the dosage was high enough to overcome a patient's resistance threshold, it could induce a hypnotic state.

It also numbed the body's central and nervous systems, and with an overdose could lead to a coma, and then death.

Rose remembered the silent children, depersonalised as 'residents' by Sunnyside's staff, passing him almost as if in a trance in the high-ceilinged corridors of the main building.

Were those children freely walking around on a dosage high enough to sedate them, yet controlled enough to allow them to remain mobile and responsive?

And were there others in the Cavendish Wing- including Dorothy- who were now doped up so powerfully that they could do little save make the occasional cry for help? Was Dorothy Hopkins a prisoner there, perhaps with little remaining of her personality? Or could she still be saved?

And had Isabel been given just enough Luminal to make her mind so irrational and paranoid that she died by her own hand, wading into the pond and drowning?

As he left the library and walked towards the seafront to clear his troubled mind, Rose didn't notice the rain hitting his hatless head and face until he was almost on the promenade, and then had to make his way back to the library where he'd left behind his trilby on a desk.

30

The same verbose driver took Rose back to the spot on the Milston Road where he could climb over the fence into the farmer's field, across which he could walk towards the woods and then on to Sunnyside's terrace on the other side.

"Do you really want to be dropped here again, sir? It's brass monkeys."

"I could do with the fresh air, even if it's bracing."

Rose waited for the taxi to depart before he entered the field as he had the previous morning because it might be difficult to explain why he was trespassing on private land.

When he was dropped off it was still light, but by the time he came out of the other side of the woods the lowering sky was darkening. It was ten minutes to five as he started out across the ever-misty terrace.

He hadn't been idle that day and had typed out a first draft of the Jack the Ripper story on his Remington Portable typewriter, ready to show Flanagan should he have to return to London at short notice, a real possibility now, he feared.

It was a mystery piece, a filler or puffer story, with no confirmation or real evidence, but it would fill four or five pages of *Travesties* if required. And due to the subject matter, it would undoubtedly be a cover story in the next issue, or perhaps the one after if he ever did get to the truth about Dorothy and could write up that far more important piece.

Rose knew exactly what he was going to ask Edwin as he sensed he was nearing the gazebo, which was still not visible in the thick white haze. It was exactly five o'clock when the criss-cross stonework finally came into view.

Inside he sat down on the bench, realising that Edwin was late this time. Several minutes had passed when he almost jumped through the gazebo's turreted roof, as a loud "Boo!" jolted him out of solitude.

"Sorry, Mr Rose. It was just too good an opportunity to miss."

Rose looked at Edwin, who was smiling widely, a rare sight, and one which served as a reminder that this truly was a boy standing next to him.

"Boys will be boys," said Rose.

"That phrase comes from Latin and was originally 'children will be children,' you know."

Rose nodded thoughtfully, marvelling at how quickly Edwin had reasserted his precocious intellect after his prank. "Well I never," he said.

"I hope you've had time to think about what we talked about yesterday," I said.

"I certainly have, and I wondered where Mr Bannister's death comes into the picture."

I confess I hadn't expected that. "Oh, poor Mr Bannister. He was too moral for his own good."

"Are you saying that his fall down the stairs was in some way assisted?"

"That's what many say... You see, Mr Bannister, or Old Bannister as we affectionately nicknamed him, must have discovered the truth about Shadowside and became a threat to *them*."

"But wasn't he one of them?"

"He thought he was I'm sure, until he learned the awful reality."

"So, who do you think pushed him?"

"I wouldn't like to say, sir."

"Mr Dodwell? Dr Sharland?"

"I doubt either of them would have to do such cleaning up themselves. It's more likely to be someone lower in the pecking order, someone eager to please *them*."

"Mr Leadbetter?" said Rose.

"He wouldn't have the spunk to do that."

"Mr Tucker? Mr Baxter? Mr Lewis?"

"I doubt it, none of them would have it in them to do somebody in."

"You'd be surprised at what people are capable of," said Rose.

"I wouldn't be as surprised as Old Bannister when Mrs Benson made him eat marble."

"Mrs Benson?!!!?"

"Yes. I saw her. I was on the way to the library at the top of the stairs when I saw her walking up and Old Bannister walking down, and then his fearful cry as he toppled."

"Did you tell the police this?"

"Of course not! That copper's in with *them*... why do you think nothing ever gets solved around here?"

"But still- it was murder."

"It would mean the end of me. I'd be drugged up and in the Cavendish Wing in no time."

"I can see what you mean. But you sound paranoid."

"Shadowside's a place that makes most paranoid, but not me."

"May I ask why you were sent here?" said Rose.

"I had some trouble at home."

"With your parents?"

"No, with my mother. My father did away with himself, but he always understood me."

"I'm sorry to hear that."

"I've long learned to live with it- I'm strong Mr Rose, I've had to be."

Rose detected a harshness in Edwin's voice and paused before speaking. "It seems to me that the only way to prove what you are saying about the conspiracy here is to gain access to the Cavendish Wing."

"Impossible! there are always staff in there and the doors are bolted from the inside- I and others have heard the lock-up many times, especially the girls in South."

"But Dorothy and others could be in real danger inside there," said Rose, with some urgency.

"That's most definitely true- but you'll have to find another way," I said.

"I'll have a good think on it."

"There must be a way- and then we'll bring down *them* and Shadowside."

"Let's just see what I can find out first," said Rose, as I left him on the bench once again.

31

Back at the Gables that evening after a greasy fish and chip supper and limiting himself to a pint of beer in a packed pub on the promenade, Rose asked Antonia Smith in the reception area whether Madame Sosostris was still in residence.

"She certainly is, I'll tell Mrs Manningham you were asking after her if you'd like."

Rose was momentarily confused, but then remembered that Manningham was Madame Sosostris's real name, or at least the one she said was real. "There's no need to do that, I'm sure I'll run into her."

"As you wish," said Antonia. "By the way, I've put a fresh towel and soap in your room. Enjoy your evening, Mr Rose."

"Thank you. Good evening to you too."

Rose went straight up to his room, feeling the need for space to think more than he had for a long time. He still hadn't called in to Flanagan, who was sure to be becoming agitated at the lack of contact, but felt he needed more to report before he did so.

He thought of Edwin and his theory about Sunnyside, and whether there really could be any truth in the nefarious motives he attributed to Mr Dodwell, Dr Sharland, and all those working under them.

Was Shadowside, this demonic version of Sunnyside, a reality, or a figment of a boy's imagination? And Rose kept reminding himself that it was a juvenile mental institute, and Edwin was indeed a mental patient there.

He had no real idea what was exactly wrong with Edwin, who seemed perfectly controlled if very self-absorbed, but he knew that the latter was normal for many boys of that age, as he himself had been, he was sure.

He pondered on the 'trouble at home' that Edwin had mentioned, and while he'd wanted to ask more questions about that, it seemed wrong to press somebody with issues. You didn't get sent to a place like Sunnyside for apple scrumping or stealing gobstoppers, after all.

But Rose was torn now, between brushing away Edwin's revelations as the product of a vivid and overactive imagination and the frightening possibility that children could be being experimented on in the secretive Cavendish Wing, including Dorothy- the whole reason he had gone to Sunnyside in the first place of course. He just had to do something.

He knew that he had only one option, although it would be risky. But he was conflicted now and needed reassurance somehow. Flanagan couldn't help as he hadn't been to Sunnyside and seen or felt what he had. That was the problem-there *was* something eerie and mysterious about the place.

Dorothy Hopkins had been gone for almost eight weeks now, with no sign or rumour of her, except for Edwin's insistence that she'd been taken by Mr Dodwell and Dr Sharland- *'them'* as he called them, but why?

Rose's instincts told him that Bernard Bannister had undoubtedly been murdered. But could it really have been Mrs Benson, who was always so ready to impress Mr Dodwell? Could she have killed Mr Bannister as he was a threat to *them*?

And Isabel Haarman, who Rose knew had descended into a nervous wreck and was then found drowned, either by her own hand or by that of another.

But how did this all link together? In the space of less than four months since Mr Bannister tumbled down the main stairs the previous October, there had been very strange and unexplained goings-on at Sunnyside, resulting in two deaths and a disappearance.

And then there was the note to Dorothy signed 'O,' the lock of hair and Dorothy's bracelet, that was apparently so important to her. Who had left the box outside his cottage? Did Isabel put it there to help him, as he'd long thought? And who was 'O'? Or could it be somebody trying to point to somebody with a name beginning with the letter 'O'?

He had to find the link- he was sure it was all connected, but how? Getting inside the Cavendish Wing would be the quickest way to get to the truth about Edwin's story at least, but that was impractical- he'd seen how guarded it was.

He told himself again that he knew what he had to do, but for now he could only drift off to sleep on the bed, fully clothed.

*

In the breakfast room, Rose, still unshaven and wearing the previous day's clothes, drank his tea and ate while looking around the room at the three other guests at the other tables.

Two looked like travelling salesmen, one a young man in an immaculate three-piece and a nervous look on his face, the other a man at least fifteen years older than Rose and wearing tweed and pince-nez, who seemed totally at ease as he looked through what had to be his appointments book.

Then there was Madame Sosostris, sitting with her back to him as she had the last time he stayed there. Rose wanted to talk to her but decided to wait until she went back upstairs.

In his room again, he had a shave and a wash-down before getting dressed, realising that he would have to ask Antonia where he could get his clothes washed and then rinsed in a clothes mangle. But such mundane matters soon evaporated from his mind.

He'd never believed in psychics or the tarot, but now truly felt he needed to speak to Madame Sosostris, a woman who had been investigated by the police for being a fake, but who had told Rose that he could be in emotional chaos, would face darkness and obsession, and something about a persecution complex.

And that was how he felt- persecuted by Mr Dodwell and Dr Sharland, and still feeling guilty about Isabel's death so soon after he'd tried to get information from her- not quite emotional chaos but going that way if he didn't find out why she had been so terrified. Darkness- he'd been around a surplus of that. And obsession? His need to find Dorothy never left his mind...

It would certainly be worth the ten shillings of expenses, or even if he had to pay for it himself. He didn't want to find out about himself now though, but about Dorothy. Whether Madame Sosostris was a fraud or not hardly mattered now- he needed any guidance he could get, however questionable.

He left his room and walked across the landing to the medium's room and knocked on the door softly. She came to

241

the door promptly, her big blue eyes staring out of the doorway at him, her expression solemn.

"I thought I'd see you again," she said. "I didn't think you'd go away."

"I need your guidance, Madame Sosostris."

"I told you before, I never give second readings."

"But it's not about me- it's about a missing girl."

She gave him a long stare.

"I can't help you, I'm afraid. I can only say that the girl is close and never went very far."

"Have you seen the girl?" said Rose.

She made no attempt to answer.

"She was wearing a green dress with white flowers on it. She's fifteen years old with long dark hair and her name is Dorothy," said Rose.

"She hasn't got long hair anymore. That's all I can tell you. Take good care, Mr Rose."

"But Madame Sosostris- I can pay you…"

"Goodbye, Mr Rose."

With that she shut the door. Rose walked back towards his room, wondering if Dorothy really had cut her hair, or perhaps had it cut for her.

But the idea that Dorothy was 'close and never went very far' was enough for him. He'd be making his move that night.

32

It was just after nine o'clock when Rose got into the taxi outside the Gables.

"I'm meeting a friend at the same place you took me yesterday," said Rose, and when they arrived next to the fence on the very quiet road, "He doesn't seem to have arrived yet, but he'll be along soon, so please drop me now."

"Say no more, sir," said his new regular driver, who had talked about a variety of subjects along the way and was now seeking to reassure him that there was no need to explain why he was asking to be left there in the near-freezing darkness. But his conspiratorial wink was a little too much for Rose and wasn't reciprocated, a smile having to suffice.

Rose walked across the field and into the woods, his hat, heavy coat, and muffler staving off the worst of the weather, but he was actually sweating by the time he got to the terrace and made towards the back of Sunnyside's main building, instead of carrying on towards the gazebo in the mist. He stopped and took a swig of Gilbey's Gin Spey Whisky from his silver hip flask, feeling that he truly deserved it.

He knew that the hardest part would be getting inside the main building and remaining hidden until all had gone to bed. With the building looming above him, he crept around the upper terrace, trying to stay on the grass and avoid gravel wherever possible, but not always managing to do so.

There were lights on above, and he realised that as even the older residents had lights out at nine o'clock, it must be the staff inside those illuminated windows, and they could be up for some time yet.

But he had to get inside the building now, as he surmised that final checks would be made all over before Mr Tucker locked the main doors at eleven o'clock and all became perfectly still.

Approaching the main door from the side, the island of undergrowth which lay sprawled between him, and his now vacated cottage looked like a dark unruly shape almost cut out against the slightly lighter sky.

He heard male voices in the main courtyard, less than twenty yards from where he stood outside of it, in the shadow of a gargoyle atop the stone pillared wall.

Once the voices had died away, he lingered there for a handful of minutes, knowing that his next move into the courtyard and through the main door was the riskiest part of his clandestine journey.

Finally, he told himself that there never would be a perfect time to make the dash, so he ran from the shadows, through the gates and into the courtyard lights, two motorcars glistening as he passed, every crunching of gravel beneath his feet making his heart lurch.

And then somebody spoke, and it was a voice that Rose now knew well.

"Good evening, sir."

It was Carstairs, standing there just outside the main doors.

Rose shushed him and waved his hand to come back into the shadows with him, which Carstairs did.

"I haven't seen you around here lately, sir." Carstairs had modulated his slow voice to a whisper, prompted by Rose putting a finger to his own lips as a warning to be quiet.

"I haven't been around for a while," said Rose.

"Have you been away, sir?"

"Not quite."

"I've been thinking about what you said to me sir, about the missing girl from South."

"Dorothy Hopkins?"

"Yes, sir. Well, I did see her around from time to time, as I told you. She was usually alone. But more than twice, I saw her talking to another boy from North outside the library."

"Who?" said Rose a little impatiently.

"Edwin Castleton, sir."

Rose shuddered, and for once it wasn't because of the cold.

"Thank you for letting me know Carstairs, that's very helpful," said Rose in a measured tone, even though he could have kissed Carstairs.

"That's quite all right, sir. I'd best be getting back to North now. Goodnight."

"Take care Carstairs," said Rose, his mind reeling from the revelation that Edwin knew Dorothy, something that the boy had never mentioned, and had always spoken about the girl as if he didn't know her.

Or could Carstairs be trying to incriminate Edwin for some reason? Rose hadn't forgotten that it was also Carstairs who'd told him about Edwin's fascination with the Indian vulture, which had revealed the Zenith wristwatch.

And if Isabel had left the box outside his cottage, Carstairs could really be 'O.' And if Dorothy truly were pregnant, could either he or Edwin be the father of her baby?

But there were just too many 'ifs' for Rose to take in properly, there in the cold and tense night.

Gathering himself back into action as it was almost eleven, Rose ran for Sunnyside's entrance, slowing down as he went through the main doors, and seeing nobody around, went directly to the right, turning the handle on the first door, which thankfully opened easily, and it was soon closed again behind him once he was inside.

It was pitch black in the cloakroom, the one which he remembered Edwin saying was hardly used and always unlocked. He looked at his wristwatch, but couldn't make out the time, so moved closer to the window, the lights outside allowing him to see that it was just after ten-thirty.

Forcing himself to exhale as shallowly as he could, Rose sat on what felt like a wooden crate, glancing at his watch at regular intervals. Some footsteps in the courtyard at just before the hour, which he thought were Mr Tucker coming to lock the doors, proved a false alarm.

When the bolts at last thudded across, it was almost quarter past eleven, and Rose smiled to himself as he was sure that the janitor had been at the Golden Bell, where he too would much rather have been, instead of cowering in a dusty storeroom like a stowaway.

There were more voices and footsteps over the next half an hour, and he decided that he would wait until midnight to leave the safety of that room. He was ready by the door as the hour passed, and opened it as carefully as he could, poking his head out and looking down the corridor towards the main stairs. There was nobody there.

Out in the corridor, Rose tiptoed across the shining chessboard floor, from black to white squares and back to black again, past the Drummond family portraits on the right-hand wall. Soon he was next to the main stairs, but he carried on, through the double doors and into the next corridor, where he turned right as he had many times before on the way to Dr Sharland's office.

That was his destination. He knew that if there was any written information about the terrible experiments being done to the children of which Edwin was so sure, Dr Sharland would have the records in his office, as he was in sole charge of clinical treatment at Sunnyside. If Edwin could still be trusted at all, after what Carstairs had just told him.

But Rose felt he had to carry on now. He scanned the long corridor both ways before he approached the office. Just as he'd thought, there was only a large old-fashioned rim lock with a single lever and a sliding bolt, which had probably been fixed to the door when the house was built.

Rose reached inside his jacket pocket and removed the rolled-up handkerchief in which he kept a tension wrench, not dissimilar to a woman's tweezers in appearance, and a longer hook pick, both given to him during his *Herald* days by a prolific cat burglar named Bumper Johnson, on account of his great dexterity in bumping locks.

Johnson had given Rose and a colleague a demonstration of basic lockpicking in his east London workshop for a piece they worked on about sneakthieves and porch-climbers. Johnson was residing at His Majesty's Pleasure the last time Rose heard, although he would undoubtedly be trying to find a way to get out of his cell.

Having used the tools several times before when no other means of entry was possible, Rose immediately placed his little finger on the tension wrench which he'd inserted in the lock and began to apply just a little pressure to turn it, then used the hook pick to manipulate. He worked it backwards and forwards, following advice Bumper Johnson given him- "Keep the pressure low, or your top will blow." Apparently, many beginner lockpickers got frustrated and applied too much force, damaging the lock, and so never unlocking it.

Slowly Rose worked the gold lock's keyhole, knowing that Johnson would've had that open in thirty seconds at the outside. It was more than seven minutes before he eventually felt the lock turning and the door opened. He looked around again, replacing the tools and handkerchief in his pocket, and then had one last look down the corridor to the left and right before he went into the room.

He went to the window and closed the curtains before turning on the light. It looked the same as it always did, and after having a look at Dr Sharland's desk, which he saw had no drawers, he focused on the two filing cabinets.

He was amazed to see that there were no locks on the cabinets, and that they opened freely, with just a slight creak. He stopped and listened for any noise outside the office, but hearing none, began to rummage through the first cabinet drawer.

As he'd expected, it was all labelled and well-organized, each drawer covering a specific area. There were three drawers in each cabinet-six in all- the North Wing, the South Wing, the East Wing, the West Wing, General Treatment Methodologies and one marked Medication. Each was filled with files.

There was no drawer for the Cavendish Wing, and Rose wondered just why that could be. Perhaps it was so secret and the experiments so unethical that there were no records? But Rose couldn't accept this- Dr Sharland was a man who thrived on order and details, and he would have everything recorded.

He looked around the room again, and just the bookshelves remained, which held a range of psychiatry, psychology, and clinical practice books- nothing out of the ordinary there.

Rose returned to the cabinets. He had plenty of time and would spend the whole night going through every file and making notes until he had what he wanted if necessary- if it was there, he'd find it.

33

The trudge back across the wet grass of the terrace towards the woods should have been tiring after being up all night, but Rose felt more alive than he had for a very long time.

It was adrenaline, tingling the back of his neck and coursing down his spine, the butterflies in his stomach doing cartwheels, what his mother used to call the collywobbles. He hadn't seen what he'd been looking for, but what he had discovered in Dr Sharland's office was what led him to the breakthrough.

After hours scan-reading countless General Treatment Methodologies and Medication files, Rose had found nothing to support Edwin's claims about the evil goings-on at 'Shadowside.' But he knew that meant nothing- those engaged in such acts would be foolish to have paper records detailing them he'd finally reasoned, as the hours rolled by towards the dawn.

Rose had next turned to the records of individual 'residents', as they were labelled in Sunnyside-speak. It was what Carstairs had told him just hours before that made him turn to the North Wing cabinet first. He looked for Edwin's file, and there it was, midway in the pile, marked Edwin Castleton. Rose devoured the main points and meticulously wrote them down in his notebook, his eyes ever widening as he did so.

Then he'd focused on the South Wing files and looked up Dorothy, Isabel, and Caitlin, and found nothing there that surprised him, in fact less information about those children than had already been supplied to him by Dorothy's mother, Dr Sanderson, Dr Sharland, and even Mrs Benson.

Back in the cloakroom, where he'd returned after pulling the office door to just after five in the morning, Rose sat in the near darkness using his Zippo lighter to read his notes about Edwin, until Mr Tucker came to unlock the main doors.

Resident Name: Edwin Castleton
Wing: North (formerly East)
Date of Birth: 16th August 1920

Admitted: 8th *March 1931*

Next of Kin Address: Mr Thomas Castleton (father), The Albany, Mayfair, London W1

Diagnosis: Infant/ Adolescent Psychopathy- no diagnosed family history, though the subject himself said in therapy that his mother was hectoring

Traits:

-Lack of scruples inwardly

-Controlled within his own world, but can react violently if the fantasy world he builds is threatened

-Acutely self-centred

-Lacks sensitivity for the feelings of others

-Delusions of grandeur

-Presents well outwardly

Treatment:

-Priority clinical monitoring

-Classified as E6 due to his history pre-admission and potential danger of repeating violent behaviour in compromised circumstances

-Medication found ineffective after runs of Morphine (April-May 1931) and Luminal (October 1931-January 1932)

Infractions:

-Questioned by the Principal over the tragic incident of the fatal fire in the chapel (25th December 1932)- the resident was seen in the vicinity with another resident (Hugo Latimer-East/North 1929-released to the Denton Institute 4th September 1936) but no further action was taken when the resident denied all involvement, and that they were near the chapel as the glow of the fire had attracted them there. Both residents put on close monitoring for six months until 1st June 1933

-Two infractions reported of the resident defying his E6 status (March/April 1936)- no further action taken, but resident was warned by his Wing Supervisor

Recommendation: Not recommended for release back into society until at least the age of twenty-one, so will be admitted to a further institution before his seventeenth birthday on 16th August 1937

There were still as many questions as answers, but it showed that Edwin was a very unwell boy, thought Rose, and he *had* been given the drug Luminal. How had he been violent before coming to Sunnyside? Could he possibly have been involved in that terrible chapel fire where three boys had died?

And he remembered that Dr Sharland had explained what an E6 was when he'd spoken about Dorothy's psychological problems to him weeks before- it meant that a child was to be kept away from the opposite sex, whether fellow children or staff. So, was Edwin dangerous to females?

There had been two 'infractions' of the E6 rule by Edwin, and he'd been reprimanded by his Wing Supervisor, which the file stated was none other than Bernard Bannister, who conducted the review with Dr Sharland, just weeks before his death.

Something else also troubled Rose- Edwin's father was obviously alive and well, while Edwin had said that he had taken his own life. Added to that, he seemed to live at the Albany, an exclusive and upper-crust block of apartments just off Piccadilly, which Rose knew only allowed male residents. So, had Edwin's parents separated?

Edwin was connected to the Zenith wristwatch, and in Rose's mind, could well be Bernard Bannister's killer. Or was it a coincidence that Edwin had been warned off talking to a female by Bernard Bannister, who fell down the stairs about five months later?

And had Mr Bannister seen Edwin talking to Dorothy? More importantly, could Edwin be the father of Dorothy's child, if she were pregnant of course?

And now Carstairs had told him that he'd seen Edwin talking to Dorothy outside the library on several occasions. Everything pointed to Edwin.

By the time he neared Milston, having walked several miles yet still filled with energy, Rose at last felt as if he was getting some real answers.

34

As he cleaned his mud-caked shoes over the washbasin in his room at the Gables, Rose was fully aware that Antonia would be less than pleased that he was using the nail brush provided to do so, but she need never know once it was rinsed off.

Once his shoes were half-acceptable for public gaze, he left the boarding house and walked down Milston's promenade. There were a few people doing just like him- thinking, clearing cobwebs from their heads and stretching legs, or perhaps going about their daily routine.

The white crest of each wave that landed close to the shoreline on the sodden sand, and the wet-glazed pebbles from the rain which had just stopped lashing made everything seem very fresh- just as Rose was now feeling too.

Weeks of being overwhelmed by Sunnyside and its insular inner world and often stymied in his search for gen on Dorothy had taken a toll. And his early paranoia and feeling of being followed and watched there became a sense of inertia, treading furiously to prevent himself from drowning in his own mind.

But just a few days away from the place had given him a new perspective, and now he had a juicy bone to gnaw on. Edwin dominated his thoughts, but Rose was also mindful that the boy's claims about 'Shadowside' couldn't be completely dismissed yet- there was still possibly some truth to it.

Firstly however, he had to look deeper into Edwin. His file showed that he was immoral and weaved a rich fantasy world for himself, never mind being potentially violent if confronted, so speaking to Edwin about himself would scarcely be fruitful and possibly dangerous.

One course of action would be to go and tell Dr Sharland and Mr Dodwell everything he had learned, but then he would probably have to admit breaking into the office. And if, unlikely as it now seemed, there were terrible things going on at 'Shadowside,' he could be in danger from what Edwin called '*them*' too.

There was Dorothy's former psychiatrist Dr Sanderson back in London, who might be able to guide him on how to handle Edwin and open him up to tell the truth. But that just wouldn't be practical, as Sanderson was a close associate of Dr Sharland and could well be aware of or involved in any potential misdeeds at Sunnyside himself.

There was only one person who could advance his knowledge of Edwin, Rose decided- Mr Thomas Castleton, Edwin's father. But how could he approach him with no introduction or help from Dr Sharland and Mr Dodwell at Sunnyside?

Rose looked across the pavement suddenly when he heard a loud clattering noise, then seeing that it was a man shuttering up his jellied eel and whelk stall in front of the fishmongers opposite.

Gazing back out to the choppy almost heaving sea, he went back to the problem of Edwin's father, and soon reassured himself that he could ingratiate himself with the man. He'd interviewed murderers and all sorts of criminals, both before and after they were arrested, or once when on the run, plus his fair share of victims.

This was a man who had committed no crime, and just happened to be the father of a sixteen-year-old mental patient who was now a murder suspect in Rose's mind.

But he needed a persona to gain entry to Thomas Castleton's world, a man who had been publicly deemed a suicide by his son. There was no telling how Mr Castleton would react when a stranger came to talk to him about Edwin.

He could pose as a policeman, but that was risky, and Slattery on the *Evening News* had served proper time for doing just that to get access to a possible poisoner, who unfortunately for him turned out to be innocent. And especially after his recent warning from Inspector Alexander at Sunnyside, it would be a very foolhardy charade.

He would have to pretend to be a member of Dr Sharland's clinical team, that was his only option, he decided. As he was already persona non grata at Sunnyside, he had little to lose there. And hopefully Mr Castleton would take him at face value and speak to him about Edwin without contacting Dr Sharland.

There was still a chance of being exposed, and he could still be arrested, but it seemed the best cause of action. He was banking on the fact that a father would do anything to aid his son's treatment, and he'd have to rely on both his professional and personal guile to pull it off successfully.

That meant a trip back up to London, which was most welcome anyway. But he wouldn't be able to go anywhere near his usual haunts, as everyone would want to know where he'd been and what story he was now on so that they could have a piece of it too.

It would just be a day visit, and he would have to be prepared to leave quickly if Mr Castleton rumbled his little deception.

Looking at his wristwatch, it was just after nine o'clock, so he could go that day. Although as he walked back along the almost-deserted pavement towards the seafront shops, heavy rain now falling again almost as if the man on the now-closed stall had foreseen it coming, Rose was very conscious of having something else to do first.

35

The poster advertising the Post Office Savings Bank had the advice 'Be Prepared- Be Thrifty,' but Rose knew that he had never had any money to spare, so was soon dreamily gazing out of the blurred wet window of the telephone box.

He was back in the same box on the seafront, the one he'd used last on first arrival in Milston, as the one outside the library would mean walking in the opposite direction of the railway station, where he was heading next.

The operator connected the call after a couple of minutes, and Flanagan finally came on the line, his voice monotone yet dripping with aggression.

"Where have you been? I haven't heard from you for an age?"

"I've been rather tied up, Mr Flanagan."

"Well, I hope you've made an inroad by now, or I'm afraid I'm pulling you out today- there's a white slavery piece brewing here with Harold Rose written all over it."

"I need a few more days- I'm nearly there…"

"You mean you haven't found the girl- Doris, wasn't it?"

"Dorothy," said Rose, a little miffed, but less than surprised that his boss couldn't even remember her name. "Dorothy Hopkins."

"Oh, that's the one. So… what have you got for me?"

Rose slotted another sixpence as he knew it could take some time, and that he had no choice but to take the chance of the operator hearing what he said if she should be listening- it was still less risky than sending a telegram which could be read by anybody.

He told Flanagan about Isabel's suicide, finding the Zenith wristwatch, and how it all pointed to Edwin having been involved in Bernard Bannister's murder.

"And how does that relate to Dorothy- please enlighten me," said Flanagan.

"Isabel was the closest person to Dorothy at Sunnyside, and she was terrified before she died."

"You think she knew something about where Dorothy went?"

"That's my line," said Rose, pumping a further sixpence into the box. "And it also looks as if Dorothy was pregnant, and the boy Edwin could be the father."

"Well, that could be a good motive for the girl to go into hiding, I grant you," said Flanagan.

Rose then went on to detail Edwin's story about the murky experiments, controlled drugging and sedation going on at Sunnyside.

"Quite a story," said Flanagan, finally. "But it suspiciously sounds rather like a book I read a few years ago."

"Which book?"

"*Brave New World* by Huxley. Good writer too- I've wanted to get him to do a piece for us about the Eugenics Movement, but he's just penned one for *Nash's Pall Mall* magazine about improving the world for their Christmas issue...they pay far more than we can."

"Aldous Huxley?" said Rose, taken aback, recalling Edwin mentioning that he'd read Huxley the same day he admitted placing the razor in the billiards room. "Isn't he a writer of fiction?"

"Yes, mainly." said Flanagan.

"What happens in the book?"

"Well, the people who live in what's called the World State are doped with a drug called Soma, which controls them-they think it makes them happy, but it takes away all their individuality and the ability to think for themselves- they have no passion too."

"It does sound similar," said Rose. "And the boy Edwin told me that he'd read Huxley I remember now."

"There you have it. Sounds like he's fantasising."

"He also says that secret experiments on children are going on within a closed-off wing at Sunnyside."

"A great story for us that would be- but it's a little like the Cyprus Experiment in the book."

"What's that?" said Rose.

255

"The most intelligent people are kept isolated on the island of Cyprus- it was an experiment to see if a whole society could be populated by the best minds- that's why I wanted Huxley to write about eugenics and its dangers."

"Erm..." Rose was trying to take it all in.

"Seems like the boy might just have been spinning you a yarn- unless you can find anything to support what he says."

"I haven't managed to yet, and I doubt I will. The boy's medical notes say that he's manipulative and creates his own inner world."

"Little wonder- he's in a mental institute, after all. Do you think you can bring the story in?"

"I'm nearly there, Mr Flanagan. Just a few more days should do it- I just need some proof."

"Isn't that the job of the police?"

"It's not the right time to bring them in yet- they've hardly got any closer to finding Dorothy anyhow, and it's almost two months ago that she went missing. And her mother must be even more anxious by now, poor woman."

"There's no denying that, she calls me regularly to ask on your progress. Look- I can give you three more days, after that you'll have to take what you have to the police. How about the Jack the Ripper Story?"

"It's already written up for subbing- I can let you have it as soon as I come back."

"That will help fill the next edition, and I'm also running your piece about the madman who threw a revolver at the King."

"George McMahon? I filed that last September," said Rose.

"About time we made use of it then."

"Could I have another twenty pounds for expenses?"

"For three days? In the countryside?"

"Well, I do have to go back to London too- I need to speak to the boy's father about his early childhood- he lives at the Albany."

"I know the manager at the Albany, you know. Do you want me to telephone him and say you're coming?" Flanagan's voice betrayed his satisfaction at having such well-to-do connections.

256

"That would be appreciated, thank you. I'm getting the train to Waterloo soon."

"I'll get straight on to it. The manager at the Albany is Mr Armitage-Gaines. And I'll wire you fifteen pounds- you can pick it up at the post office in Piccadilly."

"Thank you, Mr Flanagan." As usual, Flanagan didn't say goodbye and put down his receiver.

As Rose left the telephone box, pulling his coat collar further up his neck and ensuring that his trilby was on tight from the wind, he felt oblivious to the storm around him, even the thunder crashing down.

He had a few more days, and still had no evidence of what really happened to Dorothy. But he was sure in his own mind that the answer would come through Edwin, who was obviously close to Dorothy, possibly her lover, and if she were with child, its' father.

The realisation that Edwin had created his story of 'Shadowside' and taken some key elements from a book, by a writer he'd said he read. It was just too coincidental- Edwin was obviously trying to thicken the swamp to prevent anybody getting to the truth.

Rose now suspected that it had been Edwin who'd left the box with the note, hair, and bracelet outside the cottage, digging a false path for him to follow, which he had for some time, before ruling out Oscar Lewis and Oliver Carstairs.

Again, it was the bracelet that troubled Rose most of all- if Edwin had planted it, he must have got it from Dorothy as she always wore it, and would she ever have let him have it, the only hopeful reason being that it was a memento of her while she was away from him somewhere. But then the horse charm had fallen from it in the woods...

And Rose's mind kept replaying the words of Madame Sosostris in her own voice- "I can only say that the girl is close and never went very far."

As he came towards the ramp leading up to the railway station, Rose decided that he had to focus purely on Edwin now and forget Sunnyside and 'Shadowside' for the time being.

36

The small parade of once sumptuous shopfronts on the eastern side of the Albany's entrance looked half-gutted as Rose turned into Albany Court Yard, just off Piccadilly.

It was a symptom of the ever-changing city, but the two cloth-capped workmen smoking and idly chatting on the pavement didn't look in any rush to get on with the job.

After collecting Flanagan's money and knowing that even in a dream luncheon at nearby Fortnum and Mason would render him short once again, he'd had a quick bite at the Lyon's Corner House in Coventry Street, where Eileen, a Nippy he knew well, gave him extra mashed potato and a free refill of coffee.

The large hoardings selling Wills's Goldflake and Craven A cigarettes dominated the scene of hustle and bustle on the opposite side of the road, but Rose was very firmly fixated on the superb Georgian architecture of the building which Mr Thomas Castleton called home as he walked into the forecourt.

Five floors including the basement and attic, and seven large bay windows across, the Albany was a sight to rival the rural Sunnyside, although far smaller in size and built decades before. Walking towards the shining black door centred between two pillars at the top of the white steps, Rose felt like a strange fish in a foreign ocean.

Turning away from the polished brass knocker, Rose decided to ring the bell instead. All around him was almost silent as he stood there save for a background hum, caused by the thousands of hearts and feet pounding and omnibuses and motorcars chugging through Piccadilly about a hundred yards away.

The man who opened the immaculately oiled door was an inch or two taller and stockier than Rose, with thinning summer-sand hair, dressed as well as any resident of the building might be expected to be, although his ruddy cheeks gave him the look of a slightly tipsy farmer.

But Rose would have gambled the entire fifteen pounds just sent by Flanagan that this was Mr Armitage-Gaines, the Albany's manager, and he would have won the bet if he'd been able to find a bookie's runner to place it.

"Can I be of assistance to you, sir?" It was a voice of breeding, one cultivated in only a handful of English schools, and Rose could imagine how proud his very socially conscious boss would be to know somebody of that ilk.

"Erm- yes, please. I'm Mr Rose, a friend of Mr Flanagan."

"Splendid, I thought it must be you, sir. Invited guests usually use the back entrance on Vigo Street. Willie told me you'd be paying a visit- please come in."

Rose almost touched Mr Armitage-Gaines's outstretched palm, which didn't move as he tried to brush past through the front door. And once inside, he was still smirking to himself that his editor was known as Willie- it just didn't suit the precise Flanagan, whom he'd always assumed was a born-William, not a Willie, Billy, or Bill.

They were soon in a large reception room, beautifully furnished down to every detail, a mixture of Georgian, Victorian, and Edwardian pieces, but going together as if they were originally made to sit side-by-side. Rose knew that this was the mark of true class, and you just couldn't buy that.

There were loud chimes from the tall mahogany grandfather clock in the corner of the room, prompting Rose to look at his wristwatch. It was three o'clock, but one of the timepieces was two minutes fast or slow.

"What can I do for you sir- Willie only said that you wished to speak to one of our proprietors, but I know not which," said Mr Armitage-Gaines.

"It's one of your residents actually," said Rose, immediately aware he'd just used the same word used at Sunnyside for its patients.

"Our proprietors are all resident, sir. I require his name so that I can direct you to the relevant set."

"It's Mr Thomas Castleton."

259

"I see, sir. Mr Castleton resides in set No. 16, and I believe him to be in presently. Please follow me."

Rose assumed that a 'set' was a set of rooms in the building, which meant that the father lived in a set at the Albany while the son lived in a section at Sunnyside.

They walked up a wooden staircase, a mixture of landscapes and portraits lining the wall as they ascended.

"I take it that Mr Castleton doesn't know you are coming, sir. I can direct you to his set, but of course he must decide if he wishes to entertain you."

"That's perfectly fine," said Rose, as they walked over the red and gold flowers of the Axminster carpet laid beneath their feet, passing several large wooden doors before Mr Armitage-Gaines stopped at the fourth.

"Here we are, No.16. Shall I knock now, sir?"

"Please do," said Rose, knowing that in any other situation, Mr Armitage-Gaines would never call him 'sir,' as the Albany's manager was two classes above him in the pecking order.

Armitage-Gaines gave the door a genteel double knock, just audible enough to be heard, but in no way stirring.

Rose found himself staring at the gold number sixteen on the door as if it had some importance, but just wanted the door to open. He was about to turn to Armitage-Gaines again, to see if there would be a second knocking attempt when it finally did open, just enough for the man in the doorway to see who was there.

He was tall, thin, and wearing a light blue tie and a navy waistcoat with a gold chain hanging from it, the matching trousers meaning that it was two-thirds of a three-piece suit, very well-cut in obviously expensive Savile Row cloth, but perhaps ordered on nearby Jermyn Street.

"You have a Mr Rose to see you, sir."

Mr Castleton looked Rose up and down circumspectly as if he was weighing up making a bid for an Objet d'art at an exclusive auction.

"What can I do for you, Mr Rose? Have we met before?" said Mr Castleton, his voice well-spoken, but less than commanding.

"No, we've never met before now, Mr Castleton. I've come from Sunnyside about Edwin." As he said it, Rose was thinking about Edwin telling him that his father, the man standing in front of him now, had killed himself.

His son's name clearly startled Mr Castleton, his small eyes widening, Rose realising that he looked nothing like Edwin, who must take after his mother, he thought.

"Thank you, Peter. I'll take it from here."

"Very well, sir." And with that Armitage-Gaines immediately turned and walked back down the hallway.

"Will you come in?" said Mr Castleton.

"Thank you," said Rose, relieved that he hadn't been sent away.

The huge bay windows with the long cream pulled-back curtains framing them took Rose's eye as he entered what looked like a sitting room, tastefully furnished with antiques, from the walnut book cases which reached the ceiling to the gilt mirror above the marbled mantelpiece, and the twin leather sofas which matched the curtains in colour, completed by blue patterned cushions which were obviously made of silk, the same colour as the three Georgian armchairs spaced around the long glass coffee table.

Then there were the three lamps, also in cream, each on its own gleaming small round table, along with a tall standard lamp in the corner, and the large rug, beige and green and patterned with a floral design, almost covering the polished wooden floor.

"Please take a seat," said Mr Castleton. "Can I get you a drink of any variety? I'm afraid that my help's not here today."

"I'm fine thank you," said Rose, taking a seat on one of the blue armchairs, while Mr Castleton lowered himself onto a sofa.

Rose noticed that there was a box of Cadbury's King Edward chocolates on the table, carrying the promise 'An entirely new assortment'. He wanted one, knowing they would be delicious, but they were of course already out of date and would be superseded by the King George VI selection, he presumed. His rumination was soon interrupted by Mr Castleton, however.

"Do you work with Dr Sharland? Is Edwin in trouble? I haven't heard anything from Sunnyside since I got Edwin's quarterly assessment in November- everything appeared fine then."

"There's no problem at all with Edwin currently, I can assure you," said Rose, disingenuously in his own mind. "And yes, I work with Dr Sharland on the clinical staff at Sunnyside. We're doing some follow-up enquiries of all residents who have reached the age of sixteen, as they will be due for release soon."

"I do know that Edwin will be leaving Sunnyside sometime this summer, but he will still be going on to another place for treatment, won't he?"

Rose could detect a nervous tension in Mr Castleton's voice, as if he feared that Edwin could be released back out into his care.

"Yes, Edwin will be going to another institution, probably the Denton Institute, until he's twenty-one." Rose was just following what was in Edwin's file.

Mr Castleton looked visibly relieved, but Rose decided not to ask him how he felt about his son just yet.

"But what can I tell you?" said Mr Castleton. "I told Dr Sharland everything when Edwin was first sent to Sunnyside. Nothing has changed of course- I haven't seen Edwin for almost three years now."

"Do you choose never to visit Edwin?"

"No- as Dr Sharland knows, it was on his advice. Edwin asked Dr Sharland, it must have been at the end of 1933- I think- for my visits to stop, and Dr Sharland said on my last visit there that it would be best for Edwin's treatment if I didn't go to see him again, as it conflicted him."

"Do you write to him still?"

"Not anymore. I gave up in October- I used to write every two weeks, but I never got one letter back. Not one letter from Edwin since he went there in 1931!"

"That is a shame, I'm sorry."

"There's nothing can be done about it, at least until Edwin gets better." Mr Castleton's voice had dropped to almost a whisper, each word of the sentence less audible than the last.

"Still, Edwin's in the right place to get better," said Rose.

"And I'm thankful to Dr Sharland and all of you for taking care of him. There really was no other choice after *it* happened."

"Quite," said Rose, having no idea what *it* was, but very aware that he couldn't let Edwin's father know that he wasn't familiar with the reason Edwin was finally sent to Sunnyside.

"I never thought it would come to that. He was always a strange boy, but murder? It never occurred to me that Edwin could be capable of that."

So, Edwin had killed somebody before his admission.

"It must have been a great shock to you," said Rose.

"That's an understatement- your child taking another life is terrible enough, but his own mother?"

The word 'mother' shook Rose, and he did all he could not to show it. Luckily, Mr Castleton wasn't looking at him when he shuddered.

"What happened that day?" he finally said. "It will help me build a better picture for Edwin's notes if you don't mind."

Mr Castleton looked Rose directly in the eye. "It's not easy to talk about, but it'll always be branded on my mind. I'd been away on business to Manchester, where the family's factory is. I was only gone for three days."

"Was this in 1931?"

"Yes- the 30th of January- it was a Friday evening when I came home to our house in Mayfair, not too far from here. It's all locked up now. The nanny wasn't there, which surprised me, but I found out later that Alice, that's Edwin's mother, had sent her home the day before, giving her a long weekend off, as she sometimes did. Nobody was around- it was all so quiet. I called after Alice and then Edwin, nobody answered, but all the lights were on...."

Mr Castleton stopped abruptly, holding his face in his hands.

"Please take your time," said Rose, and after a pause Edwin's father continued.

"Everything appeared in order in the drawing room, sitting room and kitchen, so there were no signs of anyone breaking in or anything like that."

"That must have reassured you a little at the time."

"Yes, it did for a moment. I thought perhaps they might have gone out somewhere and left the lights on, although that was most unlike Alice, who ran the household very carefully and scolded the daily maid if she left lights on after leaving rooms. Then I walked down the hallway, and Edwin's bedroom door was open. He was there lying on his bed, reading a book-*Gulliver's Travels* I think it was."

"Did he say anything to you?" said Rose, playing the part of a psychiatrist on Dr Sharland's clinical staff.

"No, nothing. He just stared at me and smiled. I asked him why he hadn't answered, and he just shrugged. Then I asked where his mother was, and he said she was in our bedroom. I left Edwin there, and walked further down the hallway, finding our bedroom door closed. I opened the door, and there was no light on inside. I wondered if Alice might be sick and having a lie-down. I called her name, and no answer came again. Then I turned on the light…"

Mr Castleton now had his hand over his mouth, as if he might be sick.

"Are you all right?" said Rose.

He nodded his head unconvincingly. "I turned on the light and I saw the scene of horror I can never forget. She was sprawled over the bed, fully clothed, with her head caved in- she was face-down- I couldn't turn her over- I didn't want to see her face. There was blood all over the sheets around her, and all over the wall behind the bed, even some on the ceiling."

"What a terrible thing to have to see."

"Yes. And I ran. I ran out of the house, leaving Edwin in his bedroom. It hadn't dawned on me that it could be Edwin yet- I was still taking it all in. Our neighbours called for the police, and then I went back to my house with them. We sat with Edwin in the sitting room until the police arrived."

"How did Edwin seem?"

"He sat in silence. We told him that his mother had passed away, and he showed little emotion, he just asked if that meant he wouldn't be going to school the next week- he pleaded with me to let him go. It was all so astonishing."

"Extraordinary," said Rose. "What did the police think?

"They were sure it was Edwin. There was no sign of anyone else having been in the house, let alone an intruder. And then it all came out when the police interviewed the staff at Edwin's school."

"What did they say?"

"The headmaster said that Edwin was somewhat withdrawn but had certainly never lacked confidence. His house master described Edwin as a boy who lived in his imagination. But then they spoke to his English teacher."

"What did he say?"

"She, actually. A young woman, Miss Jenkins. It seems that about a week before, Edwin had asked her if she would be his mother. She was of course rather taken aback, but she told him that she couldn't be his mother as he already had one. Miss Jenkins had even met Alice at parents' evenings."

"What did Edwin say when he was confronted with this?"

"He admitted killing Alice. He'd used a small bronze bust we had on a sideboard in the sitting room to bludgeon her- there were at least twelve blows in all. They found the bust still covered in blood wrapped in a towel and put in a cupboard in the kitchen. Edwin had taken a bath and cleaned himself up too before I arrived home. Alice had only been dead about three hours- it seems that Edwin killed her after he came home from school that day."

"Did he give any reason for killing his mother?"

"Yes. He wanted Alice to not exist so that Miss Jenkins would be able to be his mother."

"He must have had a fixation on her," said Rose.

"That's what the police psychiatrist said."

"Was there a trial?"

"No. As Edwin admitted it and due to his age- he was only ten- it was recommended that he be sent to Sunnyside, so of course I agreed."

"What was Edwin's relationship like with your wife and yourself before this happened?"

"Well, he always had a difficult relationship with Alice. She was strict with him, always trying to mould him, keep him in line. He even complained to me a few times, saying that I should do something, that his mother controlled everything. But I never did anything- I thought that Alice was doing a good job, and she seemed to be dealing with Edwin well enough."

"Did Edwin ever threaten you in any way?"

"Never. But he did once tell me that I was a weakling, and I should be more like Captain Scott or somebody."

"Did Edwin ever show any other signs of violence?" said Rose.

"Only once, and never to a person. We had a cat called Chester that Alice doted on, and one morning we found it lying dead on the kitchen floor near its bowl of milk. Edwin was sitting at the table watching it. The daily maid had laid the milk out, but we found out that Edwin had added Smith's weed killer to it."

"What did Edwin say when you asked him about it?"

"He showed no emotion at all," said Mr Castleton, "and said something about it only being a cat."

"How old was Edwin then?"

"He must have been... eight, I think. I've often wondered if we should have had another child, a brother or sister for Edwin. He must have been lonely. But then again, I'm an only child myself."

"Me too," said Rose, "and I've never killed either an animal or human being. I don't feel that has anything to do with what happened, Mr Castleton. Edwin is just a very unwell boy."

"And nearly a man now. I do hope he's cured before he comes out. It's a relief that he'll be going somewhere else, safe until he's twenty-one, I must say. I'm not sure I can handle him, you know."

"He's getting the best treatment. And he's a very bright boy- he displays knowledge and reads books far beyond his age. Do you know that he's been reading Mr Aldous Huxley?"

Mr Castleton looked surprised. "That's interesting. Mr Huxley was resident here at the Albany last summer, I spoke to him several times. I told Edwin in a letter. Of course, he never answered."

"So perhaps Edwin started reading his books after reading your letter," said Rose, completely certain that this was the case. "Thank you for your time today, Mr Castleton, I understand that it can't have been easy going over this old ground. But it will help Dr Sharland and myself prepare Edwin for his new institution. We will of course keep you informed of any developments as always."

They shook hands at the door, and Rose felt deeply sorry for Thomas Castleton, who was obviously a broken man.

Rose made his way down the hallway, deciding to leave by the back entrance to avoid Mr Armitage-Gaines.

And as he walked down the roped walkway, past a liveried porter and out on to Vigo Street, he could only think about how dangerous Edwin really was, and how he'd almost been taken in by him.

There was no doubt in Rose's mind now that Edwin had killed Bernard Bannister, terrified Isabel Haarman in some way, and knew Dorothy's whereabouts, as well as perhaps being the father of her child.

37

Back at Sunnyside at nine o'clock the next morning, Rose went straight to Mr Dodwell's office- the meeting had been arranged on the telephone the evening before with Dr Sharland, as Rose stood in a box at Milston's railway station, having just arrived back from London.

With Mr Dodwell seated behind his desk, and Dr Sharland in the blue upright chair, Rose stood and began to explain himself.

"I realise that I left here under something of a cloud, and understandably so. But I think once you hear what I have to say, you may think differently. My goal has always been to find Dorothy Hopkins and that is all, and I think I may know who was involved in her disappearance."

He told them that everything pointed to Edwin Castleton and produced Mr Bannister's Zenith wristwatch from his coat pocket, explaining how he'd found it with Carstairs's help.

"That means the boy may well have killed Bernard Bannister!" said Mr Dodwell. "Or at least was with him just after he fell down the stairs."

"We already know that Edwin is capable of murder, of course. And Mr Bannister did tell me of his concerns that Castleton had violated his conditions as an E6, but he sadly didn't tell me who with," said Dr Sharland.

"Dorothy Hopkins?" said Mr Dodwell.

"My thoughts exactly. And perhaps Isabel Haarman. One girl missing and one dead," said Rose.

Sunnyside's principal and the head of the clinical staff looked on with great curiosity as Rose continued to unfurl an edited version of what he'd learned, without mentioning breaking into Dr Sharland's office or the visit to Edwin's father.

But he did tell them Edwin's story about the drugging of the residents and the secret experiments going on in the Cavendish Wing.

"That's all lies," said Mr Dodwell.

"Yes. the Cavendish Wing is where we treat our most acute cases. The children in there are separated from the other residents because they are unable to function well enough day-to- day. Many suffer from epilepsy and some from hypertension with convulsions. There are no experiments, I can assure you, and drugs are only used to alleviate pain and prevent fits and spasms. That's why we keep it locked up and isolated," said Dr Sharland.

"We can take you to the Cavendish Wing and show you what we do in there if you'd like," said Mr Dodwell.

"I'd rather there was no intrusion on the Cavendish Wing... It could adversely affect the residents there who are very sensitive to any change in routine," said Dr Sharland, slightly indignantly.

"That won't be necessary," said Rose. "I can take your word on that over Edwin Castleton's now."

"That's one of the dangers of fraternising with residents-they often have their own agendas," said Mr Dodwell. "I think it's time I should call Inspector Alexander and have Edwin Castleton questioned."

"Edwin can lead us to Dorothy Hopkins, I'm sure that he knows where she is. But he'll never tell *you* or a policeman the truth. Let me get it from him- he sees me as an ally of a sort, and he doesn't know that I've rumbled him," said Rose.

"It does make some sense," said Dr Sharland. "Edwin lives inside his own fantasy world and any intervention from us, or the police will just put up his defences, which are formidable."

Mr Dodwell considered it for a few moments. "Very well. Mr Tucker will let you into the cottage again. You have a week. After that, if we know nothing more about Dorothy Hopkins's disappearance, I'll have no choice but to bring in the police."

"Oh, and there's something else, which is rather sensitive," said Rose.

"What is that may I ask?" said Mr Dodwell, a little exasperated.

"I'm afraid that Dorothy Hopkins may be pregnant."

"And why do you say that?" said Dr Sharland. "I don't see how that could have happened."

Rose took out the folded-up pregnancy and maternal advice article from his wallet, telling them where he'd discovered it as he passed it over to Dr Sharland.

"This doesn't mean that the girl is pregnant- she had a fixation on babies of course. It may just have been her obsession playing out," said Dr Sharland.

"But it is a possibility that she is pregnant. I take it that you think that Castleton could be the father?" said Mr Dodwell.

Rose nodded.

"You'd better get to it, Mr Rose. We need to find the girl as quickly as possible, and stop Castleton doing any further damage," said Mr Dodwell, his voice uncharacteristically quiet.

As Rose left the office, he realised that Mr Dodwell had given him more time than Flanagan had. He'd expected more resistance to his theory, but the information he'd supplied them, and the presentation of the missing wristwatch and the article were obviously enough to both convince and trouble.

38

It only took a trip to the chapel graveyard to provide the scribbler with his little surprise.

Once I saw him going into his cottage again this morning with the deadly doctor and Mr Tucker, I knew he was back, and that could only mean one thing. He really is one of *them*.

I went immediately to the library and found a book, *The Enemies of the Rose* by Frederick Vincent Theobald, which I read with relish.

I realised that I'm not a mere caterpillar, nor even a greenfly or blackfly, but a rose maggot, especially designed to attack and eat away at Rose from the outside in and then inside out until there's nothing of him left.

I found it on a grave, all shrivelled and dry, the petals almost dust to the touch. It must have been white when it was placed there, but now was yellowed and decayed.

I left the dead rose just outside the miserable muckraker's cottage, on top of the stone dog where he leaves his key.

I saw him return just a few minutes ago. He took his key from the dog's mouth but didn't see my present. Still, it's pitch-black out here tonight. I'm sure he'll see it in the morning.

Welcome back, Mr Rose, you won't be leaving Shadowside again.

39

The sky was black with every star cloaked. Rose was at the kitchen sink, washing his socks in a bucket, thinking of little apart from how he would next approach Edwin.

He'd decided, in the hours since he came back to Sunnyside, to keep Edwin on his side by telling him he'd discovered what went on in the Cavendish Wing, and that he believed that Dorothy was incarcerated in there. And once he'd gained Edwin's trust in him and been invited wholeheartedly into the boy's strange inner world of Shadowside, he could begin to probe and hopefully find out the truth.

Rose firmly believed now that Shadowside was an invention of Edwin's twisted mind and that nobody else had ever uttered that word. It came from the depths of the boy's dark imagination, where there was no light, just like that very evening outside.

Then as he looked out onto the blackness in front of his cottage, Rose's eye caught a tiny glimmer, a pin-prick glow, out there in the near distance, where he knew the island of undergrowth stood. Where he thought he'd seen movement weeks before, but thought he was seeing things, or if anything an animal of some kind.

But this minuscule gleam remained as he continued gazing out of the window, and it was static. It couldn't be an animal or a bird, he was sure of that. He knew that he had to go out there and see for himself just what it could be.

Throwing on his thick overcoat over his jacket, but leaving his hat behind, Rose walked out of the cottage into the blindness, keeping his steps towards the island as quiet as he possibly could.

He could barely see his cold hands in front of him but looking ahead he saw that the small light was still there and becoming slightly larger and clearer as he approached. It was his beacon, but he wasn't yet certain if it really should be his guide or a signal to somebody else.

When he stood just outside the moat of the island itself, he paused and saw through the overhanging branches and bushes that it looked like a miniature flame of some kind.

He leaped over the moat- he wasn't sure if there was any water in it because of the dark, but it had rained heavily earlier that day.

Now on the edge of the island, he pulled himself up on a bough he'd felt out with both hands. He could hear the squidge of the mud beneath his brogues and was glad as it lessened the sound he was making, as there was no other noise around him.

Rose moved forward, crouching as he pushed through the outer foliage, the flame now visible just perhaps ten feet away from him now. And then a twig beneath his right foot snapped, and he stood there, still bent over, trying to not breathe heavily. And then the light went out and everything went haywire.

Something or somebody pushed into him with great force, knocking him over. Rose tried to stand up on the soggy ground but hadn't managed to scramble to his feet when he was punched in the face, a fist hitting his right cheekbone.

Now laying on his back, Rose could see the outline of someone on top of him, but there was no possibility of seeing who it was. The person was panting, as if they were frantic.

Then hands, strong ones, were round Rose's neck, throttling him and pushing the back of his head into the mud. There was no pain, but he couldn't breathe, and began to gasp for air. Rose knew that the man- it had to be a man due to his strength- was getting the better of him, and he was in real danger.

The panting continued, and Rose could hear his own gurgling, as he desperately tried to push his attacker off him, but it was no good.

Then he gave up fighting with his hands and tried to lever the man off with his knees, but the weight was just too much.

Rose's free right hand was patting the earth around him, striving to find an object- any stray object- with which to clobber the man.

And then he found what felt like a largish stone, but small enough that he could hold it in the middle of his hand and tighten his grasp around it. It felt like its jagged edges were cutting into his palm as he pressed into it, while the man continued to squeeze the life out of him, which was now making him disorientated.

Rose knew he had just one chance with the stone, or the man would knock it from his grip, and he really would be finished then. With all the strength he could summon, he lifted the back of his hand from the ground and brought the stone in his hand up towards the man and hit him as hard as he possibly could.

There was a dull thud, and then a groan with an exclamation of air coming from the man's lungs, as the hands around his throat went limp and his attacker fell on top of him.

Rose managed to push him off to the side, but his neck was burning very intensely. Pulling himself to his unsteady feet, he kicked the man, and he was relieved to see that there was no sound or movement.

Reaching into his coat pocket, he pulled out his Zippo lighter, flipped back the lid and held the unwavering flame close to the prone body next to him.

The person was face-down, but Rose was now even more confused. Whoever it was seemed to be wearing a dress, green in colour, with white flowers upon it. It couldn't be- that was the dress that Dorothy had last been seen wearing- it was emblazoned on his mind by now.

It couldn't be- Dorothy certainly wouldn't have had the strength of his attacker, even if she had wanted to stop being discovered if she'd been hiding there.

Rose closed the Zippo and turned the body over. Then he trained the lighter's flame on the person's face, and what he saw he couldn't believe.

It was Edwin, his eyes closed, with a trickle of blood coming from the top of his head. But that wasn't the only redness he saw, as Edwin's lips were painted bright red. The boy was wearing Dorothy's dress and possibly lipstick.

Rose was truly perturbed now and holding his throbbing throat with one shaking hand and the Zippo with the other.

He had to go and get help. If Edwin should wake up, he wasn't sure that he could win another battle, as the boy had the strength of a thoroughbred ox.

274

He kicked Edwin in his side to see if there was any reaction or sound, but there was none. Although Rose could see that he was still breathing.

Rather than trying to carry the boy off the island, he made the decision to run for the main building and find somebody to help.

He dragged himself through the undergrowth and over the moat, holding his neck and throat all the while. Looking at his wristwatch he saw that it was only twenty past eight, so the main doors would be unlocked still.

Through the courtyard and onto the chessboard floor of the main corridor he ran, but it wasn't until he reached the stairs that he saw Mr Leadbetter coming down them.

"Call the police please! I've been attacked by Edwin Castleton- he's unconscious outside!"

"Castleton?" said Mr Leadbetter.

"Yes! Please hurry- he may come around any minute..."

Within minutes, Mr Leadbetter had pulled the cord which set off the bell alarm all over the building, and while he rushed off to call the police, Dr Sharland, Mrs Benson, and Mr Lewis appeared, with Mr Tucker close behind.

They all went back outside, and Rose took them onto the island where Edwin thankfully still lay. Rose tried to explain what had happened, but it was all too much, and his throat felt like it was on fire. Mrs Benson insisted that he went back into the main building with her so that she could apply some balm to it.

Rose agreed, and he could just see Mr Tucker and Mr Lewis beginning to pick up the still out-cold Edwin as he left the island.

Within half an hour, Inspector Alexander and two constables arrived in the Wolseley police motorcar, by which time Edwin was beginning to regain consciousness where he'd been laid on the couch in Dr Sharland's office.

They would sit with him, guarding and questioning him for hours, his head bandaged up by a member of the clinical staff from the Cavendish Wing, the place which Edwin had deemed so destructive. Edwin said nothing.

275

As the light arrived at about seven o'clock, a thorough search of the island was made, and they found Edwin's sack, which contained some tuppenny blood magazines. Nearby under a bush was a discarded shovel. It seemed that the island had been Edwin's refuge.

They also came across a large candle, recently snuffed out, that Rose surmised must have been the light he'd seen and followed. There was also a lipstick, which Edwin had evidently used, for the same inexplicable reason he'd been wearing the dress.

But like Rose, Inspector Alexander was acutely aware that if Edwin was wearing Dorothy's dress, he must know where she had gone.

At just after eight o'clock, a Triumph police motorcycle arrived with a sidecar attached containing a police detection dog, which eagerly barked and stretched itself on all fours as it waited to do its job, undoubtedly anticipating the treat it would get for carrying out the task for which it had been trained.

Once let off its muzzle on the mound, the Alsatian made light work of its search, his handler needing to do little to direct him.

Within minutes, the dog had sniffed something out while growling loudly, and begun to kick up leaves which uncovered a sunken cavity in the ground, about ten feet from where Edwin's sack had been found. It was marked with a small flag on a pin by the handler.

And just minutes later, perhaps ten feet from that, a second hollowness was exposed by the canine detective, covered with leaves and other woodland debris. The handler placed another flagged pin there and led the well-stroked dog off the mound for its reward.

Inspector Alexander was called, and he soon appeared with a constable, the other one he'd arrived with remaining inside with Edwin, Mrs Benson, Dr Sharland, and Mr Dodwell, who had just arrived from his quarters.

At the Inspector's instruction, the constable started digging up the smaller hole, and it was found to contain a dog carcass, which would later prove to be of the same breed as Mr Tucker's dog, Pepper, that had gone missing, and which Edwin had done so much to help try to find.

Attention then turned to the first hole, and each of the wiry constable's shovel-strokes caused the debris to fall in and increasingly showed it to be much larger than the first, around six feet by three feet, but only about twenty inches deep.

And with the surface bed of leaves, bark, moss, and soggy earth removed, the shallow grave revealed its awful secret.

Lying within it upon a black woollen coat was the body of a girl or young woman, still very well-preserved and wearing just underclothes, with a black bandit mask over her eyes. It would soon be proven to be Dorothy Hopkins.

When Rose heard the news, he had to sit down on the steps outside the main doors of Sunnyside and held his head in his hands there for some time, the pain around his throat and neck now replaced by a deep melancholy, the physical trauma trumped by a true sense of helplessness.

Madame Sosostris had been right- Dorothy was close by and hadn't gone very far. But she was dead.

And for the first time since he was around Edwin's age, Rose found himself silently saying a prayer, for Dorothy.

40

They manacled Edwin, hands, and feet, and loaded him into the Wolseley. He never looked back at Sunnyside, nor Rose or the members of staff, including Dr Sharland, Mrs Benson, Mr Leadbetter, Mr Lewis, and Mr Dodwell, gathered there in shared and shocked silence.

Edwin was sullen, head bowed, defeated.

Mr Tucker was absent now. Rose surmised he was having to deal with the fact that Edwin, who had pretended to help him find his beloved dog, had murdered Pepper, that realisation coming less than a week after he'd discovered Isabel's floating body.

Rose now had to tell Mrs Hopkins about how he'd uncovered the trail to her daughter's death, after which he had to write up the whole story for *Travesties*. Luckily for him, the police would be breaking the news of Dorothy's passing and the arrest of Edwin to her mother by telephone that day, before Rose got back to London.

The Jack the Ripper/Lawrence Drummond story would forever remain a figment of Edwin's depraved mind as far as Rose was concerned unless Flanagan forced him to finish writing it up for a future issue.

Edwin would tell the police later that he'd sat in the dark for over an hour that morning weeks before with Dorothy beside him dead. Just sat there, in the middle of that mound, at the centre of the darkness.

He'd waited two days for a night with no light, keeping Dorothy in the woods where he'd choked her that early morning of 22nd November, before carrying her to the mound.

And there was still no light and no sound there apart from his breathing as he dug, and the grating of the shovel he'd taken from Mr Tucker's shed slicing into the sodden earth.

Dorothy had looked up at him, having no choice but to stare, her raven eyes still strangely glinting despite there being no light, just like the stuffed birds in the cabinets upstairs in the main building nearby.

"Didn't you close her eyes?" said Inspector Alexander when he later took his statement at the police station.

"There was no need to, she was dead," Edwin said, so Rose was told.

"So why did you put the black mask over her eyes before you buried her?' said Inspector Alexander.

"I didn't want her beautiful eyes damaged by all the earth on top of her," said Edwin.

The sweat had poured from Edwin's temples and down the back of his neck. It had surprised him just how deep he had to dig. But Edwin told the police it had astonished him even more how much effort it took to bury someone you were 'supposed to love.'

That was the true measure of Edwin Castleton thought Rose, as they took the boy killer away. He hadn't needed to hear it from Edwin's own cruel lips.

As Rose stood in the main courtyard just behind the main gates, watching Edwin being driven up that long drive away from Sunnyside on the way to the police station, he already knew that the boy was a confection, a composite, a perfect vision of what Edwin thought he should be.

It was all about control. That's why Edwin had killed his mother, Mr Bannister, and Dorothy. He wasn't capable of love or true affection. But he was an expert at masking his own emotional coldness, from watching others and copying them.

Edwin's mother had come to recognise this in her only child and stopped giving him the affection he craved. Once Edwin saw that he couldn't control her, he'd looked for a surrogate, a replacement mother, whom he thought he could control. When Miss Jenkins told him that she couldn't be his mother as he already had one, he'd bludgeoned his own mother to death.

Bernard Bannister had to go as he knew Edwin's true history and nature, and just how dangerous he could be if not controlled. It was a battle of wits that Bannister ultimately lost as he wasn't murderous like Edwin.

The boy won back control over his own warped world, but it wasn't long before he had to assert himself again. Dorothy had

279

to die as she'd somehow found the Zenith wristwatch, realised he'd done away with Mr Bannister and was now frightened of him. And Edwin had taken the Zenith back from Dorothy and hidden it in the Indian vulture's nest.

Then Edwin had almost definitely driven Isabel to her death as he feared she could expose him, Dorothy having told her about him.

Rose believed that Edwin had never loved Dorothy. He only wanted to be loved on his terms, under his own control. She was just the vessel to achieve his designs.

Edwin could recognise and appreciate beauty on a surface level, such as Dorothy's striking eyes, but there was only a stalking malevolence behind Edwin's own eyes, and certainly no beauty in his soul.

That's why he was able to sit on that island wearing the dress and the lipstick of the girl he'd murdered.

There was also one incredibly sad truth to come- Dorothy *had* been with child- it was confirmed by Sir Bernard Spilsbury, who was called from London to perform the post-mortem examination. It made the whole affair even more tragic and senseless.

And Mr Bannister's murder and Dorothy's pregnancy had obviously preoccupied Edwin. There were no new editions of tuppenny bloods placed his sack on his secret island after September 1936. Until that month, they had been purchased regularly.

It was as if Edwin had no longer felt any need for the fantasy world of Red Circle School, of soldiers, G-men, and aces of the air. Edwin had moved from fantasy into his own complete and terrible reality, of which he was very much in control.

For sixteen-year-old Edwin it would be the noose that spring of 1937, but not a judicial hanging. The judge couldn't send him to the scaffold because of his age, but Edwin tried to take matters into his own hands, ripping up a bedsheet in his prison cell, suspending himself, then twisting and attempting to slowly choke into oblivion on his own terms.

But a warder had found Edwin and cut him down, just in time. From then on, he was closely watched, a prisoner with control over nothing but his own mind.

Rose turned and looked up at the main building, the gravel walls, triangular frontage and two turrets high above, simultaneously taking a discreet swig from his hip flask, fooling himself that it was just for numbing the pain of his sore neck.

He was very aware he'd been lucky not to have been Edwin's fifth victim after Alice Castleton, Bernard Bannister, Dorothy, and their baby, and sixth if you included Pepper. And if Edwin did indeed set the chapel fire that killed those three boys, he would have been the boy's tenth human casualty. Edwin never admitted to any involvement in Isabel Haarman's death, but Rose had strong suspicions that he'd hounded her to her end.

Now having almost been asphyxiated himself, it just reminded Rose of the adage he'd forged over years and went by- "If it happens, it happens."

Rose knew that we are all struggling for control in one way or another and hurt others in pursuit of that dominance every day, whether knowingly or unknowingly. In some ways, Edwin was less complicated and more honest in his deadly actions.

The words of Oscar Wilde flooded Rose's thoughts.
Yet each man kills the thing he loves
By each let this be heard,
Some do it with a bitter look,
Some with a flattering word,
The coward does it with a kiss,
The brave man with a sword!

Although Edwin had never loved anybody or anything- he was incapable of love. That was his great tragedy, and the great misfortune of others who got in the way of his own survival.

But Rose understood that Edwin too was a victim in his own way, just as we all are, in one way or another, clasping for our own truths, but only just holding on.

When Rose looked around and back up the long drive, the Wolseley had faded from view, into the ever-misty distance.

But he knew that when Edwin's story was old news, no longer even used for wrapping fish and chip suppers or helping keep coal fires burning, and the boy himself rotted away the years in a cold cell, his existence in the outside world could not altogether be extinguished.

In Rose's scrapbook full of cuttings of his own words in print, charting the timeline of an astonishing and often chilling career, Edwin's presence would still be felt and through that collection of pages it always cast a very dark and lasting shadow.

***

Acknowledgements

Many thanks and appreciation must go to my agent Trevor Dolby, and his colleague Sara O'Keefe, at Aevitas Creative Management. Their support, encouragement, and excellent reading and editing expertise have been invaluable.

Ingram Content Group UK Ltd.
Milton Keynes UK
UKHW022248010523
421021UK00006B/21